Kidnapping Elephants

ALSO BY
MARGARET DAVIS MOOSE
Happy Days

Kidnapping Elephants

A NOVEL BY

Margaret Davis Moose

ROSEDALE

2020

Typset in Minion & Beachman Script
Book Design by John Balkwill

Kidnapping Elephants
First Edition
PRINTED IN THE USA

Kidnapping Elephants is available from
Amazon.com, Barnes & Noble.com
and at most bookstores, through Ingram.

ACKNOWLEDGMENTS

I could not have published this novel without the remarkable efforts and patience of my daughter, Amanda Moose, as well as the artistic genius of my son, Jeffrey Menifee Moose, who created the book cover with help from his friends, Dave Stewart, graphic designer; and Steve Schneider, photographer. My daughter-in-law, Laurie Moose, was hugely supportive and always encouraging. My son-in-law, Edward Lazarus, generously provided legal assistance and counseled calmness of mind.

Huge thanks to longtime friends Leslie and Judith Gelb, Howard and Mary Hurtig, Hodding Carter III, Rosemarie Howe, Nancy Ely, Guy de Selliers, Walter and Joanne Riddick, Joseph and Donna Bates, Gwynn Meden, Jane Watkins, David and Nancy Barbour, Eldon Boes, and the Alexandria Literary Society, my beloved book club of 37 years.

Special thanks to my grandchildren, Elias Menifee Moose, Lea Grover, Sam Henry Lazarus and Lily Lazarus, who were my cheerleaders. Also thanks to Gertrude Russi for her assistance with the Polish language and her delightful company.

Thanks also to my beloved brother, Atley Gene Davis, and my beloved sister, Miriam Arlene Dent.

I was very fortunate to graduate from Little Rock Senior High School in 1949 under the tutelage of superior teachers and remain grateful for their guidance.

I am deeply indebted to the brilliant help of my dear friends, Anthony Weller and his wife, Kylee. Anthony's patience, creative suggestions, and good humor, even when I woke him, and were of enormous assistance. He inspired an old lady to continue to write her story.

Kidnapping Elephants

PROLOGUE

It was still dark when he woke her. He was saying his name for her in the language her grandmother didn't like, but he seemed different that morning, his eyes sad, his voice husky. "Wake up, moj maly ptak," he whispered. "We'll climb to see the sun rise, and return before it shines on earth."

He helped her peel off her warm pajamas and put on the little flying outfit that was just like his, and she shivered as he pulled up the jodhpurs and buttoned the khaki shirt and zipped up the brown leather jacket and tied the white silk scarf around her neck before they tiptoed down the stairs and out of the house with fingers pressed to lips, and she slid her leather-booted feet across the silvery grass, and slid her small self to her side of the car seat, as her father climbed in the driver's side, closed the door with the smallest click, started the engine, and drove away so fast it felt like they were escaping from something.

When they arrived at the airport, he lifted her to the passenger seat of the Ryan, the very best plane for acrobatic tricks, and he climbed in the pilot's seat, buckled her belt, then his, lifted her goggles in place, then his, lit a cigarette, and winked at her. They both knew he wasn't supposed to smoke in the plane.

But he didn't smile as he usually did.

The sleepy mechanic, Glenn Larkin—her father called him Lark—heaved on the wooden propeller, still shiny with dew, and Lark grunted when he heaved, and he heaved and grunted until the engine came to life with a sputtering racket, and Lark yelled, "Contact!" and her father yelled "Contact!" right back with a snappy salute.

But she always wondered about that salute. Her father had

11

told her that in the Great War, pilots saluted their opponents before they began to shoot.

He took his time coaxing the engine. "We have to let our good friend warm up," he said, smiling a bit, though his eyes remained sad. The plane rolled slowly at first, then faster, the slipstream washing cold on her face, and the runway rushing toward them like an animal about to leap, and she felt a fierce joy when they escaped the earth and merged with the sky like a fish in the ocean.

Her father settled back, breathing deeply. Life was better in the sky, he always said, we're free up here, the sky is our friend. She never stopped to think that perhaps the earth was not.

The buildings below became doll-sized, and the orange LITTLE ROCK sign vanished on top of the big hangar, and the sky turned cobalt blue, the color of her mother's eyes.

"Look." Her father pointed to the clouds. "Mares' tails!" And he banked and climbed again, ready to corral the wild mares for her pleasure. He shouted "Bedziemy fruwac jak ptaki!" as he usually did. "But we won't get too close to the sun today. Our wings might melt!"

He motioned toward her goggles, and she pulled them tighter over her eyes and pressed her lips together. They tried hard to keep the plane clean, but when it turned upside down, specks of dirt or paper would tear loose and dive for eyes or open mouths like bees into a hive. Her father's pockets were always empty when he performed his tricks.

He performed a few snap rolls. "Just somersaults," he said, as though the sky were his playground, and he started a slight dive, beginning the Immelmann, then climbing at full power until they were almost upside down, and her small body was hanging from the strap, and she could see the sun beginning to show against the earth's dark edge.

Then he rolled the plane, and they were higher, and he rolled it right side up, and they were flying in the opposite di-

rection. He knew she loved that trick, but he didn't laugh with her as he usually did, because maybe, she thought, maybe he was thinking about the bad soldiers who had marched into his country and were mean to the people.

Po Land was his country. The people there were po. Tom Self and his wife, Jessie, who worked for her grandmother, talked about the po.

Her Papa banked to the right. "This is a pretty spot," he called. "Let's put down here for a minute," and he banked again, and she knew he was looking for a cow, cows were good weather vanes, they aimed their tails to the wind, and he shot the plane way up like a rocket, shouted, "Hold your nose! The water's deep!" and turned to dive that plane straight toward the earth.

He was a great death diver. He could do ten complete revolutions, and when he was performing, he wouldn't pull out of the dive until he could see the terror-stricken faces of the people below. Only then would he pull up in a loop just above their heads and flap his wings when he was high enough.

But today there were only cows on the ground.

The engine sputtered a little and started to cough, but she didn't worry. Her Papa was a great stick-and-rudder man. The plane always sputtered when they were upside down, and sometimes when they were right side up.

"Psiakrew!" he growled (she was never supposed to repeat this word), and he slid his hands over the controls and glared at the dials. The cows were running in clumsy confusion.

"Ty pieprzony kawalek smieci, sluchaj mnie!" he barked, pounding the control panel with his fist, spitting the cigarette from his mouth, and muttering more words she couldn't understand, except one word, SHIT, she understood that bad word, and he was really yelling now, "NIE! NIE! NIE!" because the Ryan wasn't behaving, not at all, the Ryan was wobbling and spinning, and her father was shouting, "Hold on, Shelby, HOLD ON!"

And she was afraid it had finally happened, the sun had melted the wax on the wings, but she didn't scream, she didn't have to scream, because the engine was screaming, and her father's face was red, and he was shouting more bad words and wrenching the steering so hard the plane straightened enough to skid and hop and bang across the field in a shuddering, terrifying slide, and she was trembling, but she wouldn't cry, even though her father was unstrapping her and throwing her onto the wing and vaulting out of the cockpit and jumping to the earth with her in such a rough way it made him limp, but he was running so fast in spite of the limp that she felt they were still in the air.

There was a jarring boom behind them, and when she looked over his shoulder, the plane, their Ryan, was on fire the way it seemed when they flew straight into the sunset. At first it was a ball of fire, then it was trees of fire, boom, boom, boom!

Which was when she began to cry.

And that was the day her father left. Flew away and disappeared. Just like Amelia Earhardt.

1

"It's Faubus behind that school board, and don't tell me it's not, with only one member to stem the Nigra tide! And don't tell me slow mixing will make it any better. I know about weeds. You let a few dandelions in your garden, they take over before you can say 'Jack Robinson.' We fixed those people a separate park just a few years back, and we just built them a brand new high school. What more do those people want?"

Eulalia's voice was soft but wry. "I wonder how the city fathers found the money to build that new high school in Pulaski Heights for the rich white people the minute that Supreme Court decision was handed down."

Her mother adjusted her girdle and *humphed* in response. "That school was already scheduled to be built. I know that for a fact. Anyhow, it was Orval Faubus caused all this trouble. I didn't vote for the man. I would never vote for anyone who went to that Communist school up in Mena that was full of Yankee rabble rousers and . . ." Baldwin paused to make certain she couldn't be heard from her granddaughter's window, and whispered, "*free lovers!*"

Eulalia fingered her thick, black hair more securely into its knot. "I wish you wouldn't spit in my ear, Momma." Eulalia was seated in the driver's seat of the old, red Volkswagen convertible in the driveway. "And I couldn't hear that thing you said about free lovers. Say it louder."

Baldwin squirmed her plump buttocks on the hot seat and ignored her daughter. "There was some big ruckus years ago about that Commonwealth College. The state had to put it out of business it was so un-American. And that tacky name. Or . . . val . . . Fau . . . bus." Baldwin pronounced each syllable in a sarcastic monotone, jerking her head in time to the beat. "It sounds like a flat tire bumping along. I don't care how long he was in Paris, France during the war. He'll never be anything but a redneck from Greasy Creek."

Her hand moved to the Victorian pin on her collar embedded with seed pearls and rubies. The pin was shaped like a delicate gold flower. Her younger sister, Ernestine, coveted that pin. She had inherited a similar one, but with fewer rubies. "I suppose Ernestine will be at the train station to see Shelby off. Shelby is her only niece, and I expect important people will be there. Ernestine loves to be around important people."

When Eulalia didn't comment, Baldwin turned toward her impatiently. "You think Ernestine will be there?"

"Why would you want her there, Momma? You don't like her."

Baldwin gave a soft snort. Liking Ernestine had nothing to do with it. *Showing* Ernestine that her granddaughter's participation in the beauty contest had turned out splendidly was what mattered. *Showing* Ernestine that her fine Pulaski Heights friends were at the station, waving to Shelby and congratulating Baldwin—who gave her girdle another surreptitious tug and changed the subject again.

"Orval Faubus can't tell me what to do just because he's governor."

"But the federal government can, Momma. We have to obey the federal government."

Shelby knew she was dressing too slowly, but the closer the time came for departure, the more slowly she dressed. She had heard a small plane a while back, which was not a

16

good omen. The sound of small planes always created a tightness in her gut, a shiver of fear.

She eased down the ancient shade so it wouldn't pop out of her hand. The room was hotter now, but the drawn shade muted her grandmother's voice, though it didn't mute the voice in her mind that said, "I once knew a girl, Merrinelle Merriwether, related to a lot of rice money. Merrinelle got a hangnail because she didn't cut straight across, and it got so bad she had to have the toe cut clean off. *Clean off her foot!* And she never got a husband after that, Shelby Howell."

Never got a husband after that. The phrase stuck to Shelby's aching head as she pulled hose up her newly-shaved legs, straightening the seams with little pinches of her fingers, which wasn't easy to do with legs damp from the heat, then tugging up her new lace-trimmed nylon panties that matched her garter belt, wincing and twisting to remove the pin from the price tag while *Never got a husband* twanged in her ears like a phrase in a country song.

She had scrubbed, tweezed, polished and perfumed every inch of her body, even cleaned out her navel with a Q-tip.

She was more than ready to leave. She reached for the crown on her bedside table, placed it on top of her platinum hair, stretched her mouth in a wide smile and bowed to the crowd she envisioned greeting her in New York City.

She would be just fine when she got to New York City.

She had won almost enough money to go to that faraway place to become a famous actress, where her father would see her name on a billboard and rush backstage to tell her . . . what? That his plane had been shot down during the war? That he had been imprisoned on a small Pacific island and escaped after all these years?

She had been eight years old when his last postcard dropped through the silver slot in her grandmother's big front door. The postcard had a color picture of the Chrysler Building postmarked New York City, with a message printed in block letters big enough for a little girl to read: "I'VE BEEN TO THE TOP!" the message said.

But she wouldn't think about that postcard today. She would think about Charlie Billington pulling her close to his side, floorboarding his Oldsmobile toward Lake Nixon and calling to Shelby to "Watch out for the law!"

Charlie was the young lawyer whose smile was slow and sweet and whose eyes promised that she would always be safe with him, he would never fly away. But four nights ago he was driving that Oldsmobile like a racecar, his free hand moving to Shelby's breasts, which was just fine with Shelby, Charlie and her breasts had kept company before, and she was thrilled by his reckless driving and by his hand on her breasts, wanted his hand to stay there forever. Maybe.

They had turned onto the dirt road and sped toward the deserted lake where they stripped to swimsuits and ran neck-deep into the water, ready to swim to the raft, but stopped just as quickly, staring at one another, until Charlie pulled down her swimsuit and kissed her nipples, which floated near the surface of the warm lake water, and she didn't stop him, because there was something about the evening air and the aqueous warmth and her imminent departure that created an atmosphere of abandon and bliss so vast that Baldwin's anxious eyes couldn't emerge in her mind to whimper and shout and deny the luxuriant feelings that were invading her body, and Charlie's calm, grey eyes fused with hers, even when he slipped underwater, his strong hands hastening that wet suit down her hips far easier than she ever could have done, which was okay, because this was Charlie Billington, whom she could trust, or maybe she couldn't, which was okay too, she was ready for a turning point, needed a turning point that would give her delicious pleasure and save her from the dread of leaving all she had ever known, and, yes, she *needed* Charlie's mouth that was sliding down her body, and to her astonishment, she knew where she wanted his mouth to be, though how in heaven's name it could be managed underwater was beyond her, *how had Charlie learned to do such things,* though she didn't care, she only knew it had to happen, and she thrust her pelvis toward his fish body, and dug her toes deeper into the luxuriant mud, no longer worried he might drown, he was a champion swimmer, wanting only for him to hurry, hurry, *HURRY, CHARLIE! LET THE DEED BE DONE AND QUICKLY!*

And Shelby might have stayed in Little Rock and agreed to marry Charlie that very night if an ancient, two-toned Pontiac hadn't halted at the lake's edge, its radio blasting away with "You ain't nothin' but a hound dog," and its spotlight, a hideous jacklight, hadn't pinioned her face like a deer, just as she thrust her neck to the stars and closed her eyes in ecstatic anticipation.

But Charlie, gentleman Charlie, also heard the music, even as he was about to shove his body into hers, and he dropped deeper into the lake, appearing some distance away, he was indeed a champion swimmer, inhaling great gulps of air and waving his hand, hail-fellow-well-met, so that the occupants of the Pontiac turned their eyes to him, providing time for his beloved to pull and jiggle and jerk up her pale blue Lastex swimsuit that must have shrunk under water.

A male voice in the Pontiac yelled, "Isn't that Miss Little Rock? Isn't that Shelby Howell? Hey, Miss Little Rock! Give us a smile!"

And the spotlight was Shelby's once more as she straightened a strap and stood up, smiling a bit shakily but decently clad in the nick of time, and waving the back of her hand back and forth, like the royalty she was.

"Now I know you lovely ladies ain't having trouble with

the law." Julien Hutchins high-stepped over her grandmother's watery garden, protecting the cuffs of his hand-tailored trousers and his highly polished Florsheim Imperials, smoothing back his slick hair with his hand as he talked, and carefully wiping his sticky palm on his handkerchief.

Shelby watched from beneath the shade, her body still cooling from the memory of Charlie's lovely, wandering mouth.

Nothing Julien could say would be interesting to her. He and his wife, Lettie, had lived next door all of Shelby's life, and he and his funeral parlor had always given her the creeps.

Still . . . she sat on the floor and watched from the corner of the decrepit shade.

Julien was bowing his head, hands pressed together in a Southern salaam, fingernails clipped and clean. Eulalia, who was still at the wheel, concentrated on a fingernail that needed attention. She seldom spoke much with people outside the family, and the family was small.

Eulalia was almost as tall and as slender as her daughter, but her coloring was the opposite. Hair black, skin pale. She wore no makeup, and despite something almost ghostly about her containment, there was a provocative aura to her looks. Men stared if only to determine what it was that compelled them to stare. Her cotton dress fit rather loosely, but revealed the curves of breasts and hips, and the blue color of the dress mirrored the blue of her eyes in an almost shocking manner. When those eyes were closed, she looked like a sensual Madonna, except for a startling streak of white hair at her forehead that had drained of color the day after her husband disappeared.

Julien's eyes caught Eulalia's, but she turned her head as though she couldn't abide his perpetually pleasant smile, always trying to impart the impression that he would never overcharge, even as he steered folks from cherry wood and polished oak and mahogany and steel, which, of course, would corrode, to that shiny, copper, top-of-the-line model that was a rock of ages, as he would say in his creamy tenor voice, smiling sadly and running a manicured fingernail along the gum-rubber gasket. If he was talking to Protestants, which was usually the case, a mournful "Rock of Ages" would magically emerge from the elaborate sound system, installed by engineers from the radio station KARK. The music was as mellifluous as the motor of Julien's new Cadillac hearse idling in his driveway.

"The question is, will the law do us any good, Julien? We got ourselves beat with that last school board, letting those liberals sneak on. Talk about *weeds*." Baldwin glanced pointedly at Eulalia, who was looking out the other side of the car as though she hadn't heard her mother.

Julien flashed his quick smile and gave three heavy pats to Baldwin's pudgy hand. His voice, too deep for his height, made him seem top-heavy. "Didn't I tell you not to fret about this subject? We're not going to let anything bad happen to our chirrun." His speech skated between proper verbs and Southern idioms with the skill of long practice. "That *Brown II* ruling says we can integrate *slowly*." His smile was knowing. "I promise we can string this thing out for a *very* long time. And . . ." his voice was a bit hesitant, "while I know you don't like to hear this," he puckered his lips sympathetically as he might with a grieving client, "Eldridge Cartwright is swinging into action with his White Citizen's Council. And Buster Crosby is with us too."

Baldwin's face took on the pain of someone who has stepped in a cow pie while inhaling the perfume of a late summer garden. Eldridge Cartright and Buster Crosby were men she would never let enter her massive front door. She was opposed to integration, but neither did she favor mixing social classes. Eldridge Cartright was a failed plumber, now working behind the counter of his father-in-law's hardware store; and Crosby, a swaggering social climber who owned a men's clothing shop, sold the same clothes to coloreds as whites, though the coloreds did have to enter through the back door.

"You told me Josh Reynolds was with us on this Nigra issue, Julien, and I know Billy Beaumont is. Those are the kind of people you need to be talking to. Those kind of people are respected."

"But those folks don't talk loud enough, Baldwin. We got to have loud talkers like Eldridge and Buster. Those gentlemen have a lot of followers."

Baldwin gave a louder "humph" at the word "gentlemen."

"And . . ." Julien's voice descended to its most reassuring depths, "I've also been in touch with Governor Faubus . . . now wait, now wait, Miss Baldwin . . . I *assure* you, Orval's going to do the right thing!"

"That man's a crook! He got a hundred and *three* percent of the votes in his county when he won! *And* he's let Nigras inside every state-run college I can name! How could you talk to that man?"

"Orval don't cotton to that left-wing school board any more than you do, I promise he don't. I've talked personal to the man. You must let us men take care of this situation—and breathe a little slower like the doctor told you to do. You're looking a little bit pink. All you got to think on today is getting your beautiful granddaughter to the train station, even though it near kills us to let that young'n go. I predict we'll see her name in big flashing lights before long! Why, she'll be another Lana Turner!"

Baldwin rolled her eyes. Julien's meeting with Orval Faubus was treachery, but the thought of Shelby's last name (which was also Baldwin's) flashing before crowds of perfect strangers was worse. She pulled at the fingers of her right hand, adorned with the large star sapphire her father had sent from the Orient, and she pulled at the other hand, bedecked with her mother's marquise-cut pink diamond engagement ring. The moment her mother died, Baldwin, who was living with her at the time, had slipped the rings from the still-warm fingers and put them on her own. She had been compelled to make the move, she reasoned to herself, before sister Ernestine arrived and took the rings for herself.

Then Baldwin changed the troublesome subject, lifted her head coquettishly, and flirted with this man so many years her junior. It was a small pleasure she indulged in, though never acknowledged to herself.

"I thank you for all the trouble you went to, Julien. I know they don't usually give those beauty contest winners first-class train tickets with air-conditioned sleepers. *And* you got Shelby that apartment for the first weeks in that city."

"Oh, well." Julien's small eyes grew round with sincerity. "My friend Justine likes to have someone living there while she's overseas taking snapshots for National Geographic."

"And I also appreciate that top berth you got for her. I've heard too many stories about Nigra porters and young white girls in lower berths."

Eulalia's book clattered to the floorboard, and her eyes caught Julien's for a fierce second before she turned her head, leaving him to blink uncertainly at the back of her neck.

"But where is our beautiful actress?" he asked.

"SHELBY HOWELLLLL . . . " Baldwin yelled. A startled Julien hopped back from the car.

"Don't bother her, Miz Baldwin!" he whined, but loud enough for Shelby to hear. "I just wanted to say goodbye to her personal!" He grinned foolishly toward Shelby's window, and turned back to Baldwin as though he hadn't. "You sure you all don't need a ride? I got the fanciest transportation in town over there in my driveway, all-leather upholstery, air-conditioning, power steering, and a tailgate in back that can pick up that trunk so easy. I got to make one quick stop at the funeral home, but after that I can deliver you ladies straight to the station door."

Baldwin couldn't suppress a shudder. "*Nooo*, I don't think so. We don't need a ride in that . . . vehicle. My car is down, but Eulalia's is fine this week. We're just waiting for Tommy Self to carry the trunk from Shelby's room. He wouldn't miss her going away."

"Well, you be sure and tell Shelby I'll bring anything she forgets when I go to the undertaker's convention up there in December."

Eulalia interrupted with sudden energy, "Shelby won't forget a *thing*."

"Of course, she won't, of course, she won't. I was just saying in *case* she did." Julien raised his hands the way he did when he was about to conduct the church choir, which he did every Sunday.

Shelby giggled at the sight of Julien's upraised hands. Years ago she had spied in his bedroom window and watched him directing an invisible choir in front of a mirror, his shiny brown hair perfectly combed, and the gaiters of his socks precisely hooked to his starched BVDs. He had smiled at himself in the mirror, entranced by his superior directing technique and his handsome self.

Shelby began to conduct in front of her own mirror, mocking Julien, humming "The Little Rock Getaway." She could play the ragtime tune on the piano. She was ready to leave, but under no circumstances would she make her getaway in a hearse.

Julien waved to people on the sidewalk as he drove with

the decorum of a man who hoped people would use his new hearse when their time came, but he was daydreaming about Miss Little Rock. Naked.

Julien knew everybody who was anybody in this city that still retained the comfortable atmosphere of a small town. It was his business to know everybody.

Here a wave, there a wave.

In fact, almost everyone in Little Rock knew one another, or knew *of* one another. People were friendly in that smiling, Southern way that seemed to include all comers.

It didn't, of course. What counted for people in the *better* class was who your ancestors were, what your daddy did, how much money your daddy had (or how much money your daddy left you). And the part of town you lived in mattered: how big your house was, which church you attended. Universal questions, by and large.

However, in Little Rock people smiled at one another as though those differences didn't matter, so long as everyone behaved appropriately and remembered the pecking order. No one of consequence mentioned skin color. It was taken for granted that white was the only color that mattered.

A little wave to Hugh Smith who sold Oldsmobiles. Julien would never buy an Oldsmobile. He preferred the look of a Cadillac car. Another little wave to Hugh to keep him happy, but in his mind, Julien was caressing Shelby's breasts that would soon rest beneath an Arkansas Razorback cheerleader's sweater. He had given her this cherished gift to wear when it got cold in New York City.

He turned the air-conditioning up a bit. He loved the ease with which he could twist the knob and create the perfect temperature as he fantasized about Miss Little Rock's long legs.

But he didn't forget to flutter his fingers at old Miss Pembleton, who was not long for this world and had ample money for a first-class funeral.

Hello, there, dear old Miss Pembleton!

Miss Pembleton waved back, but with polite restraint. A hearse was a hearse to Miss Pembleton, no matter who drove it.

And thus he continued his one-man parade, smiling, waving, planning how he could use Baldwin's social connections to smack down this integration effort. He was acquainted with the city fathers; but, alas, he was merely their undertaker, hovering in the background, limousines and hearses polished and always at the ready. He understood too well why Orval Faubus didn't like these country club people. They made it plain, without saying a word, that neither he nor Orval would ever be a part of their set.

But soon they would pay more attention to Julien Hutchins, who wasn't afraid to express his feelings about niggers, and, more importantly, wasn't afraid to do something about it. The small group of influential men who pushed business and civic efforts on behalf of the city—and themselves, of course—had organized to attract new industry with the help of that rich, liberal Yankee interloper, Winthrop Rockefeller, who had moved down to make a name for himself, and would surely be flown north when he died, and buried in an expensive gold coffin purchased from a New York City undertaker. Winthrop was spreading money around Arkansas like fertilizer; he had fallen in love with the state, he said, and wanted to do what he could for the public good, which of course meant running for office and catering to nigger lovers.

The rest of the Little Rock elite was composed, for the most part, of people who understood the importance of providing a work force that wouldn't cause trouble, people who, for the most part, took pride in their civic duty and believed the Supreme Court ruling had to be obeyed. They might not believe in integration, but they believed in the Constitution—if it were interpreted to their liking.

However, even the most passionate of those people couldn't foster segregation publicly. That would be bad for business. But they could hide behind Julien, who would wave the segregationist banner, and in so doing, would surely be invited into their inner sanctum. He imagined them assembled in one of their fine houses and raising their glasses to him, Julien Hutchins, the bravest of them all.

He gave his hair an affectionate pat at this delicious thought.

How he loved the fine vehicle he was driving! How he enjoyed the hum of the engine that was almost as quiet as the dead he transported! It was easy to imagine Shelby on the gurney in the back that was big enough for two very live bodies. The thought made him giggle and drive a little faster.

The lights were on in the handsome *Arkansas Gazette* building, which didn't surprise him. That paper stayed open day and night to print lies. Harry Ashmore, the paper's editor, was a pinko and a nigger lover. Julien only read the afternoon paper, the *Arkansas Democrat*, the politics of which were more to his liking.

He was so deep in fantasy he almost forgot to make his turn, which was important, because the cantankerous Arkansas River lay ahead. The river was filled with alligator gar big enough to bite off a man's hand, and the thought of those feisty gar caused Julien's body to tingle with more erotic images of the beautiful Miss Little Rock. It was, however, a feeling mingled with sadness, because Miss Little Rock would soon depart the bedroom where, if a certain shade was raised, he could observe her ablutions from a bathroom window in his own house. If he stood on a chair. And used his binoculars.

He would miss that view. It was much harder to look into Eulalia's window. Eulalia kept her shade lowered.

But in a few months he would see Shelby in New York

City, and he was certain that in the big city, it would be safe for both of them to fulfill the longing that, if given the opportunity to express it, she also harbored for him.

Shelby stared at the elegant, ocher leather traveling trunk in her room, brass fittings newly polished by Tom Self. She was thinking the heavy lid might rise to reveal a smiling man wearing a leather flying helmet, his arms outspread toward her, and she quickly covered her breasts with crossed arms.

The trunk had been a gift to Baldwin on her nineteenth birthday in preparation for a grand tour of Europe. But when the Great War began, the tour was canceled, and the soldier Baldwin was engaged to marry was blown apart in France while sitting astride his horse. The family was never informed that soldier and horse were so commingled in death that they were buried together in Flanders Field.

It was unfair that Baldwin's trousseau had to be stored in her travelling trunk: the beautiful satin wedding dress, yellowed with age; the intricately tatted, rotting veil, stitched with seed pearls; the embroidered tablecloths; the crocheted bedspreads, the initialed linen sheets, also yellowing. A photograph of Baldwin's sweetheart, dressed in his uniform, had rested on the bottom of the trunk until recently, when Baldwin removed the photograph and her trousseau, and Shelby replaced them with her own clothes.

The photograph of Baldwin's soldier now rested in the bottom drawer of her cherrywood bureau, and the photograph of Shelby's father took its place in the bottom of the trunk that was ready, at last, to make its maiden journey.

Shelby's Arkansas Razorback pennant was also packed in the trunk, but the pennant's shadowy shape was imprinted on her bedroom wall, and would probably stay there forever. But Shelby's life, *please God,* would never be the same.

In grammar school, when the teacher tugged the map of the United States from its long, skinny black case, Shelby would stare at New York City, imagining a place high on a hill at the center of the universe. The omphalos, her high school English teacher, Miss Finney, called the city. The belly button of the world.

Little Rock was the meadow at the bottom of the hill.

To go to Texas, which Shelby never considered, meant going downhill on a dirty bus crowded with people, by way of Malvern and Arkadelphia and Texarkana. To go to New York City meant going uphill all the way.

Two centuries ago, Indians told explorers that an enormous emerald glowed green on the riverbank at the place that would become Little Rock. But when the greedy, fever-ridden Frenchmen arrived at the destination, they found only an outcropping of schist and sandstone that glittered like the eyes of an old crocodile.

Fool's gold, Shelby's father laughed, throwing his daughter so high she nearly touched the fourteen-foot ceiling of her grandmother's living room. *Beware the old crocodile, Shelby! Remember that when you seek your own fortune!*

Then her father had left her to seek his own.

" . . . and Orval Faubus never got beyond the eighth grade," Baldwin droned on. "Sold squirrels and muskrats and so forth. He says he learned some lawyering, but I don't believe it. Always has that matchstick in his mouth. I even hear he's taking speech lessons to get the country out of his voice so he can sound good on the TV thing.

"I would *never* let that man snoop around my living room on one of those TV things, no matter what he sounds like. And to think my own daughter is working for him! There's not a proper family in this town will have him over for a meal, Eulalia!"

Baldwin readjusted her girdle, pretending she was removing a piece of lint from her navy-blue two-piece with it's peplum. The shantung silk of the two-piece followed the contours of her stomach like the permanent waves that seemed sculpted to her head. This time she leaned out the window and yoo-hooed demurely, jiggling her fingers up at the second floor.

"Yoo hoo, Shelby Howell . . ."

When there still was no answer, she pretended it didn't matter. "They ought to start that train right here in Little Rock where there's plenty of people wanting to go places early in the day instead of making us get on some Texas train in the evening." She raised each arm to fan the half-moon circles of perspiration beneath, which made her damp arm flesh rhumba about. "I'm about to melt in this car waiting for that child."

Eulalia folded the corner of a page, rested her head on the back of the seat, and closed her eyes. "We'd be too early if we left now, Momma." The book was enclosed in a brown paper wrapper.

"It's because of that beauty contest business. Did she ever give us a minute's trouble before that beauty contest? People watching her snap her fingers beneath that Lastex bathing outfit and showing her tan line? Ernestine said she would pay for her debut at the country club if Shelby would give up that Miss Little Rock business, but you said, 'No thank you.'"

Eulalia sat up straighter. "She made her debut. She presented herself to the public."

"And using the money she won to learn to act in New York City, like she doesn't already know how to act? I've seen her act! I thought Julien was going to hurt himself he clapped so hard at her acting, crowing about how great her makeup looked. I grant he knows how to put on makeup, though I shudder to think how he learned. And now she's going to a faraway place wearing that makeup, and Nigras on every street corner, staring at the color of her hair!"

Eulalia closed her eyes. "She will soon be twenty-two years old, Momma. And she's not just going to be an actress, she's going to be a *method* actress. I'm sure they mix with a higher class of people."

"And that's something else that bothers me. Who knows what that 'method' business is? Have we investigated it? I know she's going there because of that Marlon Brando, she thinks he acts so good, you letting her see that *Waterfront* picture show I don't know how many times. And that same director making that *Baby Doll* movie in Mississippi, with that girl in a shorty nightdress and her thumb in her mouth." Baldwin tried to crank her window further down. "They would all behave a lot better in Greenville," She removed her glove to get a better grip on the recalcitrant handle, "if they didn't have that Communist newspaper in that town, telling people to love Nigras and the United Nations." When the window wouldn't budge, she scolded it with a slap of her glove.

Eulalia suppressed a grin. "Why, Momma . . . did you slip off and see that movie?"

"Shelby *cannot* mix with people like that. Why didn't she use the money to go to the University? There are so many fine boys at the University. *And* she refused to learn to play bridge, would *not* learn the game that makes a person welcome in any proper household. SHELBY HOWELLLLL!" Baldwin bellowed the name this time, skittering across "Shelby" and landing on the last name so hard the emerging sound came out HOWL.

Eulalia grimaced. "She's too old for the University, Momma. Once a girl gets to be twenty-one years old, she can't be a freshman up there. She would look like an old maid."

Baldwin turned her head so quickly the wooden cherries on her hat rattled. "She will *not* be an old maid! She would meet graduate students up there! And law professors! Why she won't marry that sweet Charlie Billington is beyond me. She won't even let him take her to the train station. Everything seemed jim-dandy between them until a few nights ago. Maybe . . . *maybe* if Charlie talked a little more, Shelby would like him better. He's such a quiet man."

"He talks plenty, Momma, and he's as smart as they come. He's just a better listener. Hardly anybody listens."

"He does have everything else in his favor, and he's going to have more, with his daddy owning all those rice fields. Of course, Herbert *is* a Republican, I don't know what Charlie is, I pray he's a Democrat, but whatever he is, he brought me that little toad lily I love so much." Baldwin's voice veered toward baby talk as her toad lily came to mind. Then her eyes narrowed thoughtfully. "If Shelby would get a permanent and curl her hair, she could be one of those Breck Girls and not have to go anywhere. The Breck people would come down here and take her picture, she's so pretty."

Eulalia looked at her mother with amused eyes. "You want her picture on shampoo ads? Why is that better than being Miss Little Rock?"

"Those Breck Girls are pure, Lalie, with their pure gold hair and their pure faces looking up to God. I wouldn't use anything but Breck."

Shelby ceased listening to the voices. She was thinking about the evening before when her mother had appeared at her bedroom door, her frayed nightgown revealing a remarkably young-looking body, the white streak at her forehead luminescent in the moonlight. She looked like a ghost.

"Here," she said in a sleepwalker's voice. "Take this picture with you. It's your Papa."

The women stared at one another until Eulalia backed out of the room as quietly as she had entered.

The moment the door shut, the young woman whirled to look at the picture. Looked away. Looked back again, but the face in the photograph stayed the same. The man's hair was platinum and straight, the cheeks high-boned, and yes, the lips were full, like hers, with the sensuality that Shelby knew made men look at her. And the clothing seemed familiar: khaki jodhpurs, leather boots, leather flyer's helmet dangling from one hand. And he was smiling, his hand outstretched as though inviting her to join him. *Smiling and beckoning as he had when she was a child.*

Shelby stood, looking in the mirror from her face to his face. She stretched her lips into his smile, which made her look macabre.

My land, Shelby Howell, people would say when she answered the telephone. *You sound just like your momma.*

They had neglected to mention she looked just like her father.

Then a disturbing image altered the picture she was holding: two lines etched along each side of the mouth, a frown cleaving the forehead, sorrow or fear in the eyes that gazed down at her six-year-old half-asleep self. When Shelby described the strange encounter the following day, Baldwin, whose face also looked haggard, snapped that it was just a bad dream, and walked away.

But Shelby knew better. She knew her father had come to take her with him. *And why hadn't he?* Shelby's grown-up face grew as tight as the glass that encased the photograph. She raised the frame high, prepared to shatter the glass.

But she couldn't destroy the face. She who, like her mother, never became angry, now bit the inside of her mouth so hard, she tasted blood.

He could have taken her with him. He knew she would have gone.

After he left, his name was never spoken. The women moved around his silent space like dancers in a pavane.

Papa, Shelby thought ferociously. *Papa* was what she called him, not Daddy, the small word her friends used for father.

"Papa!" she started to yell, but choked back the sound when she heard her grandmother creak down the hall on bunioned feet, turning at the painting of her grandfather who was dressed in a beaver hat and breeches of ivory silk. Grandfather Shelby had posed for the portrait before fighting a duel at Arkansas Post, and Baldwin always added, when she told the story, that he had killed the man in three minutes. He always won his duels.

The granddaughter followed the sound of her grandmother's journey down the creaking stairs and to the lonely kitchen where she would gorge on sweets, and pick scale from her houseplants the way a monkey picks lice from its young.

Shelby shoved her father's photograph inside the trunk and lay naked on the cool oak boards, her eyes wide open.

"She can't have a garden in New York City." Baldwin stared morosely at the stump of her beloved walnut tree, weeds drooping from her fingers.

"She doesn't garden, Momma."

"Someday she'll want to garden. Then she'll come back home."

When Baldwin turned her head to conceal the moisture that welled in her eyes, Eulalia opened the car door, walked to her mother, and placed a consoling hand on top of the old hand that bore the heavy weight of a spectacular pink diamond ring.

On the first day of grammar school, the new teacher asked Shelby her father's name. Shelby stood up straight and replied, accent impeccable, *Teodor Korzeniowski!*

Her classmates laughed out loud, even those who knew her name, and the teacher frowned, though not at the laughter. She asked Shelby to spell the name, which was easy, because her father had repeated the letters over and over as they flew above the white dogwoods that covered Pinnacle Mountain in the springtime, and over the sinuous ditches that irrigated the bright green rice fields in the delta.

The teacher wrinkled her nose. "What kind of name is that?"

"It's a *Polish* name," Shelby replied, standing taller.

The children laughed louder. They knew it was the name of the man who never said "yes ma'am" or "yes sir" to ladies or gentlemen, a man who bowed from the waist with a click of his heels and kissed ladies' hands before they could snatch them away . . . though never quickly. And he was the only man in town who, in winter, wore a long, navy-blue coat with a velvet collar, the hem swirling dramatically as he strode along.

At recess that day the children danced around Shelby, shouting:

What's your name/ Puddin' n' tame/

Ask me again/ And I'll tell you the same!

"But I know the longest word in the world," she shouted back, and screamed the word across the playground:

OWNEESWAKEEMOLLYPANTS!

And, astonishingly, the word shut them up like her papa

promised it would whenever she needed a little magic.

So she survived that day and more, until a few years later, long after her father disappeared. Baldwin took her to the courthouse and had the Korzeniowski surname changed to her own last name, mumbling that it made no difference, *a rose by any other name,* etcetera. Since Baldwin had custodial charge at that time, she also changed Eulalia's last name to its virginal beginning. It didn't take long to fill out the forms. The man behind the counter stamped the papers with a resounding thump and said, smiling, "Now their last names are just like yours, Miz Howell."

But not to be "Korzeniowski" left Shelby mourning, though never out loud. Grief had to be swallowed whole in Baldwin's house.

2

THERE WERE TIMES after Shelby's father disappeared, when her mother would rush out the door, coatless in the coldest weather, top down on the red convertible, and drive toward Sweet Home Pike, the blue blaze from her eyes fueling her body. Baldwin would rush to her own car, Shelby seated by her side, and, with a hunter's eye, track down her daughter.

On the day of the last search, they found Eulalia at Adams Field, where her husband's plane used to take off and land. She was standing outside the fence at the end of a runway, humming and scratching at her arms with a kitchen knife, with the serenity of a saint and the abandon of a small child scrawling on a fence. She would wipe the blood off the knife with her skirt . . . she was always neat . . . pause to watch the searchlight sweep back and forth against the early evening sky, and proceed with her message, letter by bloody letter.

Shelby stared at her mother and at the hangar where her father's Ryan had been housed. Baldwin seemed mesmerized by her daughter's behavior. The plane from Memphis roared onto the runway, the propellers whipping the air into a frenzy. The old woman flailed at her exposed knickers, whimpering, "What else can I do? How can they expect me to do anything else?"

Oddly, it was Eulalia who took Baldwin's hand and led her to the wheel of the car while Shelby burrowed into the recess behind the front seat like a small bird against the rain. Her mother then sat herself on the passenger side, closed her door, and Baldwin turned the key, stripping the gears, moaning about the things she had done for her family. All the things she had done.

The light was faint when they made a halting drive through the gates and up the winding hill to the State Hospital. Shelby would always remember the figures on the lawn, floating like ghosts in long white gowns, their faces bland as thumbs. She studied them carefully, her young visage pinched, already forming the habit of looking for her father.

But it was her mother they left inside the big white building, and they didn't look back.

"I wish you'd look! My Mr. Lincoln rose has black spot! It's this terrible weather. I'll have to spray my own self for mildew pretty soon."

"Go take off your girdle, Momma. You'll feel a lot better."

Baldwin glared at her daughter as though she had been asked to perform an unnatural act and said, in consequence of nothing, "New York City is *not* like Little Rock." It was hard to listen to her without feeling compelled to march to the beat or run from it. "That place is full to the brim with Nigras and Catholics and Jews."

"You have Jewish friends, Momma. Bert Stein is Jewish."

"Of course he is, and I know every single member of his family, don't I? His people might as well be Episcopalian, they're so upright. And that rabbi here in town is not so bad. He has good Christian manners, and he sounds like we do. You'll have to admit that none of those Yankees talk right. I know they can't help it, and I don't hold it against them. But they sound like foreigners."

Foreigners. Baldwin twitched as though the Korzeniowski name had given her a poke. "She'll be lonely up there."

Eulalia stifled a sigh. "We're all lonely sometimes."

Loneliness stilled the air until Baldwin changed the subject. "And Arkansans do *not* go up there to act on the stage. Do you know of a soul?"

Eulalia walked up the steps and sat on the porch swing, book still in hand.

"Sister!" Baldwin's voice was sharp. "I'm speaking to you!"

"I heard you, Momma. James Simms is up there. I heard he was on the Chesterfield Supper Club. I told Shelby to look him up."

"Tell me you did no such thing!"

"He's a working actor from Little Rock. Maybe he can help her."

"You *know* what they say about that man!"

"I know he used to sing in the choir," Eulalia responded evenly. "People said back then he was Broadway-bound. You said it yourself. And he helped you find flowers along the roadside, dug them up, illegally too, and planted them for you. You loved him then."

"And did I know any better? People say he's a . . . that he's not a real man, Lalie. Does Shelby know about that kind?"

"I imagine she does." Eulalia never contradicted her mother, though her attitude had become edgy as Shelby's departure grew nigh. "I've also heard William Warfield is living in New York City. He's a famous singer from Arkansas."

Baldwin's face grew pink. "That's not a bit funny, Lalie. William Warfield is a *colored*. The only person who's connected to acting around here is Al Jolson's second wife from Hot Springs, and I don't know a thing about her family."

"We've got Senator Fulbright."

"Oh, well. We have plenty of politicians in this state who behave like actors. As for Bill Fulbright, he pretends to live here when it's voting time, *and* he's halfway a Communist, trying to turn our government over to the United Nations. I only vote for him because he's a Democrat."

Eulalia's voice had a slight edge when she said, "Senator

Fulbright was the only one who voted against the money for McCarthy's witch hunt. I thought that vote was for everyone's good."

Baldwin gave her a sharp look. "What's come over you lately? Are you feeling alright?"

"Yes, ma'am, I am," Eulalia replied demurely.

"Well, I don't want to hear another word against Joe McCarthy. He did his best to save us from the Communists and got no thanks for it. And Bill Fulbright's mother has gone wild, running that newspaper up there in Fayetteville. Roberta has plenty of money. She doesn't have to work. She acts for all the world like Eleanor Roosevelt. And no more had they announced that *Brown Decision* Supreme Court thing on the airwaves than they put the coloreds up there in the same schools with our little white children, and I *know* that was Roberta Fulbright's doing!" Baldwin stomped her foot at this indignity, which made her bunions vibrate with pain. With some difficulty, she restrained the urge to remove her shoe. "It's the law," Eulalia said quietly.

"If she's just got to be an actress, why can't she be the old-fashioned kind? Old-fashioned ways are always the best. I'm going upstairs to get her."

"Dick Powell."

"What?"

"Dick Powell is an actor from Arkansas. I think."

I'm coming down with something, and I'll have to travel with a fever, and what will happen to Momma and Baldwin if I die?

The flowers in the rug in Shelby's bedroom reached toward her. What was their name? Baldwin's phantom voice whispered, *Rose of Sharon.*

They had grown together, she and her grandmother and

her mother. They were choked by a girdling root, and Shelby had to cut it.

She thrust her hands to the ceiling, thinking of Sarah Bernhardt. Shelby could be anyone, pretend anything. She would lock the bathroom door, stare into the mirror, and practice the entire range of human emotions. It was hard for her to think of something so funny, she could have a good, spontaneous laugh, but she could win the Academy Award for crying. She began to swirl around the room, breasts flying, half-naked body glistening with perspiration, spirit soaring toward Broadway.

When Baldwin barged into the room and saw her granddaughter behaving in such a bawdy fashion, she slapped her hand against her heart. "My stars, child! You're bare *nekkid!*" She snatched Shelby's new green felt picture hat from the bureau and sailed it across the room.

A startled Shelby caught the hat and held it high.

"Cover yourself, child!" Baldwin croaked, focusing her eyes on the ceiling. "You didn't get those things from my side of the family! We don't come like that!"

"How do I know?" Shelby asked in a near whisper.

Baldwin cupped her ear to hear better.

"How do I *know?*" Shelby repeated. "You're always covered with a big white nightgown that belonged to your *mother. Everything belonging to your mother* or your *father. . . .*"

The room vibrated so violently with the unfamiliar sound of that grim whisper, it made Baldwin's head jerk sideways. Her granddaughter, of all people, had just denigrated the memory of Baldwin Josephine Shelby Howell's parents. The mean words that had spilled from sweet Shelby's lips were so improbable, they caused time to stop with an unearthly silence, and wobble and lurch until it could kick-start again.

Tears welled in Baldwin's eyes for the second time that day, and she couldn't have that, could never have that. She

41

grabbed a pair of yellow footwarmers from the floor, heaved up the trunk lid with a surge of angry strength, and stuffed them inside.

Shelby sucked in her breath at the proximity of her father's photograph to her grandmother's hand.

"If you don't take these footwarmers with you, you'll regret it. It gets too cold for Southern feet up north." She backed out of the room, slamming the door, slamming her finger against her lips, demanding *omerta* for the cold truth that had just been uttered by her beloved granddaughter.

Shelby plonked her green hat on top of her head, brought her hands to her breasts, squeezed until they hurt, grabbed a gossamer runner from the top of her dresser, heaved up the window so fiercely it shed some rotting wood, and threw the runner out the window where the only breeze of the day carried it to the spiky branches of a quince bush. The yellow footwarmers followed the runner.

She was ready to leave.

She leaned toward the mirror, darkening her pale lashes with grim, calligraphic skill. After she left, Shelby was certain her grandmother would join even more committees, and garden into the evening in the glare of the new outdoor lights. And, once again, she would start to organize the photographs stored in the back of her armoire, though she would never complete that chore. Those haughty faces would drown in the deep seas of Baldwin's memory.

Shelby feared her mother, however, would retreat to her bedroom, saying she needed to write letters, read books, mend clothes; when, in fact, she would lie on her bed for hours, brain scorched with memories she could only keep at bay when her daughter was near. Without that daughter close by, the terror that had once sucked Eulalia's breath might smother her again.

Shelby punched her fingers against her forehead and jerked them back, hoping she hadn't damaged her make-up. Maybe she was just hungry. She had been too nervous to eat the hot tamales her mother had bought for her at Tammy's on Twelfth Street, corn shucks steaming and wrapped in newspaper, though Baldwin, plump Baldwin, had eaten them all, licking her fingers with feline fastidiousness to preserve the sanctity of the starched white, monogrammed, linen napkin.

"I'm getting out of here," Shelby hissed, shimmying fiercely, raising her fists. "Outta here!"

She kicked the trunk that rested in the sunlight like a heavy-lidded cat. She kicked her great-grandmother's rug. Dusty pennies rolled like bugs. And, still braless, but now green-hatted, Shelby kicked the rug over the goal line and out the window.

3

BALDWIN LANDED BESIDE her daughter, speaking in breathless spasms. The porch swing groaned with her added weight. "I've never said it before, sister . . . and I hate to say it now . . . but Shelby is just like her father."

The gentle dark beneath Eulalia's eyes grew deeper. Her absent husband was never, ever alluded to.

"You ate too many tamales, Momma. You get gas when you eat too much."

"Well, somebody had to eat those tamales!" Baldwin's voice was shrill. "I can't let good food go to waste with people starving in China. And would that cat of Shelby's eat those tamales? No, indeed! I'm telling you right now, I won't feed that thing when she leaves, sister! Whole house smells like cat."

"You have to let Alfred out when he meows at the door." Eulalia moved her hand impatiently, causing her book to fall on the floor and the brown wrapping to rip.

"I will *not* take orders from a cat. Look at that thing lying there so we have to step over him." Baldwin glared at the large grey Persian cat sprawled on the porch stairs like a magnified amoeba.

"You know you like him."

"Humph, I do! Cat fur all over the place. And he's fat." Baldwin placed her hands on her own waist, as though proving to herself *she* was not. Her voice clamored like the old Frigidaire in the butler's pantry. "And Faubus is still going around the state in that lavender Cadillac. He's an embarrassment to every person in this state."

"It was Senator McClellan who campaigned in the Cadillac, Momma, and that was the last election."

"Well, Faubus had the calliope. Or the helicopter. Whatever he rode in, he looked like a clown. Tacky is tacky in Little Rock, Arkansas or Paris, France." Her voice rose another octave. "Go on up there and get her, sister. She'll just have to leave the trunk for Tommy to send later. Why is that man late today of all days? He's the only Nigra I know who keeps his word . . . but then he is part Indian."

She rose, peered at the street, opened the front screen and switched on lights that, when it got dark, would illuminate the house like a football field. Then she lumbered down the stairs to her garden where her hand hopped from weed to weed like a plump toad.

The garden had been her father's pride. Now it belonged to her, a longtime president of the Little Rock Garden Club, more constant than the seasons because she was never dormant. She tended her garden with a passion, with the exception of the back acres. Briars and poison ivy crept from those back acres, even though Tommy Self, gardener and handy man for thirty-five years, fought them with hoe and axe.

The back acres had once been carefully landscaped, the pride of the place, with a gazebo, a pond filled with koi and water lilies, and a statue of Cupid shipped all the way from Italy . . . though, of course, his private parts were plastered over when he reached Little Rock. But poor neutered Cupid was now lost in the brush, the gazebo had collapsed, and the pond filled in. There was a sad sense of abandonment down the slope where flora had flourished and beautiful koi had lazed in the pond.

Baldwin straightened from her work, hands to the small of her aching back, and absorbed the beauty of her flower-bedazzled garden. The light, moving toward dusk, spawned the golden haze that appeared when late-summer days die; and her face looked almost young in that bewitching illumination. She raised one ring-laden hand, and the luminescent phlox seemed to rise like a flock of white birds. She raised both hands, and the roses, their late colors deepened to a ruby red, flaunted their own aged beauty. There was something alarming about the fierce force of the old woman whispering, "Grow . . . grow. . . ." to the sluggish roots.

The same light captured the silvery glimmer of spiderwebs spiraling between the cherry tree and the house, but when the sky suddenly darkened, the spotlights revealed globs of eggs burgeoning with worms in the bulbs.

Baldwin's eyes narrowed at the sight of the eggs that would hatch their evil progeny and destroy her floral prizes. She snatched up an old broom, its straw worn to an angle, and hacked at the webs, once again an old woman dressed in a proper two-piece that strained at the seams. When she finished the chore, she drew a handkerchief from her bosom, wiped her brow, tucked the handkerchief back in its private place, and bent over the flowerbed, tossing words and weeds over her shoulder.

"Your granddaddy would turn over in his grave if he knew you were working for a Communist, Lalie." But her voice trailed off when she spotted a space in the garden where there might be enough sun to plant a peony. Then, "My stars! Here's that trowel I lost last spring." She leaned down farther, exposing garters above her knees, and straightened triumphantly, clutching a dirt-encrusted trowel, "Right where I planted my ferns! I looked for that thing, and Tommy looked for that thing, and it was here all the time!"

A large, white dog with dirty, tangled hair bounded into the yard, trampling the day lilies and causing Baldwin to jump awkwardly. The motion jostled her pearls and made the wooden cherries clatter on her hat. She shook her ring-heavy fingers at the dog and shouted, "Shoosh! SHOOSH! Those Langleys letting that mongrel run wild! Get out of my garden! SHOOSH, I say!"

"He's digging up bones someplace in back." Eulalia swallowed a yawn. "He had a big one in his mouth the other day."

A flicker of anxiety crossed Baldwin's face, and her screams grew louder, just as a new yellow MG roadster roared down the gravel drive. She was waving at the dog, but she seemed to be greeting the driver, which surely could not be the case, because the driver was a Negro.

4

THE DRIVER HONKED HIS horn in sassy syncopation and waved back to Baldwin, his long arm merging with the sycamore branches.

Colored men never waved like that to Baldwin Josephine Shelby Howell, nor did they speed up her front driveway in fancy automobiles. They parked in the alley and walked to the back door with hat in hand. But this Negro had invaded her front garden like a knight astride a bright yellow steed he could barely keep reined in. When he stepped from the car, his spotlit shadow strode before him, engulfing the old woman, who, in her agitation, crushed a clump of budding chrysanthemums. Their scent perfumed the air.

"Hello there, Miss Baldwin!" the man boomed. The spotlights caught the gleam of the gold ring on the man's right finger and the gold watch on his left wrist. "How nice to see you, too!" He was smiling, his teeth white against his dark skin, and he seemed intent on not just shaking her hand, but embracing her.

However, Baldwin's old legs maneuvered her body behind a tea rose where she could see the man's fine Roman nose, and his green eyes stippled with yellow flecks, and his skin the color of burnished brass and his shirt stitched with cording around the neck and sleeves, that matched the whirligig red and pink and green of the fabric. And there was something around his neck that appeared to be a necklace of dangling teeth, though it couldn't be a necklace. Men didn't wear necklaces.

And still he came with lengthening steps, his arms moving to an inner rhythm, his voice rumbling from deep within his chest. "Hey, Miss Baldwin!" he said, holding his arms toward her.

Baldwin glared at him over the rosebush. "Are you making a delivery?" she demanded.

The man came to an abrupt halt, sighed, reached into his shirt pocket and removed a pair of sunglasses. The glasses had a mirrored surface that concealed his eyes and reflected back to Baldwin her own tiny, distorted image.

"Take those things off your face! I've never seen the like!"

The man inhaled deeply, but didn't remove the glasses. "I'm not making a delivery." His accent was that of an educated white man from the East.

"And don't dilate your nostrils at me!"

"Momma . . ." Eulalia rose from the swing.

"Making me hurt my back, messing up my gravel with that . . . that . . . whatchamacallit! You get that thing out of my driveway!" Baldwin waved the trowel at the car with a sweep of her hand. "Where did you get that kind of car?"

"*Momma!*" Eulalia spoke more sternly.

The man's voice verged on sarcasm. "You want the nigger to leave, or you want the nigger to tell you how he got his car and his Yankee accent, Miz Baldwin?"

Baldwin jerked her chin toward Eulalia. "Didn't I tell you? It's Orville Faubus and that N-DOUBLE-A-C-P that brought us to this pass!"

The man removed his glasses, again revealing those green eyes, and he smiled at Eulalia, who snapped her fingers with a sound so loud it caused Baldwin to close her mouth. She had never heard Eulalia snap her fingers.

"Saracen. . . ." Eulalia smiled hesitantly. "You're Saracen Self. You see those eyes, Momma? You're Tommy's boy."

The man nodded. "It's been a long time, Mrs. Korzeniowski. A very long time."

The name "Korzeniowski," unspoken for thirteen years, had just been uttered by a giant black man who was smiling at Eulalia. The golden-hazed garden seemed dark again.

Eulalia's voice was flat as the Dead Sea. "I use my maiden name now. I haven't used that . . . other name for years."

The man grimaced, admonishing himself. "Of course not. Of course not. Forgive me."

She jiggled a hand as though it didn't matter. "You sure have grown. You weren't much taller than Shelby when you left, and she was younger than you by what . . . five years? Hasn't he grown, Momma?" Her voice was too controlled, too proper.

Baldwin glared at her daughter. "I want him out of my driveway," she said, as though it were up to Eulalia to carry out her command.

"Momma . . . this is *Tommy's* boy. . ."

"I don't have a prayer who this man is!"

"Look at those *eyes*, Momma."

The man was still staring at Eulalia, who slowly turned from him to speak to her mother. "And the scar on his forehead, how it makes an 'S?' See the scar? Remember when he and Shelby made that cat elevator, and Alfred jumped out of it from the second floor, and Saracen fell into the dahlia bed trying to catch the cat, and he cut his forehead in the shape of an 'S?'"

The man smiled at Eulalia again. "And I said the scar was 'S' for Superman, because the fall didn't kill me or the cat."

Baldwin squinted at the man with her head averted, trying to divine the boy superimposed on the man.

"Yes, and he ruined my dahlias when he fell. I didn't have a dahlia bloom that summer. Swinging on my wisteria like he was Tarzan." She gave another furtive look. "And how did he come by that kind of vehicle, I'd like to know?"

The man slipped back into the conversation with acrobatic

ease. "He got it in Chicago. That's where he lives now. After his momma died, his daddy sent him to Detroit to live with his aunt and uncle who talked like Yankees. He picked up the Yankee talk from them. As for the yellow car, he bought it with money he earned as a reporter for writing about a big nigger over in Africa named Kwame Nkrumah who's about to set his country *free*. In fact, all those black countries over there gonna be *free*. . . ." His deep voice fogged the air when he spoke the word "free!"

"You should visit Africa, Miss Baldwin. Visit Ouagadougou, where I got this beautiful shirt. They would just eat you up in Ouagadougou!" He tried to suppress a smile. "But right now I'm visiting my Daddy who's down in the back and shouldn't heft heavy trunks like he would have if I hadn't made him stay home. I said, 'Take care of your back, Daddy. I'd like to see the ladies after all these years. Miss Baldwin and I used to be friends. She used to call me her' sweet patootie.'"

"I did no such thing!" Baldwin huffed.

The man shook his head wearily. "It doesn't matter. This reporter is beset with a pain in his own back, not to mention other parts of his anatomy, and he thinks he'll return to his part of town where he feels just a little more welcome." He gave Baldwin a brief bow and took a short cut through a bed filled with pink obedient plants.

Baldwin wailed as the flowers collapsed, and wailed louder when Shelby called from her window, "What's going on down there?"

Baldwin's flushed face swung like a scythe between her granddaughter's voice and the man opening his car door.

"It's nothing, honey," Eulalia called in a bright voice. "I mean . . . it's just Saracen Self."

"Harrison *who?*"

"*Nothing!*" shrieked Baldwin. "*It's nothing!*" She strode from behind the rosebush.

"Saracen!" The man's voice was so loud it made Baldwin jump and caused Alfred, the old cat, to leap to the top of the walnut tree stump with an angry, twitching tail. There was a satisfying, expensive sounding "click" when he closed the car door. "Saracen Self!" he called again, walking back toward the house, eyes focused on Shelby's window.

Eulalia's wary eyes were on Baldwin.

"Saracen? You mean *Sary*? Tommy's boy?" Shelby pushed the old shade too hastily, and it clattered from its socket, emitting a cloud of dust and revealing the hazy sight of a young woman grasping at her unbuttoned blouse before she disappeared into the room and reappeared a minute later, blouse properly buttoned. "Well, Saracen!" she declaimed too cheerfully.

"Lord, help us," Baldwin moaned.

"Look at you! You've grown *up*, Saracen!"

"Well, *Shelby!*" The man grinned back. "And so have you!"

"*Miss* Shelby! *Miss* Shelby!" Baldwin cried. But she couldn't stop the young people from grinning at one another, or from Shelby shouting, "Stay right there! I'm coming down!"

"No! *No,* you are *NOT!*" Baldwin pounded the air with her fist. "You are *NOT* coming down! You . . . you don't have time!"

"Yes, she does," Eulalia interjected. "She has time, Momma."

Shelby was still tucking her blouse into her skirt as she ran out the front screen, scooting forward on one pump, pausing to pull up the sling on the other pump, racing down the porch stairs, and heading straight for Saracen, arms wide open, with Baldwin screaming at the top of her lungs, "Stop it! Stop it! *STOP, YOUNG LADY!*"

And Shelby stopped, but still smiled broadly.

Saracen's eyes were glowing like the cat's. "My God. It's

true. You look exactly like your father."

Baldwin swiveled her head as though she were on a mountaintop gazing at a distant valley. The grey cat hopped from the tree stump and rubbed against the man's legs. Saracen bent to pick up the cat, the necklace free-floating its menacing teeth.

"It must be ten years since I've seen you, Sary!"

"Oh, it's been more," Eulalia said. "Maybe fourteen. We still miss your sweet Momma. There never was a woman as good as Jessie, was there, Momma?"

Baldwin didn't respond. She was still on her mountaintop, looking into the distance, but words tap danced from Shelby's mouth. "Where did you get those glasses, Sary? I've never seen anything like them!"

Saracen, who had been staring at Eulalia who was staring at her mother, turned back to Shelby. "These are my African shades. The better to see you, my dear," he grinned.

"You've been to *Africa?*"

When Baldwin began to sputter, Eulalia spoke with excessive cheer, as though they were all seated properly in the living room. "We have distant relatives in South Africa, don't we, Momma? De Venter, isn't that their last name? Maybe you met them on your travels, Saracen."

Saracen chuckled. "There are two reasons I haven't been to South Africa to meet your relatives, Miss Eulalia," thus letting her know how he would address her in the future. "The first is, the South Africans wouldn't let me *inside* their country. The second is, if I did get in, they wouldn't let me *out* of their country, so, thank God, I have my *own* country right here." He swooped a long arm around Baldwin's property. "You do remember, Miss Baldwin, that the land I'm standing on originally belonged to the Quapaw Indians, who I doubt were paid when our great country stole the land from them. And since my great-granddaddy, Saracen, was Quapaw, I think by rights I can say this is *my* property too. Don't you agree?" His smile grew to an unabashed grin.

Baldwin spoke so emphatically her jowls trembled. "*My* granddaddy *bought* this property and I have a deed to prove it! Every speck of this American earth is mine! And old Saracen never was chief of the Quapaws like you used to brag!"

"Ah, but it says he was chief on his tombstone at Pine Bluff, *and* it says he was 'the rescuer of captive children.' *White* folks put up that tombstone to honor him, so those words must be true, Miss Baldwin." He turned back to Shelby. "Remember our games about captive children? I always saved you, didn't I? But the point is," and he turned to Baldwin again, "I believed the story about Great-Granddaddy Saracen when I needed the pride that went with what you call his legend, and what I call the truth. And the truth is, my grandfather and his *good* tribe rescued those white children from a *bad* Indian tribe, and my great-granddaddy's *good tribe* returned the children to their *perfect white families.*"

Baldwin snorted derisively, but Eulalia and Shelby didn't hear her. Their eyes were fixed on the long fingers that stroked the cat.

Shelby didn't know this black man who gave no thought to wearing a necklace and an outlandish shirt. She had known a skinny little boy who wore a rope instead of a belt, but the rope was tied in such an intricate knot it became an object to covet. He was her only close friend when she was a child, and she had loved that friend, tried to mimic everything he did. When he left to go North, she cried herself to sleep, the same way she cried a few years earlier when her father disappeared. She was so beguiled by this memory that she jumped when his deep voice ripped through the sullen air.

"Ah, but *Miss* Shelby, I see our walnut tree is gone, and how sad that is. Biggest tree I ever saw until I went to Africa. I nearly cried when Daddy told me he had to chop it down. Stupid worms destroyed it. They could have coexisted if the worms hadn't been so greedy. Those worms destroyed the very heart of that great tree. Did I ever tell you I had a hideaway up there?" The women followed his raised hand to the top of the now-phantom tree. "First time I climbed to the top, I saw the gold dome of the State Capital sparkling in the sun, and I nearly fell off the branch. I thought I was seeing Jerusalem! I clung to that branch and prayed to God to forgive my many sins! But God just laughed and told me to go back home where I belonged . . . or more than likely it was you who told me it was time to go home, Miss Baldwin."

He chuckled and turned back to Shelby.

"Remember how we used to crack open walnuts with rocks? We would pound and pound at those tough shells, and eat ourselves sick with walnut meats. Pick 'em out with a nail. Remember?"

Shelby nodded, smiling, remembering.

"And I will *never* forget the summer you cooked up a brew with walnut hulls and black shoe polish and God knows what else, and daubed it all over your hair and face and arms because you wanted to look like *me!*" He couldn't resist a lopsided grin at Baldwin. "All that platinum hair and white skin smeared with black!" His chuckle grew until he threw back his head and boomed a laugh that bounced around the garden.

The alarmed cat struggled to escape Saracen's arms, but relaxed when his fur was stroked with long, persistent fingers. "Took over a month for that stuff to wear off. You tried to scrub it off with turpentine, Miss Baldwin, but the place got infected and left a good-sized scar beneath Shelby's chin."

The front door slammed behind Baldwin when she stomped into the house.

Saracen followed her exit with narrowed eyes, chuckling with the hollow sound of a woodpecker hammering a dead tree trunk. Then, before the women's astonished eyes, he raised the mesmerized cat to his chest and began a slowdance around the ghost of the tree, humming what might have been an Indian chant. An incursion of fireflies swirled around the man and the cat, an ethereal whirl of sparkling lights that illuminated the man and the darkness until he stopped the dance and raised his voice loud enough for a person to hear inside the house. The fireflies scattered like raindrops.

"They say you're going to New York City to become an actress, Miss Shelby, and I've heard from a reliable source that the head of your school is a Communist who teaches that Russian method acting stuff. "

Baldwin exploded out the door, her voice broadcasting down the block. "It doesn't bother me if you don't get on that train, Shelby Howell!"

"We're okay on time, Momma," Eulalia said quickly. "Saracen is telling us things."

"I could hear he was telling you things! Everyone in the neighborhood can hear, and *lies* is what he's telling you! You're a child, Eulalia! You've always been a child, believing anything anybody tells you who appears out of nowhere and looks like he's from Mars. And look what it got you!"

Baldwin made no effort to hide what she was really saying: that Eulalia had eloped with a foreigner who was a pilot in a flying circus, and because the foreigner couldn't earn enough money to support a family at his ridiculous occupation, she, Baldwin Josephine Shelby Howell, had to take them into her fine house, and after her great generosity, the man had disappeared, disgracing them all.

Eulalia's face was red, her lips compressed, but Shelby came to her mother's rescue. "Oh, Baldwin . . . remember how Saracen made up poems for you? He would rattle them off on the spot, and you would laugh and call him your 'sweet patootie'."

Now Baldwin glared at Shelby.

"And he's just teasing about Communists at The Actors Studio. Victor Liebmann is a great teacher, isn't he, Saracen? . . . and he's probably a Democrat."

"Of course he is." Saracen's voice was so smooth he had to be lying. "Although that method director, Elia Kazan, did say Leibmann was a Commie when he testified before the House Un-American Committee. To refresh your memory, Miss Baldwin, Kazan directed *On the Waterfront* and *A Streetcar Named Desire*, starring that great method actor of screen and scandal, Marlon Brando. And what was that other movie I liked so much that Kazan directed?" Saracen paused, searching his memory. "*Baby Doll!*" he exclaimed. "Another great one!"

This time Baldwin glowered, not at him, but at Eulalia.

For a moment there was silence. The lightening bugs disappeared, and the muggy air enveloped all of them. It was too hot and too heavy, but it was the summer air they knew.

Saracen coughed slightly and changed the subject, like any good host at a difficult dinner party. "Do you ladies know . . ." he lowered his jaw studiously, "that this legendary cat, Alfred, has been in mortal danger his entire life?"

"In danger?" Shelby said, happy to leave the perils of method acting. "Not Alfred. Dogs don't bother to chase him anymore. Possums waddle right past."

"Remember that tamale place on 15th Street?"

"Sure. Tammy's. Better than anything I'll find in New York City." Shelby smiled coaxingly at Baldwin who turned away to deadhead geraniums with lethal twists of her wrists.

"The health department just closed him down. Found out all these years he's been making his deluxe tamales out of cat meat!"

The deadheads slipped from Baldwin's fingers.

"Yes, ma'am." His nod at Baldwin seemed sincere. "Pure

dee cat. They found piles of cat skeletons behind his shed, plus fresh kitty cooking in that big, black pot."

A mewing sound trickled from Baldwin's mouth.

"I'm not making this up, Miss Baldwin. You can read about it in this afternoon's *Democrat*."

"Oh, Baldwin " Shelby murmured. "You ate them *all*"

Baldwin turned her back on the group and walked with utmost dignity to the porch where she sat so hard on the porch swing, it squealed and sagged with her weight.

Eulalia followed her mother, chattering reassuringly. "I'm sure it's like pork, Momma. It's safe if it's well cooked. Remember when Tammy told us the secret of his recipe was how long he cooked his Grade A . . ." there was a slight quaver in Eulalia's voice when she added the word, "meat?"

Saracen raised his thick eyebrows. "Ahhhh." He spoke with great solemnity. "Miss Howell. Ma'am. I ate plenty of cat in Hong Kong, and look how tall I got to be. Cat is good for the . . . uh . . . liver." He deposited Alfred on the ground and rubbed his hands together energetically. "Now where is that trunk? I'll just load it up right quick."

"That would be lovely." Eulalia spoke too heartily. "Go up with him, Shelby. And quickly."

Saracen skirted Baldwin with utmost care and took two stairs at a time to catch up with Shelby. When he entered her bedroom, he browsed the room with his eyes, said, "Looks almost the same," and reached out his hand to her, smiling.

She smiled in return, covered his hand with hers, then, with a quick intake of breath, she stepped back. "The trunk is over there."

"Something wrong?"

"It's just . . . it's really hot up here."

He looked at her a moment, walked to the trunk, and sat

down on it.

"Saracen. . . ."

He crossed his arms and leaned back as though he had all the time in the world. "I have something to tell you."

"We've got to hurry," she insisted.

He crossed his legs. "Remember that word you taught me when we were kids? Your magic word, you called it."

Shelby nodded "yes" and pointed to her watch. "Take the trunk down. Please."

"I know when your train leaves. You're fine . . . unless," he raised his eyebrows, "unless Baldwin has a cat fit." He cleared his throat. "Remember that secret word you shared with me? *Owneeswakeemollypants,* you would scream, and wave your arms like a banshee. But," he leaned toward her conspiratorially, and honked a laugh when she backed to the door. "Are you *afraid* of me, Sheb? Your old buddy, Saracen? Afraid I'll carry you off to my den of black iniquity?"

"Of course I'm not! But I have to leave. I have a train to catch!"

He sighed. "Okay. But first you have to listen to me. When I lived in Paris, I discovered your word actually means something."

"Oh, for heaven's sake, Saracen. I don't have time for this! That was just a silly incantation my father made up for me." But there was a bit of uncertainty in her voice in the face of Saracen's absolute conviction.

"In the first place," he said, "it's not just *one* word. It's six *French* words spoken by Edward III of England in the fourteenth century." He patted the side of the trunk. "Sit by me, and I'll tell you about it. It's cooler by the window."

"I'm just fine over here," she said, too quickly.

"You're *jes fine.*" He smiled. "When you were little, you used to say you were 'jes fine' when you weren't fine at all. You would tremble like a scared puppy, and say," and he mocked her childish voice, "*I'm jes fine, Saracen, I'm jes fine.*"

"Okay, *OKAY!* What do you mean, six French words?"

"Well. In the fourteenth century these royal folks were at a big party when a lady's garter slipped down her leg. Everyone gawked and laughed, but King Edward picked up the garter, slipped it around his sleeve and proclaimed," and Saracen spoke slowly so Shelby could hear her magic word in each syllable: "*Honi soit qui mal y pense.* Get it? Your daddy took the king's words, smashed them together with an English twist and created a magical incantation for his little girl . . . an incantation, that, when we were kids, worked fine for both of us."

Shelby's mouth opened in astonishment.

"Yeah! That's your magic word, which means 'shame on you, kids, for thinking bad thoughts about an embarrassed lady'!" Then he stood to his full height, stomped his foot, sliced the air dramatically with his hand, and shouted, "*Owneeswakeemollypants!* I've been practicing," he grinned modestly. "And there's more to the story. To prove honor was above all, the king founded The Most Noble Order of the Garter and made the garter part of the insignia! It's still big stuff with the English."

Shelby grimaced and held up her hands as though she couldn't bear to be disappointed. "Would you kid me about this?"

"Kid you about our word? *Never.* I almost called you from Paris to share the tidings. It was one of those crazy moments. But I waited to tell you in person."

Shelby's entire demeanor changed. She was almost giggling. "I've got to write this down! How do you spell those French words?"

Saracen spelled the words slowly, adding, "You gotta be nice to folks when they're in a tight spot."

Shelby lifted her arms, prepared to hug him, and said,

"You solved a puzzle I didn't know existed!" Then she dropped her arms uncertainly, grabbed her purse from the bed and fumbled inside. "I . . . I've got to write down the spelling before I forget."

"It's all right, Momma."

The porch swing made a somber creak.

"You've eaten those tamales for years. They just go in one end and out the other."

Baldwin eyed Eulalia with distaste. "I tried my best, but you don't have a lick of manners, and you don't give a *fig* for my feelings and neither does Shelby. . ."

"Oh, Momma, we both do. You know we do."

" . . . and she's as good as gone from my life. Forever."

A fearful look swept Baldwin's face, then she straightened her shoulders. "If I should get sick and die, you will not tell *anyone* about those tamales, Eulalia. I will *not* go to my Maker with people snickering about cats and tamales. You make that man swear on his momma's grave he'll keep his lips sealed. And do *not* let Ernestine inside this house. She'll take anything she can get her hands on. First thing, when you see I'm gone to my Maker, slip the rings off my cold fingers and hide them in my upstairs safe. Ernestine doesn't know the combination. And remember that Shelby gets the star sapphire that's on *this* finger. She loves it best. You can have Momma's engagement ring I'm wearing on my other hand. The other pink diamonds are in the safe. They're all yours. Pink diamonds were Momma's favorites, and the house goes to you and Shelby. It's written that way in my will, and. . ."

"*You will not die from cat tamales, Momma!* You've eaten them for years! French people eat horsemeat all the time! They even eat snails that crawl on the ground! And Shelby *does* love you. She just needs to try her wings for a while. She needs . . . she needs to get away from us for a while."

A loud thump rumbled on the floor from upstairs, accompanied by a man's wild yell.

"Oh, my stars!" Baldwin struggled to her feet. "He's got Shelby in her bedroom! *Run, Eulalia! I'll get the hoe!*"

But the sound of footsteps caused Baldwin to collapse back on the swing, hand on her pounding heart. Her beloved granddaughter was walking down the stairs dressed in a suit that matched her green eyes. A green picture hat was placed on her head at a jaunty angle. Her new purse was in one hand, and a baby blue cosmetic case, purchased by Eulalia with seventeen books of laboriously pasted yellow stamps, was held in the other hand.

Saracen, the trunk hoisted on his back, followed more ponderously and less elegantly.

As they walked around the curve in the stairs, the colors in the neo-Gothic window captured the last rays of the sun and stained their young bodies with muted purples and blues and greens, transforming them into creatures from another world. They were as one with the wooden mantelpiece in the living room, which was intricately carved in an array of flowers and vines and strange beasts with human faces. The enchantment persisted as they walked over the hushed hues of worn oriental rugs, past the grand piano, its white keys yellowed like the teeth of an old man who smoked too much; and the colors hovered until they walked out the heavy front door with its silver doorbell that clanged a resounding farewell.

Baldwin put her hand to her quivering mouth. Shelby looked like a model in a magazine.

She looked like New York City.

She looked like someone who would never come back home.

Saracen maneuvered the trunk down the porch steps, kicked Eulalia's book out of the way, and dumped his heavy burden onto the back seat of the Volkswagen, which made the small car sink like a fat king's carriage. He squeezed the cosmetic case on the floor in front of the front passenger seat, and when that was done, used the tail of his many-colored shirt to wipe perspiration from his face.

Baldwin heaved herself from the porch swing, pushed Eulalia aside, and clumped down to the drive. "Hold out your palm," she commanded Saracen and dropped a quarter on it. "And tell Tommy to let me know if he can't make it on Monday. The toilet is making noises again." She marched past Saracen to Eulalia's convertible, squeezed onto the passenger seat, and propped her swollen feet on top of the cosmetic case.

Eulalia's usually distant eyes were furious, and she slammed the car door shut for her mother.

Saracen tossed the quarter high in the air, caught it one-handed, and pocketed the money. "*Honi soit qui mal y pense!*" he called to Shelby, enunciating each word carefully. He swung his long legs over the door of the MG, slid onto the leather seat, and jammed the key in the ignition. When he turned on the brights, they illuminated the old woman who was crammed in the front seat of the Volkswagen.

Shelby's heart was pounding. When she was a child, kids taunted her about her family, but Saracen would grab her by the wrist and drag her through alleys to the safety of the beloved house she was about to leave. *I'm the Rescuer of Captive Children!* he would shout as they sped to the castle keep.

"Wait." Eulalia's voice was so meek she had to clear her throat. "*Wait . . .* Saracen . . . please. *Wait!*"

He looked at her. "We . . ." Eulalia said, "we have a problem with the suitcases. They take up the entire back seat, and there's not enough room in the car for the three of us *and* the suitcases. Will . . . will you take Shelby to the station? *Please.*"

Baldwin bellowed over her shoulder, "He will not! We are *all* going to the train station in *this* vehicle!"

Eulalia placed her hands on the MG door. The car wasn't moving, but her fingers grew white with the effort of holding it in place.

"*Please* take Shelby. There isn't room with all the luggage . . . *unless* . . ." Eulalia's eyes took on a furtive hope, "unless Momma doesn't go. . . ."

"Of course, I'm going!" Baldwin roared. "Half of Little Rock is down there waiting for me to arrive! We're all three going in *this* car!"

"Where will Shelby *sit*, Momma?"

"On my lap! I've held that child on my lap plenty of times. *Come here to me, Shelby Howl!*" Baldwin gave a resounding whack to her lap to show exactly where Shelby should sit. "Or . . . or call Julien at the funeral home! Call him now, Eulalia! Tell him any kind of vehicle will do!"

Saracen put the gear in reverse.

"*Please,*" Eulalia implored him. "*Help us.*" She clutched his arm tighter.

Shelby stared at her mother's hand.

"Momma can't help the way she talks. You remember how she talks." Eulalia turned to her sputtering mother who was trying to heave herself around to open the car door. "Shelby and you and those suitcases can't fit, *so hush, Momma!*"

What was happening to the world? Shelby wondered dreamily. *Her submissive mother was telling Baldwin what to do.*

When Baldwin began to bluster again, Eulalia aimed her finger like a pistol. "*I said HUSH, Momma!*"

Baldwin's face froze.

"Saracen is a good man! He used to be your *favorite.*

I will *not* let you mess up Shelby's going away!" Eulalia whirled back to Saracen. "If Tommy were here, he'd tell you to take Shelby."

"I didn't tell Tommy goodbye. . . ." Shelby murmured.

"Tommy would carry her to the train station in his arms. And this is her first train ride." said Eulalia.

But Shelby was thinking, *Yes, I have been on a train, the little red train at the zoo, and I stuck my tongue out at Saracen and yelled nyah, nyah, nyah because the train was just for white children, and Jessie wouldn't let him yell back.* Suddenly, Shelby felt sick to her stomach.

"I'm so sorry about Momma. Please pay her no mind" Eulalia's fingers dug into his arm.

The man seemed unaware his arm was being gouged. He was staring straight ahead like a sleek black centaur with a yellow MG body. Across the way, Baldwin stomped the floorboard of the Volkswagen like an obstinate old donkey, shrieking, "*Out! Out of my yard!*"

Saracen gunned the MG's motor, and the exhaust kicked up dust and dead magnolia leaves. Then he paused, put the car in neutral, pulled on the brake, gazed at Baldwin's angry back, removed the handkerchief from his hip pocket and began to dust the seat beside him with exaggerated furls.

"No, ma'am. I won't ride Shelby to the station. But I *will* ride Miss Baldwin." He raised his voice. "When I was a boy you gave me a white linen handkerchief, Miss Baldwin, and told me I should always have one in my pocket for the necessaries. Well, I'm wiping off your seat with a white linen handkerchief right now, hoping you'll accept my personal invitation to ride in the *front* of my bus. Come on over here and be my partner, please, ma'am!"

He gave a resounding slap to the bucket seat beside him. "I'd be proud to have a country club white lady ride in my buggy!"

He began to sing in a rich baritone, "Ain't gonna ride them buses no more, ain't gonna ride no more. . ." and he jumped out of the car, still singing, rushed to the passenger side and opened the door with a handkerchiefed, many-looped bow.

Eulalia hurried to the convertible and whispered to Baldwin, who shook her head, her mouth working spastically, "*No, No, NO!*" until her lips ceased to move, and with an astonishing burst of strength, she geysered herself from the seat, reached over the door, jerked down the recalcitrant handle, scurried across the drive, and landed in the MG's passenger side.

"Ahhh," Saracen breathed very quietly, closing her door with great care. "Ahhh," he breathed again, and slipped around to the driver's seat. "Now lock your door, Miss Baldwin, please, ma'am. You're liable to fall out the way you're leaning so far to the right . . . though I'm certain you *never* lean to the left."

He closed his door, gunned the engine again and backed the yellow car out of the drive, scattering more gravel and dust. Baldwin's beringed fingers clutched her hat that was doing its best to hold down her pounding, permanent waves.

5

EULALIA SLAMMED her door too hard, forgetting in her haste that a serious jar made the window fall deep into the slot, retrievable only with a knife and a burglar's skill. She ground the wobbly shift into a too-quick reverse, and the car squealed onto the street.

When Shelby turned to grab the suitcase that was about to slide onto the street, her heart lurched at the sight of her bedroom turret poking through the trees.

She knew that turret and the house as well as she knew her own skin, its smells of wax and dried rose petals and occasional cat pee. She knew every inch of the balustrade on the balcony and the side porch's glider with its faded green cushions that bulged with stuffing like old people grown too fat. When she and Saracen were children running to safety, the house had always been there for them.

So why was she leaving it?

She sank back on her seat. The sulphurous gleam of the MG had disappeared.

"Does he know which train station?" Shelby yelled over the noise of the wind and the rattling car.

"He knows," Eulalia yelled back. Her black hair winged around her head, trying mightily to lift her into the air.

"I'm afraid he might take her to Hot Springs instead to get back at how rotten she was to him."

"He'll take her to the Missouri Pacific station. We can count on Saracen."

They clattered north down oak-lined Broadway, past turn-of-the-century houses, the city's stolid potentates. Trees, once saplings, towered over the houses, many occupied by members of the original families.

"He's huge, isn't he? It frightened me a little, the way he appeared out of nowhere."

"He used to do that when he was a child . . . just appear. But he was always kind. Always gentle. Don't be frightened of Saracen."

"What . . . what if he walks into the station with Baldwin?"

"He won't do that. Anyhow . . ." Eulalia hesitated, "he's not allowed in the 'whites only' section."

But Shelby was still left with a sorrowful unease and the faint smell of cordite.

They passed Mount Holly cemetery, pure Protestant, where the Confederate boy spy, David O. Dodd, lay buried. When a blindfold couldn't be found, the boy, a southern gentleman to the end, reached into his own pocket, retrieved a clean, white handkerchief, and handed it, with a bow, to the Yankee hangman.

Baldwin's father was also buried at Mount Holly. His body had arrived in Little Rock dressed in ragged clothes resembling those worn by Mao's early followers. The body was accompanied by a tiny Chinese woman who insisted in her broken English that she was his wife. His "life," she called herself. When her eyes lit on Baldwin's star sapphire, she stammered that the ring was hers, and she tried to wrench it from Baldwin's finger. But Baldwin Josephine Shelby Howell was not about to give up her treasure, and she kicked the little woman in the shins until members of the funeral party pulled them apart. After the funeral, the woman disappeared, perhaps to Mississippi.

Of course the woman was a fraud, because Jason Wilson Shelby already had a wife in Little Rock, Lucy Baldwin Shelby, a woman of excellent standing, who had sat on the porch swing crocheting bedspreads and decorative fringe for sheets and pillow slips for twenty-four years, waiting for her husband to return from China where he was saving the heathen.

Eulalia turned left toward the handsome State Capitol with its brass doors from Tiffany and the golden dome that had enthralled young Saracen, then turned right toward the train station where, as soon as the car stopped, Shelby's friends rushed to grab her winter coat and bags. Porters carted Baldwin's trunk that would travel Railway Express.

Shelby's best friend, Kate Norton, hugged her and whispered, "Write to me. And I do mean *everything*, Shelby Howell!" Kate was married, had a fine house in Pulaski Heights, was a member of the Junior League *and* the Aesthetic Club, *and* she was pregnant. Her life was perfect.

Inside the station, Miss Finney, Shelby's high school English teacher, had the temerity to nudge Kate aside, which was unlike Miss Finney, whose hair always struggled to escape its snood, and whose sturdy brown oxfords shuffled like two small rodents down Little Rock Senior High's halls. Her peacock laugh tended to astonish—the "Finney whinny," her students called it behind her back. But the same students fought to be included in her classes, and listened rapturously when she read passages from *Moby-Dick*, the vein on her forehead throbbing to the passionate beat of the prose.

"'I will have no man on my boat,' said Starbuck, 'who is not afraid of a whale.'" And the students became afraid of the great white that even Queequeg feared, and they caught a collective breath when tiny Miss Finney rose up on the toes of her sturdy brown shoes, raised her scrawny arm, and shouted, "There she blows! – there she blows! A hump like a snow-hill! It is Moby-Dick!" And when she intoned, "He sleeps with clenched hands; and wakes with his own bloody nails in his palms," they would stare at the vein that throbbed on her forehead and shudder at Ahab's obsession.

The vein was throbbing when Miss Finney whispered to Shelby, "Write to me. Write me *everything*. And remember that Ishmael called New York City 'Manhattoes.' He left it for the sea, but Manhattoes will become *your* ocean. Also . . ." she paused, as though gathering courage, "call me by my real name. Call me Oceana."

Oceana? Call Miss Finney *Oceana?*

"Oceana," Miss Finney repeated solemnly and bent toward Shelby, as though handing her a vial of holy water.

"Yes, ma'am," Shelby replied obediently, remembering she had heard other teachers call her "Bessie."

Miss Finney gave her a sorrowful smile.

"I mean, 'Yes,'" Shelby corrected herself.

And still Miss Finney waited.

"Yes . . . Oceana?"

Oceana's smile was beatific as she pressed a small package into Shelby's palm.

Shelby looked up from this strange encounter and saw Charlie Billington leaning against a column and staring at her. But Charlie didn't move toward her. And she wanted him to.

Why was she leaving this man who left her weak in the knees and was plenty tall, even when she wore high heels? What in heaven's name did she want that was so far away from Charlie Billington?

Baldwin's friends were tugging at Shelby's arms, murmuring, "You sweet thing, you precious thing, we could just eat you up." She embraced the old women carefully, as though they were dried flowers, and they smothered her against blowsy bosoms that smelled of talcum powder mixed with an occasional hint of bourbon.

She peered over their shoulders, looking for Charlie.

But Charlie was gone.

Kate pushed the winter coat into Shelby's arms, and plain Lettie Hutchins pressed one finger on her shoulder, as though she didn't have the right to hug. "Bless your sweet little heart," Lettie whispered. "I'll miss you, little girl. Make sure you lock your door at night. It's not like home up there in that. . ."

But Julien pushed Lettie aside, mid-sentence, and hugged Shelby, nearly, accidentally, kissing her on the lips. Eulalia jerked her daughter away before the desecration could take place.

Then there was only Baldwin looking up at tall Shelby, who hugged her grandmother; and Baldwin permitted the hug.

Shelby murmured, "I'll miss you so much."

Baldwin tried to speak, but could only manage a nearly pleading, "Write," that sounded like *riot*. She didn't say *riot* everything, and Shelby knew she never wanted to hear everything. She fumbled with her granddaughter's hand as though trying to leave a message deep within the skin, injecting the *Little Rock is your home from which you must not roam* drug one final time, and when the hand was released, the star sapphire was on Shelby's ring finger. With the exception of gardening, Baldwin wore that ring every day and had never even scratched its heavenly surface.

"*You mustn't!* This is your good luck ring! And it's too big for me. See?"

But Baldwin continued to shove the ring on each of her granddaughter's fingers, until it stayed, firmly enough, on the middle finger of the right hand.

Shelby was stunned by the depth of love and desperation in the old woman's eyes, and by how old she looked close-up: the skin on her face overlapped with wrinkles and dotted with age spots, the skin on her hands almost transparent, like a landscape seen from a distance, with blue streams just beneath the surface of very thin ice, blood trickling sluggishly, heart sputtering unsteadily, skeleton flaking, brain rotting, bit by bit.

However she was more frightened by the tears that crept down Baldwin's cheeks. Shelby had never seen her grandmother cry. *No one* should see Baldwin Josephine Shelby Howell cry, especially in public, though comfort dare not be offered to the old woman who was punching her index fingers against her cheeks, trying to stop the watery flow with pain.

It was Eulalia who came to the rescue and steered Shelby toward the stairs that led to the track. Eulalia, who always cried, had acquired a Valkyrie stance. She unwound her daughter's arms from her neck and whispered in her ear, "You'll be all right, my darling girl. You can do this thing. Now stand up straight, and smile for the people," just as the old Baldwin, the familiar Baldwin, found her voice and called to Shelby, "*Be sure you go upstairs!*"

Shelby knew Baldwin was reminding her again that the all-white ladies room was upstairs at the St. Louis station where she would change trains, as was the all-white Harvey Restaurant.

By the time she reached the platform, she was composed and waving to the crowd. She had learned, as Miss Little Rock, how to smile and wave and walk across the Robinson Auditorium stage like a Southern magnolia (whose milk-white flowers turned brown when touched by the human hand).

Five feet nine, eyes of brine.

Don't swing those hips too much, girls, but swing 'em

enough. Don't raise that bosom too high, girls, but raise it high enough. Don't open those teeth so far apart, girls. You look like you're waiting for the dentist to stick his paw in your mouth. (Or like he's stuck his paw somewhere else, Miss Beebe giggled.)

Twinkle! Sparkle! Be happy! And a one and a two and a three . . . and. . . .

    I'm looking over (kick)
    A four-leaf clover (kick)
    That I've overlooked before (step, step, step. . . .)

Waving the Arkansas flag in one hand with that great big diamond in the middle, because that's what you are, girls, Arkansas diamonds. And waving the Confederate flag in the other hand, because you are from the South, everyone looking like June Allyson, except Shelby, who was too tall and smiling so broadly she could barely close her lips over her dry teeth. She swung around the steel step of the Missouri Pacific Eagle to face the crowd, but instead of waving like Marilyn Monroe, she caught her spiked heel in one of the steel webbings and knocked her shin against the step's edge. She would have dropped her cosmetic case if someone hadn't steadied her elbow with a strong hand so she could jerk her heel free.

A photographer from the *Arkansas Gazette* shouted, "Give me a great big smile, Shelby! Say 'kiss'!"

The pain from her shin settled in the pimple on her forehead she had concealed with Max Factor, and she lifted the corners of her mouth obediently. The camera flash caused spangles to dance before her eyes, transforming Baldwin's face into an X-ray that revealed black bones and grey teeth parted in a ghastly grimace that was shouting and moving toward Shelby. But Eulalia reached out and cuffed her mother's arm, and Shelby screamed at Baldwin, though not out loud, *Stay away! Stay away!* She waved harder, her smile trembling, holding up her hand to show Baldwin the star sapphire.

It was only then she remembered she hadn't thanked the person who had steadied her arm, though she knew, even before she turned, that the next morning she would appear on the front page of the Arkansas Gazette with Saracen Self smiling up at her, his strong, brown arm gripping her arm which was, despite its deep tan, lily-white to the bone.

"Welcome, Miss Little Rock!"

The porter made his announcement loud enough for all to hear. The passengers from Texas turned to stare as Miss Little Rock entered the Pullman car. But she couldn't smile back. She handed the porter her beautiful new winter coat. She handed him her green hat. Then she collapsed on her seat, turned for a last glimpse of the city, and sat up ramrod straight, because Saracen Self was looking up at her with those astonishing green eyes, as he jogged by the side of the slow-moving train.

When the train picked up speed, Little Rock disappeared and so did Saracen.

6

EVERYONE SAW the strangely garbed Negro jogging beside the train with easy grace. There was a bewildered silence until Julien yowled and grabbed the railing as though ready to jump the twenty-five feet down to the tracks. By that time the train and the jogger were lost in the dark.

Baldwin navigated through the crowd with her chin high, though Charlie Billington was holding up most of her heft. Eulalia was on the other side, a firm hand at her mother's elbow. Then Baldwin abruptly shook off both arms to make queenly waves to her subjects. *Goodbye, my subjects*, her waves signified. *That Nigra you saw standing by Shelby does not exist. The Nigra you saw jogging by her train was a phantom.*

When the three reached the sidewalk, the heavens opened. Charlie helped Baldwin into the car and was about to raise the convertible's cranky top when Eulalia pulled off with a screech. Charlie, hands still in the air, followed the car with his eyes, bemused and drenched.

7

THE WOMEN SAT as though the top of the car were in place. Baldwin's fake smile slid from her mouth about the time the dye from her navy straw hat began trickling down her forehead. She wiped away rainwater, smearing the blue stain, which made her look like a weary warrior from the days of Robert the Bruce.

When they reached home, Eulalia hurried to close the tall windows in the rain-blown house, and fetch towels to wipe water from the beautiful hardwood floors. With the windows shut, the house grew hot, but the women didn't notice. Baldwin jerked off her hat and whispered, "I'd like a whiskey."

Eulalia's eyes widened at her mother's blue face and at her request for whiskey. Her mother was a teetotaler. "We don't have whiskey, Momma."

Baldwin sighed as though she had to tend to everything herself, and plodded to the library in her dripping clothes. Eulalia watched her mother remove a key-laden chain from her purse and unlock the bottom drawer of what had been her father's desk. She grunted, feeling into the long depths, her butt elevated like a navy-blue monadnock, her voice muffled.

"Did you see Ernestine at the train station?" She emerged with a dust-fused bottle labeled J.W. Dant.

"No, ma'am." Eulalia was mesmerized by her mother's effort to rise while embracing the whiskey bottle against her damp bosom. "We would have heard her. You know how her voice carries."

"Doesn't matter. She'll see that Nigra grinning at Shelby

on the front page of the *Gazette*. Everyone will." Baldwin slit the paper seal with a sharp slide of her fingernail and loosened the cap with several whacks on the floor. She had observed her father perform this ritual many times.

She removed two dusty, cut glass whiskey tumblers from the cupboard in the dining room, swiped the insides with her damp peplum, poured generous portions of J. W. Dant into each glass, handed a glass to Eulalia as though offering a communion cup, and sat down in her wet clothes on the very special, uncomfortable, melon-colored velvet antique sofa.

The women choked and shuddered on the first swallow, but after that swallow, Baldwin sipped steadily like a bird from a bowl. When the cat jumped on her wet lap, she let him stay.

Mother and daughter sat, unspeaking, in the rainy glow from the outside spots, until Baldwin, her voice a bit blurred, said, "That Internal Revenue Service man came by again." She gave a sonorous belch without excusing herself. "Threatening to take my property if I didn't pay. He has no manners," she said, addding inconsequentially, "and Jessie was my maid, *not* my friend like you said."

Eulalia looked at the ceiling.

"Do you think he got on that train?"

"No, Momma. There wasn't a car for coloreds."

Baldwin rose a bit unsteadily, clinging to the cat with one hand and pulling herself up the stairs with the other hand. The cat's back legs flopped with each leaden step. Eulalia followed cautiously, prepared to break her mother's fall.

At the top of the stairs, Eulalia hurried to turn down the bed, but was waved aside. She went to her own room, and when she heard shoes thump on the floor, followed by a swooshing creak, she knew her mother had collapsed on the bed without removing her wet clothes.

But it was hot. And Baldwin was drunk and humming

77

the old hymn that always gave her comfort.

She would survive.

Eulalia sighed, released her hair from its big black pins, donned her white nightgown, and lay down in the middle of the bed. Her pale face resembled the dead woman's in the poem a younger Miss Finney had read to her pupils, the vein on her forehead throbbing even then. In the poem, the inn-keeper's beautiful, black-haired daughter had died for her lover.

Eulalia was accustomed to the sounds of the house. She knew its creaks, its groans, its ghostly sighs; and the sounds comforted her. The house was her sanctuary. It kept her connected to the memories she could bear and cloaked her from the ones she couldn't. She could lie wide-eyed in her bed for hours, mind numbed by force of will.

Surely in this house she could survive Saracen's intrusive spirit.

And he would return. She was certain he would return.

She had been drawn to his radiance when he was a child, but his élan was too vital for this family now. She wanted change, but she couldn't endure more chaos.

And yet the image of his muscled stomach, revealed when he lifted his shirt to wipe his perspiration, stayed with her.

She was sure he had jumped onto one of the train's coaches, which brought to mind an article she had read about lions leaping onto rickety cabs on jungle roads and mauling drivers to death.

Saracen would never hurt Shelby intentionally. It was the unintended hurt Eulalia feared. The friendly fire.

Rain poured over the town and would continue to pour. Basements flooded. The streets near the river flooded.

Eulalia was comforted by the sound. It reminded her of how nature could animate the body, how humankind was entwined fundamentally with Mother Earth, how her blood flowed faster when rain poured in torrents. She tried not to think about the natural force of Saracen's smile, his infectious laugh, his green eyes in that dark face. He had noticed the book she was reading before she could kick it from view. A silly story, *Peyton Place*. What had he thought? And why should she care?

She stretched her arms toward the ceiling, refusing to remember how his muscles rippled when he lifted his shirt. It had been so very long since her blood burned this way. She had forgotten it could happen.

The rain slammed harder, and she sat up straight, trying not to remember.

She wasn't afraid of the rain or the night. The night was a dark eye that watched over her, and she implored this night to watch over her beautiful daughter. She prayed to the night that she hadn't harmed her beloved daughter in earlier years.

She rose, still restless. Baldwin was snoring in a broken rhythm, but when there was a different, more alien sound, Eulalia became more alert. It had to be the sough of timbers, or the groan of ancient pipes, clogged like arteries. Nothing to fear in this house.

She walked down the dark hall, paused to listen again, and climbed the creaking ladder stair. She ignored the oppressive heat in the attic, and fingered her way for the string to the bulb that had always been there. The string was shorter and dirtier and more threaded than when she had last tugged it, but the yellow light made the trunk visible in the corner where it sat, calm as a coffin.

She crept around dusty furniture and clothes bags and stacked boxes and rolled up rugs and paintings of ancestors, and she stared at the trunk before raising the heavy, dusty lid, suddenly snatching books, and slamming the lid shut with a furious iron clank that could cut off fingers. She stood awhile longer, coughing, then sat with an ungainly plop and began to slap at the trunk, and slapped faster until she was drumming to the beat of the hail that battered the attic's tin roof. When her fists began to bleed, she stopped.

8

IT TOOK THIRTY-SIX HOURS to travel to New York City from Little Rock, the City of Roses. During those hours, Shelby drifted over invisible boundaries just as Huck Finn had, straining to see rain-blurred towns that reminded her of places called Velvet Ridge and Morning Star and Evening Shade. When they were in the air, her father would call out names of the towns he liked best. "Let's land at Rose Bud," he would shout. But sometimes it was better to savor the name than to see the small, sad town up close.

As the train bore through the night, she drifted into the lovely silence that engulfed her when her father switched off the plane's engine high above the clouds. *Listen,* he would say, his hand held up as though in benediction. *Listen . . .* and the silver draught of silence would seep through her body while they floated in absolute silence above the earth.

She had forgotten to bring a book for the trip, which was annoying. She always had a book at hand, just in case. Couldn't be left alone with her thoughts. She had placed a book on the bed by her purse, but was distracted by Saracen's revelation about her father's word. Distracted by Saracen himself. She needed a book.

She massaged her temples, trying to expunge the memory. *Honi soit qui mal y pense.* Real words with real meaning. She preferred *Owneeswakeemaleepants.* A made up word that always brought her luck.

She rang the bell, and the porter appeared, a big man in a crisp white jacket and white shirt and carefully knotted black bow tie. His black hat had a bill, and the pin on his white jacket said "Jack." Smiling Jack was holding a silver-plated tray with a Coca Cola in a glass with lots of ice. Anything else Jack could do for her, just let him know.

"Why, thank you. A Coke is just what I wanted. I'm also hungry."

"Yes, ma'am," Jack smiled. "Nothin' could be finer than dinner on our diner, just two cars down." He pointed the way.

It wouldn't surprise Shelby if Jack had burst into song. Anything could happen on this journey. But Jack hurried down the aisle, stopping to hang a coat, retrieve a glass. Taking care of his domain.

She drank the Coke too quickly, which made her nose tingle with cold and carbonation. She grimaced and turned her head toward the window where her reflection merged with the early evening outline of fields and fences. It was a watery view where another creature, fishlike and phosphorescent, was swimming on the other side of the glass, and staring at her with her father's face.

She blew warm breath on the window. The face disappeared.

When the rain subsided, the sunset's afterglow settled on a slope where the name "Irene" was inscribed in whitewashed rocks. Shelby fingered the star sapphire, imagining who loved Irene with such passion that he was inspired to write her name in big white letters, so that passengers on passing trains could see it day after day and wonder about his true love.

Someone like Charlie would do that.

She placed her hand flat against the window. The blue star in the ring twinkled, *twenty carats, twenty carats.* Eastward leading. Shelby hoped IRENE wasn't buried beneath the whitewashed rocks.

Rain began to pour down again. She fell asleep and

dreamed she heard a small plane tracking the train, mile after every long mile, even in a rainstorm.

"Miss Shelby."

A firm hand grasped her shoulder. Shelby barely opened her eyes.

The deep voice rumbled again. "They gonna close the diner soon. I know you hungry."

She turned her groggy head, and sat up ramrod straight.

Saracen Self stood by her seat dressed in a porter's uniform with the name "Jack" pinned to the front. But the seams strained across his massive shoulders and the sleeves were too short and the bow tie barely encircled his neck.

And it was not just the jacket that strained at the seams. There was too much energy coursing inside Jack's uniform, and too much intelligence in the face of the man who leaned toward Shelby, ostensibly adjusting the linen cover on the arm of her seat, but also waggling his eyebrows and crossing his eyes with a face that had made her laugh as a child. She didn't laugh now.

"How did you get here?" she hissed. "And where's Jack?"

Saracen placed a cautionary finger against his lips. "Jack be back later. I come because I don't want you to miss your victuals, Miss Shelby. I know you didn't eat none of them tasty cat meat tamales."

"You're out of your mind, Saracen Self!"

Saracen leaned closer with a whispered command. "Lower your voice, Shelby Howell. And see if you can get me an autographed copy of that picture the guy took at the train station."

The large, grey-haired man seated behind Shelby spoke in a commanding Texas twang, "Are you all right, little lady? Is this porter bothering you?" The man had a neatly trimmed

Van Dyke beard and a large and mobile nose, but he had missed patches of hair along his chins, which gave him a rather moth-eaten appearance. He scrutinized Saracen with a gimlet eye. "Where's our Jack, boy? You're not our Jack."

Shelby stood up slowly. Saracen was foolhardy to defy the rules, but he was most certainly *not* a "boy." She focused her allure on the Texan.

"I . . . asked to be awakened if I fell asleep." She smiled at the Texan, but turned cold eyes toward Saracen. He knew this was a dangerous game, and that the rules were not his to make. She had never thought about the rules, had simply absorbed them, but she knew Saracen Self couldn't disappear inside the uniform he was wearing like a Halloween costume. He was too astonishing. He looked like a green-eyed black actor performing a porter's role with the confidence of a white man. And he had laughter in his eyes, which was against all the rules. He was double-dog daring the white man in the white man's own redoubt. There was no reason she should feel jittery just because Saracen liked to jump on trains. And yet. . . .

"I asked the porter to wake me when it was time for dinner." Shelby's speech slowed and her smile became less dazzling, as she watched Saracen hunch his shoulders, lower his head and dissolve into subservience.

The fat man seemed immune to Shelby's charms. His focus was on Saracen, and he listened with narrowed eyes to Saracen's mumbling speech.

"I was just telling this lady if she don't get herself on up to the diner right quick, she gonna miss her supper. They closing in another five minute."

Shelby loathed Saracen's posture and the groveling accent. It made her want to hit him. *How dare he demean himself like that!*

The Texan, his eyes barely visible beneath drooping lids,

focused on the large gold ring on Saracen's finger and the fine gold watch on his wrist. He nodded with slow menace. "You aren't Jack. I don't know what you're doing on this train, but I'll find out. *And look at me when I talk to you, boy!*" His wattles quivered as he spat the words.

Saracen raised hooded green eyes just enough to look at the Texan. His voice was barely audible. "Yassuh. Excuse me, suh. Excuse me." And before either the Texan or Shelby could respond, he was down the aisle and out the door with liquid speed.

Shelby stared at his departing figure for a second, snapped up her purse, and hurried after him in a high-heeled, long-legged sway, grabbing at the edges of seats to stay balanced as the train hurled toward St. Louis.

His eyes, hunter-alert, the Texan heaved to a standing position and followed Shelby in a cautious Texas two-step that revealed cowboy boots with yellow roses climbing up their sides.

Shelby sailed ahead, relishing the strength it took to shove open the doors, relishing the rush of air between the cars. Relishing the excitement of the hunt.

But she couldn't find Saracen. Saracen Self had disappeared. When she arrived at the baggage car at the end of the train, she banged on the locked door and shouted, "Let me in, Saracen! I know you're in there!"

However it was the door behind her that swung open to reveal the big Texan, who was breathing hard and dabbing at his flushed face with a handkerchief. Shelby was grateful he would be in the lower berth in the Pullman car. If he were in the top berth and it broke, she would die when he crashed on top of her.

"Dear me. The diner's the other way, isn't it?" She gave him a bright smile and squeezed past his sweaty bulk, wondering, as she hurried, if Saracen could have swung himself to the top of the train, which wouldn't surprise her; he had done crazier things as a child.

She was considering other options when the door of a roomette swung open, and she was jerked inside, her mouth clamped shut with a large, sweaty hand, and her body pinioned to the wall. When she clamped her teeth on a finger, a familiar voice sputtered, "Goddammit, Sheb, *that hurt! And hush!* He's coming!"

The Texan, snorting and wheezing, was moving as fast as his immensity could take him. He hesitated in front of the roomette, but only to gain his breath before charging on to the next car.

As soon as the sounds faded, Saracen hissed in Shelby's ear, "You *bit* me, you little twit! And if you scream when I take my hand away, I'll bite you back, and you'll yell bloody murder, and that fat guy will have us both arrested. And won't that headline look great in the *Arkansas Gazette!*" But his rough voice was good-humored. "So think about that when I take my hand away, and for God's sake, *do not scream. . . .*"

The instant she was free, she whirled furiously, tucking herself together with angry yanks and tugs, but she didn't scream.

"Are you crazy? How did you even get on this train?"

Saracen's jaw twitched. "You mean how did I have the audacity to board your *optic white* Missouri Pacific Eagle?" He wiped lipstick from his hand with the same white handkerchief he had used to dust the car seat for Baldwin. "I *climbed* on it, Miss Fancy Pants. I grabbed the bar by the door and swung on up. You should try it sometime. You're sure strong enough."

He thrust his handkerchief at her, and she sputtered, "I wouldn't touch that nasty thing."

"Oh, for God's sake, Shelby. You can't sashay through the train with lipstick smeared all over your face after that big guy heard you whispering with a porter who doesn't look like Jack. And you ask me what I'm doing? Why, I'm having a little fun. If I planned my life, I wouldn't get half the stories I've nailed. And it was worth the risk to see the look on your face when you first saw me!"

"My stars, Saracen! That man will report you to the conductor!"

Saracen put his hands on his chest in mock fear. "My stars, Shelby! You think they'll come with dogs and chains? But never fear. The guys who work on this train are my friends, including the white conductor. The engineer would probably lynch me, but he'll never know I was here. Later my guys and I will play some cards before I hop off and catch the next freight south. I'll be rounding the bend into Little Rock by 5:30 a.m.

"And where's *your* spirit of adventure, Shebbie? We had us some escapades when we were kids. God knows how many times I saved you from the Chickasaw Indians! We could have us a 'captive child' reunion right here in this nice roomette."

Shelby's voice was icy. "I'm not a child anymore."

"I've noticed," he grinned. When she made an exasperated sound, he added, too innocently, "But I would *never* think what you think I was thinking about a beautiful white woman. That would be wrong. I was thinking that you are . . . a lot like me. Yeah. I was thinking you're just another white-washed Negro."

Shelby looked astonished.

"Ah, yes . . . she remembers where that's from. Melville called a white man a white-washed Negro in *Moby-Dick*. Daddy kept me up to speed on the books you read with that mousy little English teacher. I saw her at the train station, seeing you off. She's a little weird looking, but that lady sure can read. I grew to like ole Melville because of her. He was a democrat, small 'd,' writing about a white boy who made friends with a tattooed cannibal. Actually, Ishmael and Queequeg became soul mates, like you and me, Sheb. Remember when Ishmael said," and Saracen raised a dramatic hand: "'*I felt a melting in me. No more my splintered heart and maddened hand were turned against the wolfish world. This soothing savage had redeemed it.*'"

It seemed incongruous to Shelby that Saracen Self, standing in front of her in a Missouri Pacific roomette, was quoting Melville with Miss Finney's fervor. There was no way he could have been inside her classroom. Had he listened outside her door? Had he posed as a janitor? Had he actually *been* a janitor at her school?

"That's me!" Saracen declared. "The soothing savage! Remember when Queequeg was planting a hook on top of the whale, and Ishmael was tied with a rope to Queequeq's harness in case the savage fell? A monkey rope it was called. If one of those guys stumbled, they were both goners. Melville said they were hooked together like Siamese twins."

Saracen was staring at Shelby with eyes so penetrating, she had to look the other way. "Ropes can get tangled," she muttered, took a deep breath, and began to spew words at him: "And you're acting like being on this train is a lark, like it's all right for you to jump on a train with no place for a Negr. . . ." Her voice trailed off, then erupted again, " . . . *and impersonate a porter and kidnap me! You could be put in jail!*"

"Which is where I'll be if you keep yelling. No one knows I'm holed up in one of the optic white roomettes with a white woman, so pipe down!"

"Where do you get this 'optic white' stuff?"

"I read, my dear. I read. But look at you . . . you've grown up tall, and I like tall women. I don't have to double up when I talk to a tall woman. And I remember your gorgeous hair. . . ."

He reached to touch her hair, but she jerked back.

"Oh, for God's sake, Sheb, this is *me*, Saracen Self, the kid who used to save your hide nine times a day. You were happy to see me when you ran into the garden . . . until Baldwin called you to heel."

But Baldwin's name made her more aware that he and she were alone in another bedroom. And that he was very handsome. *And black.* She took a step away and bumped into the bunk.

"Lord God." Saracen sighed. "Poor Shelby. She hasn't had a real conversation with a black adult since she grew up."

Shelby glared at him. "You don't know squat."

But it was true. She barely talked with Tommy any more, and he had been as much a father to her as was permissible. Anyhow, a white woman in Little Rock didn't talk socially with a black man. Why would she, unless the woman needed someone to mow the lawn or carry out trash?

And yet, Shelby knew she wasn't prejudiced. Baldwin was the person in the family who was prejudiced.

Saracen was leaning against the wall, observing her. "So why did you let Baldwin talk to me the way she did?"

"I ignore her when she talks like that, and so should you. And seeing you was . . . dizzy-making."

Saracen rolled his eyes.

"It was! If it hadn't been for your eyes and the scar on your face, I wouldn't have recognized you! It was weird to see you in that grown-up body."

"Yeah. We've both grown up. But it's easier in this room-ette. No one to judge us here. And it's pouring outside, but we're dry in our hidey hole. We could talk here for days."

"Hidey hole" was a phrase from their childhood. She smiled at him, then came to her senses. "My stars, Saracen! What would people say?"

"About what?" His voice was dry.

"You know what I mean . . . being in this little room by

ourselves. People in Little Rock are already upset about the prospect of whites and Negroes going to school in the same classroom. And, even worse, this is like a bedroom!"

"Ahhh. Well. Actually, we are in a bedroom. And I'm a reporter who went to Little Rock to interview people about this 'sort of thing.'" There was an amused glint in his eye. "I'd sure like to quote you about how whites in Little Rock feel about integration."

"Quote *me?* In some colored newspaper?"

"*Woooo...*" Saracen sounded very serious. "There's a decent *colored* newspaper in Little Rock, but I happen to work for the *very* white *Chicago Tribune.* The powers that be hired me because they think I can talk to black folks . . . though never to white folks like you. I could never do that.

"So come on, Sheb." He waved a big hand as though clearing the air. "Let's you and me forget about this black race, white race stuff... though if it were a real race," he said, grinning, "I would win. I can still run like a jackrabbit. But we can talk in here just like old times. I won't let the booger bears get you in here."

Shelby almost smiled. Another phrase from their childhood. Saracen was always protecting her from "booger bears" when they were little. Always rescuing her.

"When I looked up at your window today and saw that beautiful woman, I thought to myself, that can't be Shelby Baldwin Howell. That woman looks like a *queen* . . . and she's almost as tan as me!"

Shelby gave him a hard look, and he shrugged. "It's true. And that same tanned, green-eyed darlin' probably looked too much like that light-skinned, green-eyed darkie who was smiling up at her at the train station. And everyone knows a black man mustn't smile at a white woman. It ain't right." As he spoke, he moved closer to her.

Shelby thrust out the flat of both hands. "Don't come any

closer, Saracen . . . *I mean it . . .*"

He ignored her and tipped up her chin with big fingers "Aha!" he crowed. "It's still there! The scar Baldwin made when she tried to scrub off the black stain! It's smaller, but it's there."

Shelby twisted from his touch, but she smiled in spite of herself. It was true. She had plastered her body with black gook, especially her navel. Saracen had convinced her that to get into heaven her belly button had to be black, and as a result of painting her navel black with a Q-tip and using the Q-tip like a plunger, her newly blackened navel had swollen until it resembled an umbilical hernia.

But the mention of something as intimate as belly buttons in this space, and with this man, made her even more nervous, and she sidestepped around him to the door. "I've got to get out of here," she mumbled. "There's not room for both of us in here."

"Wait a minute." He was fumbling with the buttons on his jacket.

"What are you doing?" Shelby gasped.

"This jacket is killing me," he grunted, immune to his exposed chest and the lion-toothed necklace revealed beneath the jacket. "It's too small and my necklace is poking me beneath the jacket. How would you like to have to disguise yourself and act like a field hand so you could talk to me?" He worked a sleeve from a muscled arm. "Wouldn't like that, would you, Miss Little Rock? But sometimes I have to act like a *Neegrow*."

He peeled off the jacket and brushed at it clumsily. "Jack needs to wear this tonight." When he caught Shelby staring, she blushed. "Like that skin, don't you, Sheb?" he grinned. "Always liked my skin."

He reached into the closet, retrieved his many-colored shirt, pulled it over his head, and when his face reappeared, he said, "And you're thinking the colors in the shirt look like Queequeg's tattooed skin, I'll bet. And you *love* the necklace. Admit it." He held the necklace toward her. "Take it. It's a good luck charm."

She looked at the necklace with mild horror.

He shrugged and motioned toward the couch-cum-bed. "Okay. Have a seat in my parlor. Let's talk."

She frowned, but sat as instructed.

The truth was, she wanted to study the constellation of yellow flecks against the green of Saracen's irises. His eyes had intrigued her when she was a child. There was something magnetic and well-deep about those eyes set against his dark skin. If he had appeared in a jungle, the natives would have called him a god. When she realized she was staring too intently, she stood up.

"Relax, Sheb," he teased. "We'll behave ourselves."

"I'm hungry," she insisted. "I'm going to the diner."

"I'll see that you're fed." His voice was quiet, reassuring.

Shelby felt disquieted, and at the same time oddly comforted to be with someone with whom she didn't have to smile and pirouette, someone who wouldn't laugh at the Korzeniowski name. Someone she could trust. She felt a flurry of excitement when it occurred to her that Saracen might answer questions about her father's disappearance. She had so many questions.

She wished he would look away from her. Move farther away.

"This is crazy," she muttered. "You aren't playing fair. You are. . . ."

"Black." There was no resonance in Saracen's voice. "You're alone with a big, black man in a bedroom that's far from your grandmother."

Shelby sucked in her breath and spoke rapidly before he could hold forth in his ironic, wise man's voice.

"You were older than me when my father disappeared. You must have heard things."

Saracen squinted at her as if at the sun.

"No one mentioned the plane crash or why my father left or where he went, and I was afraid if I asked about him . . . if I *named* his absence . . . he would never return. I know that doesn't make sense, but I was a *child*. It was all so confusing. And it hurt. *Physically, emotionally.* There was this weird silence everywhere I went about what had happened to him. People behaved as though he had never existed. His name was never mentioned after he disappeared, even by Baldwin and my mother. I kept telling myself he would come back, life would be okay again, and it would be okay to say his name out loud. But he didn't come back. And life never was okay again.

"I had a child's fantasy that nothing bad could happen when I was with him. But then the plane crashed." Her words emerged more slowly. "I have no idea how we got home on that dreadful day. All I remember is that he wrapped ice in a kitchen towel, crushed the ice with a hammer like he always did, fixed me a Coke with a lot of ice the way I liked, put me to bed, sang a Polish song I loved, and when I woke up, he was *gone*. Forever."

The make of the plane suddenly emerged from very deep waters. "A Ryan," she murmured, and looked up at Saracen. "His plane was a Ryan. The best plane for acrobatics."

Saracen nodded. "I was with him once when he flew beneath the Broadway Bridge. I was so scared I peed in my pants, but he didn't complain. He said it happened to grown men sometimes. When we landed, he helped me clean the plane."

But Shelby wasn't listening. "When my mother returned from the hospital after she went batty, I didn't ask her where my father was for fear she would have to go back to that place. The one time I asked Baldwin, she got really angry, which she never did with me. She said she didn't know and never wanted me to ask again. And she meant it.

"I wasn't brave enough to run away, so I hid beneath my bed, which was ridiculous, but that was as far as I had the guts to go. Why didn't I ask Jessie or Tom what happened? Or you?"

Saracen squatted in front of her, his legs pressed against hers in the limited space. When he scooped up her hands, her eyes overflowed.

"Then Jessie died, and you left me. . . ."

"But I didn't want to leave. I cut myself with that Indian flint, because I didn't want to leave, remember? The place got infected, but when it got better, I still had to leave. And I hated it up north. I was so homesick, I cried, too. Every night."

He laid a hand against her cheek, and she clutched it with both of hers. "And now I'm the one who's leaving. I didn't think I would be so scared. I thought I wanted to leave."

Saracen enveloped her in his huge arms, and rocked her back and forth. When his mouth moved to her hair, he released his arms abruptly and stood up.

Shelby looked up, confused, tears streaming.

"You were right." His voice was gruff. "This place is too small." Rain had begun to slam against the glass and drop like stunned birds. He spoke louder to be heard. "If you want to look for your daddy in New York City, begin with the phone book. *Korzeniowski*. Knock on doors. But not by yourself."

Shelby swiped at her eyes and nose with the back of her hands. "Oh, I'll find some big, strong man to help me. I couldn't possibly do anything that dangerous by myself. And I know what his name is. I even have his picture in my trunk."

"Ah, Sheb . . . you don't need the picture. Just look in the mirror. You'll see what your father looks like." He offered the damp handkerchief again. "You still have lipstick on your face."

This time she took it, wiped her face briskly, stood up,

and held out the handkerchief.

"Keep it. I have plenty of white handkerchiefs."

She shoved it into her purse. Her eyes were still angry. "We're friends, Saracen Self. *Friends.*"

"Absolutely." He unlocked the door. "Absolutely. But watch out when you get to the big city. Queequeg won't be around to help."

When Shelby reached a ladies' room, she stepped inside, stared at the face in the mirror, gave it another vigorous scrub with soap and water, applied lipstick, darkened her eyebrows, and smoothed down her skirt. When she exited, she was Miss Little Rock again.

9

THE NEARLY EMPTY dining car was lovely, with a silvery opalesque ceiling, silvery rose-colored drapes, and a wine-red carpet. The heavy china and silver and glassware, all monogrammed with the Missouri Pacific logo, stayed in place when the car swayed. The steward's stance was equally steady as he unfurled a large white, monogrammed linen napkin that sailed into the air and onto Shelby's lap in a three-point landing.

She picked at the delicious dinner made by a cook who, in a cramped train kitchen, had prepared chicken and dumplings and butter beans and pickled beets and homemade rolls and lemon meringue pie, all foods she had loved as a child. Saracen must have ordered for her . . . though the pie wasn't as good as Jessie's.

After the meal she felt revived and sought out the club car Baldwin had forbidden her to enter, which was even more cosmopolitan than the diner. She had seen club cars like this in movies . . . leather upholstered seats with a mural of a Missouri Pacific eagle soaring behind the bar. She sucked in her cheeks and her stomach, assumed a model's face, and sauntered casually, she hoped, onto the movie set.

Most passengers were men, with cigarettes dangling from their fingers. There was glamour in the way they palmed the pack like Clark Gable did, and slid the cigarette from the cellophane-covered paper, and tamped it two times before placing it between their lips. Her eyes glazed at the memory of smoke rings blown for a little girl who looked like her father.

A burst of laughter broke the spell. The men in the club

car were joshing one another, drinks in hand, as though their Texas and Arkansas selves had required too much restraint, too many neckties, too many Protestant churches. Their club car selves laughed too loud, and drank too much Jack Daniels, and looked around, and looked around, and when they saw Shelby, they stopped looking and stared.

She knew they were looking at her, and she was glad to escape the furor of Saracen's presence, and relieved to remember she was a beauty queen. She felt emboldened in the club car that sailed through the dark and the rain like a ship. An orchestra should have been playing Cole Porter songs, and people should have been dancing and drinking champagne, and an ocean should have been lapping against the hull of this luxury liner, instead of rain slamming against a train swaying its way to St Louis. She grinned at the miracle of being in a fancy club car at night in the middle of a rainstorm on her way to New York City.

The train picked up speed, but the Negro bartender continued to flip glasses and bottles with a juggler's skill, scooping up dimes and buffalo nickels from the counter, his arms surrounded by red-tipped cigarettes that glowed like signals from a campfire.

Shelby asked for a Coke with crushed ice. The bartender nodded, stuck a silver swizzle into the frosted glass and added two maraschino cherries. When she handed him money, he waved his hand. "Saracen say drinks and maraschino cherries are on him. He say you like those cherries."

The atmosphere turned as cold as the glass Shelby now held too tightly. Her heart raced at the thought of Saracen, in Jack's uniform, entering this car full of white people. She sat in a chair, pulled her skirt over her knees, placed her thighs tight together, and put her Coke in the receptacle by her chair. She opened her new alligator skin purse, removed Miss Finney's gift, turned back the cover of the leather diary, and frowned to show anyone looking that she was gathering her thoughts. But when she turned the first page, her jaw dropped at the quotation from *Moby-Dick*:

"as . . . for me, I am tormented with an everlasting itch for things remote. I love to sail forbidden seas, and land on barbarous coasts . . ."
Sail the New York seas for me, Shelby Howell!
Your friend, Oceana.

Shelby chuckled out loud at the notion of Miss Finney in her brown oxfords, hopping like a small kangaroo onto barbarous coasts. But she stopped smiling at the sight of yellow roses climbing a pair of very large boots. The big Texan was staring down at her like a half-drunk inquisitor.

The longer she stared at the yellow roses, the more certain she was that Oceana would escape this barbarous coast and seek forbidden seas.

She grabbed the diary and her purse, rose straight-backed from the chair and strode from the club car, relishing the strength it took to open doors, relishing the grinding noise and damp, grimy air between cars. When the train slowed to a crawl, signals clanging to a jerking stop, she knew the porters were waving goodbye to a big, black man who jumped to the ground, ready to hop on the next freight to Little Rock.

Which was the moment she realized she would miss Saracen Self.

The rain blended with the train's jerking clank, threatening to pitch her out the door between cars, and she yelled a defiant speech from *Saint Joan* she had prepared for The Acting School. Joan, a peasant girl who heard voices, had burned like a comet through the medieval world, obeying Saint Michael's instruction to save France by lopping off heads with her sword, and, equally important, preserving her virginity.

Or perhaps she should perform a scene where she had to

cry. She was good at crying. Instead, she began to sing in a lonely, quavering voice,

I'm looking over / a four leaf clover,
That I've overlooked before

People in Little Rock knew she could act, and they wanted her to strut her stuff for those Yankees, but *never* become one of them. She sang louder.

No need explaining / the one remaining
Is somebody I adore . . .

Her Little Rock fans wanted her to be one of *them*, never better than they were, but somehow perfect, which was confusing, because if she never had been one of them, and never would be one of them—especially if she was in cahoots with a Negro —they wouldn't want to know.

Saracen stood in the downpour, his hand held high to the departing train. Once he and Shelby had begun to relax with one another, he knew he had to keep his distance. She was too white. Too desirable.

He pulled his wet shirt from his body and wrung it out a bit. The dye from the cloth ran, and the colors stained his flesh and his trousers. He barked a laugh, and shouted, "Queequeg!" If she could see him now, she might laugh, and she needed to laugh.

He waved his hand higher at the departing train.

When Shelby entered her Pullman car, the lights were dim, and dark blue curtains had been pulled across the berths. Our Jack, with his name on his hat, was wearing a slightly wrinkled shirt, and standing at the entry. He put his finger to his lips and led her to the roomette she and Saracen had occupied.

"A friend say I should put you in this roomette," he whispered. "It got a good lock on the door. Your bags in there too. I'll see they get put on the Spirit of St. Louis in the morning, so's they go with you all the way to New York City. And I got you a bottle of Mountain Valley Mineral Water from Hot Springs in there . . . best water on this earth . . . and you want your breakfast in bed before we come to the Eagle's Nest, you let me know."

"The Eagle's Nest?"

"The St. Louis station. We roosting in the Eagle's Nest 8:10 a.m. in the morning. But it ain't as fancy as it used to be. They melted down that big chandelier in the Grand Hall for guns during the war, plus that there iron fence between the Midway and. . . ."

"Did he jump off the train?"

Jack put his finger to his lips again and looked toward the Texan's berth. "Yes, ma'am," he whispered. "He hop off like he do. That boy so full of tricks. You hear he in one of them foreign places, and before you lace up your shoes, he in Lonoke, Arkansas, calling you to hightail it down to a good fried catfish place he found. That boy got the habit of disappearance." Jack swallowed his burgeoning laugh. "This sure been some day." Then he straightened his back and stood at his station like one of the Queen's own guards.

When Shelby opened the closet in the roomette, the lion-toothed necklace was on a hanger with a note attached: *Guaranteed to keep away predators.*

She stared at the necklace, and she stared at the way the script marched across the paper with confident, matter-of-fact letters. She removed her father's photograph from the suitcase and stared at it, then she wrapped Saracen's note around the necklace and packed photograph and necklace, side by side.

10

EULALIA MOVED a folded length of sheet to the floor.

She never slept on the floor naked like Shelby did, with only a pillow beneath her head. Eulalia needed a slight cushion, and she lay down cautiously, adjusting her body.

She knew she wouldn't sleep. She would lie there until she heard the 5:30 a.m. freight whistle. She was often awake when the train whistled its way into Little Rock.

Then, without warning, she began to wail, rocking from side to side, arms wrapped around her body, aching for her daughter to be sleeping down the hall. In the best of times, sleep didn't come until she could hear Shelby climbing the creaking stairs after a date. She mourned the loss of the sound of those creaking stairs.

Shelby would look for her father in that city. Eulalia knew she would. And if she learned the truth? Eulalia voyaged through Shelby's mind until her husband's face rose to confront her as it often did. She groaned, longing to be released from that vision and so much more. She stretched her fingers wider, welcoming the hurt inflicted when she pounded the trunk. She yearned to drift until memory became so thin she could feel nothing, aware that the same aptitude for forgetting had infected her thoughts in general, that she could appear to be listening intently, when, in fact, her attention had stilled like a black lake. The sensation was as frightening as it was seductive. She had nearly drowned in that lake once before. She mustn't walk into Lethe's deep waters again.

In spite of herself, her thoughts leaped to the image of

Saracen jogging alongside Shelby's train. When he appeared in the garden today, it seemed he had risen from the earth. He looked so strange. So beautiful. Then he called her by the name.

It was so terribly hot in her bedroom.

Suddenly, she thrust herself upward, barking a laugh, her back arching, her body thrumming with desire that had seized her body like a thief. The feelings lingered and ebbed and reemerged, and for a while she relished what she couldn't stop, then stood, too abruptly, as though it hadn't happened, flinging her arms, her long black hair flying.

She needed fresh air. She needed to be outside.

She hurried to the door that led to the emergency stair, hammered her hand on the rusted hook on the screen, dislodged the screen, leaving behind blood and skin, and shoved the door open. Compacted leaves and twigs scraped across the porch. She stopped and listened for fear she had been heard. But Baldwin's snores didn't diminish. Dogs didn't bark. She thought she heard a door closing in Julien's house, but she was imagining too many sounds. She sat on the damp step in the softening dark, hands throbbing in her lap.

When the 5:30 a.m. sounded its whistle, a light went on in Julien's house. Eulalia stood up, tugged the screen back into place, hooked it, and bolted the outside door with a fierce shove. It was the only door in the house that was ever locked, and it had been locked for many years.

She watched the light in Julien's house go off again. She knew he was always watching her.

Baldwin woke up when the cat purred in her ear and pestered her miserable body. The old fan drilled its sound into her pounding head. But she wasn't one to surrender to physical discomfort. She forced herself to stand, and was mortified to realize she was still wearing her good fall outfit. It was as rumpled as the spread and the navy-smeared sheets she had slept on.

The spread and the sheets would need a soak in peroxide. She would take her suit to the cleaners when there were no customers.

No. She would have Eulalia take the suit.

She pulled off her clothes, tugged off the stubborn girdle, sighing in relief, and put on a housedress and old slippers. She gave a swipe to her hair without looking in the mirror, which was just as well. Her blue face would have startled her more than the dye on the sheets.

Eulalia's door was still closed, and Baldwin didn't wake her, even though it was a workday. This was, more importantly, a day of mourning for the departed and should be treated as such. She made it down the stairs, one careful step at a time, the cat trailing her heels.

The telephone didn't ring all day. The photograph of the Negro smiling at Shelby on the front page of the *Gazette* was the cause of many calls around town, though none to Baldwin. It was much more enjoyable to gossip with others about the photograph.

When Eulalia finally appeared, neither she nor her mother mentioned the events at the train station. Or the J.W. Dant whiskey. Or the fact that Baldwin's face was streaked with navy dye. Eulalia kept her wounded hands out of sight.

It would be hard to exist without the energy Shelby had infused into the household. The two older women would have to make do as they always had. And so, on the surface, Baldwin's order prevailed.

11

ACCORDING TO THE pamphlet Jack gave Shelby, the St. Louis station boasted more tracks on one level than any other station in the world, and Shelby strode through this "Gateway to the United States of America," her yellow pleats whirling like butterflies. Accordion pleats were perfect for travel, because, according to the instructions, they were "guaranteed not to wrinkle. When washed, the skirt should be wrapped around a broom handle to dry the pleats perfectly in place." Tom had sawed off a broom handle, sanded it smooth, and Shelby had packed it in her trunk, prepared to keep her pleats in place.

Straight ahead a sign said:

WELCOME TO ST. LOUIS

It was the comma after ST. LOUIS and the message beneath that caused Shelby to gasp.

WELCOME TO ST. LOUIS, MISS LITTLE ROCK, SHELBY KORZENIOWSKI!

Except for the signatures inside her father's books, she hadn't seen her real last name spelled out since her first years in grammar school. Since that time, the name had existed like the silent letter in *deceit*, or *grief*. It hadn't been mentioned in her presence since she was eight and a half years old, and Baldwin had marched her to the courthouse to have it changed. A group had gathered, alerted by a tattling clerk, curious to see the participants in the strange ceremony: the middle-aged and almost-slender socialite clutching the hand of her tow-headed granddaughter, whose enormous green eyes stared back at the crowd, as though memorizing faces for future retribution.

Shelby turned around in place on the St. Louis station floor, antennae alert, scanning the station's echoing space. Saracen had to be close by.

And yet—though her eyes searched for Saracen—Charlie Billington could be reminding her that he was in the air, so to speak. His father, Herbert, could have arranged it. Herbert was a Republican, a rare breed in Arkansas, and Herbert had connections. He had dined with President Eisenhower at the White House, which impressed even the Democrats, because everyone liked Ike.

But his son, dear Charlie, whom she missed more than she thought she would, would never embarrass her. She didn't think Charlie even knew about the Korzeniowski name.

She continued to stand very still, trying to decipher the message's meaning. As a child, she had heard Tom tell Jessie that more bad luck was sure to come once Shelby's name was changed. Though it had to be okay to change the last name, Shelby thought. Married women did.

Still, the message unnerved her.

She hurried past the cigar stand with its Roi Tan advertisement: *A Woman is Just a Woman but a Good Cigar is a Smoke*, and she ran up the stairs to the Grand Hall where people waited for trains, or gawked at the gaudy ceiling and the stained-glass maidens over the main staircase that represented the great train stations of America: New York City and San Francisco, with St. Louis, of course, in the middle. She stood quietly, looking around.

Across the way, a young man with wavy black hair, dressed in a light-blue seersucker suit, white shirt, and red bow tie, was surrounded by a group of laughing young men who all wore scuffed white shoes. They were tanned, with sunglasses perched atop crew cuts or dangling from fingers, and they moved in a certain moneyed way, with summertime ease, their laughter careening through the vast space and bouncing from the ceiling toward the stained-glass maidens.

The handsome young man must have been telling a funny story with dramatic loops of his arms, but when he noticed Shelby, he, and then his friends, turned to look at her. Handsome, happy young men, Charlie's kind of people, gazing at a beautiful girl in a pretty yellow dress.

The young man with wavy black hair smiled at her, and Shelby smiled back, emboldened by her journey and by the grand train station, and she willed the young man to board her train. They would sit in the club car and hold hands and drink a New York City cocktail, and he wouldn't have to flee in the middle of a rainstorm because the club car was off limits to him.

The young man glanced at his watch and hurried toward the stairs, stopped, looked back, and beckoned to Shelby.

She looked at her own watch and realized she, too, had to board; it was too late to eat at the Harvery Restaurant, sorry, Baldwin, and she rushed down the stairs, glancing at the message board as she passed, grateful that *Miss Little Rock* and *Korzeniowski* had disappeared.

But the handsome young man wasn't moving toward her train. "Get on *this* train!" he called as she ran another way. "This is a better train!"

The conductor on her train was calling, "All aboard," and Shelby was laughing, yellow accordion pleats twirling, platinum hair swirling like a Breck Girl's.

The handsome young man called louder, "What's your name? How can I get in touch?" And his friends hooted, *"Stop her train! Stop her train!"*

"My name is Shelby!" she called.

"Last name! Address!"

But Shelby didn't know her new address by heart, and for a terrible moment, she couldn't remember her last name.

12

IT WAS THE MIDDLE of the following night. Baldwin trod downstairs like a heavy-footed ghost, holding tight to the bannister with one hand, and carrying the cat under her other arm. She was wearing one of her mother's voluminous white nightgowns.

When Eulalia appeared sometime later, Baldwin made no effort to hide the empty Snickers wrappers scattered on the kitchen table.

" . . . And when I was in my nonage," she was mumbling to the cat, "my daddy took the entire family on a train, *first class*, mind you, to the St. Louis Fair in 19 aught 4, and I got lost in that train station for hours." She dropped her chin woefully. "I was frightened. I was hungry."

Eulalia had heard the story many times, but sister Ernestine insisted that Baldwin, who was almost sixteen at the time, was lost less than ten minutes, and when found, was downing free jellybeans at Travelers Aid.

Baldwin began to hum the refrain to an old hymn, "Beulah Land," and then she took a noisy gulp of iced tea and tore open the paper of another melting candy bar.

"She's on the Spirit of St. Louis now, leaving us forever. Why wouldn't she marry that sweet Charlie Billington? My mother's spindle crib is in the attic, and the christening gown is packed in lavender."

Her words were thick with chocolate. "But at least she's in the top berth." She took another sloppy swallow of tea.

"May I have a sip?" Eulalia asked politely.

Baldwin shrugged as though it made no difference, and slid the glass across the table to Eulalia, who took a good sip and choked. The tea was generously laced with whiskey.

Baldwin reached back across the table, slid the glass to her side like a hockey puck, snatched it without spilling a drop, and took another swallow.

"And the Quapaw Indians never did own my Daddy's property like that big Nigra said." Water beads slid down the glass, and onto the cat, who gave his fur a vigorous shake. "The Indians just squatted on this property. They didn't improve it in any way whatsoever, and they didn't pay a red cent for it."

"That's funny, Momma."

"What's funny?"

"Your joke. Wasn't it a joke? You said the Indians didn't pay a red cent for the property, and sometimes people call Indians "redskins". You seldom make a joke. I thought you meant to be funny."

Baldwin stared at her daughter. "The only reds I know are the Communists, and I already told Tommy to keep his big Nigra off my land."

Eulalia's lips tightened. "How could you say that to Tommy? And the man's name is *Saracen*. You know his name. You used to spoil him when he was young. He composed clever ditties extemporaneously for you, and you would give him a nickel when he did. Remember? He was the one who kidnapped that elephant, Ruth, in the middle of the night and led her down the road to those crazy missionaries, who had convinced him they would take Ruth with them to Africa and set her free. He loved that elephant."

"Don't start talking about how nice that man is." Baldwin waved a sticky hand in warning. Alfred took the wave as an invitation, and pulled himself onto the table, foraging for chocolate.

"And you were rude to me yesterday, sister. Don't think

I didn't notice. You talked back to me more than once." Baldwin struggled from the chair, thus ending a troublesome subject.

Eulalia sighed, walked around the table to help her mother with one hand, and lift the cat with the other. The women trudged up the stairs, Baldwin clinging again to the banister, stopping to catch her breath before proceeding. When they reached Baldwin's room, Eulalia put the cat on the floor and folded back the chenille spread and the sheet that had been bleached of navy-blue dye in the sunshine that followed yesterday's rain. Before she got her mother settled, Alfred hopped on the bed—not an easy leap for an old cat—curled up and began to purr. This time Eulalia remembered to prop the windows open with sticks before she plugged in the squawking fan. But the room was still hot.

When she returned to her own bedroom, she lay in the middle of the bed and stared at the ceiling. Baldwin's drinking wouldn't last longer than the bottle of J.W. Dant. The notion of her going to a liquor store to replenish the supply was unthinkable, and that was one chore Tommy wouldn't perform for her. But Eulalia would speak to him to make certain.

Her thoughts then turned to Shelby, as they so often did. Charlie had come by Eulalia's desk at the State House, and, with restrained humor, told her about Saracen's appearance on the train to St. Louis. Charlie seemed to be apprised of everything concerning Arkansas.

The news about Saracen didn't surprise Eulalia. Disguising himself as a porter was dangerous in more ways than one, but exciting to consider. How sweet it would be to have such a grand and dangerous adventure. She felt a sudden urge to do something wild herself, get in the car maybe, and drive to . . . where?

She felt so restless. She would go to work and type and file and keep to herself, ignoring the men, the way they looked at her, bumped against her. Tried to touch her.

She climbed out of bed, and released her hair from its big black pins. Her hair cascaded down her back, which made her too hot, but those feelings began to invade her body again, and the man whose face was like Shelby's pushed itself into memory, and his voice with its lovely accent murmured into her hair. She grabbed long strands of hair with fierce fingers and pulled until it hurt.

Maybe it was the hair that caused this disquiet. Maybe she should cut it off.

She looked down at the sheet that was still on the floor, and her heavy fingers moved over her breasts . . . and paused . . . and moved down her body.

Maybe she would lie on the floor for a while . . . but only until the 5:30 a.m. train whistle from St. Louis sounded. Then she would get up and make the coffee and go to work, as she did each day.

13

SHELBY ENTERED the train at St. Louis and brushed against an older man who was dressed to be noticed in a white suit that matched his white hair. He eyed her retreating figure appreciatively before turning back to lecture a porter, tapping his fancy cane on the floor to make his point. The cane was an ebony beauty, decorated with a silver band around the neck, its knob a growling, ivory lion.

She slid onto her seat in time to see the handsome young man waving to his friends, and waving higher to her train, just in case. She rested wistful fingers against the glass.

The white-haired man straightened his red tie with its gold stick pin and continued to harangue the porter.

"That kid who was waving. He your boyfriend? He's real cute." The woman who spoke sat across from Shelby. It was hard to tell her age, but she was probably older than she thought she looked in her low-necked purple blouse and a purple skirt that hugged her hips. The ring on her left hand was set with a purple stone so large it had to be fake, and her peroxided Betty Grable curls were swept to the top of her head. She tugged at her spangled outfit with her long, purple-polished fingernails.

"No," Shelby said, her voice distant. "He's not my boyfriend."

The white-haired man limped down the aisle, swinging his cane and twinkling at Shelby as he passed. He sat down by a big-bosomed woman who clutched his arm and glared at the back of Shelby's head.

The same porter came to Shelby's seat, introduced himself as Marvin, and advised the ladies that the diner would open in another twenty minutes.

"My friend and I will be there in a little while," Shelby's seatmate answered.

Shelby rose quickly, followed Marvin down the aisle and spoke *sotto voce*. "Is there an empty roomette on the train? Or a berth in another car? I would like to change seats if possible."

Marvin responded, just as softly, "Ain't no more berths, but I'm working on a roomette. I got me a little complication this trip, but Saracen say get Miss Little Rock a roomette, and I'm doing my best."

Shelby's throat contracted. She felt oddly vulnerable without Saracen, but she couldn't deal with him on another whites-only train, or anywhere else, for that matter. "Is he here? On this train?"

Marvin seemed distracted. "No, ma'am. He ain't."

Shelby breathed more easily and followed his gaze. The man with white hair stood and called to the porter:

"I need that roomette, George!" The man's voice was too loud, too ripe with good cheer, but his finger pointed imperiously. The big-bosomed woman tugged at his other hand.

Marvin tipped his hat and called back, "I'm working on it, judge! Doing my best, sir!" Marvin nodded toward the other passengers, smiling, excusing his loud voice.

The judge gave the porter a brisk salute as though he knew the roomette would be his, and walked toward the diner, flicking his cane nonchalantly on the forward step, as though the cane were merely decorative. The woman followed, swinging her ample hips. Both her clothes and her hips looked expensive.

Shelby's eyes followed the parade. "Is that man after the same roomette? I don't want to cause you trouble."

"No'm. You don't cause me no trouble. The judge, *he* cause me trouble every time he make this trip, pretending he hear good when he don't hear nothing in his bad ear. Anyhow, he don't know who got a roomette and who don't."

Shelby looked doubtful. "He called you George. It says Marvin on your jacket."

"Marvin my name, but the judge call all us porters George."

"Why?"

"After Mr. George Pullman, the Pullman car man. He the one started sleepers."

"That's ridiculous! Ask the judge to call you by your real name. Marvin is a fine name."

The porter stretched his neck and his chin as though his collar were too tight. "Lots of menfolks on the sleepers calls us George. That just their way."

Shelby returned to her seat, troubled and exhausted, and pretended sleep before the woman across from her could speak. A nightmarish sleep came too quickly in the form of a hellish storm battering a one-engine pilotless plane that emitted an unearthly scream. Shelby woke in a groggy sweat, rain pounding the window, lightening splitting the sky, and a baby screaming down the aisle.

The woman across from her said, "You been moaning and jerking in your sleep, honey! I hope you don't feel bad? People jerk in their sleep when they feel bad? I seen it happen lots. My name's Cherie?" Cherie's shrill voice carried over the sound of the train and the wind and the rain and the scream-ing baby. "I been travelling all the way from Plano, Texas, to get on a big, ole boat in New York City, so's I can go see my hubby, Bobby? He's a soldier boy over in Germany?" It seemed Cherie seldom made a statement that didn't end with a question mark. The querulousness in her voice belied the toughness of her looks. Her hands fumbled in her capacious knitting bag as she spoke, eyes never leaving Shelby's face, and then emerged with a threaded needle.

Shelby pulled out her new diary and stared intently at the first page, thinking of Miss Finney's alias, Oceana, hopping onto faraway islands, and wishing she, Shelby Baldwin Howell, were hopping beside her at that moment.

But Cherie was undeterred. "I know I look a sight. I didn't have time to put on my eyelashes this morning? I'm just thankful the rest of my makeup stays put for a few days? I been working in Dallas, and that's where I met my Bobby! My Bobby is the cutest thing!

"When I become an exotic dancer—" Cherie cocked her gaudy head at Shelby to determine if she knew what exotic dancer meant, which Shelby was beginning to guess, "—I took Cherie Denise, White Goddess of the Jungle for my moniker because of my hair and all? We could be twins, you and me, don't you think?" The woman's long purple fingernail pointed from her coarse, dyed hair to Shelby's shining platinum locks. "What I'm fixing here, in case you wanted to know, is a new costume for my act? I already have me a whole entire suitcase filled with costumes checked safe on this train? And there's always a place for my line of work, don't you think? At the end of my act, I snatch off this top I'm fixing so all I have left is the little purple spots I paste on myself in special places?" She wrinkled her nose and pointed with the needle to the two special places. "My favorite color is purple."

Shelby nodded. "I thought it might be."

Cherie became even more enthusiastic upon Shelby's entry into the conversation. "And I'm never buck naked on stage? I always have on my G-string and my littlest pasties? But I *never* take off my littlest pasties. You can go to jail if you don't have on your pasties!" She giggled at that unwelcome possibility and removed a battered card from her purse.

"Since we're new friends and all, I want you to have this card in case you ever want to go into my line of business in New York City? You never know, is what I say? My friend, Arnie Grady, has got a place up there you wouldn't believe? And men'd go bonkers over your hair and your knockers! Arnie is meeting me at the station, and I'll tell him about you."

The card read:

ARNIE'S HOT HOUSE AND HIS GIRLS! GIRLS! GIRLS!!!

WHERE FLOWERS DROP THEIR PETALS ON STAGE!!!

Shelby stabbed her thigh with her fingernail to keep from laughing, tucked Arnie's card in her purse, but jerked back when a black hand emerged in front of her face.

Marvin stumbled back. "I . . . I wasn't going to touch you, Miss Shelby. I was just fixing to show you the supper menus and say I got you a roomette."

"No, no, no, no," Shelby stammered. "I was just . . . I didn't think you were trying . . ."

Cherie grabbed her costume and tossed the naughty thing into the bag. "You're not going to leave me, are you?"

To reassure Shelby, Marvin pressed both hands firmly against a stack of linen sheets he carried, and he spoke mechanically, as though delivering a telegram. "A friend told me there ain't no charges for Miss Shelby on the Spirit of St. Louis. You order whatever you want."

Cherie's eyes narrowed at Shelby. "You're somebody, ain't you? Who is she?" she demanded of Marvin. But before her question could be answered, the white-haired judge appeared and crowded Marvin to the side.

"Yes, George." The judge had the shoulder twitch of a fellow who thought himself especially charming after a dry martini. "Tell us who she is." Etched lines exploded from the sides of the man's twinkling, near-sighted eyes, and he leaned nonchalantly against the seat, accommodating his lame leg. "Who *is* this beautiful blonde?"

"This here's Miss Little Rock, judge," Marvin said, eager to please. "She going to New York City."

The man nodded as though he had heard every word.

"Oh, my goodness!" Cherie's purple fingernails spread like a fan across her ample bosom. "I knew you was somebody!" And she hopped to her feet with a wiggle, lining up all body parts just right.

The judge's attention was diverted briefly by Cherie's undulations, but he twinkled more aggressively at Shelby, who was trapped in her seat.

"George!" he boomed, though Marvin stood right beside him.

Shelby winced at the name.

"You got my roomette yet? That baby up the aisle will keep my wife awake all night." His shoulders winged out self-importantly as he confided to Shelby that, "George is a good man. You want anything, just ask him. Or me." He gave her a broad wink. "I know all the conductors on this line."

"Well, there ain't no more roomettes, mister!" Cherie's shrill voice carried the knowledge of dealing with his kind before. "This lady right here just got the last one!"

The judge shot Marvin an astonished and scathing look. "You gave away my roomette?"

Marvin plucked at the sheets with his large hands. "I got you lots of roomettes afore this, judge." His voice was barely audible.

Meyers frowned as though he couldn't have heard correctly. His careful words were round as plums. "You know my wife needs her rest. I don't want to have to complain to the conductor about this inconvenience." He took a fifty-cent piece from his pocket and held it between two manicured fingers. "I want to see this blonde lady's ticket."

When the train gave a sudden jolt, the judge grabbed Marvin's shoulder and dropped the money, but Marvin stood with a sailor's balance, holding the sheets like prayer cloths, as the cars slowed to a crawl around a switchback curve, and people looked out of their windows at the opposite side of their own train, strangers waving and smiling at people they didn't know and probably would never see again.

The smoldering group in car 410 didn't wave back: the white-haired, red-faced man dressed in a white suit and a red tie, clinging to a porter, the wide-eyed blonde in a haze of yellow pleats clutching the seat, and the big-bosomed purple apparition smiling at people she could barely see with her near-sighted eyes. The four held their poses when the U was at its apex and the audience was largest, but when the train rounded the curve, and the spectators' eyes disappeared, Judge Meyers shoved Marvin aside.

"Alright, *George*. Pull me a roomette out of your porter's hat, and make it quick! I don't have all day."

Marvin's nose was heaving and subsiding like the ventricles of a racing heart. Shelby was still holding on to an upper berth, trying to keep her balance. She had already had too much action on this trip, but this arrogant man was being a jerk to Marvin, and Marvin was doing his brave best to help her.

She cleared her throat. "That baby back there won't cry again. I'll bet . . . I'll bet that baby will sleep all night."

Marvin became a little more confident. "Yassuh, judge. That baby won't cry. I sure don't think so."

"You do as I tell you, George! You find me a roomette!"

"Don't talk to him that way," Shelby snapped back. "And his name is Marvin, his name is on his jacket! You should call him Marvin!"

Both Meyers and Marvin looked at her with confounded eyes.

"His . . . his name is Marvin," she repeated less confidently. "Marvin is a fine name."

Cherie put two fingers in her mouth and let out a screeching whistle of approval.

"It don't bother me if His Honor call. . . ."

"Who *is* this *woman, George?*" Annoyance whistled between the judge's teeth. "Who is this . . . *blonde?*"

"This here . . . this here . . ." Marvin was in a painful state, perspiration oozing down his face, sheets clutched to his chest like armor. "This here ain't no woman, Your Honor." His voice grew loud enough to carry to the man's good ear. "THIS HERE LADY IS MISS LITTLE ROCK, AND . . ."

But Meyers cut him off. "Don't you talk back to me, nigger! You find me a roomette or you won't have a job by the time we reach New York City!"

Then Shelby remembered who this man was. He was from Marianna, Arkansas, and had lots of cotton money or rice money, though she thought the money belonged to his wife. Herbert Billington had mentioned something about a judgeship this bully didn't get because of a scandal years ago; but Herbert had changed the subject quickly. Shelby remembered, however, that Meyers' real first name was *Judd*. He just liked the sound of "Judge" better, a title he still secretly hoped would become his.

"Give him my roomette, Marvin." Shelby's voice was firm. "And don't worry about your job. *Herbert Billington* will make sure you keep your job." She enunciated Billington's name like a spear hurled toward the enemy's heart.

"Just when did this woman get a roomette, *George?*" He spoke the name with unadulterated scorn. "Tell me, *George!*"

"I've always had one." Shelby was amazed at the confident sound that emerged from her lying mouth. "I was just sitting with my friend in the sleeper section so we could talk."

"You hear that, you old bastard!" Cherie hollered. "Me and her are best friends!"

Shelby tried not to wince. "However, I'm giving my room-ette," and her verve increased with each syllable she uttered, "to you and your *wife*." And she threw the last word at Meyers as his "wife" entered the car.

"You been gone too long, sugar," the woman called. Her mascaraed eyes resembled a raccoon's. "Come along now. I know you want an early to bed!'

Meyers glared at her venomously.

"Or whatever," the woman shrugged. "It's your nickel,"she said ironically, and she exited the car with hips rolling.

But Meyers hardly noticed. He was peering at Shelby as though some awful truth had just dawned on him. He limped a step closer to her.

"Miss Little Rock," he almost whispered. "Jesus God. Of course. *Shelby Howell. . . .*"

He leaned his cane against a seat, removed his glasses from an inside jacket pocket, attached the delicate earpiec-es one at a time, stepped squarely in front of Shelby, and croaked a laugh so jagged it could have drawn blood. "God knows, you look like *him. . . .*"

Shelby was pressed against the arm of the seat, unable to escape, thinking this wasn't what she had hoped for on this journey. She had hoped for the resolution of enigmas and good times and bright lights and standing ovations. Ad-venture, absolutely, but not this . . . whatever it was. Terror. This was terror. She felt terrorized by the reflection in this old man's glasses, where she saw her own green eyes staring back at her tiny, frightened face mirrored in his magnified pupils. They looked trapped, the old man and the young woman, inside the other's eyes.

"You're that famous *blonde*." His voice was rich with sarcasm. "*The Polish blonde!*" He spat a tortured laugh.

Shelby jerked a palm in front of her face, certain Meyers's words bore spittle. She was vaguely aware that Cherie was wrapping an arm around her waist.

"You don't use your real name, do you? Baldwin tried to hide you and your mother in plain sight by changing your names, didn't she?" But it wasn't really a question.

Shelby's head jerked fearfully, as though by merely speaking Baldwin's name, Meyers had put her grandmother in harm's way.

"She thought she could *command* people to forget, like she *commanded* people to do everything else. *But people will never forget.*" And he disgorged the name in a bitter catarrh, "*Korzeniowski!* That's your real name, isn't it? *KORZENIOWSKI! AND WHERE'S YOUR DADDY* NOW, LITTLE GIRL?"

Shelby hated the way this man diminished that raffish, exotic name. She hated the man himself. She needed to look away from him, but her head wouldn't move.

A group entered the car laughing at someone's joke, crowding past the foursome and uttering derisive animal hoots that lingered after they exited the far door. But the lively interruption seemed to increase, rather than diminish the tension amongst the travelers, who remained standing rigidly in the aisle.

Martin did move to place the stack of starched white sheets on the arm of a chair with great care, as though that quiet chore might create peace amongst the two contestants. But Meyers was as oblivious to Marvin as he had been to the passing circus of friends. Shelby was his focus, and he stared at her, his lids heavy as though finally comprehending a malicious truth.

"And you don't know about it, do you?" He snorted sarcastically. "They were ashamed to tell their little girl, weren't they?" He then added with cruel relish, "And how's your *momma* these days, little girl? She was a looker and then some before Granny put her in the looney bin! Does she still cut herself with knives?"

Shelby made a guttural sound and lunged toward the evil man, but Cherie held her back with a surprisingly strong grip.

"Well, you be sure and tell her you met her old friend, Judd Meyers. And tell her he'll get to know her daughter *much* better, like he used to know *her*. She'll like to hear that." And because he could no longer contain his fury over the thing that really drove him mad, he limped even closer to Shelby and thrust a rigid finger at his damaged leg. "Your old man made me a goddamn *cripple! Look what the bastard did to me!*" Then he added with a departing sneer, "*And where, oh, where did he go?*"

Shelby grabbed at the back of his jacket. "*Tell me where! Where did he go! Tell me!*"

Meyers jerked from her grip and kept on limping, his flashy red tie askew, barely held with its gold stickpin. His expensive white linen suit now drooped like a clown's. Flailing his angry hands at the sheets, he caused a flurry of white linen to shroud the aisle; and he stumbled over the tangled heap, muttering, "God damn you all to hell." in a louder, commanding taunt, he shouted, "You better clean up this place, *George*, before I sue you for bodily harm! And I'm a damn good lawyer!"

He limped away, strengthened by fury, but forgetting his cane that now was covered with a pile of rumpled sheets, detritus left by a storm. When he returned to retrieve the cane, the storm erupted again, because the cane had disappeared.

14

Marvin collected baggage the next morning, his face glum, his step sluggish. Shelby's fatigued eyes were fixed on the train tracks oozing past gasoline storage tanks, looking for Oz, but seeing Esso. She grew alert when the Chrysler Building came into view. The photo of the building had been on her father's last post card, with a message that read: *I've been to the top!*

She would go to the top of the Chrysler Building while she was in New York City.

She hugged Cherie one more time and rushed to be first to step from the train into Pennsylvania Station, where bright light poured from the skylights, and hurrying voices rose toward the ceiling and hovered like chirping birds.

She ran to catch up with the porter, who was carrying her bags toward the tiers of steel stairs that floated in the vast space, listening as she ran for the clump of a man with a gimpy leg, and at the same time trying to look composed. But her heavy coat kept sliding off her shoulder. Rita Hayworth's fur coat had hung sexily on her shoulder in *Gilda*, but Rita must have used some kind of movie trick.

At the top of the stairs, she paused to stare at a mammoth clock, EASTERN STANDARD TIME emblazoned in the middle. That was her time now, EASTERN STANDARD, though she felt no richer for the extra hour. CENTRAL TIME had been just fine with her.

The porter hailed a taxi with a driver she could barely understand. "Brooklyn," he shouted, when she asked where he was from. He laughed uproariously when she told him she was from Little Rock, Arkansas, and he sang at the top of his lungs, "I'm just a little girl from Little Rock . . ." He dumped her cherished blue leather suitcase in front of Justine's apartment building and sped away.

Shelby dragged the heavy bag inside the building, burdened also with purse and cosmetic case, and she scrounged in her purse for the key Julien had given her. She unlocked the door, flicked on the light, and yelped when a neon sculpture sprang from the wall in a throbbing pink incandescence. But once her eyes adjusted, she stared, open-mouthed, at the huge photographs that seemed to undulate in the flickering light. Only then did she remember to pull the bag inside and close the door behind her, still dumbstruck by what the photographs revealed.

Three days later, Cherie Denise, White Goddess of the Jungle, boarded the transport for Germany. Cherie high-stepped up the gangplank, dressed in purple satin and twirling an ebony cane that sported an ivory handle carved in the shape of a lion.

15

"IF YOU DON'T sell it to me, Baldwin Josephine, a stranger will buy it for back taxes and tear it down to build a drive-in. And wouldn't our daddy turn over in his grave?"

Ernestine, the "pretty one," was talking through the front screen door. She was a tennis player who never let the opposition rattle her. Only Baldwin, just in from the garden and holding a pair of garden clippers aimed at her younger sister, could do that.

"*My* house," Baldwin replied. "This is *my* house. Daddy put it in *my* name You got the money."

For a moment Ernestine found it hard to breathe. If her leathery skin had been flayed and cured, it might have been thick enough, and almost the right color, to cover a football. With her blood pressure raging, the mahogany color was turning purple.

Ernestine took such good care of herself. It was unfair that she, the younger sister, had high blood pressure. Baldwin, whose blood pressure was like a teenager's, was overweight and never exercised, except to pull the occasional weed. What's more, Ernestine was scheduled to play tennis in forty-five minutes and needed to be in control to win. And she always wanted to win, always *would* win, because she knew she was better and smarter, no matter how young the opponent. She flexed her stringy legs to relieve the tension and wiggled her manicured fingers just a bit, so Baldwin wouldn't notice.

But the effort to relax her fingers made Ernestine think yet again about her mother's rings, which increased her agitation. The rings were also in Baldwin's keeping. The circular inevitability of her relationship with her sister always returned to the fact that the older sister had what the younger sister wanted.

"This is the house we both grew up in, Baldwin Josephine." Ernestine's voice was adamantine with reason, even as the urge increased to tear out the screen and pull out her sister's ridiculously permed hair. Instead, she punctuated each sentence with a sharp stab of her tennis racket on the porch floor. "Important people have dined in this house. The great Nellie Melba sang by that beautiful piano over there, which you've let get horribly out of tune. We both took lessons on it. I cannot in good faith watch this beloved, *historic* place rot before my very eyes. I was talking to an architect just the other day who said we could hoist the house on a trailer and move it to Pulaski Heights near where I live. And I mean the entire house! He did say we would have to fix the kitchen floor first, because it would collapse en route. I'm afraid to walk across it."

"Good," Baldwin said emphatically.

Ernestine wailed, reverting to nature. "How can you be so wicked to me? We're *sisters!* What would Daddy say?"

"Daddy would tell you to stay away from me."

"Listen to her, I wish you would! How many times have I said I would build you a nice little place on one level? How many times have I said it won't be long before the stairs in this house will be too much for you? How many times have I said. . . ." and here Ernestine's effort to be nice to her sister reached its limit, "THAT YOU HAVE LET OUR ANCESTRAL HOME ROT BENEATH YOUR UGLY, BUNIONED FEET!" She closed her eyes, counted to ten, and continued in a sweet-as-pie voice. "In a couple of years, there's not a soul in this world will look out for you but me. Eulalia can barely care for herself."

At that moment the Langley dog bounded from the back

yard with a slobber-dripping bone in his mouth.

"And look at that tacky dog in Daddy's garden! Where did he get that bone, will you tell me? Are you feeding that dog, Baldwin Josephine? Is that bone from your kitchen?"

Baldwin's left hand began to tremble. She tried to hold it still with her other hand, but the garden clippers got in the way. "Goodbye, Ernestine." She raised dismissive eyes to the ceiling, then lowered them. She didn't want Ernestine to look up and see the cracked plaster.

"I'm *serious*, Baldwin Josephine!"

Baldwin snapped the clippers closed, but placed them gently on the treasured curly maple side table her father had inherited from his Aunt Alicia. She didn't want to scratch the table's beautiful surface. "This is *my* house, Ernestine." Baldwin's right hand gripped the wayward hand harder. "It will be my house until they carry me out in a pine box, and when I pass, it will be Eulalia's house, and after that it will be Shelby's house. It's written that way in my will."

Ernestine glared at Baldwin, who looked ominous behind the latticed shadows of the screen. "Shelby's never coming back to this place. She'll stay in that city and forget about you. And pine box indeed! I'll bet a dollar to a doughnut you've already bought Julien's top-of-the-line. You could at the very least sell me those back acres you've let go to ruin. People use them as a dump!"

Ernestine's eyes narrowed further and her voice grew sing-song. "This town is beginning to wonder about you, Baldwin Josephine, letting this fine house run down, putting your grand-daughter on a train to New York City with a big darkie. People wonder if you're *competent* to care for this historic house."

Which was when Baldwin slammed the big front door in her sister's face, the silver bell jingling *Good riddance*, which made Ernestine bellow all the way to her Lincoln. The sound of tires slinging gravel from the drive made Baldwin's hand flutter like a leaf in a strong wind. She couldn't afford more gravel.

She stood very still, trying not to panic about the gravel, trying not to panic about her quivering hand. It was just a little palsy. Her Uncle Bert had suffered from a little palsy. She watched the hand move against her thigh like an insect, interesting to observe.

But she felt comforted by the morning sun that spilled through the transom window and onto the faded wallpaper and over the worn Persian rug. The blues in that rug were so intense they could almost be tasted. Baldwin loved the rug, loved this hall, loved the doorbell with its sterling flowers, embossed and shining in the midst of the door's dark wood. During both World Wars, Baldwin had neglected to mention to guests that her father had ordered the bell from Germany.

Most facts regarding the house were too revered to alter. The stained glass window at the bend in the stairs came from a seventeenth-century church in southern France. The grand piano was a Collard & Collard, made in 1879 from a rare burled walnut. The furniture, the china, the silver, everything in the house had a history, and was, therefore, precious.

However Ernestine was right about one thing: in 1917 the great coloratura, Melba, had raised her magnificent voice to the accompaniment of the Collard & Collard, and had sung her famous aria from *La Traviata* for the assembled grandees of Little Rock. Baldwin, then nineteen, had been enthralled by the voice and by the man standing beside her. After that man was blasted to smithereens in the Great War, she was lucky to settle at twenty-four for a second-best husband who had gambled away almost all of his money, along with hers, by the time he died.

The house and all its objects now belonged to Baldwin Josephine Shelby Howell. She had always revered the house, and her father knew she had. It was none of Ernestine's business that Baldwin's life insurance, and the policy on the house, and those pesky federal taxes hadn't been paid.

She had to remember to ask Julien's advice about money matters. Her memory had become a bit slippery of late, though she would never let Ernestine know.

And Ernestine had no right to call Saracen Self a big darkie. Baldwin could do it, but Ernestine had no right. She knew Baldwin had been fond of young Saracen. Baldwin could admit that to herself in the confines of the front hall. He had possessed a remarkable memory, that boy had, and a gift for discerning what brought her peace of mind, like leaving chickfoot violets in a mason jar at the kitchen door or sassafras root for tea, especially during Eulalia's confinement at the State Hospital. It was clear that his particular cranium held plenty of brains . . . a fact that caused Baldwin a quiver of doubt about the size of the Negro brain in general.

Of course, part of Saracen's childish appeal had been his striking appearance: that lovely brown skin and Roman nose and those strange, green eyes that seemed to absorb people's thoughts. But he had grown up to be a smart-alecky colored man, hadn't he, driving that snippy little yellow car right up to her front door, and she couldn't allow that behavior from a colored.

And yet . . . as a child . . . Saracen had been very polite, and even brave. Brave to kidnap that elephant from the zoo, yes, he was. It was not the right thing to do—it was theft—but it took an unusual boy to do it. She pictured him leading that big elephant along that potholed highway in the middle of the night, probably talking to the animal like she was human, telling her she was going home soon, that everything would be better for her when she got back to the jungle. Rose was the elephant's name. But she had died in her cage in Little Rock, poor old Rose, a prisoner to the end.

Baldwin walked to the living room, settled herself on

the rose-colored settee, and crossed her legs by lifting one thigh with both hands and flopping it over the other. She and Shelby often sat on that settee for afternoon tea. She sighed at the loss of that ritual, and sighed again at how hard it might be to keep the Negroes in their place. Maybe too hard for an old lady. She didn't have the energy she used to have, and she was aggravated at Julien for enlisting members of the Citizens' Council, who didn't wear neckties and spat on her walk when they came to meetings. She had watched them from a window as they walked to her front door. It was such a disgusting breach of etiquette. And that silly real estate husband of Kate's, Bruce Norton, was buttering her up, because he hoped to sell her house one day. Baldwin knew what he was doing.

Maybe what she needed was tea in one of the Canton cups her father had sent back from China. Baldwin loved that china. It was fragile as old silk, with its painted flowers and butterflies and little Chinese ladies bowing from the waist. And, no, she wouldn't add whiskey to the tea this time. She had to stop that whiskey business.

Although . . . maybe just a splash of J.W. Dant. She deserved a splash after Ernestine's visit. And whiskey seemed to help the palsy.

But the one thing she absolutely had to remember was to tell Tom that the Langley dog was digging for bones in the back acres. He had to do something about that dog.

However, first she would seek out a bottle of her dead Daddy's whiskey. It was like a little game he had left for her to play. She started down the stairs, humming the hymn she loved, "I'm living on the mountain, underneath a cloudless sky. . ."

This would be a good day in spite of Ernestine's visit.

16

IN JUSTINE'S APARTMENT Shelby had a recurring dream. A giant with Judd Meyers's face would limp toward a little girl who was frantically flapping her arms, trying to fly to the safety of her father's voice. But the voice would dart like a bird just out of reach. When she woke, the dream would close inward like a sea creature protecting itself from a predator, and she would throw off the hot, sweaty, black satin sheets and wander aimlessly around the apartment.

It was strange to hear ocean liners braying from their dockings on the Hudson River. Once she heard a frantic, female scream on the sidewalk just outside the apartment. Her impulse was to rush out and save the woman, but she was too afraid to be a good citizen. This place was not her home.

"*Those streets up there are dark,*" Baldwin hummed in Shelby's ear as they drank their tea, silver teaspoons tinkling in Canton cups. "*Your place is here, Shelby Howell. This is your home. We could build a wall around this state and survive forever on the goods we produce right here inside our borders.*" Baldwin would reposition her feet ever so daintily, fix Shelby with faded blue eyes, and speak with the wide-eyed whispery little girl voice she used when most determined to get her way: "*THIS is your place, Shelby Howell. THIS place is in your blood.*"

The voice was silenced when Shelby flipped through Justine's fashion magazines, and sniffed moldy cheeses with foreign labels in the refrigerator, and stared at real silk dresses . . . and stared at the explicit photographs on the living room walls. No one could see her, so it was okay to stare.

A red satin robe in the closet smelled curiously of oregano, and in a fit of loneliness, she stripped off her pajamas, drew the robe over her nakedness, and, opening the robe wide, stared at her body in the full-length mirror. Familiar feelings emerged to ache and swell and migrate with delicious languor, but when Saracen's image came to mind, she ripped off the robe, threw her pajamas back on, and curled up on the bed, knees to chin.

It was hard to imagine that Julien had a friend like Justine, who slept on black satin sheets and displayed huge photographs of entangled nude bodies on the living room walls.

Justine would return in four days. Shelby had to find her own place in a hurry.

17

THE OUTSIDE OF Tom Self's white frame house looked as neat and starched as a Sunday shirt.

However, once inside the front door, one was greeted with an astonishment of African masks hanging on the living room walls, rendered more astonishing by the red and green Christmas tree lights flickering in their eye holes. Some masks were painted in bright colors, some were scarified, some had bulbous cheeks and warthog tusks and exaggerated lips and mouths filled with animal teeth sharpened to a point. One formidable mask had rusted nails pounded into the face and neck. And in the middle of this startling assemblage, an unadorned ebony beauty presided with heavy-lidded, all-seeing, sparkling-white Christmas tree eyes.

The collection was interspersed with cheap china angels and a china Jesus whose halo glittered with crystals found in caves near Hot Springs, Arkansas. The mélange of religions and cultures and folk art and cheap china was joyous—and a little scary.

Tom was taking deep pulls on his Lucky Strike and watching Saracen, who was striding back and forth in front of the masks.

Tom was proud of his son's achievements. The entire black population of Little Rock was proud of Saracen. He had seen the world, and not just as a soldier. L.C. Bates, the Negro publisher of the state's largest black newspaper, even reprinted some of the articles Saracen wrote for that big paper in Chicago. But neither Bates, nor his wife, Daisy, nor Saracen, for that matter, took white people's power seriously enough. Saracen drove that yellow convertible right down Main Street, and Tom knew white people wouldn't ignore that sass from a black man much longer. Little Rock had a reputation for being racially moderate, but the city had never been put to a real test, and Tom felt that test was coming soon.

Tom knew that white men thought their color was God's color. His china Jesus had a white face, which he could tolerate, because a china Jesus with a black face wasn't available. He also knew that white folks . . . and they had the money and the power. . .might be forced to integrate, but their true thinking would pop out in mean ways; dangerous ways, and what couldn't be changed for a very long while might as well be endured. It was one thing if you could use hate to change the white man's mind, but hate usually bit a man in his own ass. Not even that Martin Luther King folks talked so much about these days could convince whites to accept the black man just by marching down streets and singing hymns.

Saracen had quit pacing and was standing still, chin raised, lips pressed tight together. Tom knew he was about to say something annoying. It was the look Saracen wore as a child when he was provoked and about to spill it out. Tom smiled at the memory and waited for his son to speak.

"He must have said something to you, Daddy. A person doesn't disappear without a word to the people he loves. And Teddy loved Eulalia. When I was a kid, I saw them kissing . . . long kisses too."

Tom moved uneasily in his chair. "You was spying, son . . . and it ain't *right* to talk like that about Eulalia. She almost old enough to be your momma."

"She's just a couple of years older than I am, and she *ain't* my momma. She's one gorgeous woman who doesn't look much older than her daughter."

Tom made a sound like angry wasps.

"Teddy used to take me places. White places. Did you know that?"

"I know where he take you."

Saracen nodded as though he should have realized his father's reach was wide. "He was married to a society daughter and could get away with it, and he was handsome and charming and smart. The man was *smart*. People tolerated his eccentricities, and I guess I was one of them.

"Remember his long, black winter coat with that velvet collar, and the scarf he flung around his neck? The man looked *dashing* when he strode down the sidewalk. And he was always reading leather-bound books. He said they were worth a lot of money, but even as a kid, I could tell he liked to exaggerate.

"*And . . .*" Saracen laughed as this memory emerged, "he had a little knife concealed in that fancy belt buckle he wore. The buckle had a lever, and when he pushed it, a stiletto would pop out like a snake's tongue. And the thing was sharp! When I was a kid, I could watch that stiletto pop out for hours!"

Tom's shoulders sagged.

"So how in the world could a man that outrageous just disappear? And Shelby is *still* torn up about it. Her beloved papa crashed his plane with her in it, dropped out of her life the same day, and nobody said a word about it to her!" Saracen leaned closer to his father. "And you know what happened to him, don't you?"

The nostrils of Tom's fleshy nose rose and fell with each arduous breath he took. He didn't respond, which made Saracen anxious. "You okay, Daddy?"

Tom roused himself with an effort. "I been working all day digging up Baldwin's dahlia bulbs for wintertime. You just been writing down stuff in that little book you got." The big man clutched the chair arms. "But I'm mostly whupped from you talking about *Teddy.* I got my *fill* of you talking about *Teddy. Talk about something else."*

Saracen eased his father's calloused hands from the chair, rubbed them with skilled fingers, and Tom sighed and settled back.

"Okay." But Saracen couldn't resist a small tease. "I'll talk about Eulalia."

Tom threw off the hands of his astonished son. "I can't listen to this talk no more! You calling her 'Eulalia' like you know her personal? You better call her *Miss* Eulalia, and don't you say a word about how good she look!"

"*You* call her Eulalia!"

"I'se a *old* man, know her the day she born. Tired old man can say things. Strong young black man best keep his mouth shut. They's something in you looking for trouble, Saracen Self, making the boys think you got magic in your blood. Oh, yes, indeedy! They tell me about it. You best watch out for that magic talk."

"They want to *think* I have magic, Daddy. I wear African clothes sometimes, I've got a sports car like a rich white boy, I travel to strange places . . . so I must be magic. There's a guy in a play I read who claims he can call spirits from the deep, and another guy in the play says, 'Yeah, I can too, but will they come when you call them?'

"My friends down here don't ask that question. They want to think the spirits *will* come when I call. They say they believe in Jesus, but they really believe in spirits. They've got to believe in something better than their own bony existence." Saracen sighed, placed his hands at his waist, and rotated his shoulders to ease his own tension. There was the sound of bones cracking while muscles relaxed.

"I sure hope you got some magic to keep your own self safe," Tom said. "You better think on that boy, Emmett Till, tore to pieces in the Tallahatchie River, President Ike not even answering the telegram the poor boy's momma sent asking for help. I guess it's going to happen here, this integration thing, they's some good white people in this town. But it will cause a mess of trouble with them other kind." He picked up the Lucky Strike, inhaled deeply, coughed up brown mucous, swallowed it, and stubbed out the cigarette. Tom refused to see a doctor about the cough.

"But just tell me this one thing . . ." his son persisted. "Why would a man go down the rabbit hole when he adored his wife and daughter? Something terrible had to happen to make that man leave his family the way he did, and I *know* he said something to you and Momma about it. You knew everything that went on in that house. The main reason Shelby went to New York City was to find Teddy . . . and *you* know if he's there!"

Tom slumped back in his chair, groaning and stretching his long legs. "Don't ask me no more questions, *and I mean it, boy* . . . you making me mad. Let Teddy alone. *He gone!*" The startling green of Saracen's eyes seemed a blessing when the boy was born, but now those unrelenting green eyes bothered Tom.

"Dammit!" Saracen slammed one big fist into his other hand. "If Momma were here, *she* would tell me!"

Tom bellowed back, "Well, she ain't here! Your momma died on me!"

Saracen breathed deeply. His voice was grim. "She died on me too, Daddy."

Tom winced and placed his hand on Saracen's knee with a surprisingly strong grip. "Yes, she did. Both us suffer . . . and this ain't no way to talk between us, son. Your momma wouldn't like it, so let's leave this be. Stay out of Shelby's business. Put yourself in that yellow car and go down to Pine Bluff, talk to that there black lawyer man, Wiley Branton, family owns taxi cabs. Or talk to that there lawyer, Thurgood what's-his-name, coming and going these days. Brave man. Big man with a moustache. Tell funny stories, they say. I shook his hand at church. Or talk to Daisy Bates, trying to get them black chirrun into the white man's school. But don't pester me no more about a man been gone so long he oughta be *forgot*."

Saracen knew his father couldn't be forced to talk about Teodore Korzeniowski any more than he could be forced to go to the doctor about his health. And maybe there never would be an answer to Korzeniowski's disappearance. Sometimes people got off the streetcar at the end of the line and were never seen again.

"I have to go to New York City soon." Saracen's voice was calmer. "I would like to be able to tell Shelby something about Teddy. Even if it's just how he looked when you last saw him, what he was wearing, how he sounded . . . anything. I think it would be helpful to her."

Tom groaned and stretched his legs out from the chair. "You too thick with Shelby, son. You see her two minutes after all those years, and you already too thick. You better think on that boy Emmett Till when you jump on white trains and make out like a porter. You think I don't hear about that? Everybody hear. Baldwin after me like a scalded dog about you jumping on that train."

Tom tugged an old quilt over his legs, even though the weather was pleasant. He fidgeted with the quilt, looked at the ceiling and said, "Shelby got Marvin Williams fired from his Pullman car job."

The mumbling way Tom relayed the news made it hard to grasp.

"Did you say *Shelby* got Marvin fired?"

"She the one."

"How in God's name could she get Marvin Williams fired?"

"She didn't aim to, I don't think, and Marvin don't think.

139

But she got herself into some kind of fight on the Spirit of St. Louis with Judd Meyers, and Marvin try to help her. Do his best for her, he say. And that sonuvabitch Meyers got Marvin fired because of it." Tom Self never cursed. It was against his religion. "I tell you for certain, Shelby and her doings gonna cause trouble. I love that child, but I see trouble running with her like a greyhound down at the dog tracks. And Marvin just got hisself head porter, and that's a good job. Now I have to say Shelby do try to fix his job back with help from her boyfriend's daddy, Herbert Billington."

"Who's that?"

"Who Herbert?"

"Naw. Everybody knows who he is. What's the name of Shelby's boyfriend?"

"Name of Charlie. And Charlie think he fix it up for Marvin, but Herbert see a way to get hisself some Mississippi bottom land, never mind Marvin. Rich people never got enough *stuff*, do they. Proud of their *stuff*. Like to show off their *stuff*. And Marvin's got four littleuns."

"Ah, yes . . . *that* Charlie. The Charlie who's trying to convince Virgil Blossom to support integration. I've heard about that Charlie. But he'll never convince Virgil. School superintendent is just a stepping stone for our Virgil. He sounds like he's gung-ho about integration, but he really plays to the rich, white bigots, because he hopes they will recruit him to run for governor. He won't push integration in a serious way."

"All I know is, Herbert Billington finally see a way to get hisself some rich, black bottom land. Bottom land's the one black thing the man like."

Saracen stared grim-faced at the mocking eyes in the masks that covered the perky red and blue flowers on the wallpaper, thinking that Shelby didn't understand the true nature of the divide between blacks and whites. She had grown up with prejudice and thought no more about it than the air she breathed. She had surely cost Marvin his job.

"Okay," he said. "I'll fix Judd Meyers. It will take a while, but he'll pay for what he did, and with luck, maybe you and I can help Marvin get his job back."

Tom's calloused hands caressed the quilt. The quilt was worn but precious, because Jessie had made it. He looked up at Saracen. "You a good boy, Saracen. Smart like your momma, good-looking like your momma." Tom paused. "But you stay away from Charlie Billington."

Saracen laughed. "I don't even know the man. I never heard about him until he began to pressure Blossom."

Tom's voice became more stern. "Look at me, boy, and listen to what I'm saying . . ."

"*Okay*, Daddy. I'm looking and listening."

"And keep yourself out of New York City." Tom pointed a long finger at his son. "And don't give me no shine about that."

When Saracen began to protest, Tom's finger jabbed more firmly.

"Listen to me! *Stay away from Shelby and her town.*"

18

SHELBY WAS WEARING a white silk dress she thought made her look a little like Marilyn Monroe, and she was running as fast as she could in her green high-heeled sling-backs, holding her green hat with one hand and Saracen's necklace with the other so it wouldn't bounce and stab her with its teeth. Baldwin's star sapphire was on the hand that grabbed the necklace. She wore the necklace and the ring for luck.

The high heels were becoming instruments of torture, and when she bent to ease the strap on a shoe, a piece of paper bound with a rubber band landed in front of her feet. The paper was accompanied by a shrill voice screaming, "Honey! *Honey!* Pick up that paper and call the number on it. *Willya, honey?* Tell him Tina needs. . . ."

But Tina's voice was drowned by a torrent of female voices yelling obscenities until they all stopped abruptly, like animals in the jungle that sense a more dangerous beast is on the way.

"Get me outta here . . ." a woman howled, her voice seared with pain. "Get me outta here . . . GET ME OUTTA HERE . . . GET . . . ME . . ." And the screams stopped with a gagged gurgle.

Most pedestrians hurried on their way as though accustomed to the rage, but Shelby couldn't move. Her feet stayed fixed to the sidewalk until she turned toward the end of the block where people were laughing and taxis were honking and flowers were displayed in a riot of color, and she raced on blistering feet toward those better blocks, and clambered down the stairs to the subway where a tall, red-headed, freckle-faced man was leaping over the turnstile, his back straight, his toes pointed, as though he might fly through the tunnel in a perfect *grand jeté* all the way to the Times Square stop.

The gazelle-like leap dazzled Shelby. She had hoped to find this kind of verve and daring in New York City. She felt giddy at the man's defiance of convention and the laws of gravity, and she stood at respectful attention and applauded his daring, determined not to be cowed by voices, no matter how near or far away.

The freckle-faced young man leaned against a Chiclet machine, pressed a sneaker-clad foot against his knee with the awkward grace of a crane in shallow water, and bowed to her.

When Shelby arrived at Forty-Second Street, she rushed to change trains, but some wag had switched the signs to the shuttle, causing the uninitiated to scurry in confused circles around a stall with exotic flowers for sale. It seemed incongruous to see such alien, natural beauty in this underworld, and Shelby leaned to inhale their perfume, but grimaced in disappointment. The perfect flowers were made of paper.

When she exited the subway stop closest to The Acting School, she was glad to breathe open air, and began to sprint down the sidewalk until she felt a wobble on the heel of the shoe that got ensnared in the train steps in Little Rock. But she couldn't be late on the first day of school, and she continued to run uptown, then whirling to run downtown when she realized it was the wrong way, stopping once to relieve her aching feet and look up tall buildings to the cloudless sky where a small plane was skywriting. She paused, wiggling her aching toes, remembering.

It was on such a cloudless day that she and her mother watched a plane skywrite with the same cloudy, cursive loops: DRINK DR. PEPPER AT 10 2 AND 4.

On that long-ago day the plane made a turn and wrote another message:

I LOVE LALIE AND SHELBY!

Shelby had sounded out the words of the dreamy script, and her mother had grabbed her hands and twirled her around and around, shouting to her, and the man in the sky, "You are the smartest thing!" When her father began a nose-dive toward the two of them, her mother looked up again, shouting, "You'll get in trouble!" seeming to revel in her husband's fearlessness. He leveled off just above the trees, wings waggling, and headed toward the Arkansas River to fly beneath the Broadway Bridge and break another law.

On the hot sidewalk in New York City, Shelby began to sprint in earnest, ignoring her burning feet, ignoring the shoe's precarious heel, until she stood, panting, in front of a discreet bronze plaque that identified the building as The Acting School.

She stared at the sign, heart pounding, fanned her flushed face with her gloves, removed her hat, and ran fingers through her hair. She was discreetly adjusting her panties when a hand appeared over her shoulder.

"May I?" a pleasant male voice asked. The hand turned the knob of the heavy door and held it open.

The tall man, who looked like Gregory Peck, must have seen her jerk her panties in place, and she could feel her face turn red. Then the tall, handsome man nodded to the woman at the desk, and began to walk up the stairs. When he turned at the landing, he looked back at her and winked.

He definitely was Gregory Peck.

19

THE WOMAN SAT behind a Regency-style desk. She was dressed in lavender silk, and a string of pearls gleamed white against her black skin. She lifted her elegant neck when Shelby entered, and arched the painted lines of her eyebrows. If she had clapped her hands with their long, manicured fingernails, a butler surely would have appeared with tea in Canton cups on a silver tray.

Shelby tried not to stare. "Shelby Howell. . . ." She cleared her throat. "My name is Shelby Howell. I'm a new student."

The woman didn't look up.

"Is this . . . Do I need to sign anything?"

"You're late," the woman said, and raised cold eyes to Shelby's.

Shelby felt an eyelid flutter and imagined Saracen observing her with sardonic eyes. *How does it feel, little lady, to be confronted with black authority? How does it feel to be a whitewashed Negro, little white girl?*

"I'm sorry," she began to prattle, "I changed subways at Forty-second Street, but someone switched the sign, and I asked the lady at the flower stand for directions, and went uptown when I should. . . ." Her voice trailed off, though she feared she might begin to tell stories about Judd Meyers, and her missing father, and her mother who went to the State Hospital and wore a long, white robe. "I'm new in New York City," she added, determined to maintain eye contact.

The woman's eyes moved to Shelby's white gloves that she now held in one hand, palm up, the proper way Baldwin held her gloves.

"Where are you from?" the woman asked.

"Little Rock, Arkansas."

"Ah, yes," the woman said, as though that explained everything. "You're Shelby Howell."

For a bewildering second Shelby had an overwhelming impulse to say that, no . . . *actually* . . . her last name was "Korzeniowski" . . . that there must have been a mix-up on the application, that the small sounds of "Howell" *actually* composed her middle name, that the great and resounding "Korzeniowski" *actually* was her true surname.

And why not? She was in another world, a foreigner in a strange land. She would stay true to Baldwin by carrying white gloves, but she would roll the forbidden name from her tongue like a dissonant symphony. The woman interrupted Shelby's near brush with treason.

"Victor Liebmann doesn't permit his students to be late. And you may call him Victor in class. My name is *Mrs.* D'Arcy." When her eyes fixed on Shelby's heathen necklace, she pursed her mouth and touched the tips of her manicured fingers to her own perfect, white pearls.

Shelby was accustomed to colored people. Baldwin always said black hands were best when you were sick. And just a few weeks ago Shelby had been locked in a roomette with a big colored man and had emerged just fine. Different somehow, but fine. But she had never encountered carefully manicured nails on black hands attached to the arms of a beautiful Cerberus.

She took a deep breath and tried to stuff her gloves into her purse unobserved. "Where do I go?"

Mrs. D'Arcy raised her shiny eyebrows toward the downstairs in silent dismissal.

The tap of Shelby's high heels ricocheted against the walls like bullets. The sandal heel was still wobbly, and she was desperate to remove a pebble spearing her toe, but she refused to stop until she was out of Mrs. D'Arcy's line of vision.

The moment she turned the corner, she paused at the top of the stairs. She removed the shoe and the grit, balancing on the unstable shoe, and peered down at the fifteen or so people in the hall below, who were leaning against a wall or seated on the floor. When her heel suddenly collapsed, she stumbled, yelped, clutched at the railing, almost righted herself, then bumped awkwardly down the stairs, white silk billowing, arms flapping for balance.

A tall, very slender young man with curly red hair and a freckled face swept up to her.

"You all right?"

She couldn't speak.

"Shall I pull down your skirt? Pull up your stockings? Rearrange that funky necklace hanging down your back?" He turned and announced to the group behind him, "She's got monster teeth hanging down her back!" then whirled back to her. "Your fall was almost as good as my turnstile broad jump, and wasn't it a thing of beauty? I loved your applause! We were fated to meet here! Can you move?"

She thought she could move, but wished she were dead.

"Stay where you are!" Horn-rimmed glasses and a receding hairline made the new speaker look older than he was. "Move aside, Boojie." He gave the turnstile leaper a friendly shove and squatted by Shelby. "My name is Hank," he said. Hank was earnest and efficient as he removed the damaged shoe and slid his hands along arms and legs.

"Wait . . ." she pleaded, shoving down her skirt. "Please! I'm okay!" And, vision whirling, she rose to a standing position, teetering on the good shoe and the unshod toes of her other foot. She hobbled to pick up her purse, the damaged shoe, and the green hat that made the journey solo. She whacked the hat on her hip to restore some of its shape. "I'm okay." She flicked back her hair. "I'm just fine."

"You most certainly are," Boojie agreed.

"Yeah, Hank, she's okay," said the female voice Shelby had heard from the landing. "You can take your hand from . . . wherever it landed . . . but I doubt ambulance drivers qualify as doctors."

Hank tightened his grip on Shelby's elbow. "Those stairs are a menace," and adding good-naturedly over his shoulder, "and ambulance drivers get paid good money when they work at night, Max."

The girl called Max planted her hands at her waist, released a whooping laugh, scissor-kicked a shapely leg in Hank's direction, straddled her legs as though prepared to belt out the finale to a musical, and stared as Hank led Shelby to a chair.

Another girl was using the back of the chair to practice ballet exercises. Her auburn hair dangled over one shoulder in a long braid, her skin was very white and unblemished, and her blue eyes exuded a doll's unblinking innocence.

"My name is Jan," the ballerina said to Shelby in a whipped cream whisper, then pushed her back to the wall, lifted her leg to the side, and pressed one hand against her stomach as though reassuring herself it was perfectly flat. She smoothed her sleek waistline with the other hand, like a trainer calming a thoroughbred. Occasionally, she made humming sounds. It was hard to tell whether she was about to erupt into song or was simply exulting in her perfect physical condition.

"Sit." Hank commanded Shelby. Shelby sat gratefully, removed the shoe that was still intact, and turned her head to smile at Jan.

"My name is Shelby Howell."

"Be still my heart!" Boojie crooned and dropped to one

knee in front of her. "I thought I heard Southern diphthongs emerging from your lovely mouth! Have you read that poem, 'Howl,' by Allen Ginsberg? We're all wild about 'Howl.' Incidentally, I'm Gordon Hunt the 3rd, but call me Boojie. And where are you from, dear child?"

Shelby's face was expressionless, and she did her best to keep it that way. "Little Rock, Arkansas."

"Oh, my, *Gawd!* Can you believe?" Boojie grinned at someone at the end of the hall and turned back to Shelby. "Ginsberg mentions Arkansas in *Howl*: ' . . . hallucinating Arkansas,' he writes! I'll bet he saw you while he was tripping out down there and *howled* with inspiration!"

"How-well." Shelby over-enunciated. "Not Howl."

Boojie shrugged. "You should change it to Howl. I change things about myself all the time."

"Actually . . ." and Shelby breathed very carefully, "Howell is my middle name. My last name is actually . . . Korzeniowski." She said the name softly at first, then repeated it more confidently, hissing a bit when she came down on the 's,' which gave her an almost savage pleasure. "KorzeniowS-S-S-KI is my last name."

"Wow. Yeah. That *is* a name. But I'll bet your agent makes you use Howell. Or better still, *Howl.* Shelby HOWL would look great on a marquee. I can see it now . . ." and he posed, hand extended, pointing to the sign with the name HOWL in big, flashing lights.

Max, really Maxine, rolled her eyes and turned back to the other two males she had been favoring with her company. One bore a faint resemblance to Marlon Brando, a look intensified by his scuffed leather jacket, short leather boots, and faded jeans so tight they could cause genital damage. The young man's name was Robert, but Max called him Roberto, trilling the r's and caressing the "o" with her lips, which clearly pleased him.

The other man, whose name was Paul, was anywhere between twenty-five to fifty-five years old. His thick glasses had steel frames, his shoes were highly polished, and he wore the only suit in the hall. The jacket's bulge was caused by a tie stuffed in the pocket as soon as he saw that everyone else was more casually dressed . . . with the exception of Maxine, whose fingernails were painted silver, whose wild curls looked struck by lightning, and whose outfit would have looked great on a Rockette.

"Listen, ducks," Maxine said to Roberto in her ersatz English accent, "Hollywood *destroys* your creativity. Look what happened to that cute Franchot Tone, a great actor who sold his soul in exchange for starlets and red carpets. The *stage alone* produces true art." Max plunged her silver fingernails into her black hair, and her curls bounced enthusiastically.

"Brando has made movies." Paul scrunched up his nose in an unsuccessful effort to push his glasses in place. "We cannot dismiss his brilliant performance in *On the Waterfront.*"

"But my dear friend, *Bud,*" Max retorted, making it clear she knew Brando well enough to call him by his nickname, "has made a couple of movies that are nothing compared to his stage perform. . . ."

"I saw him in person two days ago," Boojie interrupted. "He was so close I could have touched him."

"You *always* think you see someone famous, Booj. . . ." Max's voice faded, as she turned to smile at a man who was entering the hall, but her smile dissolved when he looked at Shelby instead. He was about five feet, nine inches in height, so it wasn't the height that made him unique, and his long, still face wasn't especially handsome. Perhaps it was his black eyes or his older age that made him seem a bit mysterious, like Humphrey Bogart.

Shelby hardly noticed the man. She was looking at a Negro across the hall. Could he be a student? It hadn't occurred to her that a Negro might be in the class, especially one who was dark-skinned, had a broad nose, big lips, and the pocked skin of pimples at a younger age. But, and this was important to her, because it showed respect, his blue jeans were neatly pressed, his white shirt carefully ironed, and his worn shoes highly polished.

Boojie moved to the Negro's side, pointed in Shelby's direction, and slapped his knee gleefully. The black man's face revealed nothing.

Shelby knew she was barefoot and overdressed and disheveled, but it was cruel for the subway leaper to make fun of her, especially with a Negro. She turned her head, and her eyes connected with the mystery man who was staring at her. Did she look that awful? The minute he turned his head, she brushed at her wrinkled dress.

Max was talking again to the two men, jiggling a lovely leg. The silver-painted nails of one hand were splayed against the wall like a Chinese fan. "Bud told me *not* to go to the Actor's Studio. He said that after an improv, Strasberg lets the class tear you apart before he moves in to finish the kill himself. Plus, you wait years for an audition to get in the Studio, and if you fail, you have to audition again, *and* again." She scampered her nails against the wall like little silver bugs, but the man continued to stare at Shelby.

Max swung her leg higher and spoke even more vivaciously to Roberto, promising, by innuendo, so many things if he would be her friend, join her club (whatever the club was). Max was pudgy, but she had great legs and used them to her advantage.

"So, Maxie," Boojie turned to her again. "Sounds like you didn't pass the audition for the Actor's Studio. All that moaning and groaning and jumping around with that sword you borrowed. You were lucky you didn't stab yourself, dear heart! I told you that scene from *Saint Joan* was wrong for you."

Wicked Boojie began to imitate Max, hopping like a toad with a sword, and Max's brown eyes thickened and bubbled to the color of blood. But at the mention of *Saint Joan*, Shelby's interest quickened.

"*Bud*," Max continued, nose to the air, "said I should study with Liebman, that he would anoint me with his holy oils."

A skinny man, with a military cut and nervous arms and legs, giggled and said, "I hope he anoints me, but I only have enough G.I. Bill for one year, so I have to be anointed in a hurry. My name . . ." he said to one and all, "is Billy Spencer." Billy's smile was shy.

Boojie ignored Billy and confiscated Max's audience. "I've heard that Liebmann doesn't have any hair on his body, *anywhere*, and that he's *really* old, and that if he ever quit teaching, he would age like that woman in *Shangri-La*. Remember that movie with Ronald Colman and Jane Wyatt? The plane crashes and Ronald is standing in a Himalayan snowstorm wearing his fedora when Chang miraculously appears and leads the survivors to the fantastical Valley of the Blue Moon;but then Ronald lets his silly brother talk him into escaping with Maria, who claims she's thirty, but is really three hundred, and when she leaves the enchanted valley and stumbles into the freezing mountains, she turns into an ancient hag, and Ronnie's brother jumps off a cliff when he sees his true love turn into an old. . . ."

Max stomped a silver sling-back. "I will *not* listen to another of your movie synopses, Boojie! And who told you Liebmann has no hair? You make him sound like a Chihuahua!"

"My sources," said Boojie archly, "are impeccable." He turned back to Shelby. "Isn't she gorgeous? Don't we like her,

Hank? And have you met Bernard Crossroads," turning to the Negro. "And, yes, Crossroads *is* his last name, and won't *that* name look great in lights! Much better than Kowcowski, I'm afraid."

"*Korzeniowski*," Shelby corrected curtly.

"Okay. But imagine this billboard on The Great White Way: SHELBY HOWL AND BERNARD CROSSROADS STARRING IN *OTHELLO*!"

Shelby's face grew hot.

"And you'll never guess where Bernard is from. Tell her, Bernard."

Bernard shook his head no.

Boojie shrugged and dipped closer to Shelby. "You really are smashing. We like her, don't we, Hank?" A pleading quality entered Boojie's verbal cataract.

Shelby stepped to the side.

Hank said, "Let her alone, Booj."

The older man wearing the Army boots stood quietly, eyeing the scene through a smoke exhalation.

"Wait!" Boojie commanded, and pinioned her shoulders. "You need my magic hands! My daddy kicked me out of the house, but my talented fingers pay my bills. Hold still, hold still!" he cried. "This is doing you good, my love!" He dug his fingers into Shelby's back and grinned at the older man. "Wanna turn, Ben Vaughn? I take it you're here to observe. You were great in *Dinner's Ready*. You deserved the Tony for that performance."

Ben's lips smiled enigmatically, but the smile didn't reach his eyes.

Shelby took a step to the side, and Boojie blocked her move with a dancer's grace.

"Don't move, Shelby Howl, and listen to me! Hank and I want you to *live* with us, don't we, Hank? If we add one more person, we can rent this gorgeous, ever-so-slightly run-down apartment on Riverside Drive. Remember how our eyes connected when I flew over the turnstile? We were *fated* to live together on Riverside Drive!"

Shelby made an exasperated huff.

"Hank and I *need* you! You'll fix us fried chicken, and tell us sad, Southern stories. You will love living with us!" He sounded ebullient, but his fists were clenched as though the ante had become serious.

"I couldn't live with you," she sputtered. "I'm a *girl.*"

"You bet you're a girl! That's the beauty of it!" Boojie exclaimed, as though she finally understood. "You'll be our Wendy!"

She tried to turn, but Boojie grabbed her arm. "We need one more person to share the rent. And absolutely no hanky panky. That clause will be in the contract. We already have Max, who knows her cute little tantrums aren't allowed."

"Wait just a minute. . . ." Max protested, eyes aflame.

"No harm intended, Max, baby!" And Boojie turned to coax Max with snake charmer fingers. "Little Rock will take care of us, Maxine. She'll fix us biscuits and fried chicken. *And* think of *one-fifty-five a month split four ways!* When you do your long division you get thirty-eight dollars and seventy-five cents per person!" He turned back to Shelby. "Don't you love it? Don't you want to live with *me*?"

The plaintive note in his glib voice increased. "At night you can even see the Spry sign winking on the Jersey side. *And* you can see the Hudson River . . . if you stick your head out the window while I hold on to your feet!"

Shelby was frowning, shaking her head, *No, no, no.*

"I was joking about the view," Boojie added quickly. "You can see the river all the way to Poughkeepsie . . ." Boojie's accent was perfect when he crooned, "Shelby *Korzeniowski.* . . ."

She tried not to smile.

"And I've changed my mind about your name. You *must*

use it professionally, and we'll cook together and dance together on Riverside Drive, but, we'll never do *it* together.
Never. That will be a bylaw in the contract, won't it, Hank?
And Hank's daddy is a doctor in Minnesota, so we'll almost
have a doctor in the house."

Before she could protest, Boojie slipped his hand around
her waist and pushed her along in a dance, singing, "I'm just
a little girl, from Little Rock . . . *da, da, de da da da da da. . . .*"
As she swirled, the lion-tooth necklace floated in a grin behind
her body.

It was at that moment that Max placed her hand on her
diaphragm and let loose a long Ethel Merman note that was
loud enough to bring the house down and cause the closed
door to burst open. Max silenced the note with the harsh
sound of a phonograph needle scratching across a record.

A man rushed out the door so quickly, he skidded on the
polished floor. He had longish brown hair and a shaggy beard
composed of a palette of red colors, and he was followed by
an angry voice inside the room, shouting, "But that fucking
screech caused me to break my concentration!"

A deeper male voice, infused with condescension, said,
"*Use* the scream, or forget the theatre and sell vacuum
cleaners!" The same voice calling, "And Stanley, tell those
children out there kindergarten is over! If they want to go to
kindergarten, they can study with Stella. Or Sandy. Or God
forbid, Lee!"

The bearded man in the hall nodded his head with a "did
you hear that" expression on his face. "We've got the sec-
ond-year class in there! You want your balls chopped off?"
He pointed his finger at Shelby's forehead. "Screech like that
one more time, and you're *out!*"

His glare encompassed everyone in the hall until it came
to Ben, whereupon his eyes widened in awe. He gave Ben a
jerky wave and stepped back into the room, closing the door

with infinite care.

The hall was now silent.

Boojie and Shelby were still frozen in a dancing pose.

Ben was looking at Shelby with a bemused expression.

Then Boojie raised his hands and backed away from Shelby as though she radiated danger.

Max hissed, "You can't sing like that! Why did he think it was *you*?"

Shelby stared at her in disbelief, but Boojie turned to Max in a fury. "Then why didn't you say it was *you!*"

Shelby's lungs were in dire need of oxygen. "Yeah, why . . . why didn't you tell him *you* were the one who made that sound?"

"*Note!*" Max retorted. "It was a perfect A flat note!" She wheeled from Shelby, leaned toward a glowering Boojie, grabbed his head with both hands, and kissed him at length on the mouth.

Shelby was terrified by the bearded man's lecture, but she was furious at Max. She would never share an apartment with this snake-haired Medusa who forced men to French-kiss her in public, even if it meant sleeping at the YWCA, which she had heard was revolting. She hated this rotten school and all of its crazy people. She wanted to go back home. She was a fool to come to this loathsome city.

And yet . . . if she returned after just one day at the school, what would people say? Her mother might be able to bear it, but Baldwin couldn't, no matter how happy she would be to see her granddaughter. Shelby would be an embarrassment to her family if she went back home. She had to stay and suffer, at least for a while. A month maybe.

Max stepped back, and Boojie wiped his lips with the back of a trembling hand and attempted a cynical smile. "You got to practice more, Maxie."

Shelby took a deep breath, brushed feebly at her once-beautiful dress, scooped up her belongings, touched the star sapphire with the tip of a finger, and clutched Saracen's lethal necklace to her bosom.

Jan the ballerina seized her own hands as though strangling an invisible throat.

Roberto cracked his knuckles until, without looking, Paul reached over and gave the knuckles a sharp slap.

Ben Vaughn extinguished his cigarette with the broad toe of his boot.

And then they all waited.

A young man with a rose tattoo on his arm stalked from the classroom, but his eyes torched the waiting students as he passed. A blade-thin girl in pigtails trotted beside him and spat words at Shelby. "Jake was in the middle of a really heavy improv and you . . ." she had to call over her shoulder to keep up with Jake, "*destroyed it!*"

Shelby cringed. With the exception of Ben, the group turned as one to glower at Max before they filed into the room like a herd of frightened goats climbing over very steep rocks.

20

VICTOR LIEBMANN sat at a makeshift desk made from a plywood door that rested on sawhorses. It was situated to the side of a three-level platform where the students sat at secondhand high school desks covered with initials beavered into the wood. The desks faced a makeshift stage furnished with two single beds and a banged-up chest of drawers. The layers of gouged paint on the chest resembled an archeological dig.

Hank was seated at one of the desks writing in a notebook. He would glance at Victor Liebmann and return to the notebook like a sketch artist.

Shelby cowered in the back row, trying not to gape at Liebmann for visible hairs, none of which she could see, even at the neckline. His high forehead and cheekbones echoed the patrician dome of his bald head, and the flowing sleeves of his bloused shirt were reminiscent of the Romantic poets. His cigarette, ensconced in a carved ivory holder, dangled from the corner of his mouth, and he watched the smoke rise with half-closed eyes, inhaling deeply, and blowing smoke rings, one inside the other.

When his performance was over, he looked at his attentive audience with eyes so clear of color they were nearly invisible. It seemed possible that his head, magically severed, might float like the Cheshire Cat's and stare at each person in the room before it returned to rest obediently on his neck.

Ben was the only one in the audience who appeared at

ease, and his doleful eyes looked as though they were about to observe something that probably would be a waste of his time. He raised one boot occasionally and dropped it softly to the floor. The boot would rise, pause, and drop again. Shelby watched it from her higher perch.

"So. You are here." A smile of *crisis sardonicus* flickered across Liebmann's mouth.

Hank scribbled faster.

"And you want to learn to act. Or you think you do." He paused for a beat, the tight smile lingering. "Chekhov famously said if you want to be an actor, you must have iron in your blood." He tipped the ash from his cigarette into a tin can that, with his offering, seemed to glow like crystal. "We shall see what your blood count is. Whether you have what it takes to endure the long journey before you."

Mental muscles flexed around the room.

"Acting is a spooky art." Liebmann savored the timbre that flowed around each of his perfectly chosen words. "We play with the soul when we act on stage, and . . . if we are lucky . . . we bring forth demons from the deep and angels from on high." He swirled a hand around his head. "But when the performance is over . . ." He opened his palms, and hunched his shoulders like an old man, "we are alone again.

"However . . . in those moments when the actor is truly transformed, the audience is also transformed. They collude—actors on stage and the audience before them—to imbibe this communal wine, because the audience yearns, not just to be entertained, but to be transformed. People yearn for the elucidation of feelings that make us human." Liebmann's pale eyes continued to journey from face to face. "A great performance can astonish our hearts. It can burn like sulfur into our souls. It can create a single entity of the actors on stage and the strangers who sit in the dark, hoping for magic."

Shelby leaned forward, breathing quietly. She was already prepared to enter a cave where the mysteries of a cult would be revealed, and where she wouldn't be permitted to escape, and wouldn't want to escape. She already knew that she loved this man . . . and feared him, equally.

He raised his arms like a high priest and let them drop, full sleeves flowing to the desktop, knowing his subjects were under his sway.

"Of course, the magic I'm talking about comes from the power of the imagination. It's about instinct. About how to capture inspiration and use it on stage, night after night, after every night."

For some reason, Shelby was reminded of the traps she and Saracen had created as children: empty cigar boxes baited with peanut butter and propped up with a stick, ready to ensnare a greedy squirrel. Thereafter, the capturing instinct became fixed in her mind with small, elusive animals.

Liebmann took a long moment to inhale more cigarette smoke and exhale it slowly. Mere oxygen was not enough for his lungs. There had to be smoke. There had to be fire.

"Of course, the key to your talent lies deep within your own being. The question is: Can you permit yourselves to connect with those very secret, very primitive places? Can you learn how to ensnare your own feelings in order to comprehend your stage character's and bring them to life? Can you learn to laugh and cry *on demand* in order to create what Stanislavski called 'the illusion of the first time'?"

As he spoke, Shelby was thinking, *I can do that. Yes. I can do that. I will do that for the great one who sits behind his scruffy throne.* Only Ben seemed immune to Liebmann's spell, and even a bit amused. And yet he stayed, one booted foot swaying back and forth on top the other.

"Observation. Betrayal. That's the core of serious acting. Betrayal of the habits of anyone who resides in your memory.

You will file away the grating sound of your beloved friend's voice. You will note a stranger's peculiar laugh. You will steal your grandmother's squint, you will remember the agony of a grieving parent. And if you store this detritus of everyday life *in your brain and reveal it on stage at the right moment . . .* you will become a good actor. *If* you have the guts."

Shelby folded her hands together and said, though not out loud, *I have the guts. I can do this for you.*

"And if you're a serious actor, you will betray your own self in every role you play. You will reveal secrets about yourself you didn't know existed. You will dance with your own demons in your effort to become somebody else on stage. You will be the puppeteer, while you, yourself, are the puppet." Leibmann jiggled his fingers as though manipulating puppet strings. "And I will know when you're forcing an emotion, because your acting will be *empty. Your eyes will be empty.*" He tossed his glasses onto the desk in a soft landing.

A woman, who had just entered the room laughed nervously. The sound startled the air, and Liebmann almost recoiled, as though recognizing the woman by the laugh. She looked to be in her thirties, but there were no highlights in her dyed red hair, and too much make-up on a face that seemed too young to look so old.

"So," he said briskly. "Too many words. Let's get to work."

There followed a quick rustling of changed positions and deep inhalations.

"We'll start with a couple of improvisations today. Tomorrow we'll begin the basics." He raised his chin like a scepter toward Max. "*You.* On the front row." He lowered the scepter. "Come here."

Max stood up, sucked in her stomach and walked toward Liebmann, high heels tapping like a pony's hooves. When she reached his desk, she posed, weight on one hip. She didn't need a spotlight. The only danger was of spontaneous combustion.

Liebmann looked at her with amused irony, as though foretelling her future. "What's your name?"

"Maxine. My friends call me Max."

"Are you listening to me, Maxine?"

Max nodded, ignoring the slight. After all, she was the first chosen. Her shining brown eyes, her wild black hair, her silver-tipped fingers were raring to go. She fluttered her hands, bracelets jangling.

"*Really* listening? Listening is as important as betrayal in this profession."

She nodded harder with her most adorable smile.

"Well, *listen* to this: Your boyfriend is in the living room talking on the phone. He thinks you're taking a shower after the two of you have made love. You got all that?"

Maxine rolled her eyes at such a brazen concept, raised one shoulder a bit coyly, and said, "Yes . . . Victor."

Shelby groaned inwardly. She could never call this man by his first name. "Exalted One" maybe, "Your Highness," "Master" maybe, but never "Victor." She detested this Maxine person. She was like the mean girls in high school who whispered behind her back, knew about sex, wore tight sweaters, cheated on tests, and never got caught.

"You turn on the water, but you aren't really showering, because . . ." Liebmann continued, "you suspect your boyfriend has another girlfriend, and he may be talking to her on the phone. So you pick up the extension in the bedroom. And you listen."

"I just . . . listen?"

"You just listen."

"Okay," she said. "You're the boss!"

"You're right." Liebmann eyed her without expression. "I am."

Maxine's smile wavered only slightly before she removed

her silver shoes and leaned against the bed to display her great legs to their best advantage. She captured her naughty bracelets with one hand, gave Leibmann an apologetic grimace, raised her eyebrows dramatically, picked up the phone . . . and pretended to listen.

Stanley quietly left the room.

"Enough." Liebmann's voice was brusque.

"Oh, but I've just begun. I can do lots more expressions. And I've done lots of summer stock. I worked with *Bud*. . . ." She paused to allow the full force of Brando's nickname to register with Liebmann's impassive face. "I've done lots of television, I. . . ."

He cut her off mid-sentence. "Sit back on the bed."

She blinked rapidly, but sat, tugging her skirt a little nervously.

"And let us say, Maxine," and Liebmann was patience personified, "that you have . . . and without those bracelets, which you will never wear to this class again . . . let us say you haven't picked up the phone yet. So pick up the phone. And this time *listen*."

Maxine turned her crumpled chin from Liebmann, removed the bracelets with a flourish, clunked them on the bedside table, one at a time, and settled herself on the bed. When she put the phone to her ear, her leg stopped its motion, and she slammed down the receiver.

"Who is that *creep*?" she demanded of Liebmann.

"That creep," he said calmly, "was your boyfriend, Maxine. He was talking about you to another woman, because he thought you were in the shower. And you *listened* to what he was saying. *You really listened.* You reacted because of what your acting partner was saying on the phone, not because of how you thought you should react to impress me. You can return to your seat now."

Max's eyes were very bright. She stood up, sucked in her

stomach again, and returned to her seat, chin high, heels clacking too rapidly.

When Stanley returned, Liebmann was still speaking with the measured authority of the master. "To become a good actor, you must learn to listen." He leaned toward the class. "Are you listening to me now?" He banged his fist hard on the desk, and the class jumped, except for Ben and Stanley, who sat, unruffled, as though they had witnessed this act before.

"Yes," Leibmann nodded. "You were listening, and you re-acted appropriately. Remember that. So. We'll have one more exercise today. And we'll use Bernard." Liebmann pointed to Bernard Crossroads.

Bernard rose slowly, medium height, built like a wrestler, clumping from the second level, eyes on his worn, polished oxfords. He was blowing a silent stream of air through his lips like a safety vent for a furnace stoked too hot.

Then Liebmann pointed to Shelby. "You. The blonde singer in the back row. Come down here."

Shelby couldn't breathe, yet forced herself to breathe, and to stand, because she had to. She always did what she had to do. She cleared her throat. "I don't sing." Her voice was barely audible.

"Ah don' sing." Liebmann mocked her accent.

There was a pause before Shelby almost whispered, "No, sir."

"No, *suh*," Liebmann mocked again. "And I bet you say 'Yes, *suh*' and 'Yes, *ma'am*' as well."

Shelby could feel the blush rising. Maybe he was less per-fect than she thought. "Yes, sir, I do. To my elders."

There was an intake of breath among the students. Liebmann's low chortle at her comment was without hu-mor. "Ah, but we heard you sing . . . or whatever you call that sound you made in the hall, and, in so doing, you

164

destroyed a very good scene."

"I can't sing," Shelby repeated, trying not to choke on her own words.

Maxine studied a wall.

"Well," said Liebmann, sensing a mystery that wouldn't be solved instantly, "come down anyhow."

Shelby descended the platform in her stockinged feet, her platinum hair shining down the back of her dirt-streaked, chic white dress. But her descent was okay. She had learned, as Miss Little Rock, how to descend.

Liebmann eyed her for a moment. "When you go to Hollywood," he said, "they'll tell you to curl your hair. Don't. Tell them Greta Garbo wouldn't curl hers, so why should you?"

"I don't want to go to Hollywood." Her left thumb was glued to the star sapphire. "I want to act on the stage in New York City."

Liebmann made an unbelieving sound. "You young people all want to go to Hollywood. What's your name?"

"Shelby." She tried to keep her voice steady. "Shelby Howell. . . ." Her eyes wavered toward the floor and her voice lowered when she added, "Korzeniowski."

Liebmann repeated, "Korzeniowski," as softly as she said the name, and with an accent as good as hers. "I don't remember that name on the list of new students. Howell, I remember, but Korzeniowski . . ." and this time he spun out the name with the ease of a fisherman swirling a silvery line into the morning air, " . . . I don't remember. But keep it. Your public will remember it belongs to the tall blonde with green eyes. The name is Polish." It wasn't a question.

Shelby nodded weakly.

"Stanislavski is a Polish name. Did you know that?"

"No," she replied. She needed to sit down.

"Do you know who Stanislavski was?"

She was afraid to lie. "No."

There was a buzz among other students eager to present their superior knowledge. Liebmann ignored them.

"Good. That means you probably haven't had acting lessons, and as a result, may have fewer bad acting habits. Actually, Stanislavski's real name was Constantin Sergeyevich Alexeiev." Liebmann spoke as though he were also acquainted with the complicated music of the Russian language. "His father was a well-to-do Muscovite who owned a factory that made gold thread. A rather romantic enterprise, I've always thought, spinning gold . . . though I am reminded of Rumpelstiltskin and his fate.

"However, Stanislavski actually did spin gold thread in his father's factory, but he loved the theatre more and joined a vaudeville company, using a Polish stage name to protect his family. In those days, as it will be forever more, the Russians thought themselves superior to the Poles. But the name change was just a bit of subterfuge on Stanislavski's part. Actors change their names for various reasons."

Shelby caught her breath. Could this man intuit that she had changed her own name . . . no, *retrieved* her name . . . about ten minutes ago?

"And where are you from, Shelby Howell Korzeniowski, with that southern accent and that rather ominous garnish you're clutching to your neck? Not Poland, I presume."

Shelby dropped her hand from the lions' teeth as though they were poisonous. "Little Rock, Arkansas," she said and waited for a response she knew would be sarcastic.

"Ah . . . well . . . of course." Liebmann turned to the class and extended a carnival barker's arm. "We have Miss Little Rock with us, dear students! A Polish Miss Little Rock!"

There was an amused stir among his new disciples.

Shelby straightened her back. "I won enough money as Miss Little Rock to come to your school," she said, chin tilted upward and with more than a little dignity.

Liebmann lifted his eyebrows, and gave a "touché" nod with his chin.

"And I'm not Polish. I'm American. I was born in Little Rock. My father . . . is . . . Polish."

"Are you related to that great Polish writer, Joseph Conrad, whose birth name was Korzeniowski? Josef Teodor Konrad Korzeniowski?"

"The man who wrote *Lord Jim*?" she blurted. "His last name was really Korzeniowski?"

"Ahhhh. You're learning something in the big city."

She found it ever harder to concentrate. Her father's first name was Teodore. Teddy.

"And why did you leave Little Rock, Miss Korzeniowski, and journey all the way to Gomorrah?"

"I . . . I read that you were a good acting teacher." She didn't add that she had read about him in a movie magazine. He might think that was beneath his dignity.

Liebmann cocked his head and changed the subject. "Do you know Bernie?"

The young Negro interrupted him. "My name is Bernard. You know my name."

"Yes. Bernard *is* your name. Do you know *Bernard*, Miss Korzeniowski?"

Shelby searched the floor with her eyes. "We met in the hall."

"And do you know where he's from?"

"No, sir."

There was an amused stir as though everyone else in the room knew, coupled with the fact that Shelby had once again called Liebmann "sir." She corrected herself quickly, like a witness on the stand, blood gushing to her face again. "I mean 'No.' I do not."

"Tell Shelby Korzeniowski where you're from, Bernard

Crossroads." And Liebmann lounged back in his chair to observe her reaction.

Bernard's voice was as soft and as Southern as Shelby's, but the vowels were longer and tinged with a soft slur. "I come from Pine Bluff. Pine Bluff, Arkansas."

Shelby couldn't look at Bernard or Liebmann or her classmates.

"And how far is Pine Bluff from Little Rock?" Liebmann asked.

"About fifty mile," omitting the final "s" in the way of country folk in the South.

"You take the bus in Pine Bluff and catch the train in Little Rock?"

Bernard smoothed the sides of his jeans with his large, calloused hands, and nodded "Yes."

"Imagine. Riding all those miles, perhaps on the same train, unaware that you and Miss Korzeniowski would wind up at The Acting School. Why, you could have sat together!" Liebmann's eyes twinkled sardonically. "You could have had a meal together!"

Bernard's response was sullen. "You know I been up here a while."

"Well," Liebmann's voice became brisk, "let's get down to business. I'm going to teach you to become a thief, Bernard. Good actors must be good thieves, and I'm a regular Fagin when it comes to teaching thievery. So let's think of a plot that will hit home for both of you . . . and what I think is," his twinkle reviving, " . . . *this.*

"You, Shelby Korzeniowski, will lie on that bed and go to sleep. But I don't want you to just lie there. I want you to *dream*. Something always should be happening to you on stage, even when the script says you're sound asleep. We'll talk more about that in sessions to come. But tell me . . . what you will dream about today, Shelby Korzeniowski?" The question was smug and slightly suggestive.

Shelby felt spooked each time he repeated her last name. "Do I have to tell you?"

"Noooo," he said, with an approving nod, "you do not," and he turned toward Bernard.

"You, my friend, have a difficult objective in your thieving apprenticeship." Liebmann seemed ever more pleased with the improvisation he was creating in his mind. "And probably a dangerous one, because, my dear fellow . . . "Liebmann spoke each word separately and emphasized Shelby's name with a flourish, "because you have been secretly dating Shelby *Korzeniowsssski!*"

Liebmann beamed at his, genius, and at the startled reactions of both Bernard and Shelby. "You've even been hopping into bed with the beauteous Miss Little Rock!"

The two young people looked as though they had bumped into one another accidentally and run in opposite directions.

Liebmann ignored their reactions. "You, Bernard, began sneaking into her bedroom after you became the driver of her car for the beauty contest parade. And it's a big house, isn't it, Shelby Korzeniowski, with lots of bedrooms?"

Shelby closed her eyes and ignored him, already pretending sleep.

"And people down there probably don't lock up at night, which made it easy for your *lover* to get in the house. What's *more* . . ." Leibmann was obviously enjoying his creation, his imagination rampant "Bernard, you have written passionate love letters to your southern belle . . . *all of which she has kept and begs for more!*" Liebmann chuckled at his own cleverness. "But . . ." he held up a dramatic finger, "you finally realize you were stupid to become involved with this white girl, and more stupid to leave a paper trail. In fact . . ." and Liebmann grinned at his cunning, excited by his imagination, "you've become *afraid* of this white girl, because . . . and get this . . . she wants to *marry* you!"

Shelby's lips constricted so tightly they looked glued together.

Bernard lowered his head and studied his shoes.

"She says she looooves you . . ." Liebmann teased. "You were ready for a fling with a good-looking white woman, but this one could get you hung by your neck! And your Polish daddy would organize the lynching, wouldn't he, Miss Korzeniowski?"

Shelby's eyes closed and her posture became rigid.

"Ah, yes. This should work. I see it's close to the bone. So here's the scenario: it's a hot summer night in Little Rock. You, Bernard, go into the hall, close the door behind you, wait a couple of minutes, and sneak into Shelby's bedroom to steal those letters. And I don't want either of you to say a word during the improv. Not one word. So . . . go to it."

He sat back, beaming, and folded his hands expectantly.

Bernard's mouth worked nervously. "Is this how it's gonna be? This acting stuff?"

"Depends on how good you want to be, Bernard. And you know I think you can be very good."

Bernard looked up at the ceiling, sighed, and removed his old oxfords. Shelby walked toward the bed as though it were the guillotine.

"And quit fiddling with that ring on your finger, Korzeniowski. Bernard is liable to steal that too."

Shelby lay on the bed as though it were the rack, pulled up the bedspread, and tucked it tight around her legs.

"Oh, it's too hot for covers," Leibmann said softly.

Shelby lay very still, then flung the bedspread to the floor, stood up with her back to the audience, reached beneath her full Marilyn Monroe skirt, removed stockings and garter belt with discreet jockeying, and slipped them to the floor. There was something old-fashioned and modest and, at the same time, seductive about the way she took off her stockings in front of but with her back to everyone, leaving a pile of white satin gleaming on the dark wood floor. She walked back to the bed, lay down, and aimed the blue star in the ring at Liebmann. *She would not be intimidated by voices far or near.*

The moment Bernard closed the noisy door, Liebmann motioned to Stanley, who fiddled with a screw in the door and returned to his seat. When Bernard re-entered, the door made no sound. After a moment's confused hesitation, he dropped to his knees and crawled on all fours, his eyes fixed on the bed and the silent sleeper, who flopped an arm over the side of the mattress.

Bernard froze.

The sound of a car coming to a screeching halt outside the building broke the silence, but the eyes in the acting class stayed fixed on the two figures in front of them.

When Shelby turned over, limbs sprawling, Bernard flattened his body and moved from her line of vision. She settled down, and he moved again, but his belt buckle scratched the floor. She moved once more, and he froze in place until she was still, then resumed his crab-like crawl to the side of the table where he pulled on the drawer's knob, his eyes fixed on sleeping Shelby. When the drawer wouldn't budge, he pulled harder . . . and harder . . . until the drawer flew out of the table, showering rubber bands and papers and pencils and loose cigarettes over the floor.

Shelby sat up, wide awake.

"Stop it there!" Liebmann called.

Bernard stood with downcast eyes, frowning at the waxy dirt on the front of his shirt and jeans. Shelby pulled the spread up to her neck.

"Stop it right there," Liebmann repeated, even though the two had stopped. Bernard gave his clothes a quick swipe.

"That was good," Liebmann said.

Shelby exhaled slowly, surprised she had been holding her breath, and surprised at the pleasure his comment gave her.

But why was it good? She hadn't acted, only dreamed of lying on the floor of her bedroom on a hot summer's night, not daring to dream of anything specific, certainly not how Charlie's long fingers had felt in the warm lake water. When she summoned the courage to take a quick look at Liebmann, she saw cruelty in the pale crystal eyes. But there was also approval.

"That was good," he said again. "You didn't anticipate."

Shelby had no idea what he meant.

"And . . ." he spoke with sudden lethargy . . . "that's enough for this session. We had a little fun today. We'll begin basics tomorrow." He rose from his chair somewhat unsteadily and walked toward the door, with Stanley trailing after him.

The older woman with too much makeup left almost as quickly. Ben Vaughn walked behind her. When he touched her arm, she jerked it away and walked faster.

"Was that Monique Masters who just walked out? She was in . . . what was it . . . *The Sun Goes Down*, a long time ago? She got great reviews and then disappeared." Boojie's eyes glistened with the mystery of Monique.

"She didn't disappear." Paul was nearly treading on Boojie's and Hank's heels. "She was in small parts for a while. But she looks too old to be Monique Masters."

Jan the ballerina passed the group. "It's Monique, all right," Jan said. "She's Lisa's mother in *As the World Turns*, the one whose husband jumped off a cliff because Monique accidentally got pregnant with his identical twin. Not a great part." Jan continued down the hall with a dancer's slew-footed strides, hips always poised to plié.

"Cheez," sighed Boojie. "Poor Monique. You're on top and you wind up with a dinky part on a soap. I heard she and Ben Vaughn had a fling years ago, but she freaked out when he dumped her, and she went to Europe and performed in Westerns."

"Who cares about Monique? What about Liebmann? That man's amazing!" Paul whirled to make certain Liebmann wasn't near, then whispered, "Is it really true he doesn't have any hair? Anywhere?"

"Why don't you ask him?" Boojie responded too innocently.

Shelby hurried up the stairs in her bare feet, shoes and hat dangling from one hand. She crammed torn stockings and garter belt into her purse without looking, Liebmann's words still ringing in her ears. *That was good. That was very good.*

She thought of Boojie sailing over the turnstile, she thought of stripping off her hose in front of the world, and she narrowed her eyes when she thought of her Negro acting partner. Saracen had to know that guy would be in her class and hadn't told her. Her happiness fizzled further when Maxine grabbed her arm at the top of the stairs. Her grip was tight, but her voice was subdued.

"You were nice to keep your mouth shut about the singing. I was a shithead not to speak up."

Shelby blinked at the foul language from a girl, and gave an impatient shrug to rid herself of the long fingernails biting her skin.

"I have this bad habit of doing stupid things," Max said. "And I was a little scared today."

"Everyone was scared." Shelby made no effort to be pleasant.

"So?" Her eyes bore into Shelby's. "Can we give Boojie's apartment a try? I promise to be so good. And I really need this place." Max crossed her heart and held both hands high, fingers spread wide, *See, Ma. No tricks.* She backed down the hall past Mrs. D'Arcy, opened the door with one hand behind her and left the building going backward, one hand still raised to Shelby.

Shelby's heart was pounding. She took a deep breath and looked down the hall where she saw Liebmann talking earnestly to Bernard Crossroads. Bernard was backed against a wall, his head turned toward Shelby. His sad eyes connected with hers, but he didn't move a muscle. Liebmann continued to hammer his point, whatever the point was.

21

SHELBY SCURRIED for shade in her bare feet, eyes to the sidewalk. When she looked up, she thought she saw Ben Vaughn shimmering in the sunlight, astride a shiny red motorcycle, and dangling a leather helmet from a saturnine finger.

"Got a problem?" Ben Vaughn called over the engine's roar.

"No problem," she called back too gaily.

"Looks like you have a problem." He nodded toward the back of his bike. "Climb on. I'll take you home." He put on the helmet and the goggles and revved up the engine.

Shelby was briefly immobilized by the memory of another man with sun-bleached hair who wore goggles and a helmet.

"Get on the bike!" he called again. "You try to walk four blocks on the sizzling sidewalk with no shoes, and you'll step on a nail, contract tetanus, and die on the subway. I assure you I know how to fly this thing."

Fly this thing.

Shelby peered down the interminable crosstown blocks. It was a long way to the subway, and this engine sounded steady, no coughs, no whines. She lifted her feet in long-legged hops over the hot concrete, and the great Ben Vaughn instructed her how to tuck her new purse and her battered new shoes in the side pockets, and how to put on the goggles he handed her. "They keep the dirt out," he explained.

"I think . . . I think I can put them on." And she could.

She sat on the seat, gathered her skirt beneath her butt,

positioned her feet on the footrests, and backed as far from Vaughn as possible.

"It won't work that way," he called again. "You have to put your arms around my waist and hold tight, or you'll fall off in the middle of New York City traffic. I have never heard of a passenger assaulted on a moving motorcycle, and I'll take you straight to your door. Wherever it is. Whichever country."

She clasped her hands around his waist, which was complicated, because she also had to hang on to her hat that covered the front of his trousers like a large green codpiece.

"Greenwich Village," she shouted over the noise.

"Greenwich Village it is," he shouted back, and revved up the machine again. The sound and the motion thrummed through her body like a one-engine plane. "As we get to know one another on this epic journey, perhaps you'll tell me exactly *where* in Greenwich Village. And do you want a helmet? I have an extra. The ride will mess up your hair to a fare-thee-well."

But a helmet would create another connection to the past that she didn't want. Before she finished shouting "No," the motorcycle shot down the street.

Maxine was watching with narrowed eyes.

Ben made a fast left turn, shouting, "Hold on!" and Shelby's head whirled with the memory of hurtling toward the earth and her father yelling, "Hold on, Shelby! Hold on!" And she had held on that day, as she was on this day on Fifth Avenue in New York City, with yellow cabs bellowing, and the Empire State Building wavering in the sun in the distance. When they stopped for a red light, she leaned back to see the top of the building, but couldn't.

"Thrilling, huh?" Ben called over his shoulder. "Max gives tours of the Empire State."

Shelby's groan was consumed by the noise of the motorcycle. Why would Ben Vaughn know what that woman did outside of class?

When they sped off again, her hair stung her face and blew into her mouth, and she wasn't certain she was calling the right directions until she heard women's voices screaming at the sight of a blond female flattened to the back of a man on a speeding motorcycle. Shelby shrieked directions until Ben came to a sliding cowboy halt at the curb, switched off the engine, removed his helmet and goggles, ran his hands through his golden hair, and said, with an ironic grin, "Time flies when you're having fun."

Shelby grunted, crawled off the motorcycle, pulled her hat on and way down her ears to hide the tangles, and dragged her belongings from the saddlebags.

Ben was rubbing his fingers on the back of his shirt. "I think I've been tattooed with your necklace. That thing is lethal."

She slapped the necklace to her own chest and winced when the teeth sank into her skin. "Oh, my stars . . . I'm so sorry!"

"Oh, my stars," Ben repeated, mocking the phrase. "I bet you wore it for luck."

Shelby blushed and walked backward up the sidewalk, smiling at him.

"And it worked," he grinned. "Liebmann doesn't praise often. He'll keep his eye on you . . . as will I." He stared at her with those impenetrable, obsidian eyes.

"But all I did was pretend to sleep." Her voice was warm with pleasure. "And thanks for the ride. You probably saved me from a terrible death."

"Yep," he said. "My name's Ben Vaughn, a thirsty Samaritan." His expression said the next move was up to her.

Shelby stepped back more slowly. But she couldn't let him inside the apartment with those obscene photographs on the living room walls. She mustn't do that.

"Once you get used to riding on a Harley, you'll find it's the best way to travel in the city."

When he spoke, she was also thinking that his resonant voice could project for blocks, a voice perfect for the stage.

"My bike and I are at your service."

Shelby paused. A motorcycle would provide the perfect transportation to look for her father. She was sincere when she replied, "Why, thank you. I'll remember that."

Ben gunned the motor, then let it idle again. "Max isn't so bad. You two could survive together. You might even learn something from one another." The white teeth and dimples that emerged in that brooding face were dazzling. Perhaps she should invite him in after all.

"Wait . . ." she said, though he hadn't moved. "I wanted to ask . . . who . . . who are those women who were yelling from that building we just passed?"

He shrugged as though the women were inconsequential. "That's the Women's Detention Center. It's a holding jail. The detainees yell because they're frustrated, but it's like a lot of noise in the city. After a while, you won't hear it. They get plenty to eat. Forget about those women."

That comment made him seem less intriguing. Shelby would always hear the women's voices. They brought to mind her mother when she was in the State Hospital . . . though her mother probably hadn't yelled, even when she should have. Her mother probably succumbed to circumstances.

"And don't let Victor suck you in either," Ben continued. "He's a brilliant teacher, but he can be cruel. You have to stay tough if you want to succeed in that school. Or in the theatre." He leaned across the motorcycle handles and showed those dimples again. "If you have another question, you could ask it inside your place. I recite pretty good if I'm given a drink."

"I . . . I don't think so." Shelby felt as reluctant as she

sounded. This man had nearly won a *Tony,* for heaven's sake! And he wanted a drink? *Of alcohol?* It sounded so cosmopolitan! Anyhow, all she had to offer was lemonade and one Coke. And she couldn't let him inside that apartment that reeked of sex. She *mustn't* let him inside. "I'm sorry my necklace bit you."

When a deep voice rumbled behind her, she was so entranced with the man in front of her, she jumped at the sound.

"He should be careful though," the voice behind her continued, "If he gets any closer to those lions' teeth, they'll bite him."

Shelby swung around, her purse flailing from her arm, and stood face to face with Saracen Self, who was lounging on the steps of her building as though he owned the place. "And once the teeth sink into his skin, he'll foam at the mouth."

She grabbed at the necklace so hard it stabbed her palm.

"It's still there," Saracen reassured her. "For a moment I thought you were gonna give that treasure to your friend on the Harley with the hot camshafts and the rear suspension. You been riding in style, Miss Shelby."

Ben switched off the engine, swung his leg around the seat, leaned against the motorcycle, and stared at Saracen. The gingko leaves fluttered along the street, and the Village murmured contentedly. Except for the prickly aura that wavered between the two men, the Village kingdom seemed peaceable.

Saracen's image had been floating in Shelby's mind so frequently, she was accustomed to his invisible presence, but it was startling to see the solid flesh of the man in front of her.

"How . . . how did you get here?" She was almost tongue-tied. "What are you *doing* here?"

Saracen tucked his newspaper under his arm and shot his shirt cuffs with exaggerated flair. "Is that how you greet an old friend? You said the same thing when we were hiding in that compartment together on the train." He smiled briefly at Ben, and looked back at Shelby. "'*How did you get here*,' you demanded, after I risked my neck to board that train so I could see you. How about, 'It's so nice of you to visit me so far from home, and I'd like you to meet my friend on the Harley-Davidson who was nearly maimed by the juju necklace you gave me.' Didn't your grandma teach you no manners?"

Saracen's tailored suit was a shade lighter than his skin, and his green silk tie with brown dots was perfectly knotted, and his brown oxfords had a high sheen. It was hard not to stare at this handsome man bedecked in such flattering finery.

"*This* . . ." Shelby stammered, staring at Saracen, "this is Ben Vaughn. Ben, this is Saracen Self. He's from Little Rock. Or was."

Saracen admonished her with a smile. "Once from Little Rock, always from Little Rock, my dear." He rose to his full height, towering over Vaughn on the motorcycle, but speaking to Shelby as he studied the man. "Innocent passers-by might be a little embarrassed to see your stockings and whatever else you got laid out on the sidewalk in your purse that probably also holds all of your money. A New York City thief grabs your purse, and you've had it. And you're barefoot to boot, Miss Shelby. Shame on you!"

She snatched up her belongings as Ben swung his leg around the motorcycle seat and gunned the engine. "I'll leave you to your reunion, Miss Shelby Korzeniowski, but I *will* see you again." He turned an expressionless face toward Saracen, added, "In class and out," and he took off in a rumble, leaving behind a trail of fumes.

22

Saracen's eyes followed the motorcycle. "I don't like him."

Shelby made an exasperated sound. "You don't know him, and neither do I."

"He's too slick for you." Still tracking the cycle. "And too old."

She poked at the lions' teeth, but jerked her hand away when she realized Saracen was watching. "So why *are* you here . . . other than to embarrass me?"

"Ben Vaughn," he mused. "Big actor on Broadway. I've read about him, seen posters for his play. Took you about ten minutes after you landed here to hook up with some fancy star."

Shelby stomped a bare foot on the sidewalk, which hurt. "This is *not* your business, Saracen Self! And Ben Vaughn is *not* my boyfriend."

"He will be."

"I can't believe this! You followed me on the train, and now you're spying on me in New York City so you can tattle to Momma and Baldwin that I was carrying on with a strange man in the middle of the sidewalk, and looking like a tornado hit me!"

"You do look a little frazzled. And you pulled your brand new hat out of shape, and that's a shame. It was a nice hat."

Shelby jerked off the hat to reveal a platinum snarl.

"*And* you're *barefoot* on a sidewalk in New York City!"

Saracen was so calm. And much too tall.

"Feet dirty, new dress dirty, garter belt waving at me from

your purse. You're a *mess,* Shelby Howell!"

Shelby slammed the garter belt deep inside her purse.

"Other than that . . ." Saracen shrugged, "you're looking fine. But you think I'm up here because of *you?* I have to earn a living, *Miss* Shelby. I'm flying to Egypt in a few hours to report on what's happening in that foreign land. Want to come with me?"

Shelby looked at Saracen as though he had asked her to jump in a river filled with crocodiles.

"Naw," he said mournfully. "She don't want to come. I'll have to go by my lonesome to that heathen place and learn what I can about ole Nasser, who's fussed because the U.S. and Britain bugged out on the money they promised to build his dam. But he damned them when he took over the Canal in one fell swoop! I'm sure you know all that news, just like you're keeping up with all that integration *stuff* in *our* home town."

Shelby barely listened to what Saracen said about the Suez Canal, but she was sure he said "*our* home town" to needle her.

"So you planning to ask me inside? I think we can get away with a black guy walking into a white lady's apartment up here in Sin City as long as I come out in about three minutes. But I'm proud you wouldn't let that Ben dude inside. You won't let him in until I'm gone, and then you'll tell yourself you're only seeing him so he'll ride you around on his motorcycle to help you find your daddy."

Shelby looked away, annoyed that he knew her so well he'd already guessed she had the motorcycle in mind to search for her father.

"But you better watch out for that great actor. There's something bothersome about him." Saracen barked a rueful laugh as though he knew his opinion would make no difference, picked up his briefcase and newspaper, brushing at his trousers a bit. "You and me going inside?"

Shelby studied the concrete steps. "This apartment is mine for just a few more days. It belongs to a woman named Justine, a photographer friend of Julien Hutchins. The pictures on the living room walls are . . . extreme. Bizarre even."

"I think I can handle bizarre, Miss Shelby. I've seen bizarre in my day."

She hesitated again at the door. "I guess you could call her an artist. And you know how artists are."

Saracen lifted an eyebrow. "We going inside, or we staying in this hot hall talking about crazy artists?"

She unlocked the door, and turned on the light. The pink neon sprang from the dark like a djinn, and the red roses Charlie had sent looked black in the light, but the nude photographs loomed large and eerily real.

Shelby had first thought they were sand dunes, before she realized they were of a woman's naked body and a man's naked body, with the bodies sometimes . . . together.

She escaped to the tiny kitchen, opening windows with the vague hope of cooler air, while Saracen moved silently from photograph to photograph. When he spoke, his voice carried easily to the kitchen.

"So your neighbor, Julien, is good friends with this woman. And we can just imagine what kind of good friends they are. Ole *Jul-ee-in* is the jerk who tripped me when I was a kid, and laughed when I fell. I hated that guy. He *lurked*. I'd wager a pretty penny Lettie's never with him when he visits this place."

The rattle of glasses carried from the kitchen, and after a moment, a jazz combo sounded from the living room. Saracen spoke as though he and Shelby were having a friendly conversation between the rooms. "Justine has a great record collection, but she has a heavy hand. Lots of scratches, which is a damn shame."

"I've Got You Under My Skin" began to play, and Saracen

called, "Come on in here, Shelby Howell."

When she entered the doorway, he was swaying to the music, holding his hands toward her.

"Dance with me, Miss Little Rock. I'm about to embark on a long and lonesome journey, and I'd sure like to dance with a beautiful blonde before I go. And don't back away like that! I won't step on your toes! I'm a dancer! Anyhow, you're well armed with genuine lions' teeth around your neck, and those things can hurt, as your boyfriend discovered. The only question is, will you let me lead?"

Shelby stared at him. Saracen knew a white girl didn't dance with a colored man, even one she had known all her life. He knew that for the two of them just to stand in that hot room, surrounded by hot photographs, was far too complicated, especially while Frank Sinatra crooned a love song. And it didn't help that he looked so fine, though there was something about the look in his eyes that wasn't fine.

"Okay," she demanded, hands on her hips. "What's going on?"

"I might ask the same thing of you." He dropped his arms along with his friendly voice. "Like how you got Marvin Williams fired from the good job he had. How in God's *name* did you manage to do that in the few hours you were on his train?"

"Fired? He got *fired?*" Shelby looked stricken with remorse. "I hate that beastly Meyers! Meyers said he'd get him fired! I *hate* that man! Meyers threatened me, Saracen, and he tried to make me feel like a slut. He said my momma was a terrible woman, and that everyone in town knew it, and that my father had *crippled* him! Marvin stood up for me as best he could, and I tried to stand up for Marvin too! I *did,* Saracen! I even called Charlie Billington and asked him to help, and telephone calls aren't cheap. Charlie said he would try, and I was sure Charlie could fix it. I feel *awful* for Martin, and so sorry. I'm so very sorry."

"So it was Charlie boy who tried to rescue the little white girl from the big boogie man, never mind what happened to Marvin, the nigger, who courageously stood up to a white bully on her behalf."

Shelby's face flushed. "*Don't you talk to me that way, Saracen Self!* Just because you're wearing a suit and you're in New York City, you think you're somebody, and you're *not!* You're . . . you are. . . ." For a moment she was tongue-tied.

"Say it, Shelby!" Saracen's laugh was bitter. "Spit it out! The word is *NIGGER!* Say it, *Miss* Shelby, *Queen of the World!*"

"How *dare* you talk to me like that, Saracen Self! That word has never passed my lips and never will! I even did a scene today with a Negro from Pine Bluff, and you didn't tell me he would be in my school just to be mean!"

"You acted with a *Neegrow?* From your own state? Did you have a fainting fit? And another *Neegrow* just had the temerity to ask you to dance? Well, *Miss* Shelby, you may not say 'nigger,' but you hid behind Baldwin plenty of times while she said it. Call her right now! Tell her you're with that big nigger boy in your bordello living room looking at naked pictures of men and women who are *fucking! Tell her that!* Then tell her you cost a good man his job whose life and living was working on that railroad! Will you do that, please ma'am? And I'll get in a word too. I'll ask if she'll give Marvin a job cleaning toilets alongside my daddy!"

Shelby's face jerked sideways as though Saracen had slapped her. "No . . ." she was struggling for breath. "Saracen . . . I . . . I don't think you're a . . . *Listen* a minute, Saracen . . . Judd Meyers is a *terrible* man. You wouldn't believe the way he spat out my Papa's name! *My* name." She reached a timid hand toward Saracen. "I told everybody at that school today that my last name is 'Korzeniowski.' You heard Ben Vaughn call me that. That's who I really am, how you knew me when I was little.

And I did everything I could to help Marvin, and I am *not* prejudiced like Baldwin! *I'm not!* And you're more than my friend, Saracen. You are . . . you are . . ." Shelby clutched at his arm, tears rolling down her cheeks. "You are my *best* friend . . . You've always been my best friend. . . ."

Saracen didn't try to soothe her as he had on the train. His voice was calmer, but his face was sad and weary.

"Maybe you did your best, but for God's sake . . . and Marvin's . . . stay out of it now. Don't call your rich boyfriend again. *Just stay out of it.*" He picked up his briefcase and walked toward the door.

"Don't be mad at me, Saracen. Please don't be mad. And don't go away angry. Let's dance. Okay? One dance? Sinatra's still singing. . . ."

He gave a derisive snort, but turned around.

There were dark circles beneath Shelby's eyes, and her face was tear-streaked and her hair tangled. She looked like a waif in her bare feet and bedraggled, fancy white dress. Saracen sighed, reached to pat her arm, let the briefcase slip from his hand, and touched her face instead. Then, as though there were no alternative, he wrapped both arms around her body, and kissed her full on the mouth, which caused the lions' teeth to dig into both of their skins.

Shelby struggled at first, then put her hands around his neck and returned his kiss. It was such an easy thing to do.

He stepped back first, eyes closed as though in sorrow, gently pushed her hands away, shook his head, and reached for the doorknob.

"Don't go," Shelby whispered.

He grimaced. "That was an accident, Sheb." His voice was harsh. "I shouldn't have let it happen." He twisted the knob. "I'm sorry."

"We should talk about it. We did nothing but skirmish before the . . ." But she couldn't say the word.

He leaned his head back, groaning. "I was overcome by how . . . how you've changed. And I didn't like that dude on the motorcycle. That guy is big trouble. But," he sighed, "you'll have to find that out for yourself. Won't you." His voice held no hope for the outcome.

"The one thing I ask you to do is call home. I promised your momma I'd get you to call. A couple of puny postcards haven't been enough. And you'd better get on the phone quick if you don't want Baldwin to come and storm into *this*." He brandished an arm at the photographs, then gave a slight wave of his hand in the manner of someone who is too far away to be seen, but makes the gesture just in case.

When he walked out the door, he didn't look back.

23

THE PINK LIGHT was still washing over the steamy photographs, and Frank Sinatra was still singing, "We may never, never meet again on that bumpy road to love."

Shelby jerked the needle off the record, went into the bedroom, threw herself onto Justine's black satin sheets, and pressed the back of her hand against her lips that were still fraught with the feel of the kiss. If Saracen had stayed . . . *and she had begged him to stay* . . . they would have made love.

She sat up and swung her head back and forth until her tangled hair looked like a string mop.

She had to call home. The thought of Baldwin charging into the apartment was hilarious. And painful. She couldn't let that happen. She couldn't do that to her grandmother.

Shelby would call home and play the happy child, a role at which she was adept. She sat up, preparing herself, composing the text in her mind.

She would first report the good news about her small success in the acting class, though she would, of course, ignore egregious details, like her partner's color . . . or that she had almost disrobed in a room full of people. She would never relay that news to Baldwin Josephine Shelby Howell. She would be enthusiastic about the apartment to allay their fears about where she would stay. She wouldn't mention that two of her roommates would be male, and she would *never* mention that the female roommate French-kissed men in public . . . though Baldwin probably didn't know what that meant. Baldwin had conceived a child, but most likely by

Immaculate Conception.

And Shelby would *never* mention that there were eleven Korzeniowskis in the Manhattan phone book. And she would *never ever* say that Saracen Self had appeared on her doorstep, viewed photographs in the living room of couples having sex, and grabbed her in his arms and kissed her. Ardently. Her hands moved to her lips, then jerked away. She sat up very straight.

She would ask Baldwin about Judd Meyers. She had to ask her. She might even ask her qualmy mother. It was her daughter's *right* to know what had happened, wasn't it? The more indignant she felt about her ignorance of past history, the less guilt she felt about kissing Saracen. It was in this more righteous state of mind that she reached for the phone.

It was 6:30 p.m. in Little Rock. Eulalia would be home from work, and Baldwin would be at the stove or tending her flowers, inside or out. But when the operator answered, "Mel pew," Shelby groaned. That accent would be incomprehensible to Baldwin.

"I want to make a collect call to Little Rock, Arkansas," Shelby said, articulating each word with tight, Yankee vowels.

There was a pause. "W'yew repit thet, puleeze?"

Shelby condensed the vowels into even harder pellets and tossed them into the airwaves. "I'm calling Little Rock, Arkansas, COLLECT."

The operator grunted.

"My last name is 'HOWELL,'" Shelby added just as carefully. It was the first lie she would speak during the call.

"What's that name again?"

"HOWL!"

When the phone began to ring, Shelby's heart beat faster, anxious that one of them, Baldwin or her mother, would actually take the call.

"Hello!" Baldwin shouted. The sound of that familiar voice trumpeting into her ear nearly jerked Shelby into the receiver.

The impatient, foreign-sounding operator asked if the party would accept a collect call from New York.

"You have some kind of cold?" Baldwin sounded incredulous.

"I . . . have . . . a . . . collect . . . call . . . from . . . Shelby HOWL. . . ." The operator spoke with long, exasperated pauses between each Brooklyn-accented word, which made her sound like an American speaking to a foreigner with the expectation that the foreigner would understand if the English words were spoken loud enough.

"Who *is* this?" Baldwin demanded, huffy at this stranger speaking gibberish in her ear. At which point Shelby yelled into the phone, "It's *Shelby*, Baldwin! It's your granddaughter, *Shelby Howell!*"

Baldwin murmured in a wonder-filled voice, "It's Shelby Howell . . ." then she shouted into the receiver, as though not just her voice, but her plump body was trying to slither through the line, "*It's Shelby Howl, Lalie! We've got her calling from New York City! You hang on, Shelby Howl! Your momma's in the yard, but she's coming! Hang on to the telephone!*"

The operator shouted, "Whaddya, whaddya . . . oh, fuh Gawd's sex, *tawk* tuh Noo Yoik City!" And she disconnected her line with an ear-piercing crackling sound to show who was boss.

"Shelby Howell! Honey! What happened to you? Are you alright?"

Shelby knew Baldwin was holding the receiver away from her ear like a bomb about to explode, swaying anxiously from one foot to the other.

"We haven't heard a word except little bitsy postcards!" Baldwin had never called Shelby "honey" in the twenty-one years of her life. "Honey" was her mother's endearment.

"I'm fine, Baldwin." Shelby tried to swallow a great lump in her throat. "I'm just fine." The longing to be sitting at the kitchen table with her grandmother and her mother was overwhelming. She desperately needed to see their faces and inhale the homey fragrances inside the house that was her only haven. Everything there was chipped, sagging, peeling. But there were no tigers in those woods.

Or were there? Judd Meyers said there were.

"This is a terrible line!" Baldwin continued to shout in one breath, calling to Eulalia with another breath. "You better get yourself in this house, sister! I've got to go turn off that hose before it floods the whole back. . . ."

The receiver banged from its cord against the wall, a screen door slammed, and Eulalia was on the phone, panting, "Shelby? Honey? Are you really there?"

"Yes, ma'am, it's me, Momma, and I'm . . . I'm not crying. I'm just so happy to hear your voice." Shelby eyed the satin sheets, but they were too slick for a good nose wipe. "How are you, Momma?"

She did her best to squelch the tremble in her voice, and wipe her nose with the inside of the dress's skirt. But what did it matter? Nothing mattered.

Eulalia's voice was too steady. "We're just fine down here, honey. It's still hot as firecrackers though. I hope it's cooler where you are."

There wasn't a window in the steaming, New York City bedroom, but Eulalia didn't know.

"Oh, yes, ma'am. Everything's fine up here. I've found an apartment with some students from school."

"That's wonderful, honey! And such a relief for Baldwin and me. I'm so glad you've met some nice girls to share a place. We were wondering just a little about where you would move. Everyone asks about you down here. Saracen Self even came by and asked about you, wanted to know where you were staying." There was a wry note in Eulalia's lowered voice. "Baldwin wasn't here when he came."

Shelby closed her eyes.

"But this bill is running up . . . unless . . . unless . . . there's something else you need to say. . . ."

What did her mother expect her to say? That Saracen had thrust his tongue in her mouth and that she had wanted him to do more? *So much more?* She sprawled back on the bed, exhausted.

"I'm so glad you called, honey." Shelby knew all of her mother's voices, all of her moods, and this voice was too jolly. "We were just a little worried since we hadn't heard from you. It's so nice to hear your voice."

Eulalia paused as though she, too, might be close to tears, which meant that Shelby had to be strong for her mother's sake. Then Eulalia was saying, "Momma! Just wait!" though she spoke calmly again to Shelby. "Baldwin is about to pull my arm off. She wants to say goodbye. I love you so much, honey. Take care of yourself."

"Wait a minute, Momma!" Shelby implored. "Wait a minute! There was this man on the train and he said . . . he told me. . . ."

But Eulalia had disappeared into the endless miles between New York City and Little Rock, and thank God for that. Her mother mustn't hear about Judd Meyers's ravings. Shelby was the only one in the family who couldn't bear an enigmatic past. She would have to find another way to learn what had befallen her family. Right now she had to stay calm and say goodbye to Baldwin.

"Shelby Howell!" Shelby jumped when Baldwin shouted into the phone again. "Are you wearing your gloves when you go out? You put your hands on those subway straps, and you'll get the itch for sure! And watch out for lice up there too . . . those people never wash!"

Shelby looked down at her grubby hands and her beautiful, grubby, snot-ridden dress, and she yearned to sail across the Hudson River and race through New Jersey and Delaware and Maryland and Virginia and plow through the Blue Ridge and the Smokies and hurry through the long, caddie-cornered length of Tennessee and cross the Mississippi River to Arkansas where she would wind up near the Dog Tracks in West Memphis before she could tear down Highway 70 over Crowley's Ridge, so that finally she would be in Little Rock and could sit down at that kitchen table where, no matter the weather, a bowl of fresh flowers always presided.

"Oh, yes, ma'am." Her voice was meek. "I'm wearing my gloves."

"Well, we've just been sick with worry about you up there. There's never an answer at that woman's apartment. Where have you been, dear child?" Baldwin only called Shelby pet names when she was fretting about something.

Shelby rubbed the black satin sheet between her fingers, picturing the bowl of flowers on top of the white enameled kitchen table in Baldwin's kitchen, the surface of which was also used for pencil-scribbled reminders. She was probably writing a message as she talked. *Send Shelby castor oil.*

"I'm just fine," Shelby answered, already forgetting she shouldn't ask about Judd Meyers. "But Baldwin, there was this man on the train who said. . . ."

"I can't hear a word you're saying! Speak up, Shelby Howl!"

"I wanted to ask you . . . I wanted to ask . . . what kind of flowers are on the kitchen table?"

"Flowers?" Baldwin sounded dumbfounded. "You're spending all this money on a telephone call from New York City to ask me about the cosmos?"

"Yes, ma'am. The cosmos." And the thought of the pink and orange and fuchsia and purple and yellow colors, surely arranged in an ancestor's cut-glass crystal vase on top of the plain white enamel table, created a vision of such exquisite beauty it made Shelby double up with pain.

Cosmos. The world. *And the world was home.*

There was an unaccustomed silence from Baldwin's end, until she said, somewhat uncertainly, "I'll box up some castor oil and get it in the mail to you, Shelby Howl. Right now you must fix yourself some hot water tea and have a tub soak." She changed the subject, always determined to obliterate unpleasantness. "How do those folks up there like the star sapphire?" She spoke louder so her granddaughter could hear over all those mountains and lakes and noisy trains and trucks that separated them. "I'll bet no one up there has one like it. Ernestine threw a hissy fit when I told her I gave it to you!" Baldwin's snorted complacently. "At least you're up North where it's cooler. I'm suffering from the heat down here," thus placing the worry in Shelby's court, and, as was her custom, she hung up without saying goodbye, which left her in control.

Shelby sat quietly, phone still to her ear. She could imagine her mother rinsing mint from the garden and slicing thin wafers of lemon to serve with their sun tea. Alfred would be rubbing against Baldwin, who would shout, "Get away from me!" but leave the skillet on the stove to open a can of tuna for the cat, while the skillet smoked so hot the handle had to be grabbed with several hand-crocheted pot holders and hurried outside to cool off on the stone step, with Baldwin shouting all the while at the exigencies of life and the dreadful cat she loved.

"*Puleeze* heng up ya' rece*evah!*" the operator said tartly. Shelby banged the phone into the woman's ear, marched into the bathroom, stripped off her fine, dirty, Miss Little Rock clothes, threw them on the floor, twisted the arthritic faucet as far as it would go, and stood, naked except for the juju necklace, watching the turbulent water slowly fill the tub.

At that moment, Saracen was flying over very deep water.

She slipped into the bath and submerged herself until her head was covered, one hand lingering over her breasts, the other trailing down her stomach and into her body's loam. She opened her eyes underwater, shoved her feet against the end of the tub, and watched the necklace's teeth float above her before she surfaced and stood, sputtering, shaking her wet body like a healthy young animal, and staring toward Egypt. She got out of the tub, fluttered the towel along her back and beneath her arms, and wiped the damp from beneath her breasts before she removed the necklace, hung it over the side of the tub, and watched water drip from the big yellow teeth.

24

AN OLD MAN entered the dance studio and shuffled toward the piano. He was paunchy and short-waisted and rumpled, but the twinkle in his eyes suggested he might whirl around the room on the tips of his toes at any moment. When he sat at the piano, however, his agile aura evaporated, and he slumped like a dusty philodendron in a run-down hotel lobby.

Boojie sidled excitedly up to Shelby. "That's Freddie Freyer at the piano. He's the only person in the world who can keep Ana George in line! They were lovers for years until she dumped him for a young dancer, but Ana's still the greatest modern dancer in the world, and she'll hit you if you don't move right. My sources tell me that one time when she was really angry at Freddie, she threw his dachshund at him! But the dachshund and Freddie survived."

The door opened again, and a middle-aged woman entered, dressed in black leotard and tights, with a short jersey skirt tied at the waist. Her knobby feet looked brave and hardworking, like those of peasants long in the field, and she strode purposefully on those feet to the middle of the all-seeing mirror, and captured her long hair with a quick twist of a rubber band. She turned to face the pupils, clapping her hands with the sharp sound of castanets. The noisy room became quiet.

"Sit on the floor so I can see you," she instructed. She moved briskly among them, sorting height and space with no-nonsense shoves, like a clerk arranging cans on shelves. She rolled her eyes at Maxine's hot-pink leotard and tights that glowed among the conventional black outfits, but said nothing.

Then, "My name is Linda Moore," she announced. "I'm Ana George's assistant. You may call me Linda, and you may call Ana by her first name when she arrives." She gave a quick, familiar smile to the man at the piano. "And you may call Freddie Freyer, our pianist and choreographer, by his first name." The old man gave a cocky wave with his cigar. "Now. All of you. Sit on the floor in wide stride like this . . ." and the woman sat on the floor and stretched her legs wide with what seemed amazing elasticity. Her battered feet seemed almost supple.

A jumble of bodies scrambled to the floor, spreading legs.

"Now. Bend your knees with the soles of your feet together," demonstrating as she spoke, "and sit firmly on your coccyx with your navel pressed to your backbone. Watch what I do, then repeat on a silent count of four."

Linda placed her hands on her ankles, contracted her pelvis inward, inhaled slowly and sonorously, and unfolded her back, exhaling with the sound of a distant fog horn until she was sitting straight again. She continued to contract and release with mesmerizing regularity, breathing in luxurious inhalations of oxygen, and exhaling just as noisily, while luring the new students to mimic her gyrations. Periodically, she stood and corrected form while Freddie Freyer's music shadowed the movements with the mysterious sounds of the deep sea.

Shelby exerted every one of her muscles in an effort to follow her leader, but as she struggled with a body howling with pain at the impossible twists and turns, Cherie's graphic lesson on bumps and grinds barged into her mind. The lesson had taken place between the swaying, rain-swept train cars after the pestilential meeting with Judd Meyers. There was something just as provocative about the contraction and release Linda Moore was now demonstrating: pelvis thrust out, vulnerable and waiting, then withdrawn, only to be thrust out again. Shelby was quietly convinced that this venerable dance exercise was based on an exalted stripper's bump.

In the midst of her musings and suppressed groans, a different voice festered the air. The voice, female, almost child-like, but confident it would be obeyed, inspired Freddie to abandon the magic of Ariel's enchantment and create the fury of Caliban's curses, while the woman's unseen hands gripped shoulders and her tight fists plunged down spines. She flitted among flailing bodies with a thousand pinching fingers.

Freddie Meyers, who had been so visible when he shuffled his immensity across the floor, disappeared inside his musical dissonance, as though joined at the bone with Ana George.

She was old, Ana George, and perhaps five feet, two inches in height, but she had the presence of an Amazon whose muscle-toned body had been reduced to its essence like a fine sauce. Black tights overlaid by a deep-blue jersey dance dress that swirled below her narrow hips and jet-black hair was pulled back in a bun so tight. it tugged the skin at the sides of enormous eyes that glowed preternaturally alert from their mascaraed caves. Her stringy hands looked arthritic, her jawline was too strong, her teeth were too big, her lips too livened with red paint. The sum of the parts created a fearsome whole that would have been at home among Tom Self's masks.

At the end of her journey through the room, she strode to the front and made her first pronouncement: "In this room you will be *dancers*." Her dark eyes scanned faces for unbelievers. "You will learn in this room how to connect your body's movements with your emotions. You will learn that an audience can be moved to tears by the way an actor stands . . . or merely raises an arm . . . or by the way an actor dies.

Show them how to die, Linda."

Freddie growled, *"Bang, bang!"* and the class tittered.

Ana's head turned fractionally, and there were no more sounds from Freddie.

Linda, hands loose at her sides, contracted her pelvis, bent her knees slightly, and breathed in spastically, as though she had been shot. Her hands clutched at the air, and she fell to the ground in a fetal position; but almost immediately, she inhaled a deep intake of air and rose from the dead.

Ana, her huge eyes fathomless, looked at Linda for an instant and motioned her to the side. Then the One Master, chin raised arrogantly, demonstrated the same exercise in a sinking, swaying, arms-supplicating contraction that caused her knees to collapse to the side and at the same time pulled her body inexorably to the floor. And even as she touched the floor, she began to rise, as though possessed with a succubus that would never cease its flirtation with death.

She continued to die and rise from the dead, contracting and releasing her body with the charged energy and flexibility of youth, even though some of her crooked fingers weren't tracking the undulations of her graceful, long-sleeved arms.

It didn't occur to the students she could be in pain, or that she might be driven to perform with greater skill and bravura than the younger Linda Moore.

When she stood in command again, she ignored her painful hands and proclaimed, "Bodies never lie." Her eyes scorched the hapless group as she spoke. "And never forget that I will know what you're thinking by the way you move."

The certainty of her pronouncement caused the bodies before her to freeze, remembering Liebmann's earlier words . . . that he would know if, in a scene, the students tried to conceal their true feelings. A collective shiver coursed through their bodies, like prisoners who realize they will always be observed from secret windows.

"Begin your contractions again, and this time show me *passion!*"

As the neophytes spiraled on the floor in tortured fourth positions, Ana George intoned in her penetrating half-whisper that they should work around their spines; that their blood and guts and the skin that covered their bones were nothing compared to the spine; that the pelvis provided the center, but the *spine* was the source of a dancer's energy.

Maxine did her best to obey the relentless orders. She was awed by the presence of the great dancer and was willing to suffer. For a while.

Bernard, however, encountered great difficulty. Neither his body nor his temperament were suited for these exercises. He floundered sullenly, his arms waving like tentacles, until Ana waded into the midst of the gyrating bodies, grabbed his shoulders, and almost lifted him from the floor.

"Straighten that back!" she hissed. "That's where your wings grow! That's where you'll learn to be a dancer!" She glared at him like an animal trainer who will use the whip if necessary, but retreated when Freddie Freyer began to pound chords in minor keys. She tossed off Bernard's incipient rebellion with a proud jerk of her chin, and moved to the front of the class to exhibit control in another way.

"You see this?" She swung her leg back like a horse showing his rider who was boss. The music whinnied as her leg cut through the air, arms deliberately akimbo. "You see this?" She pushed one high-arched foot onto its toes, knee wheeling to the side, body leaning toward the knee, hip thrust outward, arm stretched arrogantly. The music strutted with her.

But when she put more weight on her foot for a whirl into space, she winced, and Freddie quickly changed his tempo to a ragtime beat that caused the students to look at him instead of Ana George, which gave her time to manage a relatively smooth transition. She was aware, however, that

Bernard's mocking eyes had observed her brief agony, and she swooped a hawk-like hand in front of him, then barked at Shelby, "You! With that lumpy ring on your finger! Take it off! It will get in your way!"

When Shelby was chastised, the appreciative smile on Maxine's face reflected a new respect for the Ana George technique.

Shelby frowned, but removed the sapphire, and looked for a place to store the precious charm. Mercifully, Linda Moore took it and deposited the ring on the piano at the damp end of Freddie's cigar.

"And you . . ." Ana pointed to Maxine, "in that disgusting pink outfit. Wear black to this class! Only black!"

Maxine glowered, but Ana was the queen, now commanding Boojie to copy her stride across the floor, a stride that possessed such verve and grace it seemed she might glide through the wall and soar into thin air.

Boojie did his terrified best to match her stride with the focus of one who knows he must perform well or walk the plank. When Ana George said, "Not bad," his smile was rapturous.

"Now you . . . Miss Little Rock . . . try to walk like he just did," though her tone implied that Shelby could not perform as well.

But Freddie's jaunty, hand-holding music helped Shelby sail through the air somewhat like the woman whose voice still goaded from the side. "You're moving like a Rockette, but you're a *woman, Miss Little Rock! Move like a woman who's about to meet her lover!*"

Shelby gasped inwardly, lifted her chin, lengthened her stride, and swung her arms higher.

"Sex!" Ana shouted after Shelby's retreating form "That's what it's all about, whether you're acting or dancing or walking down a street. Walk like a woman, and think about *sex* when you walk!"

When Shelby reached the opposite corner, she kept her humiliated face to the wall.

"Now turn around and follow me." The woman's voice was more subdued. Shelby turned slowly, focusing her angry eyes above the door.

"But this time you're Joan of Arc, and you're not afraid of anything. You put a crown on the head of the Dauphin. You made the little coward a king, because it was God's will, but God talks to you alone with His voices, and *never* to that scrawny little boy. You are God's woman who fights like a man, and you will win! So walk because God *commands* you to *WALK!*"

Ana George, who was also God, raised her invisible sword, swung it over her head in exultant circles, and surged across the room. As she surged, Shelby muttered, "*Honisoitquimalypense*" . . . and Ana stumbled . . . *she actually stumbled* . . . and swung an angry profile toward Freddie, as though he was the one who had injected her perfect dancing instrument with another whiff of mortality. And dear Freddie created music to distract so that Ana George could conceal the imprecision with a willowy wave of her hands and point at Shelby to "*Begin!*"

Shelby's eyes sparkled. Her Papa's magic had worked! Saracen would be so pleased when she told him! It never occurred to the young woman that age and arthritis were Ana George's true tricksters. Shelby smoothed the sides of her svelte body with her hands, flaunting her youth, and she strode with long, confident steps, swinging her arms high, until she reached the opposite corner and turned to beam triumphantly at the great dancer.

But the first person in her line of vision was Bernard Crossroads, whose face was shining with congratulatory joy. Embarrassed by his identification with her victory, she turned her back on him. Who did he think he was? He shouldn't look at her like that! He was a *Negro!* Which caused the insufferable Saracen Self to barge into her mind and mutter sarcastically, "Poor little white girl."

Poor little white girl, he repeated, while Ana George caressed her perfect twist of dyed black hair and stared into space like a woman looking in a mirror.

"Well," Ana said with a shrug of her shoulders, "I doubt she could make it across France, but she made it across the floor. What do you think, Linda?"

"I think she moved well," her assistant said.

"I think she likes Saint Joan better than sex. What do you think, Freddie?"

Freddie grunted in response.

"Okay," Ana said, as though only Linda and Freddie were there. "You take over."

Freddie began to play "The Maple Leaf Rag," an Ana George favorite, and she strode out of the room with the grace of a hip-swinging young woman on the way to meet her lover. But before she closed the door, she gave a back-handed wave to one and all, similar to the wave Saracen gave when he walked out of Shelby's door on his way to Egypt.

25

BY THE TIME Shelby showered, spirits rising as her body cooled, her classmates had left the building. Only then did she remember the star sapphire. She groaned and sprinted back up the stairs to the empty dance studio.

There were many spots where cigars had singed the piano's surface, but the ring wasn't where Linda Moore had placed it. Shelby looked all over the surface of the piano and up and down the keyboard.

No ring.

She ran a finger along the length of the keys. She raised the lid, used her head as a prop, and peered into the piano's entrails.

No ring.

She brushed a hand against the strings, creating the buzz of angry bees. She let the hammers fall against the strings, praying for the emergence of a large, blue, unblinking eye. She got down on her hands and knees, and swept beneath the piano with her fingers.

Then she bolted up the stairs to the front entry.

"My ring. . . ." Shelby croaked.

Mrs. D'Arcy scooted back in her chair to distance herself from such excessive emotion.

"My ring was on top of the piano, and now it's gone, but it really belongs to my grandmother, her father sent it from China and. . . ."

Mrs. D'Arcy interrupted her. "Freddie took it."

"He *took* it?"

"For safekeeping," as though that should have been obvious.

"Well, I have to get it. It's my grandmother's ring and. . . ."

"I told you, *Freddie* has it. You shouldn't have worn it to class."

Shelby almost whimpered, "Where can I find Freddie?"

"We don't give out teachers' addresses. And you shouldn't have made that singing racket in the hall. That sort of behavior will not be tolerated at this school."

"I can't sing. *And it's my grandmother, Baldwin's, ring!*"

"You already said that."

"*Listen to me!*" Shelby leaned much too close to Mrs. D'arcy who had already backed her chair against the wall. "*Baldwin's father sent it from China, and that Chinese woman tried to jerk it off her finger at his funeral, and Baldwin, who is an absolute lady, kicked her, which shows how much she loves that ring! And I didn't make that racket in the hall, I told Mr. Liebmann I can't sing, I wish I could, but I can't, and I'm really, really sorry I wore the ring to class, but I have to get it now, PLEASE!*"

"I told you, we call him 'Victor' at this school. And if it wasn't you who sang, tell me who it was!"

Shelby was on the verge of becoming a quisling when she felt a hand at her elbow and heard Ben Vaughn's lovely voice saying, "I'll give you a ride home."

"I've got to get my ring," she said, not turning around. "Please, Mrs. D'Arcy, *please* give me the address! All Mr. Freyer has to do is reach his hand from his door with the ring, and I'll. . . ."

"*I told you to call him 'Freddie.'*" Mrs. D'Arcy's voice was hard as a ruler.

"Freddie. Yes, *Freddie!* I won't tell a soul where *Freddie* lives! I'll sign an oath if you want!"

Ben's hand was pushing her gently toward the door. "I'm

going to give you a ride on my bike. *Now,*" he said, and looked back at Mrs. D'Arcy. "She needs a bike ride, don't you think? A little early evening air? Good night, Monique."

When the front door closed behind them, Ben rolled his eyes. "God, you're dense. I know where Freddie lives. We'll have a bite to eat, then we'll pay him a call."

Shelby slapped her hand on her chest. "Oh, my stars! Thank you, thank you, *thank you!*"

Ben's reply was laconic. "Oh, my stars. You're welcome."

She gave him a glorious smile, stuffed her gear into the side pocket without prompting, put on the goggles, hopped onto the motorcycle and held on tight, his body no more in her mind than a subway strap.

What had Saracen said about Ben? There was something about him that was bothersome? Well, she wished Saracen could see her now. This "bothersome" man was about to help her retrieve her treasure.

26

IT WASN'T DUSK yet, but it was dark inside the restaurant. The waiter greeted Ben with great ceremony and led them to a discreet table.

Perhaps it was the preferential treatment, or the dark corner, or the lighted candles that made Shelby more conscious of Ben and caused her eyes to gravitate to the unlit cigarette he held between his thumb and forefinger, palm out. It seemed an inordinately sexy and debonair gesture, a New York City way to hold a cigarette.

"You're very quiet," he said.

"I need to get my ring." It was hard to keep her eyes from his hand and the cigarette. A black woman walked to a stool lit by a single spotlight. She sat down and began to sing a whispery version of "My Funny Valentine" to the soft ripple of a piano accompaniment. The customers grew quiet, savoring the sound of her lovely voice enveloping them with its serene, sad beauty.

A waiter brought the drink Ben ordered for Shelby. The bowl of the slender-stemmed glass was wide, and a sugar cube sizzled inside, like a creature preparing to surface. She lifted the exotic drink to her lips as though she knew what it was and smiled to herself at the notion of being in this restaurant with this man in Greenwich Village, with a fancy cocktail fizzing in her mouth.

After a while, the woman stopped singing, and the accompanist played the piano solo. Ben said, "After we pick up the ring, and once it gets dark, we'll climb to the top of the Washington Square Arch. Do you know who John Reed was?"

Shelby wanted to say she was excited to be in this place, and didn't care who John Reed was, and didn't want to go to Washington Square. She had already seen it from the outside. But she only shook her head "No."

"He was a writer. A revolutionary, you could say. Probably a Communist."

Shelby's mind veered south toward Baldwin and her rabid feelings about Communists. But thinking of Baldwin invoked the image of the star sapphire that appeared above Ben's head like a big blue eye that stared accusingly. The image made it difficult to concentrate on what he was saying.

"Reed went to Russia to report for a newspaper during the Revolution, and he died of typhus over there. But before he went to Russia, he lived in the Village. The story goes that he and Deschamps . . ." Ben didn't bother to explain who Deschamps was. She had never heard of him . . . should she have? . . . there was so much to learn. . . . "

He and Deschamps got drunk one night, climbed to the top of the Washington Square Arch where they shot a lot of caps and bellowed that Greenwich Village was a free state and that Village inhabitants should rise to its defense! The two men had to be hauled down by cops, and . . . after that unseemly invasion of public property, the only door to the Arch was padlocked. But I . . ." his black eyes absorbed the dark aura of the corner that was theirs, "I have the keys." He dangled two formidable keys from his fingers. "We'll have an adventure, you and I." And he raised his beer toward her.

Shelby raised her champagne glass more tentatively. She was sure Ben had said something more convoluted than sneaking to the top of the Washington Square Arch, but she didn't ask what it was.

She would go to the library and look up John Reed and Deschamps. There was so much to learn, and this sophisticated man might become her teacher.

27

WHEN FREDDIE FREYER opened his door in Greenwich Village, he was wearing a rumpled paisley robe tied loosely at the waist, and holding a gold-tipped cane. He squinted at Shelby as though trying to place her, ignoring the dachshund barking behind his heels.

"I'm so sorry to bother you," Shelby began to babble. "I was the person in class who had to walk across the floor like . . . like Joan of Arc? It was my ring you took from the piano for safekeeping. I would like to have the ring back now, please."

Freddie leaned his head toward her as though he didn't quite understand the language she was speaking. He was shorter than she was by several inches, but seemed happy to focus his eyes at her breast level.

Shelby raised her voice in an agitated spurt. "Please forgive me for bothering you, but the ring is a family heirloom." She hugged an arm across her body to divert his eyes from her breasts. "I'll just take it and leave."

Freddie lifted his wrinkled neck like a turtle and leaned further forward, which caused Shelby to retreat and back into Ben, who steadied her with his hands around her waist.

"Ah, yes. I remember. You're the blonde," Freddie smiled, exposing weathered teeth that protruded slightly, like a warped barn door. "You're the big blonde who doesn't like sex. But you brought someone with you." His face fell into a boozy pout, then brightened. "For a demonstration?"

Shelby sucked in her breath, and the little dog yapped at

a higher pitch. Ben chuckled and moved so Freddie could see him.

"It's Ben Vaughn, Freddie. We won't take much of your time. This is just a pick-up," he grinned.

"Ah, Ben . . ." Freddie projected his cane in a twitching greeting. "And a nice little pick-up she is, my boy," thumping the cane on the hall floor in approval.

Shelby exhaled in a huff and tried to move away, but Ben, one hand still around her waist, guided her back to Freddie, who said, petulantly, "But go away. Both of you. I'll bring that damn ring to school tomorrow. It's a nice little bauble, but you shouldn't wear it to class, my blonde Amazon. Now go away."

As Freddie leaned forward, perhaps to kiss her hand, the little dog barked louder and ran around the old man's legs, causing him to totter.

"Make Cupid stop that yelping!" a female voice inside the apartment demanded. "You know it makes me dizzy when he yelps!"

Cupid didn't like the female voice any more than the female voice liked his yelps, and he ran toward Shelby and jumped up on his stubby hind legs for her approval. When Shelby moved to avoid him, the dog began to hump her leg, and she stumbled into the room, trying to shake off the dog.

"Ahhh, Cupid," Ben said. He swooped up the dog as though accustomed to the exercise, took the leash hanging from the doorknob, hooked it to the dog's collar, tied the leash to a chair, put Cupid on the floor, and closed the door behind him.

Cupid crawled toward Shelby as far as the leash permitted, but Shelby didn't notice. She was staring at a photograph of a dancer who looked like a much younger Ana George. The photograph and the dancer's pose were stunning . . . torso bent parallel to the floor, one leg elevated in a reverse kick that lifted her long dress in a billowing wave. Shelby eyed other photographs of the dancer that encircled the room, but her eyes lurched to a stop when they fixed on Ana George herself, who was slumped on the side of the bed, dressed in a rumpled red satin costume, half-zipped in back and pushed up to reveal muscular legs roped with varicose veins. Her dyed-black hair had come loose from its bun to reveal wormy white roots.

But the most arresting part of her attire, as far as Shelby was concerned, was the large star sapphire that encircled a gnarled finger.

"That's my ring," Shelby whispered.

"She likes pretty things." Freddie flicked his fingers to indicate how insignificant the ring was compared to making Ana happy. "And she needed a bit of cheer."

"But it's *my* ring," Shelby said louder. Any thought of Baldwin's ownership evaporated.

"Of course, it is, but tonight it's on loan to Ana. She's like a little magpie when she sees shiny *objets*."

"I'd like my ring back *now*, please." Shelby's voice was quick and surprisingly firm.

"Tomorrow," replied Freddie. "We're playing dress-up tonight."

Ben, who had been silent, walked toward Ana. When Cupid barked at him, Ben snapped at Freddie, "Give that damn dog a biscuit."

Freddie giggled, pulled a biscuit from the pocket of his robe, tossed it to Cupid, and the barking was replaced with a slobbering crunch.

Ben's voice was placating, an actor in the role of petitioner approaching royalty. "You look beautiful tonight, my dear Ana. May I kiss your lovely hand?"

Ana raised a face that appeared to be melting beneath layers of stage makeup. She swept back her coarse mane with sluggish fingers (the better to see her supplicant) and lifted her ancient hand to her loyal subject.

Ben's eyes stayed locked on hers as he worked to remove the sapphire from her arthritic finger. But the finger had swollen, and the ring wouldn't budge.

"Shit," he said under his breath.

Ana's smile faltered. "Freddie gave me the ring. Freddie loves me."

"And I love you too, my darling," Ben crooned as he reached for the vodka bottle, and swathed the ring finger with the spirit.

The dog slurped the spill from the floor.

Shelby couldn't take her eyes from the tableau of the drunken old dancer trying to seduce the suave actor, who had the beringed finger in his mouth. The soft lamplight blurred the wrinkles in Ana George's face, and the regal tilt of her neck and her body and the blacks and reds and blues of her dress combined to create a montage of erotic longing.

When Ben stood, rather abruptly, he slipped the sapphire from his mouth, and handed it to Shelby, who jammed the ring onto her own finger and locked it there with her other hand.

Freddie chortled, "Bravo. Bravissimo!" and tapped his cane on the floor. Ba bump. Ba bump. Ba bump.

Ana turned her head toward Freddie as though surprised to see he was there. Her face was again captured in the unforgiving light of reality, but Ana didn't know, and she smiled up at Ben through the weight of her makeup, her wrinkles, and her hair's perfidious white roots.

"Don't be so long in coming, Benjamin," she whispered. Her ancient torso swayed with disturbing sensuality. "Next time I'll dance for you."

28

WHEN THEY ARRIVED at the Washington Square Arch, Ben locked the motorcycle, slung the panniers over his shoulder, opened the rusty padlocks, placed the locks on the floor, led Shelby inside, pulled the door shut with a loud thud, and felt for her hand.

The sudden dark was absolute.

Then, and only then, did Shelby feel frightened. What was she thinking . . . But of course, she wasn't thinking. She was an idiot. She could disappear forever in this dungeon, and no one, not another soul in the world, would know where she was. She could scream forever in this crypt-like place, and no one would hear. Was she about to endure the horror Baldwin feared would befall her granddaughter in this wicked city, but would never say out loud?

On the other hand . . . the waiter at the restaurant . . . and, yes, Freddie, too . . . had seen her with Ben . . . if Freddie could remember. Ana George wouldn't remember. She was drunker than Freddie. Mrs. D'Arcy had seen Ben and Shelby walking out of The Acting School. But would she testify she had? Would she rat on Ben, the Broadway star, in order to save Shelby, the latecomer nobody from Little Rock, Arkansas with the weird name, who D'Arcy thought had screeched in the hall and interrupted a very good scene? Shelby's only hope was that since Ben had rescued her grandmother's ring from an ogre, he had to be a decent human being. Still, her mouth felt like sandpaper, and her heart was kerlumping so fast, it felt like a motor boat's engine, too big and much too loud to contain in such a small space. *Can hearts actually burst, or do they deflate like a balloon, flat and defeated?*

But Ben was talking to her in his lovely, reassuring voice as they climbed from one step to the next, obliterated by darkness. He was saying, confidently, soothingly, that they were almost at the top, just a few steps to go.

Not unusual for him, Shelby supposed, this blind climb, on a staircase with no railing. He could probably fly like a bat. Big actor in New York City. Spread his arms and take off, leave her to die, alone.

But they did emerge, and he released her hand and strolled to the other side of the roof as though it were a picnic ground.

She didn't follow.

She stood by herself, inhaling great gulps of fresh air, trying to relax and gain enough confidence to look out at the Village and what she could see of the dreamlike city. Slowly, surely, she became enthralled by the panorama of the sky, made opalescent by millions of city lights. She felt she was inside an inverted, hand-blown translucent bowl. Maybe she *could* survive in a city this enchanted.

She began to step cautiously around the roof's perimeter, then more confidently, becoming mistress of the Washington Square rooftop kingdom, inhabited by two people. She nearly laughed out loud at the wonderment of swimming in a muddy lake with Charlie Billington just three weeks ago, and now ambling around the rooftop of the Washington Square Arch in New York City.

At midnight.

With a strange man.

Ben was seated on a spread-out sleeping bag he had pulled from his panniers and was smoking a cigarette, as though there were nothing extraordinary about two people making a life-threatening, illegal climb to the peak of the

Washington Arch.

He motioned her to sit beside him, which she did, and they were quiet for some time. Then,

"Who's the big black guy?"

Shelby looked away. "He's . . . from Little Rock."

"You told me that before. Is he your boyfriend?"

She jerked to a standing position. "Of course, he isn't my boyfriend! He's colored!"

It was so easy to betray Saracen. Her heart thumped even faster at how easy it was. But he had dumped her, hadn't he? He was a Negro and had the gall to dump her!

"Ahhhh," Ben said, "gets to you he's a Negro."

"Of course, it doesn't get to me! He's a . . . a . . . friend I've known forever! And he's not just a Negro. He's part Indian. And French. Maybe. *And* he's a reporter for a big newspaper. I'll probably never see him again."

"A Negro-Indian-French reporter for a big newspaper. Interesting." He patted the sleeping bag. "Sit back down."

Shelby looked away, then sat, but slowly, as though if she didn't look at him, it was okay to sit. When Ben took her hand and kissed the ring, a frisson passed through her body, and she gave a soft *ha*, remembering how he had slipped the ring from Ana's finger with his mouth. She knew she should get up and climb down those perilous stairs, and scramble for the key in that hellish dark, and flee from the man who had engineered this strange evening.

But she didn't.

She had followed him up those stairs. Willingly.

They sat without speaking, and after a while he began to undress her, and she let him, because she knew this was the night, but she didn't look at him, which sort of made it okay. She lay on the sleeping bag, eyes closed, resisting the impulse to curl into her naked body, knowing he was looking at her. She knew her body looked good because of all those dance classes.

But he didn't touch her.

A minute passed, or perhaps five, and she also knew if he didn't touch her soon, she would take his hands and place them where she needed them to be.

But then he stood and removed his own clothes unself-consciously, as though it made no difference, clothes, no clothes, naked bodies, human beings, and he lay down beside her and began to stroke her breasts. "This is the friendliest thing two people can do together," he whispered.

Her back arched at his touch and the sound of his voice, and she gasped as he entered her body, thinking, *So this is what it's like.*

His eyes widened when she winced, but that moment passed, and a demanding urgency grew and expanded until she almost forgot about Ben, except that he had to stay inside her forever, and she became part of the diaphanous air that floated all around them, as he pressed harder and harder into her body.

When they were lying apart, he said, almost accusingly, "You were a virgin."

She could feel herself blush in the dark.

Then he said, "Don't get pregnant."

She was too astonished to speak.

"Go home and take a cold shower," he said matter-of-fact-ly. The man-about-town instructing the neophyte about how to have sex without getting pregnant, facts he believed to be true. "Take a salt douche. And find a doctor who will give you a diaphragm. We can't do this again unless you have a diaphragm."

She stood up abruptly, and scrambled for her clothes. Her voice was harsh. "How can you talk like that after what we've just done. And I don't know any doctors, and I don't want to know that kind of doctor. I'm not even married!"

Ben reached up, his fingers strong around her wrist, his voice gentle. "This will get better for us. But we have to be careful." He sounded so reasonable, as though he were merely stating facts.

Shelby snatched her hand back, furious at being seduced so easily, and by someone who sounded much too experienced . . . someone who, instead of telling her how lovely it had been, talked about cold showers and diaphragms.

She was finding it hard to breathe. The big city air had become dirty, too dangerous to inhale.

But she had never been called a woman, and she liked the way he said it . . . and she had to admit, only to herself, that she loved the confident way he had touched her . . . and was embarrassed that she was already yearning for him to touch her again.

He stubbed out his cigarette, took the hand he still held, and drew her ring finger into his mouth. She felt an electrical surge between his mouth and her body. When he released the finger, he pulled her down to his side and returned the warm, wet ring to her finger with his mouth.

This time he took much longer before his body merged with hers.

29

Dear little Shelby,

I hope you will learn everything you need to know about that acting business so you can come back home real soon. Remember to eat your Wheaties and drink plenty of prune juice.

The leaves are beginning to fall but the Mr. Lincoln rose is still blooming. That rose is a regular miracle and so is Fulbright's vote for the Southern Manifesto. Our brave Senator and other southern gentlemen in Congress fixed it so we can't have any more of that nasty racial integration goings on in public places. I got down on my hands and knees over that vote.

Also, I am heartened to learn that Orval Faubus may not be as terrible a man as I thought and I will tell you why. Julien took me to the State House before the election just so I would rest better about how to vote. Your mother didn't happen to be around which provoked me a little because I told her the exact time we would drop by her desk. She never has seemed to care for Julien, and he has tried to do everything in the world to help that girl.

Anyhow, I met Orval Faubus in person and I have to confess that I even shook his hand though he does not really know how to shake a lady's hand. It's more like he is hoeing corn. He is just plain country when you come down to it, but I am pleased to say that he is one of us on this integration issue. I asked him outright how he stood and he told me the truth.

And yes I did vote for the man and I know you did the same like I said for you to do on your mail-in absentee ballot I had the State House send you. This was your Maiden Vote, and that's a big moment for a little girl.

But I am slowing down a bit on that stop-integration committee with Julien. I have to say I do not care for some of the people he asked to join us. They make water rings on my tabletops and some use coarse language, and I cannot have that kind of talk in my home. Though I guess I will let them come here a few more times, though Charlie thinks I should stop it altogether. That young man can be too outspoken sometimes. He may be one of the folks pushing this integration nonsense. Could he be a Communist?

I bet you are already wearing those foot warmers up there. I trust you are in good health. Your letters are such stingy little things it's hard to tell.

> *Your grandmother,*
> *Baldwin Josephine Shelby Howell*

P.S. This Max friend of yours. What does his father do?

Darling Daughter,
Julien is going to be in New York City in a few weeks and wanted your phone number, but I was sure you wouldn't want to be bothered by such a tiresome old undertaker, so I gave him the wrong number. If he manages to track you down, just avoid him. I want you to do that. Avoid him. You can see him at Christmas if you have to and that won't be long from now. I'll be so happy to see you.

I'm pleased your classes are going well and that Boojie and Hank and Ben . . . he's the one who has an acting job, isn't he . . . are taking good care of you.

> *I love you, my sweet child.*
> *Momma*

Dear Shelby,

What's going on up there? You haven't written in weeks! You've met a man, haven't you? I know you have! I can feel it in my bones . . . so spill the beans, Shelby Howell! No secrets from your best friend!

The only news in this town is about the School Board. Everyone is yakking, because School Superintendent Blossom wants to enforce that hideous Supreme Court decision that says the darkies have to go to school with our precious little ones. Everyone screamed when Blossom said he'd begin integration with the first grade, so he changed it to high school. He calls it the Blossom Plan, which I think is so egotistical. Of course, our sweet baby will go to the new Hall High when it opens here in Pulaski Heights. None of the dark people live in Pulaski Heights, thank heavens, they need more money to buy a house in the Heights, so we're safe up here. That's what Orval Faubus calls them . . . the dark people . . . which I think is real cute!

Bruce says that integration will just lead to mongrelization and that our precious child will never go to school with any of that kind. Our precious child is kicking me so hard right now, I can barely write this letter. I need a juicy letter from my glamorous friend up North to help get me through these months. Life gets dull when there's a baby in your belly!

Oh, and the other day, when I was buying shelving for the baby's room, I saw Saracen Self at the lumber yard. He came right up like he knew me. I prayed nobody I knew was there and saw it. He said he was about to go to Egypt again, and I thought, oh yeah, you're going to Egypt! More likely you're driving to Benton, Arkansas in your Daddy's pick-up!

We still haven't recovered down here from that picture of you and that nigger when you were getting on the train, and that's been almost three months ago. You were the talk of the town for weeks! I heard that Baldwin called Harry Ashmore at the Gazette and bawled him out real good for printing the picture, and I don't blame her a bit. That Ashmore has turned out to be such a nigger lover. I'll bet he never gets asked to Baldwin's house again. I notice how some people don't talk to him any more at the Country Club.

And listen to this . . . Bruce and your grandmomma have become phone pals, organizing this and that to keep the niggers in their place! Though Bruce does say she's not working at it like she was for a while. I told Bruce your grandmomma is getting a little old for such shenanigans. She's such a cute little thing.

The one plus about that picture of you and Saracen in the paper was that your Aunt Ernestine nearly had a heart attack! That woman is such a pill. But honestly, Shelby, it did look like he was trying to get on the same train with you, which is what I heard happened. But he didn't, did he? You would have told me. And he couldn't ride on your train, because there wasn't a car for niggers.

Anyhow, at the lumber yard, Saracen talked to me just like I was somebody he knew. I couldn't get out of that place fast enough. Remember how little he was when he used to hang around your grandmomma's house? Well, he has grown up to be one tall Nigra, hasn't he, and not at all bad to look at. But don't you ever tell Bruce Norton I even whispered such a thing!

And what in the world is going on with you and Charlie? Rumor has it that some little gold digger with red hair is trying to snare him like she tried to do last year. Charlie is a catch, Shelby Howell! He has a ton of money, and I just love his dreamy gray eyes. You better hold on to that boy. Though I hear he's telling folks we should let niggers in the school, which may get him into a lot of trouble with some people, if you know what I mean.

Gobs of love from your almost X-friend,
Kat

30

THE OFFICE MANAGER, Bobby Davidson, was leaning over Eulalia's back as she typed. Eulalia, who could type faster than any secretary in the building, had been asked to stay late to finish the Governor's daily report. It was a dubious honor, but she was paid overtime. Also, in late hours, she often heard bits of unguarded conversations that were the opposite of the news she read in the newspaper.

For instance, she overheard Orval Faubus, in a phone conversation, say he would have voted for the Brown v. Board of Education decision if he had been on the Supreme Court. But the next day, he lobbied for anti-integration measures on the November ballot. It was a shock to realize the Governor of her state lied like that to the people who voted him into office. Or at best, he played one side against the other.

However, Eulalia worked at the Capitol to earn money, not for politics, and the faster she typed, the more she could earn. At the thought of the money, her fingers darted like hummingbirds over the keys.

Bobby Davidson read the pages as soon as she ripped them from the roller, but when he stepped closer and his hands drifted around to her breasts, Eulalia stopped typing, took a breath, and backed into Bobby's crotch as hard as she could with her chair. Then she stood up very straight and glared at him with turbulent blue eyes.

Bobby stood, knock-kneed, hand raised in a moaning surrender. Eulalia cleared her throat, sat back down, ostentatiously placed the letter opener where she could reach it in a hurry, and typed even faster.

31

SHELBY READ in the *New York Times* that the Egyptians had destroyed the statue of the man responsible for negotiating the building of the Suez Canal. His marble shoes were already covered with sand.

She also read that Britain and France had attacked Egypt. When she read about the attack, she stood very still. Her mother had written that Saracen was in Egypt again.

But Shelby's attention was diverted abruptly when her eyes fastened on a Little Rock dateline. She had never seen a Little Rock dateline in a New York City newspaper. It looked big, and very important.

"Buy the paper, lady!" the vendor demanded.

She dug in her pocket for the change, her eyes still glued to the article. In his campaign for re-election, Orval Faubus had denounced *Brown v. the Board of Education*, arguing that for ninety-two years the *Plessy v. Ferguson* decision had legitimized the separate-but-equal policy in schools. Shelby understood little of the legal details, and didn't much care. She did know that her fragile mother was working for a governor who was becoming increasingly controversial.

But what could she do? She was too far from home and inhaling life in a way she never could have imagined, both at The Acting School, and with the actor whose hair was still summertime gold. She stripped her emotions in class, stripped off her clothes for Ben Vaughn, and was becoming better at both.

When she asked to see the ocean, Ben revved up his bike,

and ferried her to Montauk at the tip of Long Island. He skidded close to the deserted beach, scooped her up in his arms,
and carried her into the cold water, laughing and shouting,
"You're a big girl, but I am Zeus!" He quoted Yeats, he was
teaching her about Yeats, and he bellowed over the roar of
the waves, as though the ocean was the biggest stage:

"A sudden blow: the great wings beating still
Above the staggering girl, her thighs caressed
By the dark webs, her nape caught in his bill . . ."

At which point he stumbled and dropped her in the water, which made them both choke and laugh, their clothes
heavy with water and salt and sand, and they staggered back
to shore where they fell onto the beach, and he placed his
sucking mouth on her neck and shoved up her wet clothes,
whispering dramatically,
"He holds her helpless breast upon his breast. . . ."
And she shuddered when he placed his salty mouth on
one chilled nipple then the other, before they rose and raced
to the motel and into a hot shower and onto the squeaking,
rollicking bed.

She was sure their relationship wasn't all about sex, that
one-syllable word that ends so abruptly. It was also about desire, the softer word that connoted longing and lingered on
the lips and in the mind.

And surely that feeling was intertwined with love.

32

"I've seen the ocean, Baldwin, and . . ."

Shelby stopped speaking, afraid that thirteen hundred miles away Baldwin might sense her granddaughter had seen far more than the ocean at Montauk.

"And I . . . I've been to the Statue of Liberty. It was very . . . educational." Another pause, because Ben had whispered far more than historical fact in her ear at the Statue of Liberty. "And the teacher at The Acting School likes my work. I'm learning to move better, and to enunciate words correctly."

"What do you mean, you're learning to move? You move just fine, Shelby Howl. And you're learning to *enunciate?* You mean *tawk?* You move just fine, you tawk just fine. You'll be a stranger to me when you come home," Baldwin moaned.

"Oh, Baldwin. l could never be a stranger to you! But I have to learn to speak so people can understand me in any play, not just plays about Southerners. Southerners have accents."

"And those Yankees don't? Just who decides who has an accent? Is there a committee? If there is, it's full of Yankees."

"And I make diphthongs out of my vowels." The moment Shelby said the word, she wished she hadn't. She could never explain diphthongs to Baldwin. It was hard to concentrate on the simplest subjects while visions of wild lovemaking spun in her head. She felt delirious and depraved and anxious to get off the phone.

When Eulalia took the receiver, Shelby was more honest.

"I've met a man I like a lot, Momma."

Eulalia was silent.

"But don't tell Baldwin."

"No," Eulalia replied solemnly. "I would never do that."

33

THERE WERE STRETCHES of time when Shelby didn't see
Ben or hear from him, which made her anxious. Males had
a habit of disappearing from her life. When Ben did call, he
seemed distant, as though he had been someplace far away,
though it couldn't have been too far, because he performed
every night except Sunday.

But she forgot her niggling worries when she watched
him on stage, thrilled and proud to be his . . . companion. He
seldom smiled when they were alone, but on stage, when it
was called for, the wattage of his smile would rip across his
face and light up the entire theatre. He looked taller up there,
wider of shoulder, even more alluring up there on high.

When she realized his hair was bleached, not by the sun
but with a bottle of peroxide, she was surprised. It didn't fit
the image of the man she thought she knew. But what mattered most was the gravitational force she felt while looking
up at him on that stage. And when they were in bed.

He asked her to meet him late that November night at
the entrance of the Chrysler Building, and of course, she
was there, waiting, excited at the prospect. She had saved
the Chrysler until it could be properly savored, and a private
viewing after hours with Ben was thrilling to contemplate.
I've been to the top! her father had written on that last postcard, with a photo of the skyscraper blazing against the night
sky. But the memory gave her a guilty jolt. Her search for her
father had faltered as her relationship with Ben had soared.

When he arrived outside the Chrysler Building, the usual motorcycle panniers slung over his shoulder, Ben seemed more energized, his eyes more intensely black. The guards in the lobby saluted him, which didn't surprise Shelby. Ben knew many people. He had keys to many apartments.

The light in the lobby was muted for the night, but still reflected the red marble walls and sienna marble floors. She was enthralled by the luxuriant ambience, but gave a start when a guard's cough echoed like a shot through the empty space.

Ben squeezed her arm reassuringly and led her to an elevator with an interior that looked like a miniature parlor, walls made of a marquetry of exotic woods. She was bewitched by the beauty of this elevator. It was the perfect beginning for a perfect evening, and she reached for Ben's hand. But he responded almost formally. "I have a surprise for you upstairs. I know you like surprises."

When the elevator glided to a soundless halt, he led her down a shadowy hall, and opened a door with one of his keys.

Shelby was accustomed to seeing elegant apartments in Ben's company, but this place was extraordinary. The living room had huge windows overlooking what seemed to be an enchanted city that sparkled and wavered so close to the glass, it seemed she could touch it. The ceiling was two stories high, and the walls curved like cupped hands. It was a fantasy apartment, a set from a 30's movie, where, at any moment, John Barrymore might stagger through the door, or Fred Astaire might tap dance down the winding staircase.

However . . . when she looked more closely . . . she saw that the expensive modern blonde furniture was watermarked, and the expensive Plexiglas side tables were covered with dirty glasses, and the expensive thick cream-colored carpet was stained.

Ben seemed oblivious to the disarray. He waved an expansive arm at the grandness of it all, and said, "Welcome!"

But Shelby didn't feel welcome. She was repelled by the large photographs that hung from the vast walls, photographs of destroyed buildings, hopeless faces, mangled bodies. It took a moment to realize that what she first thought were stacks of wood, were actually charred bodies, and it took longer to realize that a smiling soldier, arms gracefully extended, a cigarette dangling negligently between two fingers, one leg raised in a balletic pose, was kicking a corpse. A first-prize blue ribbon hung from the frame of that photograph.

"A friend of mine lives here." Ben's actor's smile was too bright. "She's a renowned war photographer." He placed his panniers behind the bar. "She has the only private apartment in this august building, and it's ours for many nights."

Shelby imagined the woman on a distant battlefield, snapping scenes with the skill of a soldier shooting a weapon. The pictures would obscure the horror of the scene, and accentuate the beauty of line and shadow, and the photographer would win medals for her artistry. Shelby thought back to the dune-shaped, love-entwined bodies in Justine's apartment which now seemed far more beautiful than the images of mangled bodies on display in this grand place.

"You must have a lot of friends like her." Shelby's mouth felt dry.

Ben's return smile didn't reach his eyes, which was the moment Shelby realized she was a fool. Going to the Chrysler with Ben had seemed like the perfect introduction to this building, so legendary in her thoughts. Later they would take another elegant elevator to the observation tower that Ben was now describing as a surreal circus with undulating walls and a deep-blue ceiling adorned with glittering stars. "You'll have an out-of-body experience in an otherworldly place," he whispered, too close to her ear.

But she already felt too high in the sky, and for the first

time, she felt too alone with Ben. To be in the creepy apartment of a woman he was probably sleeping with at the same time he was sleeping with Shelby was depressing. He knew the boundaries she had transcended when they first made love. She had made the naïve assumption that, while they were doing such "friendly" things with one another, they wouldn't do them with anyone else. Either of them. Hopefully forever.

She turned to face the large windows that encircled so much of the room. From this great height, the view was of a sparkling stasis, far removed from death and evil, and the faint roar of the city was like the pleasant roar of the ocean heard from a conch shell, and the glittering ocean of lights seemed to rise and fall like the tide. She walked closer to the window, drawn to the mesmerizing lights. Ben was close behind her, reciting in his luscious voice:

"For the world, which seems
To lie before us like a land of dreams,
So various, so beautiful, so new,
Hath really neither joy, nor love, nor light,
Nor certitude, nor peace, nor help for pain;
And we are here as on a darkling plain,
Swept with confused alarms of struggle and flight,
Where ignorant armies clash by night."

Shelby moved further from Ben.

The truth of the poem was too keen on this evening, and the ignorance of armies was too much in evidence on photographs on every wall in the room.

Why did people kill one another? Why did they torture one another? Why did they lie and deceive and use one another? *Why did they yell* VICTORY *at fields of dead bodies and pulverized cities?* Why were they gratuitously mean? *Why did they betray one another, manipulate one another, re-*

joice in one anothers' pain?

And why was *she* standing on this darkling plain with this man, this *stranger*, really? She belonged in the glittering city right in front of her. Life was various and beautiful down there in that city. She had friends in that city.

Why hadn't she realized earlier that Ben's voice was too syrupy, too Victor Mature-ish? Couldn't he feel "the eternal note of sadness" resounding right here in this grand and desolate space?

She had to rid herself of the thick nap of his velvet voice. She had to get away from this apartment where a woman's shoe had been tossed into a corner. She had to get back to the reality of the city's grit. She wanted to go home.

"I don't like this surprise." She spoke so abruptly, she surprised herself.

She turned from the window and saw that a newcomer, a man, had entered the room in bare, silent feet. The man's build was wiry, and his sandy hair was balding and damp as though he had just showered. His flesh-colored trousers and his flesh-colored sweater were cashmere, expensive looking; but everything he wore was the same color as his skin, which made him appear fragile and almost transparent. He smiled at her, but the smile didn't seem real, as though he had zipped open his lips merely to reveal teeth that were very white, so different from her necklace of very real and yellow lions' teeth.

"Shelby," he said, and held out his arms as though he were the host.

She didn't like it that he knew her name, and she was weary of plummy voices.

"Shelby Korzeniowski. . . ."

She hated the flippant way he tossed out "Korzeniowski."

"And you're from *Little Rock* with a name like that. Such a delicious combination."

Shelby looked at Ben.

"This is my friend Kevin." Ben stubbed out the cigarette he had just lit. "He wanted to meet you."

Ben had mentioned someone named Kevin in passing, saying she would like his friend, Kevin. But it seemed too curious that Kevin had appeared, as though on cue, from within the apartment.

She was increasingly uncomfortable in this strange aerie. She felt surrounded by creatures that didn't mean her well.

Ben took her hand, squeezed it too hard, and held her at a distance like a prize horse on a leash. "Isn't she a beauty?" he said to Kevin.

Kevin's creamy smile hovered, and he poured himself a drink, ignoring Ben. "This is a wonderful building, isn't it, Shelby?" He spoke as though he had known her for years and was pleased they shared the same opinions. "It's like a piece of handmade jewelry created by a designer who was a little crazy. And the photographer is also remarkable," his hand swirled toward the photographs, "and she is fearless. She slides on her stomach onto those gargoyles that stick out in thin air from the sides of this building, and she snaps pictures of our great metropolis." Kevin held up his manicured hands and made rapid clicking sounds, as though taking pictures. Rat-a-tat-tat. Machine gun sounds. "She likes wars. She says they distract her. She's in Egypt now, so the apartment is ours."

Shelby imagined the woman taking her photographs in Egypt, and smiling up at Saracen, who was also in Egypt, and who would envelop her in his strong arms. And she hated this phantom woman who had no compassion. She hated this cellophane man who held a glass toward her filled with a golden liqueur. She thought of Charlie who was in her brain and telling her to get out of there.

"She'll do anything," Kevin teased, about the photographer.

Shelby said to Ben, "I'm ready to go."

"Don't go." Kevin's tone was imperative. His smile matched the bleached color of his eyes. "Ben told me all about you." He leaned against the bar as though he had many hours to stare at her. "And he was right in every regard, my Ben."

Shelby turned her back to Kevin. "How could you do this to me?" she asked Ben.

Ben put his hand on her shoulder. "The woman who lives here is a *friend,* and she's on the other side of the world and will be for many days." He began to rub her back and around to her stomach in a way that was much too intimate in front of Kevin.

A man's voice and a woman's voice were heard down the hall in the apartment. Shelby shrugged off Ben's hands, grabbed her precious winter coat, and was moving toward the door when he caught her shoulders. She could feel his breath, and his voice, murmuring hot on her neck.

"Don't leave. Give Kevin a chance. We'll have a party," and again his voice took on that excessive timbre that he used sometimes on stage, "that you'll never forget. . . ."

Shelby turned to look at him incredulously.

"But I'll send them all away if you like," he added quickly, the rich timbre gone. "This was just a . . . thought." His eyes were too cold.

Kevin called from across the room, "Oh, stay. Do stay! We have *bottles* of Veuve-Cliquot! We have Beluga caviar! We have nights and days to come! We'll pull up the drawbridge and release the portcullis to our castle!"

Shelby felt so stupid. The drink Kevin offered her was probably drugged, and, had she drunk it, she would have wound up a sex slave in this city, as Baldwin had feared but never spelled out. Shelby would go to church every Sunday if she could just get out of this place.

"Don't go." Ben's fingers dug into her shoulders. The

pleading quality in his voice was too brittle to hide his anger. "*Don't*. I'll send Kevin away. Get your stuff and leave, Kev!"

Shelby struggled with the lock.

"I don't want you to go, Shelby. *Please*."

"My, my," Kevin mocked from across the room. "As I live and breathe . . . *Ben Vaughn begs a girl to stay. . . .*"

Shelby pounded the lock with her fist. "Open this door!"

"I don't want you to go . . . Kevin is leaving. Get out of here, Kev, and tell the others to go too. *All of you! GO! This is my place! She gave it to me!*"

Somewhere in the apartment people giggled.

Kevin didn't move.

Ben rushed across the room for his panniers just as Shelby released the lock and turned the heavy knob.

"It's that Negro, isn't it?" Ben called. "You're going to be with that big Negro I met in the Village!"

Shelby raced down the dimly-lit hall, Ben yelling for her to wait, Kevin laughing and calling, "Tell the Negro to join us! I like big black guys!"

When the elevator doors closed behind her, she could hear Ben kicking them with his heavy boots, yelling for her to *Come back, goddammit! You can't leave, goddammit!*

She hurried from the exotic, handwrought elevator, and rushed past the guards and out the door, running from the high windows and winged radiator caps that circled the building like the spokes of a wheel that never stopped turning. She fled from the gargoyles with their ugly drooping beaks and vacant eyes.

It was a building best seen from a distance. Or on a postcard.

She inserted a subway token with a shaking hand, and thanked God as a train appeared at that ungodly hour, because Ben's voice was calling, Ben's steps were pounding down the stairs. The doors thumped closed, and she huddled in the empty car, terrified Ben would appear, or that Kevin would press a grinning face against the dirty glass, still thrusting a glass toward her that held a poisonous liqueur or an aphrodisiac. The bare lightbulbs in the tunnel flared, and the train's screeching brakes sprayed sparks. She was shaking with fear and fury. She was so dumb. So alone.

Her skin hurt from the moaning sound of the word, "*alone.*"

Why had she let herself become so obsessed with Ben? He didn't care for *her*. She had succumbed to his prowess, to his success. She had sold her body for a ride on a motorcycle and front-row tickets to a Broadway show. He hadn't forced her to get a diaphragm. She had gone on her own accord to the smirky doctor he recommended, had lain down on the hard, cold enamel table, placed her feet in the stirrups and slid way down, as requested, while the doctor poked around with smirking fingers longer than was needed.

Alone. She would always be alone.

Shame and anger clawed her body. This city could never be her place. It was a dirty, treacherous, no-man's-land where she could barely see the sky. She belonged in her turret bedroom where the moon shone through the trees. She belonged . . . she didn't know where she belonged. Nowhere. She would always be alone.

It was raining hard when she reached her stop. She ran down the sidewalk, hair stringing in the rain, mascara dribbling down her cheeks, choking on rain and tears and makeup. She raced up the stairs to the apartment, shoved the key in the lock with a shaking hand, and slammed the door behind her. Finally safe in her cave.

There was a message for her on the table: *A man with a deep voice phoned from Paris, France!!! I think he said he hoped Shelby was wearing her lions' teeth, but I could barely hear him!!!!! But calling from Paris, France??? Amazing!!!*

How much did that cost? Weird message, great voice. Is he an actor? Why haven't you told me about him! I didn't get his name. Hugs and kisses, Boojie

34

JULIEN WAS STANDING on a chair in the bedroom, his binoculars aimed at Eulalia's window. Lettie was attending an early-morning prayer meeting at the church. Julien had a good half hour before her return.

He had noticed that, after years of a shuttered existence, Eulalia was raising her shades in the morning, wearing new clothes in bright colors, and walking with a looser swing to her lovely hips. Julien was sure she stitched the clothes herself, because, when he stood beneath her window or crept into Baldwin's house at night, he could hear the clack of the foot-pedal sewing machine.

Julien was certain she had a man in her life after all these years, and that he was not that man was so unfair. It was his *right* to have her. *It was his turn!* And he lived right next door, which would be so convenient for both of them! It was so . . . logical.

And when he did have her, *and it would happen,* he would show her who was boss.

Right now he could only watch her change clothes. And was she shimmying as she unbuttoned her robe? Was her butt wiggling? More importantly, did she know he was watching? Was she showing off for him? It seemed that way. Was she flirting with him?

In the following days, he would make it his business to find out who her new man was. He would patrol and listen, which was an easy thing to do. He had a lot of experience watching and listening, inside and outside that house.

At this moment, however, he had to focus the binoculars with one hand. It was tricky to maintain his balance on the wobbly chair, but he needed this live entertainment before embalming a dead body. He pulled down his zipper, tooth by tooth when . . . OHO! She held up a red dress, preparing to step into it! *Now yank off that robe!* he telegraphed silently. *Get naked for me!* He could almost smell the perfume of her freshly bathed body, feel the smooth surface of her luscious skin.

When the front door shut with a bang, and Lettie's footsteps clattered down the hall, Julien snarled, lost his balance, slipped from his precarious perch, and lost his grip on his new and expensive binoculars that clattered to the floor.

Lettie looked down at him, wringing her hands, not daring to touch him. "Dear me, Julien . . . are you okay?"

"What do you think?" he snarled, standing too quickly, turning to tug up his zipper, ignoring the pain in his shoulder, patting his hair in place. "You put too much wax on this goddam floor, and look what you caused me to do! Can't you do anything right?"

Lettie backed away, hands weaving anxiously over her bosom. "I'm so sorry, Julien. So very sorry! I told Eulalia just yesterday I was worried about you watching birds on top of that rickety chair. I'll remove the wax right away."

Julien whirled to look up at Eulalia's window, and she was there, of course, she was, wearing the new red dress, and smiling triumphantly down at him before she snapped the shade shut with one quick tug.

And Julien felt curiously, though very briefly, unsettled, not because Eulalia caught him spying, but about something more elusive, and about which he had never been aware, and wished he never had been . . . how he frequently lusted after things that never would be his, and maybe shouldn't be his. About how he often planned retributions,

that, if implemented, hardly ever turned out well. About
. . . and this insight was truly alarming . . . about how
angry he felt about so many things. Almost everything.
It was a very unusual insight and it dominated his con-
sciousness for no more than a second or two, but during
those seconds, he felt sad and lonely. Bereft of illusion.

However the frisson of self-awareness was too unsettling.
He must never let himself be disturbed by ridiculous insults
to his ego, like this insignificant slight from Eulalia, who was
shunned by everyone in the community. The woman was
crazy. Always had been. And Julien deserved so much more!

Stop sniveling! he ordered himself. *Thinking too much just
fucks up the brain. It might make a man impotent!*

He turned his back to the window to show his disdain, and
in spite of the pain that ripped through his arm, he threw on
his jacket with a flourish. He pushed Lettie aside, ignoring her
yelp, mouthing words to himself as he strode toward the door.

*Smile while you can, you strumpet! But you won't smile
when I have my turn with your daughter in New York City!*

He jerked his tie straight and wished he hadn't when pain
seared his shoulder. He eased on his new navy-blue cashmere
coat. "I am *somebody!*" he said out loud, as though saying it
made it so. "I own the biggest funeral home in the state of
Arkansas, and I'll own more!" he announced to the closet.
He knotted his silk scarf precisely. He could knot that scarf
with the precision of a noose. "People around this state know
who I am. They know my name! And why? Because I drive
my hearse faster than anyone, because I can make a dead face
look alive, because everyone needs me when they die, *and*
. . . because I am never afraid to speak the truth about the
goddam niggers!"

When he slammed the front door behind him, he was
feeling in charge again, with a new and exciting thought
emerging in his mind. *I might even run for an office . . . State*

Senate, maybe . . . no . . . NO, GOVERNOR! . . . And why not? I laid the way for Faubus. I know more about politics than he does. I've got the money, and I could raise a lot more, and I'm making new friends every day with people who would do anything for the cause of the White Superman!

He straightened his spine, slicked back his hair again, slid onto the slick leather seat of his almost-new hearse, turned on the engine with a cheeky flick of his wrist, and he drove down the street, waving to people, even though it hurt to wave, smiling at people, even though it hurt to smile, reveling in the thought of his exciting future, and already looking for votes.

35

"WELL . . . HE'S EXPECTING ME."

Maxine was lying on the couch, cotton wool stuffed between each toe while the polish dried. She was gasping for air every few words as though she had been running a marathon, while doing a cruel imitation of Bernard's accent and the awkward way he clawed his hands when he was agitated.

"He told me . . . I could have the part . . . if I could get down here . . . in forty-five minutes! So pick up that phone . . . and tell him . . . I'm *HERE!*"

"Bernard was so 'in the moment,'" and Max switched back to her own phony English accent as she lay on the couch, "that every time he opened his mouth he spewed spit, and I was on the front row and got it in my face! I'll probably die of his filthy spit!"

She waved the Frosted Snow Pink fingernail polish bottle back and forth, ridding the air of the foul memory. "And as usual he smelled like he hadn't bathed in years."

"Come on, Maxine," Hank growled. "If you lived like he has to live, you would caterwaul all day long. But he never complains. Not a word."

Max scooped a finger into a bowl of hard sauce and sucked the creamy mixture of butter and sugar and brandy from her long, Frosted Snow Pink fingernail. "You want to hear what happened in the improv or you want to continue your lecture on the milk of human kindness?" Satisfied by Hank's long sigh, and another scoop of sugar and cream, she continued. "So . . . Bernard was pacing back and forth . . .

I'm sure he got those moves watching tigers at the zoo like Ana told us to do, and he had this weird, tigerish look in his eyes, which should have tipped off Jan, who was playing the secretary. But Jan just kept on chewing gum and stroking her gold cross and being her twitty self while she demeaned him. I can't stand the way that girl acts so innocent, when I know she's doing it with Freddie Freyer."

Hank groaned. "Freddie flirts with everybody. He would flirt with you if your choreography weren't so sloppy. You just lie on the floor and twitch your legs and call the dance Dreaming or Dying or Lying on the Beach in the Sun. You're too hard on people, Max. People aren't bad for the most part."

Max dug another fingernail into the hard sauce and sucked it clean. "I'm only reporting the truth, which is this: Jan wouldn't let Bernard see the director. She clapped her hands in his face and ordered him to *leave*, because people like him didn't belong in that building. She said it out loud and we all knew what she meant . . . She thought she could get away with talking to him like that, because she was just *acting*."

Then Max sat up, raised her voice to an even snippier level, and directed it toward Shelby's door. "The only reason Jan was Bernard's partner was because Shelby didn't appear in class *again. He doesn't work with anyone but Shelby, which I personally think is strange.* And why does Victor let her miss classes like she's doing now? *Is she sleeping with Victor too?*"

Hank rushed across the room and clamped his hand on Maxine's mouth. When he sat back in his seat, she yelled, "I knew Ben would dump her!"

"*Leave her alone!*" Hank hissed and raised a fist.

"Ah, you want to hear what happened so you can put it in a novel one day. You're worse than Liebmann, the way you study us all the time." Max imbibed an extra-large nail-ful of hard sauce. "If you want to hear the rest of the story, you'll have to say, 'Pretty please, Maxie.'"

Hank said a grudging, "Pretty please. But keep your voice down, for God's sake."

Max exuded a long-suffering sigh. "Well . . . our Jan just sat like Little Miss Prissy Muffet and clapped her prissy little hands and ordered him to *leave*, with that *We don't let niggers in this building* look. So Bernard reached over the desk . . . they were using that rickety table as the desk . . . and picked her up . . . she's so skinny, that girl . . . and we could see everything she had on, including really ugly underpants . . . I always wear great underwear to that class, because you never know in an improv. It wasn't until it looked like Bernard might actually throw her out the window that Victor told Stanley to stop him . . . as though Stanley, or anyone else, could manhandle Bernard. And then . . . this may be the weirdest part . . . Liebmann began to laugh, and when Bernard heard Victor laughing, he practically dumped Jan on the floor and stormed out of the room and didn't return to class for days . . ." Maxine directed a loud voice toward Shelby's room again, "just like Shelby Korzeniowski!"

Hank shook his fist at Maxine, who clapped her hands together penitently, sat up to pluck the cotton from between each toe and flick it onto the floor. "Bernard said yesterday his next improv was going to be about someone named Elston Howard. I sure hope Elston Howard doesn't promise him a part in a play and then renege. Elston would get clobbered."

Hank looked up from his notepad. "Elston Howard? He's a Negro baseball player. Plays for the Yankees with my hero, Don Larsen. Larson pitched a perfect game this fall, and got his picture taken with Jayne Mansfield hugging him."

"Big deal."

Hank grinned, pantomiming Jayne Mansfield's breasts. "Two big deals!"

"Mine are better," Max said smugly. "Want to see?"

Hank aimed his pencil at her again. "Don't start that, Maxine."

"You started it with Jayne Mansfield." She settled back on the couch. "Bernard talks about Elston Howard like he's some kind of god."

"Elston is a great ball player. Incidentally, I heard you tell Bernard you wanted to do an improvisation with him some time, and he told me he would ask you to do one in a couple of weeks. Usually he just says a flat-out 'No' to anyone but Shelby, so I'm betting it will happen."

Maxine's pleased look said there might be a gift for her beneath the tree after all.

"But when Shelby returns, who knows what Bernard will do. . . ."

Max's face fell, and Hank modified his words.

"He should be assigned to other people, but Liebmann lets Bernard do what Bernard wants to do. But you should let up on Shelby, Max. She needs a break right now."

Maxine raised one carefully plucked eyebrow, plunked the bowl of hard sauce on the floor, and rolled over for a nap.

36

THE PHONE WAS RINGING in the apartment on Riverside Drive. Boojie moved to answer it, but Shelby snapped, "*Don't! It's Ben again. Or that freaky Kevin.*" The ringing stopped, but when it began again, she picked up the receiver and slammed it back on the hook.

The wind was swirling like a dervish over the river, and the bedrock gleamed like a giant straining to hurl the city from its shoulders. Shelby faced the window and inhaled deeply, seeming to imbibe the storm. "I saw a parrot flying outside this window three days ago," she finally said. "Its feather were all puffed up from the cold, and it perched on the sill and talked to me. 'Open up,' the bird said. 'It's cold out here!'

"I wish I had opened the window and let him come inside, but I was afraid of . . . of foreigners, I guess. Then the bird said, 'I love you too!' But I hadn't said anything about love. I didn't love that bird. I told him to fly away. Fly away home. I do hope he didn't freeze to death. I feel bad about that parrot. If he comes again, I'll invite him inside. I read some place that parrots can be great companions. Very sympathetic to those in need."

Boojie continued to pare his toenails with big, dull scissors. "How did you know the bird was a he?"

"Because he was so beautiful . . . bright blue and green and red. He was beautiful, even in the cold. I read somewhere that female parrots are never as beautiful as males, which seems so unfair."

Boojie put down his scissors with a clunk. "When you

see parrots outside a third-floor window in the icy winds of New York City, it's time to go home for the holidays. But right now . . . let's brave the weather and go to the West End Bar for a beer, and tomorrow . . . for even more excitement . . . you'll come to class with me."

Shelby ignored him. "I know I saw a beautiful parrot perched on the sill outside this window. He had a big, yellow beak, and blue and green and red feathers, and he squawked in a deep voice that sounded just like a man's, 'Get out of town! Run for your life!'

"And I don't just see parrots. I see all sorts of portents outside these windows," Shelby continued. "The neon sign across the Hudson blinks SPRY SHORTENING day and night, but I'm certain it's really signaling a sinister message in code to gangsters, maybe. Or spies. I see sunsets that relay fiery messages in New Jersey windows. I see small planes trailing black-and-white banners in strange languages. I see Goodyear balloons with bears in the gondolas yelling, 'Run for your life!'"

Boojie held the scissors midair. "You sure you're okay? Hungry, maybe?"

"Of course, I'm okay. I'm fit as a fiddle!" She gave him a corrosive look. "Look at these arms." She made a muscle with an arm. "Look at this leg." She lifted a well-toned leg and wiggled a foot covered with a yellow foot-warmer.

"But you have been a little . . . cranky . . . lately," Boojie ventured. "A walk in the storm might be a good thing."

"I am not *cranky!*" The new shadows beneath her eyes were dark like her mother's. "And you won, okay. Ben is a *creep.* Quit harassing me about how I feel!"

"Ah, Shelby . . . you never win when a dear friend is hurt. And you are my dearest friend. That goddamn Ben will quit calling. He'll find another innocent."

"I wasn't innocent! I asked for it!"

Boojie stared at the cracks on the ceiling that coiled like the whorls in a fortune-teller's hand. He cleared his throat. "I saw Laurence Olivier yesterday. Vivien wasn't with him."

"You did not." Shelby blew her nose with a large, initialed white linen handkerchief.

"He was just outside the Carlyle Hotel, backlit by steam rising from a manhole. He looked like he was standing center stage. He was dressed in a smashing brown suit and a maroon silk vest with little bitty gold dots. I'm sure his hat was a Borsalino, and . . . *and* he was swinging a fancy walking stick! He looked so . . . *jaunty* I wanted to hug him. I was desperate to get his autograph, but I didn't have a scrap of paper. I would have offered my undershirt, but it's full of *holes*, so all I could do was stare at this gorgeous man whose piercing bluish gray eyes beamed back at me! As he came closer, he smiled at me, tossed me his cane and began this outrageous Charleston, arms flying, toes twirling, and singing in a quirky tenor voice,

"O, That Shakes-pea-ri-an rag
Most in-tel-li-gent, ve-ry, el-e-gant. . . ."

Boojie hopped up to repeat the ditty in his own clear tenor voice, kicking his long legs in a Charleston, slicing the scissors to a dangerous beat,

"O, that Shakes-pea-ri-an rag
Most in-tel-li-gent, ve-ry el-e-gant. . . ."

When Shelby smiled, Boojie sighed, "Ahhhh, she smiles." He stopped dancing and wound his limbs back onto the couch. "I love it when she smiles."

The wind and the rain rattled the windows harder and attacked the buildings and the cars and the people racing for shelter. The world felt vulnerable.

Shelby buttoned Julien's cheerleader cardigan tighter.

"You always see famous people, Booj. Your eyes are always wide open. When I think I see somebody, it turns out they're nobody . . . though . . . I did meet a woman on my way up here on the train who thought *I* was somebody." Shelby smiled, remembering. "You would have loved her, Booj. She was a middle-aged stripper trying to look nineteen. She called herself Cherie Denise, White Goddess of the Jungle, and said she was put on this earth to show off her big boobs to lonely men. And she meant it. She really believed that was her mission in life."

"Bravo!" Boojie yelled, fist to the ceiling. "Bully for Cherie!"

"I hope she's happy in Germany. She married a young soldier who promised she would always have enough money to live on, which was the best thing that had ever happened to her. Aside from showing off her boobs."

Shelby wrote MONEY with her finger on the cold, grimy window. "Cherie tried to help me on the train with this . . . this *monster* I met. She's one of those rare people who is filled with good will . . . like you, Booj. She showed me how to do the bumps and grinds in the middle of the night." Shelby made a slight shimmy, remembering the lesson between the train cars. Remembering the handsome young man in the St. Louis station, the perfect young man whom she would never see again. Remembering Saracen and trying not to. And Charlie. Dear Charlie. Maybe it was Charlie she really loved. She could always count on Charlie.

Then she turned on Boojie almost angrily. "Did you know Olivier thinks method acting is nonsense? Too many messy feelings, too much agony? I read in *Variety* that he dons the character with his costume. It's the results that count, he says."

"Jeez Louise," Boojie muttered. "I heard he reads Stanislavski and slaves over his parts."

Shelby threw her hands in the air, "But who cares? The

only thing that matters in this world is *money*. I would put on blackface like Olivier did in *Othello* if it would pay." She barked a laugh and moved her finger to the scar beneath her jaw. "When I was little, I made some black goop out of anything I could get my hands on, old paint, shoe polish, anything black, and I smeared it all over my body, because I wanted to be black like . . . like my friend, Saracen."

"Really?" said Boojie, very interested. "You thought it would be fun to be black? You were nuts, Shelby."

"I thought . . . I thought I wanted to be black like my friend. He was so beautiful. And he was kind. We were really, really good friends. He is. . . ." Her voice trailed off and began again with a spurt.

"I like these 'as if' things we're doing in class." She clapped an absentminded beat on her thighs. "Those justification things? You're not just saying the words of the script, 'To be or not to be . . .' You're really saying 'everybody hates me, nobody loves me, think I'll go eat some worms.' The subtext of the words. Do you realize that we seldom say what we really mean in real life? It would be dangerous to speak the truth, and most of the time it would be mean. Anyhow, people hate truth tellers. Remember that line from Emily Dickinson . . . *Tell all the truth but tell it slant . . .*"

But she wished she hadn't thought of the poem. Ben, who was nothing but subtext, had taught it to her. "We're always saying one thing and meaning another, so we can survive. Maybe most of us even think like poets and don't realize it." Then her thoughts swerved back to money. "I've *got* to find a job, and soon." When she toppled onto the couch next to Boojie, the damaged springs caused the couch to shake.

"My God, Shelby! I nearly amputated my toe with these scissors! And you're tawkin' too Arkansas agin, honey chile. Watch those diphthongs. Beats me how you can make four syllables out of one-syllable words."

Shelby jumped up, straightened her back, relaxed her jaw, hummed sonorously, and spoke in a monotone, trying to capture each vowel before it could multiply its sounds. "*Money, money, money. I need to earn more money.*" She stopped with a wailing, "What can I do to earn *MONEY*, Booj?"

"Well . . ." Boojie stroked his chin, and stretched his mouth in a bad guy leer. "I have a friend who works in a condom factory checking for holes. He could find you an opening."

Shelby stretched out a long leg and gave him a resounding kick. "Be serious."

"Okay, okay . . . you could sell your blood. And do not leap onto the couch again unless you can sew my toe back on!"

Shelby stared at him in horror. "Sell my *blood*?"

"People do it all the time, babe. I do it regularly. Keeps me fit. Bernard does it too, but he goes to different places so they won't know he's draining his red corpuscles so quickly. Be warned, however: the clinics have dirty doors and sticky green plastic curtains between beds. But the needles look clean, and you walk out with a five-dollar bill for each pint."

Shelby made a retching sound. "I can't do the blood thing. I hate needles. Maybe I'll be a stripper like Cherie, White Goddess of the Jungle."

"That'll be the day."

"Of course, I won't really do it," she added hastily. "But . . . I do have the card of a . . . of a place downtown that pays a lot better than typing. Or waiting tables. And don't waggle your bushy eyebrows like that! I would just be *acting*. And I would *never* take off my clothes."

She tried not to think about the times she had undressed slowly while Ben watched with those ironic black eyes . . . It was not so different from what stripping her clothes on a stage would be like. "Except for that gold cross, Jan took off every stitch in a private moment exercise the other day. That girl is not as innocent as she looks."

"She did it for the sake of art."

"She did it for the sake of Liebmann! I saw that look on his face. It was voyeurism, not art! And he's always goading Bernard to do private exercises that are much too revealing . . . though Bernard doesn't seem to mind. Doing an improv with that guy is so . . . fluid. It's like a dance. I take chances, because I know he'll catch me, but when he really gets going, I just hang on for dear life."

"Watch out, m'dear. You might begin to like Bernard."

"I *do* like him. I work with him a lot, don't I? But he always seems so . . . het up. What does he have to be so angry about?"

Boojie looked at her in disbelief. "He's a *Negro*, dummy. He doesn't feel he *belongs* anywhere . . . the North, the South . . . even the subway. He's the only colored person at school, except D'Arcy, and she's almost white and treats him like dirt. So Bernard stays hidden. We only see him when he's performing, and we don't really see him then, because he's being someone else."

"So who is he when he's at home?"

"He's never at home."

"But he must know he's a terrific actor. And remember in dance class when Ana George told us we would own the movement once we felt it? Bernard is *feeling* those movements. Have you noticed? And she doesn't jerk him around like she used to. Something superhuman is happening between those two. She understands superhuman. She's a witch."

"No, she's not. She's a dance evangelist."

"She's a dictator! She thinks she can do anything she wants."

"Maybe . . . but she's the divine dictator of movement. Anyhow, Bernard even inspired Max. She dragged him to the zoo today to watch the big cats. The sun was shining when they left. I bet she'll come back drenched and bitching."

"Pity. Maybe she'll melt. But she doesn't read Stanislavski the way Bernard does. He also reads that other dog-eared book he carries everywhere, *Invisible Man*. Remember that old movie about the guy who drinks this special formula and becomes invisible?"

Boojie nodded enthusiastically. "Claude Rains plays a scientist who invented stuff that makes people invisible. He even drank some of his ambrosia to give it a try, and he became invisible! But he also went bonkers, and in order to conceal his crazed, invisible self, he wore gloves on his invisible hands and wrapped gauze around his invisible head and pretended he had been in an accident. But when the maid in a hotel happened to see him unwrap the gauze and expose his . . . headlessness . . . she. . . ."

"I saw the movie, Booj! I don't need to hear the plot again!"

"*Okay.* Bernard's *Invisible Man* is not the same. The book is about a nameless Negro from the south whose granddaddy tells him he must always agree with the white man, but with an important difference: 'Agree 'em *to death and destruction*,' his granddaddy says. So this nameless Negro thinks he has to play the white man's game, for a while anyhow, and he sets out for New York City, where he hopes life will be better, but it ain't. First he works in a paint factory. 'If it's Optic White, it's the Right White' is the company's motto, but as I recall, the white paint became optic white because it was mixed with drops of black paint, and . . . I just skimmed the rest of the story."

Shelby remembered Saracen Self had said something about "optic white."

"Why did you skim the rest?"

"Because it's not *my* story. What I do remember is that

this no-name guy loves the way Louis Armstrong sings 'Black and Blue.'" Boojie lowered his chin, mimicking Louis, and sang, "*My only sin / is in my skin . . . All my life through / I've been so black and blue. . . .*"

But Shelby wasn't listening to Boojie. She was thinking about Saracen Self, who wasn't invisible to her, and who knew everything about her, understood everything about her. Their friendship didn't change when he kissed her . . . *and she kissed him back, and asked him to stay.* But she would delete the memory of the kiss, and only remember the friendship part, she could do that, had done that, she told herself. She stared at the storm that pounded the windows in what seemed like a primeval need to destroy the human world and all that was in it so that nature could rule earth once again.

"So this *Invisible Man* guy," Boojie rambled on, raising his voice to be heard over wind and rain, "hooks into the white-owned power company and lights up the ceiling of his basement hideout with a thousand bulbs, like Bernard is doing, because he, *and* Bernard, want to be *visible. To feel free.* To be themselves . . . *to be human, for God's sake!* You get that, don't you? They want to be able to look white people in the eye as equals. Such a small aspiration when you think about it."

"Lots of us have a reason not to look people in the eye."

"If you're talking about Ben, that jerk isn't worth it. And you could never be invisible, Shelby Korzeniowski."

But Shelby didn't hear him. Her mind was seething with memories that swirled in her head as fiercely as the weather. "My father disappeared when I was six years old. He was a stunt pilot. I'd forgotten what he looked like until my mother gave me his picture. I hoped . . . ridiculously . . . that I could find him in New York City. But I haven't found him."

She straightened her back, marched to her bedroom and returned with her father's photograph in its walnut frame. Boojie stared, amazed, from the photograph to Shelby's face.

"And don't say it. *I know we look alike.*" She turned the photograph face down on the floor and put her hand to one side of her mouth, as though creating a wall no one could enter. *No Entry,* the hand said. *Keep your distance.* "My grandmother changed my last name to hers when I was eight. But I took back my real name, my *Papa's* name, that first day at The Acting School. *Korzeniowski.* Remember? *That* is my real name. Mine! Korzeniowski! You mangled it when you first said it."

"I was trying to be funny, " Boojie said meekly. "I'm sorry."

"And I accept your apology. But I nearly passed out when I said the name out loud in class that first time." She placed the photograph on the floor, and curled up on the couch. From that position, she could also see the coffee cans on the table, filled with Charlie's red roses.

One of Max's high heels was propped alongside one of the cans. Shelby sputtered at the sight.

"I told Max she could kill herself clattering up the fire escape in those high heels, but she said Joan Crawford climbed on a chair in high heels in *Mildred Pierce.* 'If Joan can do it, I can do it,' she said. But someday when she forgets her key and staggers, drunk, up the fire escape to climb in the window, she'll fall. And she takes men into her room all the time. When I complain, she smirks, 'Sorry, lovey. You should try it.' And she's always grabbing you and kissing you. Why do you let her do that?"

Boojie became more intent on his toenails. "Don't worry about it."

"And you cannot crawl into my *bed* any more, Booj."

Boojie looked up in dismay. "But I get cold at night, Shelby! And I get so lonely. I get really, really lonely. I just need to snuggle."

"Well, crawl in bed with Max. Everyone else does."

Boojie's head dropped to his chest, and his legs and arms

sprawled out from his body like a long-legged spider. "I don't like to crawl in bed with Max." His voice was muffled. "I won't swirl into space when I'm close to you."

"Ah, Boojie. We're both swirling in space. I just want us to stay friends."

"Precisely," Boojie said eagerly. "Best friends. Sleeping-together friends."

Sleeping-together friends. Shelby and Ben had done "the friendliest thing," but they weren't friends. They had slept together, and used one another's bodies, like renting a room for a few hours in a cheap hotel. She began to breathe as though she had run a very long distance until she erupted into sobs she couldn't stop.

Boojie looked as though he might cry too before he stood up and raced to the bathroom for a damp cloth for Shelby's forehead. When her sobs became intermittent and she closed her eyes, he arranged her more comfortably on the couch, covered her with a blanket, and tiptoed to the record player. Louis Armstrong's trumpet began to wind around the notes of "Black and Blue" in a lonesome melancholy that slid to the next note in the nick of time. It was Louis at his best, trying to staunch the sadness about to break his heart, and create beauty in the midst of deep despair.

"What did I do, to be so black and blue?
I'm white inside / But that don't help my case,
'Cause I can't hide / What's in my face."

Boojie snuggled as close as he could to Shelby, and they both fell asleep to the sweet sounds of the sad music.

37

IT WAS EVENING when the door slammed. Maxine's black hair was plastered to her head like a seal's, her sharp nose red from the cold. She walked to the couch, high heels clicking, turning on lights, disregarding wet fingers and faulty wiring, and kicking the scissors that crashed into Teddy's photograph.

Hank took off his overcoat and shoes, shook himself like a dog, and plopped down on the battered easy chair with an exhausted whoosh. "It's *cold* out there!" he groaned cheerfully. "Your feet must be frozen, Max. How you can walk for miles in those shoes beats me. They better put a pair of high heels in your coffin."

Max was dressed in rain-shiny black leather gaucho pants. A pale blue cashmere sweater was rain-plastered to her breasts, and Shelby's prized, rust-colored winter coat was slung over her shoulder like a side of sopping beef. She stood close to the couch, clearing her throat, rubbing a thigh against Boojie's arm. When Boojie wouldn't rouse, she threw the coat on the floor, encircled him with her wet arms, and kissed him soundly, at which point, he rose from the couch, gagging.

"Ah, Max . . ." Hank protested. "He looked so comfortable."

Max aimed her chin at the ceiling. "Just doing my job, lovey."

"What's that thing on the floor?" Shelby muttered, her voice heavy with sleep. "It's making puddles." She sat up, stared down at it, and whispered in hoarse dismay, "It *can't* be my new coat. . . ."

"It rained." Max shrugged her shoulders by way of apology. "And the coat's not new. You've had it for months, and it's not even a designer coat." She tried to give Boojie another smack on the lips, but he shoved her away and stood up.

Shelby held up the drooling coat. "You've ruined it," she moaned.

"So I'll have it cleaned."

Shelby stared at Max, almost breathless with rage. "You are the most inconsiderate person I've ever met. You have a ton of great clothes that come from God knows who, and you *never* share, and you're always bringing men into your room and making horrible noises, and you kiss Boojie when it's obvious he hates it, and you hog the refrigerator, and you sing so loud the neighbors call the cops, and now you've destroyed my gorgeous new coat!"

When she saw the shattered glass on her father's picture, she screamed, "And you broke the glass on my Papa's picture! *I hate you, Maxine! I really hate you!*" She leaned down to pick up the photograph, but Maxine snatched it first, broken glass littering the floor.

"This dude is your daddy? You've been hiding this handsome dude? And you're almost the spitting image! But you need to use more color on your eyebrows, Shelby. Your daddy is prettier than you are." Max tossed the photograph to the end of the couch. "And haven't you figured out what I'm doing for Boojie? *Gawd*. You are *so* naïve!"

Shelby looked at Max as though she had landed on a planet peopled with monsters.

"Enough," Hank ordered and pushed Max toward the kitchen. "Do your K.P.!"

Max grabbed the back of the couch with both hands, her wet sweater drooling from her body. "Just one minute! Wait one more minute so Boojie can tell his little friend about our bargain!"

"You mean tell her what an ass you can be?" Boojie moved

closer to Hank. "Go do your job, Max. You're not getting out of it this time."

"I *have* been doing my job. You just aren't doing *yours!*" She turned to Shelby and announced with a grand gesture, "Boojie is *gay!*"

Shelby wasn't listening. She was removing glass from the picture frame and, with careful, pinched fingers, placing the biggest pieces on the table by the roses, as though she might be able to reassemble the broken mess.

"He's queer!" Max yelled. "Boojie is a homosexual!"

Shelby looked up and stared at Max.

"He likes men, not women! He does it with men, not women! Do you understand what I'm saying? You cannot be *that* naïve! But he hates being queer, and I'm teaching him to be a *man*. I know he can do it with a woman, because he did it with me. He just needs practice." She pointed an unmerciful finger at Boojie. "But you'll never touch me again, Gordon Hunt the Third, no matter how hard you beg!"

Boojie's freckles seemed to merge, and his face became almost featureless. He glanced woefully toward Shelby, but burst into tears when she started toward him, waving his hands fiercely, and backing away.

"Ahhhh, Max." Hank sighed. "Why did you have to do that?" And he took the Boojie by the arm and steered him gently down the hall towards Boojie's bedroom.

The only sound in the living room was the rain battering the building, until Shelby asked, not just Max, but the room, perhaps the world, "How do you keep it straight? I didn't know homosexuals existed until a couple of years ago. Sometimes I can tell, but often they look like . . . well . . . anyone else. So how can you tell? Is there a trick?"

Max's hands were pressed on either side of her head as

though it were about to split. Her sopped leather pants made a soughing sound as she tapped her toes. She ignored Shelby, perhaps didn't hear her.

"All I did was tell the truth and try to help him," Max moaned. "And I am *not* too hard on people. I'm tired of hearing that shit." She whirled toward Shelby. "Everybody loves sweet little innocent you, but I know what you've been up to with Ben, and, believe me, he needs far more than you can ever give him! He'll never settle for a *good* girl."

Shelby's voice was dull. "It's over with Ben and me. It never should have begun."

Max gave a scornful toss of her head. "You were bad news from the moment you fell down the stairs at school like it was an accident, throwing your skirt over your head, flirting with everyone. And yes, half of our class is gay! Victor is gay, but surely you know that much!"

Shelby stared at Max. "But . . . but . . . he's so sexy. And he's *married*."

Max opened her mouth to say something, then grimaced as though there were no earthly use. Her toe-tapping increased.

"Is Hank . . . ?" Shelby asked querulously.

"Oh, for God's sakes, *no*. Don't you know *anything*?" Max slumped over with a dreadful moan, her long, red fingernails gouging into her black pants. "Why did I do that to Boojie? I *love* Boojie. Why can't I keep my big mouth shut?"

Then she spun on her wet high heels and rushed out the door, clattered down the stairs, dripping water, and ran into the December cold without anyone's coat to keep her warm.

Shelby moved in a circle as though searching for an exit that didn't exist. Then she picked up the blanket from the couch and shuffled forlornly down the hall toward Boojie's room where he was lying in bed in a fetal position, his back to the open door. Hank sat in a chair by the bed.

"Is he alright?" Shelby mouthed, pointing to Boojie.

Hank shrugged his shoulders in a silent "maybe yes, maybe no."

She walked closer to Boojie's ugly Salvation Army bed.

"I'm here, Boojie," she said softy. "It's me, Shelby."

Boojie didn't move.

Hank rose quietly, and left the room. Shelby sat in the chair and put her hand on Boojie's shoulder. "You are my *friend*." She kissed his cheek and placed her cheek against his. "You will always be my very dear friend. And I already thought you might be homosexual." She drew the blanket up to his chin. "Believe it or not, there are homosexuals in Little Rock."

It was Boojie's turn to sob. When he reached out a hand from beneath the blanket, Shelby curled up against him on the narrow bed with her arm tight around him to keep them both from swirling into space.

38

SHELBY POLISHED THE star sapphire with the palm of her hand, readjusted the G-string, and tugged at the fringe on the silver bra that barely covered her breasts. There was no way the costume would cover another millimeter of flesh, and still she tugged, jiggling herself in place, sucking in her stomach, trying to conceal the lions' teeth beneath the silvery boa.

Baldwin would hate that Shelby wore the ring in this place, but Shelby needed it on her finger. And Baldwin would never know.

The drums from the little band boom-da-da-boomed, and decades of cigarette smoke seeped from every dim corner of the striptease club. But the smoke couldn't obliterate the stench of sex.

Shelby peeked from behind the dusty blue curtain. The spotlights were so bright, the audience seemed blacked out, and she nearly shouted with relief. If she couldn't see faces, she could survive. But when her vision adjusted, she groaned at the sight of open-mouthed men, heads thrust forward like the gargoyles on the Chrysler Building.

The performer on stage was beginning a series of serious bumps and grinds, her pudgy hands thrust high, her fingers lit with zircons, her screaming red hair piled high. Her cutout bra revealed pasties she rolled around her nipples like jumbo marbles, and as the grinds became more prolonged and the bumps more emphatic, she unclasped her bra with a practiced flip of the finger, and let her massive breasts pour forth. A surge of animal excitement coursed through the room. Men stood and shouted, their faces shiny and fierce. An insolent smile emerged on the dancer's tired face, and she twirled those pasties with muscular magic.

Shelby was shivering from cold and terror. She had stuck the pasties so tightly to her own nipples they hurt. Arnie had volunteered to help her. He seemed totally professional as he assisted other dancers with the same chore. *Like sticking a stamp on an envelope,* he grinned as he pushed his thumb onto a pastie. *Now she's ready to go!*

But Shelby preferred to stick her own stamps, even though Saracen's necklace got in the way like a pesky fly.

Arnie hadn't been pushy about her dance. When she appeared one afternoon at *Honey's Hot House!!!! Our Flowers Bloom All Night!!!!* he said, "Just give it a try," eyeballing her with the excitement of a trainer who has found a horse that might win the Derby. "With that hair and that body, if you don't do nothing but stand still, the boys'll go nuts. Move a little, they'll love it so much I'll prolly have to call the police. Later, maybe you'll take off the boa and wave it around like this..." And Arnie demonstrated, a big man verging on fat, moving his shoulders suggestively. "Oh. And men like to see nipples...."

Shelby rushed toward the door when Arnie said "nipples."

"No, no! Wait! Don't give nipples a thought!" Arnie shouted, hopping up surprisingly fast for a man his size. "Cherie would kill me if I don't do right by you! All you got to do is look... I don't know... mysterious? Yeah, or pretend...*just pretend*... you're in the shower... starkers."

When Shelby whirled again, he shouted, "*NO!* You don't have to pretend you're starkers! But you know how to pretend something sexy, don't you? You can move your butt a little, cain't you?" he pleaded. "Ain't you a actress?"

Move like a woman, walk like a woman about to meet her lover. Pretend. That was all she had to do, she told herself, as she waited backstage at Honey's. *Pretend* she was an

American agent in France *pretending* to be a stripper whose mission was to steal a German officer's plans to blow up the Statue of Liberty. It was her patriotic duty to move sensually, with the German—in the shower. She had to distract him so she could steal his plans. It was not a perfect improvization, but Ingrid Bergman had performed a similar role in *Notorious*. Sort of.

Then, for some unearthly reason, she thought of her father. What if he were in the audience? What if this, of all places, was where they would meet, because he happened to be in New York City and decided to go to a burlesque show? Of course, he would never do such a thing, but *if* he did, and *if* he recognized her face (which he certainly would), he would be so appalled he would disappear. Forever this time! The thought made Shelby want to beat her head against the unstable, wooden wall.

"Arnie!" she whispered frantically toward the side of the stage. "*Arnie!*"

Arnie came running to her side. "What is it? I got to pull the curtain in three minutes. They don't like to wait out there."

"I need . . . I need a cigarette!"

"You said you didn't smoke."

"I changed my mind."

He handed her his lit cigarette from his yellow-stained fingers and ran back to the curtain. Shelby mouthed the end as she might a bottle of Coca-Cola, inhaled deeply, and immediately hawked a series of ragged coughs.

The dancer onstage gave an angry backward kick toward the curtain until Shelby stopped coughing, caught her breath, and wiped tears from her cheeks with the tips of her fake, silver fingernails. She dropped the cigarette to the floor and demolished it with a silver four-inch heel.

Not just sex, she whispered to herself, still breathing hard. This was about espionage, and when it was over, she would be paid good money. *Remember the money,* she told herself.

She would act out a private moment, something she resisted in acting class. She would pretend she was in the shower with the German officer. A warm heart and a cool mind. That's what it took to be a good actor. Think of warm water falling over her body. Particularize. But keep a cool head in the warm shower.

The drummer did his best to pull the bass and the piano along to the beat of her entry music, and when the curtain opened, Shelby Howell Korzeniowski was standing tall and nearly naked on Honey's Hot House stage.

The spotlight flared into her eyes, and she drew her hand over her face in a reflexive, protective gesture. *But a stripper mustn't look startled or confused!* A stripper had to look *bold,* so she thrust her arms straight up to the ceiling and pretended that, in the service of her country, the United States of America, she was in the shower with a handsome German officer. When she could almost feel warm water raining from above, she began to move her pelvis in the way that Cherie Denise, White Goddess of the Jungle, had taught her, and Ana George, the great modern dancer, had taught her, and a big-time actor, who had a leading role on the Broadway stage, had taught her.

39

"Well, lookie here!"

Shelby nearly stumbled down the stairs of Honey's stage door exit when she heard the voice. She had been so eager to leave, she hadn't removed her inch-thick make-up, and was still struggling with her shrunken coat.

"It's Miss Little Rock!" Julien Hutchins's breath steamed into the cold from the gap between his teeth which made him look like a small dragon wearing a handsome, navy-blue cashmere overcoat. His hair was darker than Shelby remembered . . . but surely a man wouldn't dye his hair.

"I been to two county fairs, two goat ropings, and a bull-dog race, and I ain't never seen anything like you up on that stage! And all you did was take off your boa and that little jacket! We didn't even get to see your pasties! They got some good shows in Dallas, but yours took the cake, Shelby Howell! You had us stomping our feet! Why'd you run out on us boys, sugar?'"

Shelby felt stunned for an instant, then turned to run back into Honey's, but Julien lunged to grab one of her ankles with a surprisingly strong grip. "Now where we going to have us some fun?" His awkward perch made his grinning face look macabre. "You name the place! We'll have us a hot time in the old town tonight!"

Shelby gave him a hard shove with her other foot, and he landed with the lucky bones of a drunk, still holding tight to her ankle, and jerking her with clippity-clop high-heeled steps as she tried to keep her balance down the stairs to the pavement.

"What is wrong with you?" she yelled at him. "And how . . . how in the world did you find me?"

He got to his feet in a wobbly dance of cold and excitement. "I knocked at your door, that's how! Your Momma got your address wrong, but I checked with Baldwin, and she set me straight. Baldwin and me is buddies, and when some good-looking little lady with wild black hair and great legs answered your door and told me you were at Honey's Hot House, I couldn't believe my ears! Honey's is one of my regular New York City places!"

He lowered his voice to an insinuating drone. "You was just practicing in the Miss Little Rock contest, wasn't you? Getting ready to show it all in the Big City, wasn't you?"

He moved a step closer, and Shelby jerked up her purse like a battering ram. "What's come over you?"

"Come over *me?*" His rubbery lips slid sideways. "The question is what's come over *you?* But hell, whatever it is, I love it!" He winked at her, blinked at her. "Now let's you and me get ourselves in the taxi over there and go have us a good time. . . ." though it was clear Julien's good time had begun earlier in the day.

"Baldwin will kill you for talking to me like this!"

Julien's expression changed a fraction. "Let's don't go taking Baldwin's name in vain. And what you think she gonna say if she hear where I found *you?*"

Shelby caught her breath. "I'm *never* doing this again no matter how broke I get. You saw how I ran off that stage!"

"Aw, you can trust me, Shelby Howell. I'm your old buddy boy, ain't I? And I ain't never gonna tell her I saw a big nigger walk out of your apartment with a tall, red-headed skinny white boy. I been looking forward to this night with you ever since you left town!"

Shelby's voice was frigid. "I can't go out tonight. I have

to study for a class. I'm on my way to the subway right now."

"You can't go home this late on a subway."

"I take the subway any time of the day and night, and no one has ever grabbed me like you just did!"

"Come on, sweetie, relax . . ." he whined. "It's me, your ole friend, Julien Hutchins! We'll go to your apartment, you'll change your clothes, and I'll take you to the Stork Club in this taxicab. Betcha never been to the Stork Club! And you can tie my naughty hands behind my back if you want to! We'll buy us some rope, and you can drag me hogtied into the Stork Club!"

"Baldwin wouldn't like that, Julien."

"But Baldwin ain't here, baby doll. Baldwin's back in Little Rock where the sun don't shine. I got us a taxi cab waiting right over there. . . ."

Shelby stood very still, shivering from the strip club experience, and now Julien, and from the cold, but with a plan forming in her mind. In his current state, Julien might give her clues about what happened to her father. He had always lived next door, he should know something. And actually, it would be a lot easier to go home by cab this time of night.

"Okay. Take me to the apartment. But if you lay one finger on me, I'm out of the taxi. And you can't come inside. I have roommates and we have rules."

Julien held up his gloved hands. "I'm just up here to buy me some caskets. You wanna come with me tomorrow and see some fancy caskets, I'm your man. They got a makeup display at this place you won't believe, Shelby Howell, and you could use some of that makeup for your act. Guaranteed to last for a long performance! But you did a real good job on your face tonight. I like a woman who knows how to put on her makeup."

Shelby gave him an icy stare. She hated her makeup. It made her look like a whore and was beginning to itch. She had to get the stuff off her face before it gave her a rash.

"Okay, okay," he said. "Change the subject." He opened the cab door and withdrew a package. "Surprise from your grandmomma!" He giggled, threw it back inside like a bone for a dog, then, more giggling, snatched it back again.

Shelby sighed, climbed in, and backed into the far corner. Julien might have an agenda, but she was in control.

The ride was tolerable. Shelby hugged her window, and Julien kept to his side. She had planned to ask about her father in the cab, but Julien wouldn't stop bragging about the role he played in shaving the number of Negro applicants for admittance to Little Rock Central High from eighty to thirty-two, and counting. He also exulted in Orval Faubus's push for interposition, a word that took him several attempts to pronounce. She had no idea what the word meant, and doubted Julien did either. She was busy plotting how to wangle the truth about her father while standing in the hall. She would not let this besotted man set one foot inside the apartment. *And* she was worried about the makeup. She had to get it off her face.

When they arrived at her address, she dashed up the three flights; turned the lock with her key, preparing for an escape inside; and put her back to the door just as Julien appeared, panting from the climb.

She snapped her fingers and said brightly, "I just remembered something I need to ask you!"

"Wait a minute, wait a minute!" Julien cried, brandishing the package. "Baldwin gave me talking points, and I got to report back to her! She won't be happy if she don't get a report!"

"Don't worry. I'll tell her how kind you were to bring the package up three flights. But I can't wait to see what she sent. Let's open it right now!" Shelby held out an eager hand for the package. "We can't go inside. It's too late to disturb my roommates," She lied. "Like I said, we have strict rules about late hours." Lying again.

"No, ma'am!" Julien jerked the package out of reach like a child playing keep-away. "No questions until we're both inside!" And more quickly than seemed possible for a man half-inebriated, he shoved her aside, turned the knob, and squeezed himself through the doorway. "I'll just get this stuff sorted," he called, rushing to the couch as though it were home base, "and you can ask me any question you want. Anybody home?" he called proprietarily.

When there was no answer, Shelby sighed and followed him. He almost fell onto the lumpy couch, still clasping the brown package against his coat with both gloved hands, knees tight together. He looked smaller on the lumpy couch, like a harmless errand boy.

"Baldwin told me to take a good look around," which he was doing, "and what do I see but my Razorback sweater over there on that chair, and don't that make me feel good? And roses all over the place like it's summertime. Wonder who they're from? Should I tell Baldwin?" But his tease was innocuous. Nothing to worry about. "And there's Baldwin's ole travelling trunk over there. Won't she be happy when I tell her it's on show in the living room instead of packed away in that dusty corner of her attic!"

A brief grin transformed Julien into someone more devious, and the thought of his lusting after Baldwin's house, and probably prowling its spaces, made Shelby wish Boojie or Hank would come home. Even Max. She would be really happy if Max walked through the door.

"Okay," she said briskly. "You open the package while I take off this makeup. It's itching like crazy. Then I'll ask my questions."

"Whatever makes you comfortable," Julien said, in his most affable manner. He lowered his head and fumbled with the string on the package.

Shelby walked into her bedroom, slathered cold cream on her face and wiped it off with a gob of tissues. She looked like a ghost with no eyebrows, and that was good. Ghosts had no sex appeal. But when she turned from her bureau, Julien was standing in the doorway, his hands covered with red woolen footwarmers.

"Special delivery man! Knocking on your door!"

He had been drinking again. She could smell liquor from where she stood. "And this is what I call a nice little space you got for yourself. I see you got your quilt from your bed at home, you got your Razorback pennant on the wall, just like in Little Rock. . . ."

"You . . . you've been inside my room at home." Shelby's heart beat faster.

"And I sure do like to think of you wearing my sweater over your beautiful booty," Julien giggled.

Shelby moved purposefully toward the doorway. "Okay, Julien. I hear your taxi honking. Your bill must be getting really high."

Julien blocked her way with his red paws, a stupid grin on his face. "You're a beautiful woman, Shelby." His body jerked with antic energy. "You made me feel soooo good when you were on that stage, moving your hands all around your body, but never quiiiite touching it . . ." Julien pantomimed her seductive movements with the foot warmers. "And you were doing it for me, weren't you? You saw me out there. You were bumping your butt for *me!*"

When he moved toward her, she could see that his fly was unzipped, and his erection was humped against his shorts.

"Oh, my God . . ." Shelby's eyes swerved back to his face. "I wasn't looking at anyone tonight! I didn't see anyone, *and I was praying to God no one could see me!* I *hated* being on that stage! That's why I ran off! Now you turn around and go

out that door like the gentleman you've always been to me!
You're my grandmother's good friend, and you have a wife
named *Lettie!* I'll forget this happened if you leave *now!*"

Julien let the footwarmers slip from his hands, and his
manicured fingers touched one another in supplication. She
tried to keep her eyes on his face, but it was an amazement
to her that a man so skinny could have such a big erection.

"But, baby," he wheedled. "You were rubbing yourself!
You want to rub something, rub *this.* . . ." With great pride
and tenderness, he put one hand on his bulge.

"*Get out of here, Julien Hutchins! NOW!*"

"You earn chicken feed at that joint, Shelby Howell! I
know what those girls earn! And Baldwin's gonna lose that
old house of hers If I don't help her! All you gotta do to help
her is help me now! Just a little help, baby!"

Shelby stopped her tirade, confused.

Julien's mocking laugh was shrill. "Didn't know that, did
you, little lady? That old woman can't pay the taxes, and soon
I can buy that house at auction for peanuts! But Shelby . . ."
His voice oozed oleaginously again, "*Beeyootiful Shelby . . .
I could help your granny if you would pleasure me some.*"
He reached out and yanked her against his body, his laugh
triumphant, his breath nauseating.

"*Take your hands off me, you animal!*"

"Aw, sugar . . ." that guttural laugh again . . . "you're just
begging for it, ain't you!" He smashed himself harder against
her body, and each time he smashed, the lions' teeth sliced
through his Hathaway shirt. But he was impervious to lions'
teeth, impervious to anything except the rush of his own blood.

"*I'll tell every human being in Arkansas! And when I tell
Baldwin, she will kill you! You know she will! She'll call the
Marines!*"

He yanked down her sweater and tore off her brassiere
straps, but by this time, Shelby gave no thought to naked

breasts or drooling spit or the destruction of her good sweater. She wanted to survive. *She wanted to destroy.*

"Oh, my God. . . ." He moved his mouth toward her breasts. "See? *See what you do to me!*"

Shelby wriggled hard to sock Julien's grotesque front teeth, even as he ripped the buttons from her jeans, but his strength increased with her resistance, until she couldn't move her arms.

He did freeze at a sudden noisy clatter when Maxine crawled over the windowsill from the fire escape, yelling, "Anybody home?" She slammed the window shut and yelled louder, "It's cold as a witch's tit out there!"

Julien clamped an odiferous hand over Shelby's mouth, gouging deep into the side of one eye, seized both her hands with his other undertaker's hand, and tethered her with his body.

"Anybody in this place?" Max yelled louder. Her voice was followed by the clatter of a record dropping from the stack, and Sophie Tucker's booming voice expanding the already agitated air:

"Some of these days. . . .
You'll miss me, honey. . . ."

Max joined the song, her voice as voluble as Sophie's.

"Some of these daaaaaaaa . . . a . . . ays.
You'll feel so lonely. . . ."

Almost immediately there came thumping on the floor, as though the occupant in the apartment below had anticipated Max's duet, and had a stick at the ready.

Max thrust her arms in the air and sang even louder.

"You'll miss my huggin'. . . .
You'll miss my kissin'. . . ."

Sophie and Max's singing flooded the apartment, at the

same time that Julien slobbered in Shelby's ear, "Help me a little, sugar. . . ."

Help him? Shelby marshaled her forces and heaved up with her body in a snorting effort to knock him away, which only increased her pain. But when she opened a slit of a throbbing eye, she had the bewildering impression that Julien's hair was sliding to one side of his head.

"Okay." His laugh was giddy. "You'll have to give me a blow job! Won't take long, I promise . . . I'll just gonna scoot up some like this . . . put my man in your mouth . . . *and don't kick at me like that, honey! It's not nice!"*

The music grew louder as he pushed the back of her head farther into the mattress, and shoved his weight squarely onto her stomach.

Shelby tried to scream Max's name until her lungs nearly burst, but the only sound that emerged was a strangled choke. She knew Max was strutting around the living room singing to an imagined audience, waving one hand like a lasso while Shelby was being brutalized! *Hear me, Max!* she tried to scream. *Help me!*

The pounding from the apartment below increased Max's volume, while Julien's swollen penis crawled up Shelby's stomach like a separate organism with its own agenda. If he pushed it into her mouth, she knew she would vomit and strangle to death, but if she didn't open her mouth, he would smash her teeth. She kicked her legs as high as she could in a futile effort to knock him away.

The thump from the apartment below changed to banging at the front door, comingled with the sound of Max's heels hammering across the floor and screaming, "Alright! Alright, you peons! *I AM OF THE THEATAH! I MUST PERFORM!"*

She stormed out of the living room, ignoring the knocking and was belting out the last verse of the song, a cappella, as she passed Shelby's open door.

When she saw a man on top of Shelby, Max let out a whoop of approval, "Okay, Shelby! Way to go!" and slammed her own door behind her.

Julien, distracted by Max's proximity, let his hand slip a fraction, enabling Shelby to jerk herself up, and causing the sharp teeth on the necklace to scrape the side of his penis, just as his semen exploded. He was screeching even before she pulled back her fist, slammed it into his nose, and screamed, "Help me, Max! Help me!" forcing herself to holler with a throat that was bloodied and raw.

When Max ran into the room, Julien was already on his feet, pin-striped trousers dangling around his ankles, Hathaway shirt ripped, silk tie askew and sticky with semen. His flaccid member was scraped deep on one side, and his head . . . incomprehensibly to Shelby . . . was bald, with a dark brown toupee, streaked with semen, hanging from one of his ears. But Julien's eyes were fixed only on his penis, a look of agonized disbelief on his face.

The sight of those skinny white legs infuriated Shelby even more. They were the same dead-white legs she had seen as a child when Saracen lifted her to spy on Julien. Where was Saracen when she needed him? Where was Charlie? *Where was her father?*

However, on this December evening, she leapt up by herself from the bed and began to pound Julien's back with both fists, her scratched and bruised breasts bouncing painfully with each blow. But pain didn't stop her bombardment.

Julien didn't try to defend himself. He didn't even seem to feel the blows. He was crying and concentrating on stuffing his penis inside his trousers, as though tending a beloved, wounded pet.

Max ran into the room, snatched the pillow from the floor and began to pummel his head, feathers floating while she spewed venom, "You bastard! You sonuvabitch!"

The pounding from the apartment below began again.

"Call the cops!" Max screamed. "We caught a rapist up here!" She threw down the pillow, grabbed the Italian loafers and also used them to pummel. The room was alive with flailing arms and feathers and Julien crying, "Stop, for God's sakes! Stop it! I love her! Can't you tell? Tell this demon to stop, Shelby Howell!"

Shelby's breath was shallow, her torn sweater trailing from her hand. She limped after Julien, who was stumbling after Max, who was darting back into the living room from the kitchen with their only butcher knife held aloft in a threatening stance.

But Julien was staring at the toupee that had fallen onto the living room floor. He gave an anguished cry, and made frantic, motherly sweeps over the soft sprouts on top of his head, as though the toupee surely must still be there, his own small, hairy, beloved pet animal.

Shelby blinked hard, trying to clear her vision, and made a limp effort to cover her breasts with the rag of her sweater.

Max snatched the toupee, grabbed Julien's coat from the couch, flung it over her arm, and roared, "Don't take another step!" She circled the butcher knife in the air like Joan of Arc's sword.

Shelby motioned Max to stop with a gesture that wrenched her wounded body. "Wait, Max . . . please wait! I need him to tell me why my father left Little Rock. . . ."

Max looked at her, uncomprehending . . . but she waited.

"If you tell me why my father left Little Rock, I won't say a word about . . . about what you tried tonight, Julien. I'll swear in blood, if you want, and there's plenty of my blood on my body and on the bed and on you to swear with. So tell me . . . you lived next door . . . *why did my father disappear?*"

But Julien turned away with a grimace, as though encountering something disgusting. "I can't look at you like

that, Shelby Howell . . . nobody could!" His stance was unsteady, one hip and the opposite knee slumped together, trying to ease his pain. "You need to put on some clothes! If I'd
a thought you were that kinda girl, I wouldn't of come here!
And I need my shoes too. That black-headed devil took my
shoes! And tell her to give me my coat. . . ."

"You sonuvabitch!" Max hollered. "I hope she bit it off!"
Julien clutched his wounds and moaned. "And you call
her by her right name! You call her Shelby Korzeniowski!
Korzeniowski was Joseph Conrad's name!"

Julien looked so stunned, for a moment he forgot his
misery. He had no idea who Conrad was, but he knew who
Teddy Korzeniowski was. "You use that Polack name up
here?" he sneered, as though using the foreign name was
far more degrading than her stint as a stripper, or his effort
to rape her.

Shelby ignored the jibe and croaked, "Just tell me what
got my parents in the papers, and I'll never say a word about
your . . . behavior tonight. . . ."

"I don't care what you tell!" he screamed. "Tell 'em! Everyone in Little Rock saw that picture of you getting on the train
with that nigger!"

The pounding on the floor began again.

"And I'll tell people I saw a nigger boy come out of your
apartment too! And I'll tell 'em you're a whore in a sleazy
strip joint, that you're as wild as your momma and your old
man were put together! He tried to snatch you from Baldwin's
house when your momma was in the booby hatch, and betcha didn't know that! I heard him yelling at Baldwin in that
gutter language of his! But you were with Jessie and your little *nigger boyfriend in their nigger house!*" Julien was weasel-
ing his way toward Max and the toupee as he spoke.

But Max was on alert. She stomped her high heels like a
matador and ran toward Julien, knife in hand and he crabbed

out of her way, whimpering, cradling his penis.

"Wait, Max!" Shelby croaked.

Max stopped, knife aloft.

"You said my father came back to get me?"

"I know what I heard," he snarled. "The windows were open, weren't they? But I never told anyone. I'm an undertaker. I never tell about the stuff I've seen, and believe me, I've seen it all! I kept my mouth shut about that night, just like you'll keep yours shut about tonight. The bank could go easy on Baldwin if I said the word. I know those tax boys in Little Rock! They would call off the dogs for me."

Shelby hated him so profoundly she couldn't speak.

"And I need my shoes too. That's part of the deal. My bare feet could stick to that freezing sidewalk. And I need my coat. It's a brand-new coat." His eyes darted around the room. "And my cheerleader sweater . . . I want my sweater back. When I gave you that sweater, I thought you were a nice girl!"

Max snorted, "I hope it's not just your feet that fall off," and she tossed the hairpiece into the air, giggling and running to catch it on her head.

Julien scuttled, groaning, to capture the prize, but Max lunged at his wounded groin with the knife, then clattered across the floor, Julien's shoes in hand, and opened the window. Frigid air poured into the room.

When Shelby yelled a husky "No!" Max looked back at her.

"My ring! Baldwin's ring! He must have my ring!"

Max, butcher knife in hand, snarled, "Give it to her, you rat!"

Julien pointed to the toupee, eyes narrowed, "Give me *that* in exchange."

"Give him his hair, Max," Shelby rasped. "Let him have the filthy thing. But first get my grandmother's ring."

Max kicked up a petulant heel, pranced back and forth,

grabbed the ring from his hand like a greedy crow, tossed the toupee at his feet, then ran to the window and threw his shoes down the fire escape. The shoes fell in slow motion, bouncing from stair to stair, icicles breaking, shoes thumping on every stair, and Julien wailing, "Nawoooo!"

Max slammed the window shut and moved toward Julien with the knife, barking like an attack dog. Julien hugged his hairpiece to his bosom, apparently cowed, then shot out a hand and twisted her wrist with his mortician's grip. She screamed and dropped the knife, which gave him time to open the door and slip and slide, sock-footed, down the stairs and into the glacial weather, but without his shoes and without his coat, and without a taxi in sight in the wee, small, freezing hours of a Sunday New York morning.

Shelby was seated on the couch, enveloped in a faded green chenille robe and her old yellow foot warmers. The se-men-sticky red foot warmers had been thrown in the trash.

She reached for another Kleenex, spat in it, and threw it onto the bloody heap accumulating on the floor. Her tongue bled, her right eye was swollen shut, the other eye was bare-ly open, and bruises were spreading like rainbow-colored oil slicks over her skin.

"I hate him," she rasped.

Max nodded emphatically. "He should be put away. So let me call the police! He'll be the only person in Manhattan who's outside in this weather. And while we're at it, let's call his wife and your mother and your grandmother and tell them what he did! *And* let's call the casket cops and get him blackballed! We could put him in jail with all the evidence he left.

"As for what he said about your family . . ." Max hesitated, uncharacteristically searching for the right words, "He was making up stuff, Shelby. I've been around a lot of creeps who make up stuff. Anyone who works with dead bodies all the time is bound to make up weird stuff."

Max chugalugged the rest of her Ballantine, but kept her eyes on Shelby as though collapse still might be imminent. "That man would rather climb a tree and lie than stand on the ground and tell the truth. The only thing I would ask him is when he was going to jump in front of a train . . . which he'll probably want to do with his pitiful pee-pee so sore! And you notice how *little* it was? And he'll surely get pneumonia without a coat and shoes, and that wig of his will freeze to his head with his own juice!"

Max began to heave big snorts of laughter. "He wanted that toupee so bad! Did you see his face? And he'll *never* find the subway, and *never* find a cab on a night like this! We should report him to the police just to save his hide!"

When Max's laughter subsided, she looked at Shelby who still seemed totally depleted. "You need something stronger to drink, and . . . here it is!" Max waved Julien's silver flask in the air. "Excellent bourbon in a monogrammed silver flask . . . I gave it a quick taste test . . . plus a pair of loafers frozen to the fire escape, to be retrieved by Boojie tomorrow, *and* . . ." Max gave Julien's coat a kick, "a classy, navy-blue cashmere coat with his initials embroidered on the red satin lining! And, baby, it's cold outside!"

Shelby huddled deeper in her robe and balanced the sapphire on her palm. The ring wouldn't fit on her swollen finger. "I chipped my ring when I socked his nose. But it was worth it." She tried to smile at Max. "And you saved me. If you hadn't come into my bedroom . . ." Tears stung her eyes and rolled down her chapped, bruised cheeks as she considered her fate if Max hadn't appeared.

Max waved her hand uncomfortably. "Forget about it. What you need is to stomp up and down and say 'fuck' a lot. That always makes me feel better. Say *fuck, fuck, fuck!* and then

. . . *retaliate!* Sprinkle the salt of revenge on that slug! Wear his coat when you go home at Christmas! He'll tremble when he sees you wearing the coat . . . and it's a lot better looking than the one I ruined." Max looked away from Shelby. "I'm really sorry about that coat. But with your blonde hair, you'll look like Greta Garbo in this navy cashmere.

"As for your gratitude . . . no way do I want gratitude. What I deserve is a kick in the butt. First of all, I shouldn't have told that bastard you were at the strip joint. And I've done a few other things I shouldn't have. When Ben went after you, I got crazy and mean . . . even though I knew it wouldn't last. I'm sorry about all of the mean stuff."

"It didn't last with Ben," Shelby whispered. "And it shouldn't have."

"But you and I are okay now, aren't we? We're going to be friends now?" Max looked down uncomfortably. "I'd like us to be friends. I could use a friend."

40

Dear Shelby Howell,

Julien was so disappointed he did not get to lay eyes on you in New York City. But this huge Nigra stole his coat and his shoes and broke his nose so bad there is a big blue mark on it. It hurts me just to look at it.

And he got the worst croup up there in that place. Can you imagine being knocked down in the bitter cold for your coat and shoes, and by a Nigra who was at least six feet four inches tall and had big yellow teeth, and an ugly scar all the way down his cheek? I pray to God in heaven you will come home and settle down here where people love one another. Julien couldn't even order his caskets up there, which was his sole purpose in going. He's down to the bare minimum, and because that savage broke his nose and injured his right hand, his help has to do all of the . . . you know . . . body work. Let's hope nobody we know dies for a while. I hear the help is not nearly as good as Julien is with that . . . makeup. He learned how from his daddy. They used to live on top of that mortuary, which must be a terrible thing for a child to think about, all the dead people beneath his bed. Though, of course, it didn't affect Julien a bit. He said he loved living up there, because he could just walk down stairs to help his daddy paint the faces of the dead people. He loved to paint faces even then. But dear me, what a way to raise a child.

But in spite of his terrible ordeal up there in that city, Julien has been such a good friend to me in the past weeks. I have been having a little bit of trouble with some tax matters, and he is *going to get the entire mess fixed. He says the Federals will have to pay me money when he is through helping me! He wanted me to tell you that good news.*

By the by, I read in the paper that it snowed where you are, but do not make snow ice cream. They say that snow up there is radioactive.

And, Shelby Howell, you must see Charlie while you are here for the Christmas vacation. He has not said a word about it, but I think he has forgiven you for breaking up with him. If that is what happened. Of course, I don't know what happened, because you never tell me a thing, but Julien told me that Charlie has been seen with that red-headed girl they say is on the television weather show. I don't have one of those televisions, so I have not seen her with my own eyes. But that's what Julien said and I believe him, because he doesn't lie.

You will be happy to know I have already baked your fruitcake. I know you love it so.

Charlie volunteered to pick you up at the train station since it will be dark and the weather might be bad. And I am sure that girl from the television station is just seeing him for legal help.

I am glad you are coming home soon. You can take over feeding this cat. He is such a nuisance.

Your grandmother,
Baldwin Josephine Shelby Howell

41

THE MISSOURI PACIFIC station in Little Rock was noisy with families greeting students and other family members returning home for Christmas, but Shelby was oblivious to the noise. She stood very still, absorbing the feel of the place. She loved this small section of the world, even though New York City echoed in her brain like a two-fingered whistle.

A few Miss Little Rock fans smiled, but her fame was fading fast. In a few months there would be another Miss Little Rock.

Charlie took her arm over the icy sidewalk, but removed it when she flinched from the pressure on her wound. He said, "That's quite a coat you're wearing. A little . . . roomy, but the latest New York fashion, I'm sure."

Shelby looked down at the coat and grimaced. "It's borrowed. My roommate ruined my own coat," quickly adding, "but she's a great girl."

Charlie drove down Victory Street past the brightly lit crèche that was always set up on the steps of the State Capitol during the Christmas season. Mary and Joseph and Baby Jesus gleamed brightly in the lights that wavered in the icy wind, and appeared, miraculously, to be rising from the earth. Word of this holy sight had spread, but a drainage back-up had caused a Chevy pickup to zigzag across the frozen grass, climb the Capital stairs and knock over a Wise Man's camel. The camel's legs jammed the sound system, which got stuck on the first two lines of *Santa Claus is Coming to Town*, blaring,

Oh, you better watch out . . .
Oh, you better watch out . . .
Oh, you better watch out . . .
Which some people took as a bad omen.

Charlie maneuvered around the Christmas gawkers and stalled automobiles, past houses top-heavy with frosted Santas and ice-encrusted reindeer, and past trees weighed down with icicles and bright burdens of Christmas lights. The crepuscular light lent another layer of mystery to the holiday night, even though a downed telephone pole blocked the road at Fourteenth Street, causing hot wires to droop dangerously. Charlie backed cautiously over black ice and found another route.

Shelby sat silently, hands folded. Charlie wiped the inside of the fogged windshield with his glove, rolled down the window, and gave hasty swipes to the side mirror. Shelby wanted to apologize for her behavior after Lake Nixon, and for being so cool on his visit to New York City, and for showing up with her roommates when he asked her to dinner. She wanted to tell him about the awful things that had happened to her in that city. She wanted him to put his arms around her.

But she didn't say anything. She couldn't, and she didn't know why. To punish herself? Or to punish him for being a good guy, which made her more aware of her own duplicitous nature?

When they got to Baldwin's house, Charlie turned off the engine, and they sat without speaking for a while.

"Are you okay?" he finally said. "Your face looks a little . . . swollen."

"Oh, I'm fine. I just banged into a door."

He cocked his head, and pursed his lips. "Big door."

The interior of the car cooled, and Shelby wiped off a space

285

on the fogged window. She caught her breath when the house emerged, but not as she imagined it would. The outside lights were turned on full blast, and the sparkling icicled-turret transformed the house into an enchanted castle, smaller than when she had waved farewell last September, but still there. Still home. Her eyes filled with tears.

"You sound a little different," Charlie said. He pushed his hair back with the palm of his hand, a habit Shelby found endearing. She wanted to touch his hair, caress his face, especially his nose that had been broken some years back when he slipped on the apron of the pool at the state swimming finals. It gave him a rather dashing appearance, she thought, like someone who could defend himself when push came to shove.

"You'll have to be tolerant with us locals for a while," he said. "You seem a little . . . different."

"Oh, I'm the same. My accent may sound a little different, but if I'm not careful while I'm here, I'll sound Southern again."

Charlie sighed and said to the ceiling, "And we wouldn't want that to happen."

The silence was broken by the sound of sleet clicking against metal, like goblins with sharp talons. Charlie raised his voice above the clatter. "Saracen is in town."

"Saracen Self?" Her hand slid from the door handle.

"How many men do you know named Saracen?"

"I thought he was still in Africa."

"He seems to have a magic carpet. Must have been a shock to connect with him before you left." He paused. "You hadn't seen him for years." Another pause. "Had you?"

The name "Saracen" burned in the air until Charlie extinguished it with another one. "So tell me about Julien."

She brushed at the arm of the coat as though ridding it of detritus. "Why should I know about Julien?"

"I thought you might have seen him in New York. The

guy came back looking like hell. He'd been mugged."

"Julien is a shit."

"Ahhh. You're learning a lot of things in the big city. But I agree with your assessment of Julien. When he got back, his nose was broken and. . . ."

Shelby sat up straight with a smile and a satisfied "Ha!"

Charlie looked at her thoughtfully. "And he's unfriendly to me. Maybe it's because I've made my views clear about his group that opposes school integration. They meet here at Baldwin's house, even thugs like Buster Crosby. None of these people is her 'sort.' Your mother thinks the Governor manages them behind the scenes. Incidentally, your mother is looking great these days. Her new haircut is a knock-out, and these trips she's taking. . . ."

"My mother cut her hair? And she's taking trips?"

"I supposed you knew. She seems more . . . lighthearted."

Shelby frowned. She had always been the glue in the family. She was the person who knew what each woman was thinking, what each was doing. She was the favorite to whom both women turned with the few revelations they were willing to impart, and now Charlie knew more than Shelby did? For a moment she felt a mean urge to hurt him. To tell him about Ben Vaughn. About Saracen's kiss. Tell him everything. Get it out. Get it over with.

But she didn't. She couldn't. Charlie would be disappointed in her, and for some ineffable reason, she had to be perfect for Charlie who, at that moment, was exhaling a cautious breath.

"I think your Mom trusts me," he said. "She told me Julien's been courting Baldwin since he returned from New York, sending her flowers, running errands. For some reason he's gone out of his way to tell people he didn't see you up there. Too busy at first, he said, and then he got mugged."

Shelby put her hand on the door handle again. She wanted to get out of the car. She didn't want to get out of the car.

She wanted to tell Charlie the truth about everything. She wanted to hit him. She wanted him to take her in his arms. She didn't know what she wanted from dear Charlie, whose breath was visible, steady puffs of steam in the cold air, their steam intermingling.

He shoved down his unruly hair again. "I'm concerned about what Julien and his friends are up to with Baldwin. I don't like her personal attitude toward Negroes, but I think these guys are using her to lend respectability to their even more extreme positions."

Shelby's sharp words were intentionally hurtful. "What do you care? You're rich. You're a Republican."

"Oh, come on, Shelby . . ." Charlie's voice was gruff. "You're sounding so . . . tough. But your eyes are sad."

He took her hand with one of his, but removed his hand when she didn't respond. "And so what if I have money? Does that mean I don't care about the chasm between coloreds and whites . . . which is increasing, in case you haven't noticed. I've never talked about it, because you haven't seemed interested, but it's so obvious to me that it's to our advantage, even rich white peoples' advantage, for Negroes to have equal rights. Read a little history. Anger caused by subjugation leads to violence, not to mention the fact that our Constitution says all people are created equal. And I'm sure this anger will increase, it's *bound* to increase. If I had been treated the way we have treated Negroes, I would have a gun in my hand and murder in my eyes.

"But I think there's something very interesting afoot with this Negro preacher in Alabama. This Martin Luther King. Have you followed what he's saying? What he's trying to do?"

Shelby stared at the dashboard. She had heard about King, but had thought little about him. She had more important things to think about.

"Evidently, he's been influenced by Gandhi's ideas on change through nonviolence. It could be a formidable strategy for Negroes in this country." Charlie's voice gained energy. "We're about the same age, King and I. Maybe that's one reason I'm intrigued. I hear he's a terrific speaker."

Shelby could understand why Saracen could be interested in King, but why Charlie? She was certain King's philosophy could be dangerous for white people. Why would Charlie get involved with that stuff? He had a good life.

"You've never mentioned this before."

"The truth is, I haven't thought much about social struggle until recently. The law school at the University was integrated in '48 when I was an undergraduate, but I hardly noticed." Charlie shook his head, as though befuddled by his lack of interest. "They . . . the ubiquitous 'they' . . . actually built a fenced-in pen inside the classroom for the first Negro law student. A white picket fence actually *separated* that black boy from the white boys, as though he were contagious. Like touching him might make us white kids . . . what? . . . become infected with blackness? My frat brothers and I watched from a window when he left his . . . dock . . . because . . ." Charlie shrugged his shoulders uncomfortably, "because it was the thing to do. We all did it. The guy had to know we were watching.

"When I put myself in his place, I realized he had great dignity and was very brave. I felt a twinge of shame at the time, but I watched with my buddies, *and* from a safe distance. The fence was removed after a couple of years, but not because I protested.

"Anyhow," Charlie's tone became flippant, "I'm for integration because it might be good for business. Is that what you want to hear? That I only care what happens because of the money I would somehow make from the Negroes' need to be treated equally? That's the way my Daddy thinks. He says, 'Always make money when there's money to be made, and be sure and put your name above the door in capital letters.' So he sells substandard housing to Negro families and tells me I shouldn't complain about it."

Charlie abruptly switched on the engine again, but neglected to put his foot on the clutch, which caused the car to dig a muddy path in Baldwin's grass. When the car lurched forward, Charlie threw out his arm to protect Shelby, and she cried out, alarmed by Charlie's quick arm that slammed against her damaged body.

He switched off the engine, his voice sheepish. "I'm so sorry, Shelby. What I meant to say was that I lov . . ."

His half-spoken, "I love you," wavered between them, even while Shelby was silently begging, *Say it! Please say it. I need to hear it!*

But the world and the people inside the car suddenly seemed at great risk as the wind and the sleet clacked harder on the car, and the earth, and the trees, and the house. Charlie didn't reach out to protect her again. When it grew quieter, he cleared his throat and said, "You should know before we go inside that Baldwin has lost some weight. I also think she may have some financial needs. She asked me if I knew whether Eldridge Cartright's wife was a good antiques dealer, that she might sell some furniture. I told tell her I think Eldridge and his wife are crooks and absolute racists."

Shelby almost choked on her words. "Baldwin is talking about selling her *furniture?* She might sooner sell her soul!"

"Yeah, well, I talked her out of selling the furniture. She gave me some papers to study, and I think I can help her . . . *if* she'll keep Julien at arm's length. The man is determined to be her savior. But I don't trust him any more than you do."

"So you're the one who's been talking to Momma about Baldwin's tax problems! And I can't believe Baldwin had the *nerve* to ask you for money!"

"No, no! *God, no!* She hasn't asked me for money! I'm just looking over legal documents! Evidently, your mother has a friend who's willing to help with monetary problems, if it's necessary."

"What do you mean my mother has a friend who has money? And she's taking trips?" Shelby demanded, as though it were all Charlie's doing. "What's going on down here?"

Charlie twisted his long limbs uncomfortably. "I have no idea. And it's none of my business." There was a brief pause before he pounded a fist on the steering wheel. "Dammit, Shelby, I don't want to talk about your mother or your grandmother or anything *but us!* You know I want to take you in my arms!"

A nearby siren seared the cold air. There were so few to be heard in Little Rock, and so many in New York City. She shifted closer to her door. "I hear your arms aren't all that empty."

"Oh, for God's sake. This town is so damned small. And what do you expect? I never hear from you. You don't return my calls. You don't acknowledge the flowers I send. The one time I was in New York City, you brought all your damn roommates to dinner."

More silence inside the car until Shelby began to croon, *"What did I do / To be so black and blue. . . ."*

"You know that song, Charlie?"

"Goddammit, what's wrong with you?" Then, with hissing exasperation, he said, "Fats Waller."

Shelby smiled in the dark. She loved it that he knew who wrote the song. When a gust of wind caused the big car to sway again, she put out a startled hand toward Charlie, but he was staring out his window.

Finally he said, "You call me if you want to see me." He opened his door abruptly and swung her suitcase from the trunk. She opened her door and got out as though they were strangers. They walked single file, through the sleet and over the frozen grass that shattered like glass, and walked up the sand-covered stairs. The front door opened before Shelby could twist the silver bell.

She stared for a second at Baldwin, who, indeed, had lost weight, and she gaped at her mother's new haircut and her new dress that made her look like a Vogue model. Then Shelby fell upon them both, hugging and crying, and they hugged and cried back, as though she had returned from the wars.

The white streak in Eulalia's short curls wasn't in evidence. Was it the cut? Or . . . this possibility was shocking to contemplate . . . had she dyed her hair? And without telling her daughter? Shelby felt a curious tug of jealously about this woman who had survived quite nicely without her daughter. The feeling was unnerving, so she began to play her accustomed role of the happy child, laughing and hugging in the drafty hallway.

"Come on in this house!" Baldwin nearly shouted. "Tom cleaned out the chimney from birds' nests, and made us a good fire! And where on earth did you get that coat? It's too big for you, Shelby Howell!"

Shelby's smile diminished. "I . . . I borrowed it. My other coat is at the cleaners."

"If you borrowed it from that roommate, Maxine, she must have broad shoulders."

Shelby whirled around, concealing the initials with her hand. "You like the red lining?"

"Is it cashmere?" Eulalia was regarding the coat and her daughter with careful eyes. "And what's wrong with your eye, honey? And your face? It looks bruised."

Shelby turned from her mother and moved farther from Baldwin, who still didn't need glasses. "I was rushing to a class and ran smack into a door. It looked worse two weeks ago."

But Baldwin couldn't listen to anyone for long, not even her newly arrived granddaughter. "Did I write that Julien had to walk barefoot in the freezing cold in New York City, because a huge Nigra with gold teeth and a pistol and a long knife took his shoes and his coat?"

She continued to chatter as she led Charlie to a plate covered with thick slices of fruitcake. "He was lucky to get out of that city alive. And now that we've got you back home, Shelby Howell, we may just have to keep you here forever, don't you agree, Charlie?"

But Charlie had turned toward the door.

Baldwin grabbed at his arm. "I don't want you to go so soon, young man! I sliced you some of my fruitcake!"

Shelby winced. Baldwin's fruitcakes were famously inedible.

"You're very generous, Miss Baldwin, but I best leave you ladies to your homecoming. You'll have a lot to talk about." He bowed his head politely to each of them, avoiding Shelby's eyes, and walked out the door and into the storm.

Shelby watched from the window, but Charlie didn't look back. He got into his car, charged backward out of the ruts, and disappeared into the night.

42

"As I live and breathe, it's Miss Shelby, come home from New York City." Saracen Self stepped from behind the meat counter at Hanson's Corner Grocers. His big voice sailed like a net across the room and settled over Shelby.

The store smelled like sawdust and dill pickles and bacon and the blood of the stew meat that Cal, Hanson's helper, was chopping behind the counter. Cal was grinning, first at Shelby, and then at Saracen, the way he would when presenting a particularly fine T-bone steak to a customer. He was proud to have Miss Little Rock in the store along with Saracen Self, the most august card shark in town. Never mind that Saracen wrote for a big-time newspaper and traveled the world. Cards were what mattered to Cal.

Shelby began to smooth her hair, then pretended she was brushing aside a piece of lint. She had known this meeting would take place sooner or later, but not in E.J.'s store, especially when she was dressed in an old sweater and faded corduroys and had casually brushed her hair. She wrapped the navy coat closer as she studied a Christmas tin filled with squares of candy advertised as *Lenore Hanson's Heavenly Homemade Divinity Candy Chock full of Arkansas Black Walnuts one square 5 Cent.* Shelby picked up a piece and bit into it.

Saracen was regarding her from across the store with that unnerving stillness. She forced herself to stare back, squashing the candy between her teeth, trying not to smack. She put a nickel on the counter top. The wooden drawer of the cash register popped out with a good loud snap when Cal rang up the nickel. She lifted her coat, deliberately wiped her sticky hands on her corduroys, and when that didn't suffice, licked each of her fingers, and eyed another piece of candy.

"Makes your teeth rot," Saracen warned. "You used to get a stomachache eating that stuff."

She picked up a larger piece, stuffed it between her teeth, slapped another nickel on the counter, and purposefully revealed white globs of candy in her mouth when she said, "I heard you were in town with your reporter's notebook. I bet you'll be interviewed by an *Arkansas Gazette* reporter, who wants to know what you think about what white folks think about what Negroes think. They could use that picture of you and me at the train station for the article. I'm told you were cuter than I was, though no one has had the nerve to show me the picture. But people still talk about it. Whisper about it."

She swallowed the rest of the candy without choking, and added, "You certainly have a gift for disappearing when things get too hot," turning immediately toward Cal. "I want this whole box of divinity, Calvin. Will you wrap it up for me? Put it on Baldwin's bill? I do love divinity with black walnuts."

Cal smiled but looked at Saracen for confirmation.

Saracen rolled his eyes, nodded "Yes," and motioned to Shelby. "Let's go talk in my office. I see Miss Hiller barreling down the sidewalk, and she's liable to get on the phone right quick if she sees you and me chatting it up." When Shelby didn't budge, Saracen took long steps and grabbed her by the wrist. "Come on, Sheb. *Move.*" He gave a slight chuckle as he dragged her along, acknowledging the ritual from their childhood, as he saved her from the mean calls of other children.

Shelby shook her wrist loose, but she followed him out the back door.

Saracen's yellow MG was parked in the alley, top up, motor and heater running, as though he hadn't intended to stay long. He opened the passenger door with a flourish, and Shelby got in without saying a word. Before closing her door, Saracen leaned forward, and whispered, "Your coat's too big."

"I'm wearing it for . . . for a surprise party."

His huge frame swamped the driver's seat, and Shelby was reminded of the small space they had occupied together, on the train.

"Okay," he said, all business, "we'll ignore the fact you're wearing a man's expensive cashmere coat. You've proved the coat can look great on a tall, blonde female. So . . ." Saracen spoke like a doctor asking for symptoms, as though nothing intimate had happened between them. "Tell me why your face is recovering from bruises."

But bruises were not the issue for Shelby. She planned to settle that score herself. The issue was the kiss she and he had shared. It obviously had meant nothing to him. And what more should she have expected?

"What's been happening with you, Shelby Howell?" he asked again in his white radio announcer's speech. "I called from overseas, but you were always out. You were a very busy lady up there." His lips twitched. "And, by the way, your accent is a tad different."

"I probably sound like you do, Saracen." Her voice was tart. "Except for a few minor details, we could be green-eyed twins tied together with a monkey rope. Remember?" She splayed her fingers against the polished wood of the glove compartment door. When she lifted her hand, her fingerprints stayed, and she smirked with revenge. But he was donning the sunglasses he had retrieved from the top of the rearview mirror, and didn't see the smirk.

"The sun isn't shining," she said with satisfaction. "You just wear those things to conceal your thoughts."

Saracen chuckled and removed the glasses. "You're becoming too observant, my dear. Here's what I was trying to hide: that I should not, under any circumstances, have kissed you. You and I are too . . . familial . . . for kisses like that. I let my better sense go down the drain in that crazy apartment with those photographs spiking my blood pressure, and Frank Sinatra crooning a love song, and you looking like a beautiful, bedraggled witch. You *should* be angry with me. I was angry at myself, and I apologize, Sheb. Profoundly. I called a few times, but you were always out. But I hope you'll forgive me, because I need your friendship, and I want that friendship back, if you'll give it."

Shelby could feel her gorge rising.

"But is our kiss the only reason you seem different? More intense, even a little . . . tougher?" His eyes were piercing. "Has something happened . . . beginning with the bruises on your face?"

Charlie had said she seemed tough. She didn't want to hear she was tough again. She wanted to hear that Saracen had missed her, that she was irresistible. She had loved his kiss. It was exciting . . . not threatening the way Ben's kisses had been. Or loving like Charlie's. If she *was* tougher, it was because of Ben Vaughn. And Julien. When she thought of Julien she thought of his . . . death, by torture.

But she didn't feel tough with Saracen, and she wanted, or she thought she wanted, more than his friendship. She had plenty of friends. But there was Charlie, floating in her mind once again. Charlie wouldn't go away.

"I loved the kiss," she said quietly.

"And I loved the kiss. That must have been obvious."

"Well?"

"Well, we're *friends*, Sheb. The best of friends. You said so yourself, and kisses like that are too dangerous for friends."

Shelby moaned, "What's wrong with being dangerously attracted to someone. I love that feeling. It's a friendly way to feel."

"No. It's not." He sounded very certain. "Friendship has boundaries, Shebbie. Friends may feel titillated by the moment and let feelings spill over into something sexual, and that's okay . . . unless the friends are like family. But if they are, *which we are,* it's a dangerous diversion. We find one another attractive, but we can live with that. Real friends, genuine friends, live with it all the time. There are certain boundaries, though, that mature friends don't overstep, and sex is one of them. I need you to be my good friend who respects those boundaries, as I promise I will now and in the future. I want you to be my friend who makes me laugh, who helps pull me from the depths when I'm down, and who always tells me the truth, just like I'm telling you right now. And I want you to feel the same about me."

"But how does that differ from love?"

"You and I don't have *romantic* love, though I'm certain we love one another. Our friendship didn't diminish one bit over all those years. That's one of the things that amazed me when you looked down from your window last summer. I thought, with a great surge of warmth, *That's my dear friend, Shelby. I've missed her so much!*"

"But then you kissed me in New York City. And it was a passionate kiss."

"Yes. It was," he sounded deeply contrite, "and I hope you'll forgive me. But even if you don't, you're stuck with my friendship." Then Saracen sighed mightily. "Which sometimes means cleaning up the messes you cause . . . like your fight on the train with that dude that cost Marvin Williams his job."

Shelby's voice stung the air. "That's so ornery, Saracen Self! And you're changing the subject! I feel rotten about Marvin, and I did what I could to help him! But my *real* friend, Charlie Billington, asked his father to get Marvin's job back and I supposed he had!"

Saracen sat back, surprised. "Well, now. That's interesting. But listen to this: instead of helping Marvin, Charlie's father blackmailed Judd Meyers into convincing his wife to sell a chunk of her bottom land . . . deepest, richest land on earth, land Herbert has hankered after for years . . . it got turned up in the New Madrid earthquake a century ago, and in return for this black gold, Herbert promised to forget about the hanky panky Judd was up to on the Spirit of St Louis. I've also learned that Julien Hutchins helps Judd find his playmates for the train!"

Shelby muttered, "There's no end to these disgusting circles."

"I do not think Herbert will jeopardize a fabulous real estate deal to help a Negro porter keep his job, and. . . ."

"Well, *Herbert*," Shelby interrupted in a mixture of sarcasm and self-righteousness, "will have to give that land back! I know Herbert! I'll tell him to call the president of the Missouri Pacific Railroad, and I'll . . . I'll. . . ."

Her voice trailed off, mushy with remorse at the odds of Herbert Billington returning the precious, black-gold acres to reinstate a Negro's job. Saracen's car engine chugged steadily, reminding her of the sound the train made when she shirked Marvin's hand, and then, for some unearthly reason, Bernard's image popped up alongside Marvin's. She clunked her forehead against the side window, welcoming the cold discomfort. Why should she feel responsible for Bernard *or* Marvin? *Let Charlie worry about Negroes. Let Saracen worry about them. They were his people.*

"Sometimes you have to lie in the weeds and wait for the right moment, Sheb." Saracen's voice was less charged with blame. "And sometimes you have to wait a long time.

"But here's the good news. By a strange fluke, I came into possession of photographs of the Judge taken with more than one of his so-called wives, all of whom were naked and tangled up like monkeys inside a Missouri Pacific train compartment. Meyers's real wife is Mildred Anne Meyers, the heiress who gives him money for his fancy clothes and his 'business' trips. She's also a savvy lady who sold her bottom land to Herbert for a hefty price. She knew how much he wanted that land. And amazingly," and Saracen slowed his voice for dramatic effect, "very recently, Mildred Anne received copies of those same photographs with the assistance of . . . I guess you could dub her a secret agent, though some folks might call her the maid who takes the mail to Miss Mildred on a highly polished silver tray. The maid had no idea, of course," though the tone of Saracen's voice said otherwise, "that a particular envelope was filled with obscene photographs of the same boss who frequently chased her into corners, with hands like an octopus. I'm told," and by this time, Saracen was chuckling, "that Mildred Anne's explosion was of atomic proportions."

Shelby stared at Saracen, already guessing the answer to the question she was about to ask. "Who gave you the pictures?"

His face took on a kind of rapture, and he lifted his hands expansively. "*That* is a beautiful mystery! I opened the door of my daddy's house one day, and lo and behold, there was a big envelope filled with genuine, dirty pictures of a raunchy old man with a gimpy leg in the midst of two naked, equally raunchy damsels! I do hope my good fortune will become Marvin's."

Shelby was certain Charlie was Saracen's benefactor. Charlie could have managed it. Her eyes became bright with conspiracy. "What if Mildred shoots Judd?"

Saracen gave a dismissive shrug. "Marianna, Arkansas will witness a grand funeral with a beautifully dressed, dry-eyed widow who, of course, had to fire in self-defense. If Herbert lives, she'll take away his money or kick him out of her life.

Either way he won't be welcome at the country club or have money for his lady loves. And he adores the country club and his lady loves. He has always thought of himself as an irresistible stud in a hand-tailored suit who should have become a judge, at the very least."

Shelby's face grew very still. Then, "It's not enough," she sputtered, remembering how he had treated her, what he said about her father. About her mother.

"It's enough. He'll suffer. Believe me."

"And what if Judd traces the pictures back to you? Does that frighten you?" She barked a dismissive laugh. "But you're never frightened, are you. You thrive on danger. *And* deceit."

Saracen sighed mightily. "I see it will take a while for you to forgive me . . . So . . ." Saracen hesitated, "maybe it will help if I tell you something I've never told anyone. And I do mean *no one.*" Saracen cleared his throat as though about to make an important public pronouncement. His shoulders deflated, and he sighed again. "I get scared out of my knickers when angry white men like Judd are breathing down my neck. I try to conceal the fear, but I assure you that I loathe and at the same time quake, at the thought of being under someone's big, white foot."

Saracen's honest eyes bore into Shelby's. "What in hell difference does skin color make if a man is hard working and pays his bills? Or is hard working and sometimes *can't* pay his bills? But those white guys don't care. They have to stay in control. They have to feel in charge of the world. They want all the power, all the money.

"*And* they think we're all black studs after their white women!" Saracen's laugh was acrid, far removed from his usual contagious boom. "You'll never know what it's like to have to stand quietly while some ignorant sonuvabitch threatens you just because you're black . . . and in my case, because you're black and your eyes are green, which can only mean that one of their precious white women was raped by a big, black Negro." A quick grin sliced across his face. "You really have to watch out for those good-looking black girls. Those black girls will tie white boys to beds and beget mulattos like me."

Shelby bowed her head, unable or perhaps unwilling, to witness his distress. "Momma says Faubus meets secretly with members of some group called the Capital Citizens Council, and that those people hate Negroes."

Saracen nodded. "Of course, he does, and yes, they do. At the same time Faubus does his best to butter up the Negro community. He's a very tricky lad, our Orval. One day he says integration won't be an issue, the next day he allows anti-integration measures to pass the State Legislature. And then," Saracen held up the pale palms of his huge hands as though resigned to duplicity, "he turns around and appoints a couple of Negroes to the Democratic Party Central Committee to keep us on board. If I weren't one of the folks he's trying to railroad, I'd find him a fascinating study. He doesn't have real friends, just cronies like Buster Crosby, who like to be around power and drop names, and are willing to threaten people with fists, and maybe guns, when people don't do the Governor's bidding. Or he has influential associates with lots of money, like Witt Stephens, who has the biggest brokerage firm off Wall Street and runs the Arkansas Louisiana Gas Company. For his own reasons, Witt manipulates Orval, who in turn plays rinky-dink with the big planters who want to keep white blood pure and labor cheap."

"Maybe the planters use Faubus right back."

"Of course, they do. It's an incestuous merry-go-round. But I don't think he's decided to go all the way with the white supremacists yet. He hasn't entirely shaken the socialist teachings of his daddy, who was a hardscrabble farmer with a smattering of schooling and a lot of book learning on his own. Old Sam was such a committed socialist, he went to prison as a pacifist during World War I! One of the little dramas in the state occurs when Sam berates Orval's policies with letters in the *Aransas Gazette,* using the pen name Jimmie Higgens, which, by the way, is a socialist *nom de plume.* He told a reporter that Orval was taught not to hate anybody of any race, because people would look down on him if he did, and Orval has never liked to be looked down on, his Daddy says. He likes to stand on the podium looking down at people who are applauding him. He thrives on applause.

"And who knows . . . Orval may even try to do in some of the segregationist white establishment who look down on him. Though softly, softly, as we say in Africa when we track wild animals. Sometimes he forgets and exposes his need for adulation. But he has to hear the applause. Hear people shout his name.

"I personally think he'll keep on playing both sides against the middle, like the canny hillbilly he is, because he knows deep down that being Governor of Arkansas is the best job he'll ever have. But the outcome of integration in our state will mostly boil down to what happened to Orval Faubus growing up in Greasy Creek. Look to their past, and you'll usually learn how people will react.

"I also think Julien Hutchins is hiding his Klan membership until the right moment, and using Baldwin as cover with the meetings at her house."

Shelby stirred uneasily, imagining her grandmother ensnared in Julien's web of racist machinations. He had to be stopped. *Shelby had to stop him.*

When Saracen grabbed her bruised arm, she jerked back in pain. "What's wrong, Sheb?" Before she could stop him, he shoved up the sleeve of the coat and her sweater, and with narrowed eyes, lifted one of her hurt hands. "Ah, Shebbie," he sighed, "what has happened to you?" It was more a lament than a question. He positioned his other hand on top of, but not touching her skin, fingers hovering, then stroking gently.

The pain diminished.

"It's Julien, isn't it?"

Her voice broke. "He tried to rape me in New York City. It was a nightmare. He beat me up, Saracen!"

Saracen was silent, but after a while, he massaged her other arm.

"But I kept his coat." Shelby's voice was stronger, "and I'll swoop down on him in a crowd like a big bat wearing his navy-blue coat with the red satin lining embroidered with his big, navy-blue initials. I want to see him as afraid as I felt when he held me down. Everyone in Little Rock knows about his coat. He told people it was stolen by a Negro giant in New York City, but it was my roommate, Maxine, who grabbed it from him. And did you know he wears a toupee?" Her attempt to laugh sounded more like a painful hiccup. "His head is bald!"

Saracen whispered, "Shhhhh, shhhhh," like a parent to a distraught child, but Shelby continued to babble.

"My friend, Max, grabbed his toupee and whomped him with it! And she threw his shoes out the window. It was so cold they froze on the fire escape like big turds!" Shelby's laugh was too shrill. "And I got mixed up with that guy, Ben Vaughn, the one on the motorcycle you told me to stay away from, and he was hateful. And I didn't find my father. I gave up looking, because I got too involved with Ben, and I'm so sorry. So very sorry." By this time, she was sobbing.

Saracen continued his massage until she began to breathe more easily.

"I've seen the big city though." She didn't smile when Saracen handed her a clean, white linen handkerchief. She dabbed at her face as she stared at the Coca-Cola beauty painted on the back of Hanson's store. The paint was peeling on the beauty, who smiled at the world with cracked lips, smiled even when slush slid down her face from the store roof. The slush caused the crows to jerk up like six puppets and settle down in the same place again.

"You'd better watch that deep scratch on your left arm." Saracen's voice was just above a whisper. "It's not healing right."

"Yep." Her smile was cynical. "I have a great collection of scratches and bruises." She blew her nose again.

Saracen muttered something unintelligible. Then, "Stay away from him, Sheb. *Don't under any circumstances go on a vigilante mission to get that guy.* You're his *enemy* now. You know who he really is, and he can't endure that. And get rid of that coat. It must be a burden to wear that thing. It could devour you."

A crow jettisoned into the air again, followed by his croaking mates, and Shelby waited to speak until the noise subsided. "I had this fantasy of meeting my father in the street up there. I would recognize him right away, and I would walk up to him and shout, '*Why did you leave me? You're my father, and I look just like you!*' But . . . what if he did something awful? What if he's a bad man? That would break my heart."

Saracen shook his head. "No. No, no. He wasn't bad. News of badness travels, and I heard *nothing* bad about him. What I do know is this: he loved you. You can count on that. And he was always nice to me, which not many white people were. And generous. When I was a kid, he even gave me a copy of *Lord Jim*. I still have it."

Shelby stared at Saracen, remembering that Conrad's real last name was her real last name. Lord Jim disappeared because he couldn't face his own cowardice, but he redeemed himself, even though he caused great pain to the woman he loved. Maybe her father had redeemed himself for whatever crime he might have committed.

"Nothing is ever simple in this life," Miss Finney had told her class when they read *Lord Jim*. "Remember that, my young friends. Unless someone does something monstrous, you must learn to forgive. And if that doesn't work, you have to soldier through the hard times, *which you can always do*. You *must* do it! When you're older, you may read a strange play that ends with these lines: '*I can't go on. I'll go on.*' And you, too, will always be able to go on. *Always*. Remember that. Just say those words to yourself: *I'll go on*. And do it. *Go on*. Never give up!"

Miss Finney's words would always echo in her ear. But it did occur to Shelby that there hardly ever were happy endings in great literature. And were there in real life? When her father returned, would he come trailing clouds of glory? Or would he have a little Chinese wife by his side who would snatch at the sapphire on Shelby's finger . . . the ring whose star had fractured slightly when it broke Julien Hutchins's nose? A noble break that made the ring even more precious to her.

"How about supper at Daddy's house? It's soothing to be with someone who'll love you to the end of his days, no matter what. We'll try to get him to talk about your daddy, and between the two of us, we might get some answers."

Shelby's mouth lifted in a slow smile. "Supper at Tom's house. That would be nice. I haven't seen him since I got back from New York City, and I've never been to his new house."

Saracen chuckled. "Tonight you'll have your chance. Daddy still makes the best biscuits in the south. But don't be frightened by the African masks he's hung on his walls in a rather spectacular manner. I'll pick you up at six, and we'll race away before Baldwin sees me at the wheel." He tapped `a drumroll with his fingers on the steering wheel, then carefully engulfed her bruised hands with his. "Are we friends again?"

43

SARACEN'S HANDS were still on hers when a beat-up Ford pick-up skidded to a stop alongside the MG, splashing mud onto the shiny yellow paint. Saracen quickly released her hands, and placed his own hands on the steering wheel.

Two large German shepherds in the truck bed barked ferociously, their hackles raised. E.J. Hanson banged a big red fist on the window, and Saracen rolled the window down, his eyes fixed on the steering wheel.

"Well, now." E.J.'s grinning teeth looked lethal. "I hear you come back home sounding like a Yankee, and looks like you picked up more than just an accent up there. But you better park someplace else with your boyfriend. He wound hisself up in the wrong part of town."

E.J. talked across Saracen as though he weren't there.

Shelby snapped. "Cut it out, E.J.! And tell those dogs to shut up." E.J. gave a sharp whistle and looked smug when the barking grew louder. Saracen dropped his hands out of sight, and a curious clicking ensued that might have come from the crows. The dogs stopped barking.

E.J. whistled at the dogs again, at the same time, Shelby squeezed herself over a confounded Saracen and crooned out the window, "Buttercup! Baby! Hello, sweet doggies! I've missed you!" and in a stern voice, she commanded, "*Down, boys! Down!*" The dogs dropped to the bottom of the truck bed and began to slaver and whine noisily in Shelby's direction.

E. J. looked like he wanted to kill both his dogs and the

woman who subverted them.

"I just loved it when I was little and you taught me how to make your doggies mind. But they're getting a bit old now, aren't they? Probably can't knock down people and bite like they used to." Shelby smiled sweetly and settled back in her seat, ignoring Saracen's warning glance. "I came to pick up Baldwin's chicken, and look who I bumped into! Saracen Self!" Her big, green eyes were all innocence. "He and I have been having such a nice chat. You remember Saracen, don't you? He got bigger, see!" Shelby waved her hand proudly at Saracen who didn't move a muscle. "He used to haul off your spoiled meat, and boy, did you have a lot!"

E. J. was almost hopping up and down in his fury. "I never knowed this yahoo, riding around town in this fancy car. I knowed a skinny little nigger who minded hisself like he should. But this yahoo's on my private property, and I'm thinking it's time I called the *po*-lice. And maybe I'll put in a call to Miss Baldwin while I'm at it, let her know what her granddaughter learned to do with big black niggers up north! I reckon you heard what happened to poor Julien Hutchins up there when one of them New York City niggers knocked him on the head with a two-by-four, stole his shoes, stole his good coat *and* his money, and left him on the freezing street to bleed to death! Made him so mad, Julien's aiming to get rid of all the niggers in the entire state, and maybe run for a high-up office so he can get the job done right!"

Shelby made a disgusted sound. Saracen's jaw muscle was working as Cal rushed out of the back door with Shelby's groceries and the box of divinity, awkwardly wrapped in butcher's paper. But Cal's big smile faded when he heard E.J.'s angry voice directed at the MG and its occupants.

"I'll sit here as long as I want to!" Shelby folded her arms and bounced back against her seat. "And don't you move!" she ordered Saracen who was reaching for the stick shift.

All trace of middle American accent had evaporated from Shelby's mouth, leaving only slightly nasal, slightly honeyed Arkansas diphthongs.

E.J. gave another sharp whistle, and the dogs jumped out of the truck and began to bark and leap against Saracen's side of the MG, their nails scrambling and scratching at the yellow door.

Saracen made a slight sound that might have been "shit," put the car in reverse, and said, eyes still lowered, "Sorry to bother you, Mister Hanson," and backed into the alley, even as Shelby resumed her tirade at E.J., her head thrust out of the window.

"Baldwin doesn't want your old chickens! You soak 'em in water and sneak lead inside when you weigh 'em! You're a cheat, E.J. Hanson!" She now had her hands on the edge of the lowered window, and the top half of her body was hanging out the side of the car. "Stay, Buttercup! Stay, Baby! You stay, sweet boys!" she yelled. The dogs hesitated, moving their heads nervously between E.J. and Shelby, as E. J. ran after the car, yelling, "Well, you're a stuck-up Polack, nigger-loving brat with a mother who's worse! And using that Polack name again, Julien says! And you're a damn Yankee too!"

Cal jogged uncertainly after E.J., holding the box of divinity high in his hands.

"Jesus God," Saracen muttered, his eye on the rear view mirror.

"Well, that moron can't talk to me that way! And you sitting there looking at your feet! But you were just *acting*, weren't you, so demeaning yourself didn't matter! Lord, I wish I'd never come back home! It's awful down here! Everybody's changed! Everything's changed!"

Saracen enunciated his words very carefully. "If those

damn dogs scratched my car, I'll send *you* back North on a rail. Grow up, Sheb. *GROW UP!*"

"Well, you could've defended me instead of practically calling that jerk 'massa'! You could beat him up with one hand tied behind your back!"

"Oh, yeah. Yes, ma'am. Maybe you didn't see those gun racks in his cab." Saracen's mouth was grim. "'*Agree 'em to death and destruction*,' I say."

Shelby looked at him, wide-eyed. "Do *all* of your people read that *Invisible Man* book? The guy from Pine Bluff at The Acting School reads it all the time."

"I can't believe that one of *your* people has even heard about the book. What a jolt it must have been for poor Bernard to escape the prejudice in Pine Bluff, only to find people like *you* at his school up north!"

"Bernard likes me! We're friends! We perform together! You make me feel rotten about everything!"

Saracen turned his head and breathed in and out, trying to curb his anger. "Okay . . . okay. Let's both slow down." He chose his words very carefully. "I have no doubt that . . . occasionally . . . you feel as invisible as I do. Surviving in this world isn't easy for anyone. But I don't *want* to be white, inside or out. I want to be my *own* color. To be accepted as the man I am! A free human being!" The small car shook when he pounded the steering wheel.

"However . . . *however* . . . your smarty-pants talk has made me, and therefore, Daddy, bigger targets; and you have no idea what it's like to have a target on your back, day and night. You will be fine, of course. E.J. wouldn't dare do anything to the darling Miss Little Rock, except rant."

"Wait a minute . . ." Shelby sputtered. "Talk about targets! Who drives around this town in a yellow convertible and wears weird clothes?"

"Madam, as you can see, I've quit African clothes. I wear

the white man's uniform while I'm here: grey flannel trousers, white shirt, grey sweater. I'm bland as a bean. And I parked *behind* E.J.'s store and would've been long gone if you hadn't appeared. Maybe you don't know that E.J. takes pot shots at *my* people when he's drunk. And why does he do it? He likes to watch *my* people run . . . run for their lives! Maybe you don't know he has uncles who lynched a black man some years back. *Dangled him by his neck like a piece of meat!* So I don't say a harm word to that peckerwood grocer."

Saracen swerved to the curb, brakes squealing, even though he was in front of Baldwin's house in a fine white neighborhood. He turned off the motor.

Shelby blurted, "E.J.'s folks are crazy, but they wouldn't *lynch* anybody."

Saracen curbed his turmoil with a mighty effort and sat back in the seat, head pressed against the cushion. His voice was very soft and controlled. "I'm going to tell you a story, *Miss* Shelby, and if it's at all possible, keep your mouth shut until I'm finished."

Shelby started to speak, but Saracen commanded, "Goddammit, *HUSH.*" And she closed her mouth and kept it closed.

"Back in the late twenties, some of E.J.'s relatives grabbed a half-witted Negro named John Carter, who *supposedly* climbed on a wagon with some white women and hit at them. Another Negro had been jailed recently for *supposedly* raping a white woman, so folks were already riled up. When the Hanson men heard about John Carter, they grabbed the poor sucker off the street, stood him in the back of their truck bed, tied his neck from a tree branch, and let him hang. Didn't take long for the poor old guy to die, I'm told. Then, very professionally, they chopped off his arms . . . they were butchers, remember . . . and they chopped off the hands of the arms to preserve in a jar, as well as more private parts I won't name.

In those days, people paid good money to look at preserved nigger parts. And . . . because the guys were in a party mood . . . they fired a couple of hundred bullets into John Carter's lifeless body."

Shelby pressed her hands over her ears and shouted, "I've heard enough of this story," but Saracen ignored her, staring ahead as though visualizing the scene.

"The Hansons and their friends tied the body to the back of the truck and dragged it to Nigger Town where . . ." Saracen's eyes were now slits, "one of Little Rock's prominent businessmen directed traffic with one of John's severed arms. And the gathering crowd, white, of course, cheered at the sight of his trophy, and cheered louder when the Ku Klux Klan, in their full Halloween regalia, galloped down the street on horseback, exhorting the revilers to steal pews from the Bethel AME Church and build a fire on the street, which they did enthusiastically.

"Then the Grand Poobah tossed the arm on the fire as the final log, and was awarded the honor of lighting the heap with part of a church pew soaked in gasoline. And when John Carter's flesh began to sizzle and crackle and smell like beef, or maybe pork . . . the crowd howled like the hyenas at the zoo when the moon is full, exhilarated by the sight, and inspired to greater vengeance, they marched off to burn Negro businesses and homes."

Saracen's voice was so low Shelby had to lean forward to hear, her face wrenched with horror.

"For a long time afterward, Negroes stayed out of sight. Maids didn't go to work, which was a terrible inconvenience for the white ladies. And maybe there were whites who were horrified by the savagery, *maybe there were, but they did nothing to stop it that night*, and nothing to outlaw it for a much longer while."

Shelby handed the white handkerchief back to Saracen.

He wiped the perspiration from his face, and leaned his head back against the seat. "But I think the worst part of this tale is not the hanging, or even the severed arm, or that a lot of Negro businesses had to close down. The worst part was that a few white people had the itch to *murder* a black man, and knew they would get away with it."

Shelby, whose body had become rigid with the telling of the story, shrank into the corner of her seat.

"So I don't talk back to E. J. Hanson," Saracen said. "And I step off the curb when the white man wants to pass."

At that moment, the tall fir trees along the sidewalk shed their last burdens of ice and rose slowly upright with the awkward dignity of elephants climbing to their feet. Saracen and Shelby watched, amazed and silent and exhausted.

44

SHELBY CAME TO a halt inside Tom Self's house. The exterior of the red brick house was modest, but the living room ballooned with the flashing Christmas tree lights Tom had installed in the eye-holes of the African masks attached to the walls. They stared into the room and out of the picture window with the intensity of animals transfixed by a fire.

Tom shambled toward Shelby like an old bear emerging from a bizarre cave. The smell of cigarettes hung like gauze from his body and nearly smothered the delicious smells wafting from the kitchen. He was laughing in the expansive, throaty way Saracen had inherited, and that always made Shelby feel all was right with the world. He grabbed her in a hug, his laughter rumbling into her body, and she pressed her fresh young cheek against his cheek, chilled with age, and they rested together contentedly. Then Tom held her at arm's length with his big, calloused hands.

"You looking beautiful like always! And you coming into my house now, honey. See how Saracen fix me up like some ole Africa chief? He say all them play-pretties up there on the walls got souls, and they looking out for me. They vigilant watchers, he say. But that beautiful lady in the middle of them uglies? I call her Jessie. And we always safe in my house with Jessie and them uglies on the lookout."

When Tom's laughter trumpeted such good will, Shelby couldn't help but smile.

"When kids come here for Halloween, I turn off the house lights, so them eyes twinkling in the mask faces can scare 'em nearly to death. And do they love it? Those little dickens screech like panthers! But they always got time to grab the cookies I bake for them before they run out the door!

"Remember when you last visited, we lived out there past Geyer Springs and had us a outhouse? Well, I want you to take a look at my bathroom before you leave. It work better'n Baldwin's do, hers always getting stopped up in them rusty ole pipes, and clattering like a tornado. And wouldn't Jessie love that running water?"

When Tom spoke Jessie's name, Shelby laid her head against his broad chest again. But when a truck rumbled outside, he ducked his head to look out of the picture window and murmured to Saracen, "There he go again. He got the dogs this time."

"Don't worry about it," Saracen said dismissively to Shelby, who raised her head in alarm. "He's just showing off."

"E.J.," Shelby whispered, and stared out the window.

Saracen shrugged as though E.J. were nothing but initials. "A dog named 'Buttercup' won't bite when his true love is back to call him 'sweetie pie.'" He turned off the lamps in the living room, leaving the mask lights blazing.

"Daddy's going to make biscuits," Saracen smiled, his white teeth shining in the shadows, but he looked more menacing than reassuring. "You never had the patience to learn when you were little, but tonight the pro will give you a grown-up lesson."

"We going that-a-way, baby girl," Tom said, pointing toward the kitchen. Shelby looked uneasily toward the window.

"*Huh*-uh!" Saracen said, giving her a gentle shove. "Don't even *think* about running out there in the dark and screaming at that maniac. That would bolster his courage. The man doesn't have anything to do but drive back and forth like he has the whip hand, but he's not smart enough or brave enough to do us harm by himself. His wives all leave him, and his uncles are so old and worn out with drinking rotgut, they can't hold a gun steady anymore. Anyhow, the word on the street is that Daddy and I make black magic with these African masks, and E.J. believes in that stuff. He sees those twinkling lights and gets goose bumps."

"My masks is scarier than his German shepherds," Tom chuckled. "Anyhow, he just all beered up." The old man took a puff of the Lucky Strike, laid it on a saucer on the kitchen counter, opened the door of the old oak hutch, removed a bowl from a shelf, at the same time Saracen was reaching for flour and shortening and salt and baking powder and a bottle of milk from the refrigerator, and vigorously shaking the thick layer of cream into the milk. Then the two men performed a long-practiced cooking duet.

"You watch us good now, sugar," Tom said. "Watching is the best teacher."

Shelby tried to keep her eyes on his gnarled, black hands, now white with flour, but her mind churned with E.J.'s menace. The sight of him driving by the house with gun racks in his truck and whiskey on his breath was hard to dismiss, especially since it was her fault he was out there. If she had kept her mouth shut today, E.J.'s howls would have diminished quicker than his dogs. Would she ever learn to stay calm when it mattered, rather than react impulsively?

"They don't know how to make nothing this good up where you gone." Tom hummed contently, still gathering his implements. "Truth is, they ain't nothing hard to making biscuit, and it always make you feel better to make biscuit when you got the lowdown, and I mean a lot more lowdown than you got about ole E.J." Tom looked down at Shelby's concerned face. "E.J. got to have a whole string of trucks behind him before he do us any mischief. And if it come to mischief time, we got us some tricks, ain't we?" Tom smiled serenely at Saracen.

Shelby tried to keep her attention on Tom as he scooped up three or four cups of flour, and dumped them in the big bowl along with an overflowing tablespoon of baking powder and a quick splash of salt. He used the same tablespoon to dig out a glob of shortening he didn't measure.

When Shelby saw the Spry name on the tin, the sign across the Hudson River in New York City lit up in her mind, evoking the dangerous charm of Ben Vaughn, and, quite irrationally, Charlie's disappointed face, which bothered her a lot. And all the while, Tom crisscrossed two knives, combining the dry ingredients and the shortening with a steady beat that sounded faster and faster, until what evolved from the knives and Tom's own mouth was a fast moving train. Shelby added the wail of a train whistle as she had as a child, and the three of them laughed at their soundtrack.

"You see that?" Tom pointed to the small clumps of shortening and flour. "'Bout the size of nasturtium seeds. Now we ready for bidness." He dumped a cup of cold milk into the middle of the bowl. "And that there's the secret!" He held out his doughy hands, impresario-like, at the simplicity of his biscuit magic. "That's it! And nobody knows that secret but Jessie up in heaven and me and Saracen, and now you. You dump in the cold milk, *all at once,* and stir it around just enough to hold the mess together. Then you knead it a sweet nudge or two, so it holds on to itself, and you dips your hands in the flour and rolls out your dough a little bit with your hands on a floury board, then you take the best biscuit cutter in the United States of America," and he held up the old biscuit cutter, "give to me by the cutest little girl this side of the Mississippi, who found it in the alley behind her grandma's house. And you put it in the flour sack so's your cutter don't stick to the dough, and you cut out your biscuit," which he was doing with his mammoth fingers, their yellow fingernails splattered with dough. With surprising nimbleness, he

317

placed each biscuit on the pan that Saracen had greased with bacon drippings.

"But you *got* to remember this: you can't leave a scrap of biscuit dough to throw to the chickens . . ." and he continued to cut biscuits as he spoke, " . . . or you bound to be . . ." and he used the last bit of dough and placed the biscuit on the pan, "*an old maid!*"

Tom beamed, and Shelby laughed and clapped her hands while Saracen set the pan in the hot oven.

"I remember the story about biscuits and the old maid. It seemed like magic when you made that last biscuit and saved me from living in a house by myself, like old Miss Winslow down the block, who had all those cats. I always thought you and Saracen would save me from anything."

Tom paused, and looked away from her. "I did my best."

"For all of us," Saracen added softly.

Shelby laughed a bit nervously and said too cheerfully, "I hope I can remember how you put the dough together. Will you write down the recipe?"

The Lucky Strike clung to the corner of Tom's mouth with a wisp of paper, one eye narrowed from the rising smoke. "You always wanting to write things down. Some things don't work so good from a paper. You got to feel it in your fingers when the dough is right. I give you a lesson again, but I bet you got biscuit making in your brain from when you was little. That's when things stays." He looked straight into Shelby's eyes. "More stays up there from when you was a tyke than you let yourself on to." He rinsed the dough from his hands, some still stuck beneath his fingernails, and he began serving big helpings directly from the stove top onto their plates: chicken and dumplings, and green beans, and fried apples, and mashed potatoes, and hand-shucked black-eyed peas he had canned in the summer, and home-grown collard greens cooked with ham hock, and his own homemade cottage cheese. Saracen set glasses of sweetened iced tea on the red oilcloth that covered the table, along with crocks of home-made plum jam and strawberry preserves.

Shelby gazed at the sumptuous still life served in the old and familiar dishes. "Oh, Tom. It's just like it used to be," adding very softly, "almost." For a moment she was afraid she might cry.

Tom set down a dish of his churned butter. "I didn't do all this by my own self. Saracen help me. That boy a cook. He got this thing he call peanut stew from one of them jungle places, and if you can keep your mouth from burning up with a glass of cold buttermilk, it's good stuff with hot cornbread. Puts his cornbread in a hot skillet with the bacon grease smoking before he set it in the hot oven. But Saracen remember you love your chicken and biscuit best, so that's what we got." Tom smiled beatifically at the two young people. "Been a long time since we at the same supper table, and don't it feel good." Which wasn't really a question. "Now let's set ourselves down and say grace."

They held hands and bowed their heads while Tom bless-ed the food and the beloved young people who sat around an old kitchen table in a house that smelled of chicken and dump-lings and hot biscuits and apple pie, mouth-watering scents that bound all three together with sweet memories, and sad ones too, as time expanded and pitched backward so abruptly for Shelby, it burst into bright flashes.

Open a biscuit so light it breaks in two at a touch, and Shelby was back at Tom's old house, with Jessie telling her . . . what? To cry? That it was good to cry? Tom was standing by their wood cook stove in that little house near Geyer Springs, stirring up biscuits, collards cooking in a cast-iron pot, and Jessie was holding Shelby in the rocking chair, telling her to cry, to yell even. Saracen, his face a misery, was seated on the old couch Jessie had covered with the crazy quilt she had pieced to hide the holes in the couch, and Shelby's young and feverish mind was struggling to comprehend the meaning of the elaborately embroidered patterns of the quilt as though they might reveal the mystery of what had happened in the last days: the red and blue and green and gold velvets, and satins and silks and taffetas connected with a myriad of tiny stitches and irregular shaped scraps that created a magical wonderland of flowers and birds and leaves and spider webs and unicorns, and heavens with moons, and galaxies with stars, in silky, glimmering, magical stitchery. Then she fixed her gaze on the steadier horizon of Saracen's green eyes, and began to count their yellow spots, and he sat very still, his too-big hands dangling between his long, skinny legs, knowing what she was doing, knowing, even at his young age, it brought her comfort. And Jessie continued to hum that she, Jessie, was there, that Tom was there, that Saracen was there, they were all there with their sweet baby girl, and now she could cry. It was okay to cry.

But her father wasn't there. Shelby knew he wasn't there. He had flown too close to the sun. Her mother was at home, but her eyes didn't see her daughter, so she had disappeared too. And Shelby was disappearing, she could feel she was disappearing, so, of course, she couldn't cry, which was terrifying, because she was falling into the earth beneath the house, disappearing, forever; but she couldn't open her frozen mouth to tell Jessie, which made Shelby bore her fingers tighter into Jessie's neck. And Jessie let her do it.

Sixteen years later, Tom and Saracen were grim-faced again, still poised to help the young woman who was lifting her ice tea glass and raising a toast in a voice that was too shrill and too jolly. "God bless us all!" she almost shouted.

Saracen kept his eyes on Shelby's face, and Tom began,

uncustomarily, to rattle on about the Nativity traffic pileup at the State Capitol, and whether the dogwoods might be too damaged to bloom in the spring, and whether the spring at Boyle Park might be frozen so thick, folks would have to crack it with an axe to get to the delicious spring water, when Shelby interrupted him, her voice belligerent, to say, "I need to know what happened with my parents, Tom. *I need to know now.*"

Tom's forced cheerfulness immediately evaporated, and he mashed biscuit crumbs with his big fingers, and stared at his plate of uneaten food, and said, "Yes'm," and he rose from his chair, the Lucky Strike trapped between his big fingers, and walked so ponderously toward the living room, the floor shook.

Shelby rose uncertainly, but she followed Tom, who seated himself in his chair and covered his legs with the same crazy quilt Shelby had just remembered. But the much-worn quilt, interspersed with scraps of dark-blue velvet, now seemed as ominous as Julien's dark-blue coat that was hanging on a hook by the door like an oversized bat. The flickering eyes of the masks provided the only light in the cave-like room.

Shelby sat on the couch, her back rigid, and clutched her hands tight, but Saracen remained standing, facing the window like a sentinel.

And with no introduction, Tom began to quote, his voice deep and preacherly: "*The heart is deceitful above all things, and desperately wicked; who can know it?*' Jeremiah 17: 9." And having laid out his text, he began the story.

"Your daddy been flying in and out of Little Rock before he met your momma. The ladies . . ." Tom paused a long time. "The ladies . . . they liked your daddy. He . . . he was a hard man for anyone not to like." Tom tapped the cigarette ash onto his calloused palm.

"He met your momma down there in Mississippi where

she gone for schooling, and your momma was a beauty, the rich boys all after her, but the minute she met Teddy, there was nobody in the world for her but this blond Polack man who click his heels and talk so funny nobody could hardly understand him but your momma. And she say God let him fall out of the sky at her feet like a big ole angel.

"But your grandma say he warn't no angel. He more like Lucifer, that God shove down to the hot place, talking a strange language, wearing heathen clothes; but for once, Eulalia don't listen to her. She quit her schooling and her and Teddy run off and got married, because she got you in her belly."

Shelby blinked. "They *had* to get married?"

"They would of hooked up afore you got started, but Baldwin say Teddy warn't good enough. She want a high-up, country club, rich boy for her only daughter. And when your grandma hear you coming, she did something terrible in the eyes of God and man. She sneak stuff in your momma's food to make her get rid of you, and it nearly kilt your momma. But your daddy walk her round and walk her round and make her drink strong coffee and don't let her sleep, and Jessie cook up a potion, and your daddy pour it down your momma, and all the time you was hanging on like a little possum, until her and you be alright, and that was a blessing. But after that, they was even worse bad blood twixt your daddy and Baldwin."

Shelby pressed her hands to her mouth. Her head was pounding thunderously. Baldwin could have killed her mother *and* killed her unborn granddaughter. *Poisoned them both to preserve her social standing in Little Rock!*

"And when you come into the world, folks say, 'My, you was a early baby, wasn't you.' They know Baldwin fixing to slit their throats if they don't say that. And you was so cute Baldwin had to love you. She don't say nothing, but she must of been real glad her evil don't work. And as soon as you could sit, your daddy was riding you on his motorcycle, tying you round his waist with a rope, scaring the liver out of all of us, and you would set up there and giggle and wave your arms like a little monkey, loving the ride."

Shelby's voice was without inflection. "I thought he had a car."

"He had both'm for a while. He sell his motorcycle, 'cause he needed the money, but he still have his car, and he still have his airioplane to fly in them circuses, and ever chance he got, he sneak you up with him. He buy you this little flying outfit, and your grandma have a fit." Tom smiled at the thought of Baldwin's vexation.

Shelby squinted her eyes, remembering. "The jacket was leather like his. And I had goggles too."

Tom looked away from her, his voice almost sullen, as though resenting having to say more. "Yes'm, you do have. But don't stop me no more. I got to finish this telling now I started. There was something about Teddy couldn't settle. His eyes always busy, and ever time he got that airioplane landed good, there was a woman, and that's the God's truth. You say you got to know it all, and I hate to tell it, but that's the God's truth, and I'm telling it all."

Shelby closed her eyes, thinking, why am I not surprised? Who could resist her charming Papa?

"Your momma begin to hear about it, and something happen to her. She don't cry. She just got changed after a spell. She got too private. She got too quiet."

And Shelby was remembering her mother's new perfume, and the arguments between her parents while she huddled in her bed, wanting to yell, but not daring to yell, a little girl in bed, hugging herself, whispering loud, *Don't say those bad words!* Strange she had suppressed the ugly times, and only remembered the perfect family. *Don't say those bad words! We don't say those bad words!*

"Eulalia don't have to go far. All the men looking at her anyways." Tom was circling his big thumbs like pistons. "But she got the gloom real bad, and when she started it up like Teddy was doing, Jessie tell her *quit* it now. Jessie her true friend and they talk. Jessie tell her it don't mean nothing with Teddy. She say that feeling jump on him and take hold afore he can help hisself. And them men all do it, Jessie tell her."

Tom shook his head mournfully. "But my Jessie know *I* don't do it. She know I love her too much for messing around." For a moment it seemed the old man's crust might crack at the loss of his one true love. Saracen moved toward him, but Tom waved him away with fierce impatience, and he smoothed the magical quilt again, but gently, as though soothing a woman's soft skin with his calloused old hands.

"Eulalia say it mean something to *her* about those women, and Jessie say but he one of them foreigns, and they do it with anyone. Cain't help hisself. Had to prove they manhoods. But your momma wasn't no foreign, she a Methodist, and that. . . ." For a moment Tom's hoarse words tangled with phlegm . . . "that *Julien*," he spat into his hand as though sealing a curse, "always sniffing around. Your Momma wouldn't have none of him, but Julien stand in them holly bushes still out there, I keep them trimmed and watered good, staring at her window like a dog about to howl. Then that Judd man come along with all that money and his fine white suit, buying her clothes and play-pretties." Tom snorted in disgust. "Eulalia never care about any of that stuff. She just wanted your daddy to say, "Where you get them play pretties?" But your daddy don't see nothing until he walk in on her and Judd one night and couldn't stand what he see. And the onliest thing he used on that man was his flying helmet he had in his hand and that knife he got in his belt buckle. And he *struck* that man with that knife fast, like a rattlesnake do."

Tom turned to look at Saracen. "You say you saw that

knife when you was a boy? Well, Teddy knew where to slice with that knife, and how to hammer them slices with his boots that got steel in the tips until he left that mister a cripple! Left him a *cripple!*" Tom's tired face filled with sorrow, not for Judd Meyers, but for the fate of the man who had crippled Meyers.

Shelby pressed her fist hard to her mouth and bit a finger until it bled. The beautiful image of her Papa she had nurtured for so long was shaken. No. Shattered. *He could have kicked Meyers out of the house, he could have broken his jaw, he could have ruined his reputation somehow, but gouging him with a knife, knowing he was crippling the man forever? That was barbaric! Her father was a barbaric thug! And a philanderer! He wasn't a god who could fly like a bird!* She pressed her pounding head hard between her hands until it seemed her skull might crack. There couldn't have been love between two people who tortured one another in such cruel ways. And these people were her parents! A philanderer who could barely make a living flying stunts, and a vengeful tramp! A confused fury, a murderous need, something dangerous and bloody seethed deep in Shelby's being. She felt adrift in a deep and stormy sea. Alone. All alone forever.

But her father was still out there somewhere, and she would find him and make him explain why he had abandoned his only child . . . *when he knew* she *would have gone with him no matter what evil thing he had done! She would have kept his boots shined! His shirts ironed!*

Tom mashed his cigarette with a hard twist of his thumb. He looked weighed down with sorrow, not for Judd Meyers, but for the fate of the man who had done the maiming. He sounded near collapse, his voice thick with phlegm. He kept trying to clear his throat as he spoke in a very tired and old man's voice.

"Your grandma call me when it start, and I got over there

quick, but your daddy already done the deed, Judd lying there, howling and bleeding like a stuck pig on one of Baldwin's good rugs. And the very next day Teddy took you up in that airioplane. And he crash the thing and brung you home some which way, God knows how, before he walk outn the house and took off, God knows where." He pulled the quilt all the way to his chest, licked his dry lips, and whispered, "The heart can get wicked when it love too much."

Shelby wrapped her arms around her own shivering body. "The plane crashed, we nearly died, and I *forgot* all of that stuff for years." She made a guttural sound that wasn't a laugh. "He was hurt, I think he was hurt, but he grabbed me and raced across the field, and the plane blew up, it was so horrible, our beautiful plane exploding, and when we got home, he fixed me a Coke with crushed ice, because he knew that's how I liked it, as though nothing out of the ordinary had happened." She leaned forward so awkwardly it looked as though she might fall onto Tom. "He was hurt, wasn't he?"

"I don't think bad."

"He *was* hurt, but he got me away from the explosion. He cared enough to save me! He even fixed me a Coke, and put me to bed, and sang me a Polish song! But then where did he go? Where is he *now?*"

Tom shook his head again.

"Tell me where he *might* have gone! *Please, Tom!*"

Tom wouldn't look at her.

She grabbed at the crazy quilt on his lap and felt the old fabric rip. "I need to know! *Help me, Tom Self!*" She pulled harder on the quilt, but Tom wouldn't let go, even though some of the old threads were breaking at the seams, and the colorful galaxies were exploding. "*You have got to help me!*"

"North!" he bellowed. "New York City!"

Shelby dropped the quilt and sank back on her chair. "Yes." She looked bludgeoned with too much truth, and her

voice squeezed angrily from her mouth. "But if he had wanted me with him, he would have come back for me."

Saracen's eyes were glued to his father's face. "You know
more, Daddy. You know more, and you've got to say it now
while I'm here to help. I can help you!"

Tom's bitter response shocked his son with its sarcasm and
lack of love. "I forget you a *magic* man. You *divine* what folks
thinking, don't you, and this time you right. Teddy come back,
trying to break in the crazy house to get Eulalia, crawling up
that big wall like a monkey. If he could of landed that plane
he stole on the hospital roof, he would of flew her away, and
Shebbie too somehow, but the *po*-lice got him and put him in
a straitjacket. Except they don't know the man, do they? They
leaves him alone, and the man slither out of that thing like a
snake and hightail it over the roof in the dark. Then he gone
for good. And beyond that, there ain't another word to tell."

There was a sharper edge to Saracen's voice. "There *is*
more, and I'm here to help, Daddy. Tell the rest. *Please tell it
all now. I'm begging you!*"

But Shelby didn't want to hear more truth. Too much
truth was killing her. She had been so proud of her handsome
father, a man who could turn somersaults in the air. A man
who could run faster than the wind, save her from demons.
But in truth . . . in truth he was merely a handsome, philandering, self-centered, small-town circus pilot who gave people rides in his one-engine plane for twenty-five cents.

"*Tell* her, daddy," Saracen demanded, and stepped back,
as though fearing the answer.

"*There ain't nothing more to tell!*" Tom bellowed, heaving
himself upright, grabbing the quilt, shuffling to his bedroom,
and slamming the door behind him so hard, the eyes in the
masks went black.

45

SARACEN TURNED OFF the ignition in front of Baldwin's house, and hesitantly broke the forbidding silence that had had been theirs all the way from Tom's house.

"Daddy's sad tale has to be very disturbing for you, Sheb. But . . . he hasn't been well lately, and maybe what he told us is a mixture of truth and fantasy. That can happen with old people. And even if it is the truth, it happened so long ago, I think you should just . . . let it go. Try your best to close that unfortunate chapter. I do hope you can forgive your mother . . . *if* she did what Daddy said. Anyhow, why not let the dead past bury the past? There's nothing to be done about it now, except go forward."

He laid a soothing hand on one of Shelby's, who squeezed the hand too tight in return, leaned toward Saracen, grabbed his face, and kissed him hard on the lips. Saracen pushed her away slowly but surely. She stared at his blank face.

"Nothing bothers you." She sounded so bitter, so weary of life. "Nothing at all. You make people feel you care about them, but you always stay in control."

Saracen heaved a strained sigh. "God help me. I sure don't feel in control. The one thing I do know is that I'm not wise enough to counsel you, Sheb. The only thing I know for certain is that we need one another's support far more than you'll ever need my kiss. Like I told you this afternoon, I need your friendship, and I mean that from the bottom of my heart. I'll always need you as my very dear friend."

"You're such a *wizard*, aren't you," Shelby almost hissed,

"knowing exactly what's right for you *and* me! Has it ever occurred to you that you might be wrong?" She stormed out of the car without closing the door, and stalked toward the house, mopping up water with the hem of Julien's coat as she raced up the stairs, slamming the front door behind her, and dripping a trail to the kitchen where she snatched up the telephone and dialed Charlie's number with clumsy fingers. When he answered, she said, "Come and get me, Charlie. *Please come and get me.* I need to get out of this house!"

There was a brief pause before Charlie said, "Fifteen minutes. In front of the house."

She walked back toward the front door. Her mother was standing at the foot of the stairs looking lovely in a new, rose-colored dress belted tightly around her waist and curving softly around her breasts. A live red rose was pinned with a Victorian clasp at the V of the dress's neck.

Shelby hated the hair that she knew would be tousled by a man's fingers that night, and she hated the costly rose that didn't come from the frozen bushes outside.

"You going out again?" Eulalia smiled brightly at her daughter.

Shelby's voice was filled with scorn. "Yes," she said. "I am."

Eulalia looked concerned and touched Shelby's arm. "Honey, what's. . . ."

But Shelby shrugged off the touch and spoke over her shoulder as she hurried toward the door. "You're certainly . . . *decorated.* Are you going out too?"

"I am," Eulalia replied uncertainly. "For a while. What's wrong, Shelby? What can I do to help?"

The women stared at one another from opposite ends of the hall. Shelby had taken it for granted that her mother and grandmother would maintain their familiar images for her return. But Baldwin looked frail and anxious, and Eulalia looked like someone her daughter hadn't seen since she was a terrified child . . . the woman about whom Tom had just told a shattering story . . . a woman who was obviously going to meet a man.

"Well, don't let *me* keep you from your date," Shelby said flippantly, just as Baldwin called from the top of the stairs, "Where are you going, Shelby *Howl?* You just came home! It's your bedtime! Your momma's going out too, and I'll have to lie here and worry by myself until both of you girls come home!"

Shelby yelled back angrily, "It's *your* bedtime, Baldwin! Not mine!"

She slammed the front door behind her, expecting to hear Baldwin shout again. But there were no more admonitions from within the house. That routine, too, had altered, which fed Shelby's anger exponentially, and in ways she didn't understand. She wanted to pummel her chest, pull out her hair, scream that both women lived rotten, lying lives, that they didn't love her! They never had loved her!

She wrapped the cashmere coat tighter about her body, stomping her cold feet in a forlorn rage, waiting for Charlie, but fearing E.J. might pull up and drag her inside a truck that stank of unwashed bodies and wet dogs and cheap whiskey, and hide her in a cave in the Ozarks.

But Charlie, thank God, was arriving first, his big Oldsmobile gliding like a rocket ship to the rescue. As Shelby ran to meet him, a half-hidden yellow gleam caught her eye up the block, and she stopped, eyes focused like binoculars. The bright lights around Baldwin's house were extinguished, and Shelby caught her breath as her mother walked out of a side door, a phantom in a cream-colored coat, stepping cautiously over the grass in her high heels.

Whether or not Shelby loved Saracen was of no consequence. It was her mother who would be with him that night.

46

CHARLIE'S HOUSE WAS on the east side of Little Rock, in an area originally part of the thirty-two million acres designated to the Quapaw Indians in 1818. Once the Quapaws were officially presented with the land they had claimed long before the white man came, the United States subtracted another thirty-one million acres in exchange for blankets and guns and whiskey. Zebulon Pike, the American general and explorer, described that land as "the paradise terrestrial of our territories," blessed with gloriously colored wildflowers, clouds of rare butterflies, and flocks of exotic birds so numerous they could block the sun.

After the government reflected a bit, however, one million acres were too many for the handsome savages who loved to make jokes, sing native songs, wear scarlet buckskins and elaborate jewelry, and, on occasion, discard the buckskins and the jewelry, and perform lewd dances in the nude. This, of course, was against all laws of the Christian God, even though the Indians provided shelter and shared food with the white man when he was cold and starving.

But these Indians didn't deserve so much land. They were heathen.

Time went by and more "annuities" in the form of trinkets and whiskey were exchanged for more Quapaw lands, perhaps even by Baldwin's great-grandfather, until the Downstream People, which was what "Quapaw" meant, were pushed into the malarial swamps of Louisiana. The old Quapaw, Saracen, ultimately staggered back to Arkansas with the remainder of his starving tribe.

By the late nineteenth century, a small part of what had been Quapaw land in the Little Rock area was comprised of homes for the "better class," constructed in Queen Anne, Colonial Revival and Greek Revival styles. But by the mid-twentieth century, many of those homes had deteriorated like flamboyant old aunts whose once-fashionable clothes had become worn. Nevertheless, they still stood with great dignity and straight backs.

Charlie's house, located in what was evolving into the posh Quapaw District, was one of the first "old aunts" to be renovated, and he had chosen to live on-site while the flimsy walls that had divided the house into apartments were demolished. Plaster was exposed, and in one room a ten-foot-high fruitwood bookcase was revealed. In other rooms, elaborately carved fireplace mantels were exposed, along with wide-planked, center-cut pine floors. The floors were stripped and sanded and waxed until they glowed like the brown eyes of a beautiful woman.

Charlie loved the remodeling. He felt like an archeologist on the site of a promising dig.

The master bedroom on the second floor was nearly completed and temporarily furnished with elegant necessities, like a now rumpled four-poster spool bed, a mahogany Chippendale chest, and a comfortable reading chair piled with law books. A lamp, made from a nineteenth-century tea caddie, lit a mahogany Pembroke table, and a small refrigerator buzzed in the corner like a trapped wasp. The stately floor-to-ceiling windows, adorned with dentiled cornices, were still bare of curtains.

When Charlie and Shelby walked into the bedroom-cum-kitchen, he made a grand gesture, said, "Welcome to chaos," and shoved the books from the chair. But before he could turn on a light, Shelby had removed Julien's coat and began to undress.

Charlie blinked. "Wait a minute."

Shelby obeyed, her voice flat. "You don't want me?"

He shoved his hair back from his forehead. "Slow down, Shelby. You look troubled. We have plenty of time."

She looked around the room as though she hadn't heard him. "You could see me better if you turned on a light."

Charlie's voice was laconic. "I don't have curtains. The neighbors would love the show."

Shelby backed away from the windows, but continued to remove her blouse. Grey and brown and blue bruises were evident, even in the moonlight. She removed her slip and brassiere and jerked off her garter belt and hose until she was only wearing panties.

"See how flat my stomach is?" she said, slapping her hands on her bare stomach. The slap echoed in the high-ceilinged room. "We exercise a lot at school in dance class. But did you know I got fat when I was young? You should know that about me," she said. "You should know everything about me."

"Are you going to propose?" Charlie's voice echoed over the bare floor, and Shelby's voice rose a decibel, ignoring Charlie's ironic question.

"You should also know I put on eyeliner first thing in the morning, because my eyebrows have almost no color. And you definitely should know that Julien tried to rape me in New York City, and he made me into a work of art. See!" She twirled around gracefully, arms extended, to display the bruises.

Charlie's eyes narrowed.

"My mother sold *her* body to Judd Meyers," she continued, "but I doubt he got his money's worth, because when my father found them together, he crippled Judd for life. *Deliberately crippled him.* And having accomplished his mission, my father left town and abandoned me. Us. My mother and me."

Shelby began to shiver, but when Charlie moved toward her, she barked, "Don't!"

He backed away.

"My roommate, Maxine . . . you met her in New York, she flirted with you a lot. Max came back to the apartment, and the two of us beat him up. A Negro thug didn't break Julien's nose. *I did*. I broke it with Baldwin's star sapphire ring! The star cracked when I socked him, but nothing's perfect in this world." She looked at the coat on the floor. "I kept his coat."

They both stared at the navy coat, which seemed to take on the color of cyanide in the moonlight.

"No one can be trusted. Don't you agree, Charlie? Consider your father and the bottom land. Can you trust him after that transaction? And Saracen Self, who says he loves me like a *sister*. . . ." Shelby hissed the word . . . "*Saracen is sleeping with my mother!*"

Charlie's eyes grew wide. Then he said, "Stay away from that coat, Shelby. You want a man's coat, I'll give you one of mine."

"I want to make Julien suffer!"

"Stay away from him, Shelby. I'll make him suffer."

"Yeah. You and Saracen Self. Always taking care of things. Although . . ." she looked bewildered, "you did arrange for those pictures of Judd Meyers on the train with his hookers, and I love you for that. I do. I love you, Charlie."

But did the word "love" have any meaning? Shelby wondered. It didn't for Ben Vaughn, and she had learned that very evening that her grandmother, who supposedly loved her, had tried to murder her in the womb, and her mother, who supposedly loved her, had been a virtual whore and lied by omission about her relationship with Saracen; and her father, who had supposedly loved both her and her mother, was a philanderer who deserted both of them.

And Saracen Self? Saracen was a Judas.

Her mood swung again, and the words that emerged from her mouth jangled like shards of glass strung on very thin wire. "Did you know I have another last name?" She shivered again.

Charlie hesitated. "I'll get a blanket.".

Shelby's eyes flashed. "You knew that Howell wasn't really my last name?"

He made an impatient sound, nodded, "Yes," but didn't move.

"Of course you did! Why did I even ask? Everyone in town knows! That's the name I use in New York City now. My real name is *Korzeniowski*." She spat out the word as though it were poison. "But I'm going to change my name back to Howell. I don't like the sound of Korzeniowski anymore."

Charlie's grey eyes were just discernible in the gloom. "You could change your name to mine."

Shelby's eyes widened, but she ignored him Her voice, however, wavered. "I got fat and stayed that way for years after Baldwin changed my last name. I think it was too confusing for a little girl to suddenly be called such a short yowl of a name. You should also know I can be really ugly."

Charlie scoffed quietly, but didn't move.

"During the ninth grade I got a strange fever, and Baldwin called that quack doctor, Bergen. You know him? William T. Bergen?

"He prescribed bed rest, drawn shades, no visitors, and lots of cod liver oil. Sometimes, on sunless days, cod liver oil erupts in my mouth, like a volcano that can no longer be capped. I can taste it now."

"Shelby, listen to me. . . ."

"After my father left, my mother went to the State Institution for the Insane, and the few friends I had disappeared." She scoffed at her self-pity, as though friends were inconsequential. "Baldwin did her best to entrap me with country club girls who smiled like sirens behind the jails of their braces. They were all cheerleaders who leaped to the sky in flying splits, braces sparkling when they smiled, trying to vamp for pimple-faced football players. Which they did, of course. "But I couldn't be like them. I didn't even want *secretly* to be like them."

She was silent for a while, swaddling her still-aching breasts. "But I sneaked my father's forbidden books from the attic and read them under the covers with a flashlight. Some of those books were really raunchy. Titillating for a kid. I hid some of the Korzeniowski books in Baldwin's trunk and took them with me to New York City. The books are beautiful. Leather bound. That was before I knew Teddy Korzeniowski had hopped into bed with any woman who would lie down with him.

"The good news is . . ." words spilled out now . . . "I know all the answers . . . or almost all . . . to what happened to my family. I don't know where my father *is,* but who gives a fuck anymore?" Shelby moaned a laugh. "You didn't think you'd ever hear me say that word, did you, Charlie! My friend Max told me to say it when I felt frustrated, and I've been saying it a lot lately, just to get into practice. But now, I am *really* frustrated. So listen to this: *Fuck.*" She said it hesitantly, looking at the floor. Then she stomped her foot, raised her head and her arms, and said progressively louder: "Fuck! Fuck! FUCK!"

Charlie stepped close to conceal her body from the open drapes and the neighbors, and placed his fingers hard on her lips. When he removed his hand, she sounded even more frantic.

"You're a lovely man, Charlie, a really good person. But you've got to watch out for me. I'm infected with the disease of expectation, this feeling that my real life won't begin until my father reappears. I won't feel . . . *apart* then, like I'm the epitome of unfinished business. I might even relax, feel a little happy. But since the man I thought I knew as my father never really existed, I'm confused about how I feel about anything, and probably never will relax and feel happy. And you deserve better. Much better."

Then, in one singular motion, she stripped off her panties and flung them across the room. "So we're not going to make love. We're going to *fuck*. You'd like that wouldn't you? A good fuck? I learned how in New York City. I had a really great fucking teacher."

Which was when she began to cry in earnest, and she let Charlie lead her to the bed, and help her lie down, and pull the rumpled covers over her body. Then Charlie took off his shoes and belt, and crawled in beside her, and took her cold nakedness in his arms. Shelby moaned, curled closer toward him, and went to sleep.

But Charlie lay in the dark and stared at the uncurtained windows for a very long time.

47

SHELBY SHOVED OPEN the heavy sliding door to the study, and it settled in place with a ghostly sigh.

The study had been Shelby's great-grandfather's domain, and therefore was sacred, and therefore was as unchanged as the crackled nineteenth century paintings that were hanging on the walls. The painting, still vibrantly colored depicted, a full-rigged ship sailing on a turbulent ocean. Shelby imagined her great-grandfather staring at that painting, year after year, until one day he had clapped a big fist onto his desk, rose straight-backed from his chair, packed a bag . . . or did not . . . and journeyed west to board a China-bound clipper like the one on his wall.

But it was the Major's Confederate walnut desk that dominated the room. The desk hulked to the side like a large hibernating brown bear. It was five and a half feet long, and constructed of six separate sections that could be disassembled and packed with feather bedding, placed on a wagon by slaves, dragged by mules when the company headquarters moved, and reassembled at the new headquarters like a jigsaw puzzle. The desk was the symbol of the power and hubris of a white southern gentleman who wore a Confederate uniform.

A cut-glass bowl caught the light and sparkled on top of the desk. It was filled with Baldwin's favorite red dahlias, an expensive wintertime gift, surely from Julien.

Plates with slabs of untouched fruitcake were placed within easy reach.

The lesser mortals attending Baldwin's meeting were un-aware of the historical importance of this sanctuary. Jason Wilson Shelby would have lauded their stance on race, but, with one or two exceptions, he wouldn't have permitted the other socially inferior beings into his house, let alone his private space, where large bottoms had squeezed onto the big leather sofa, the leather crazed with age. Others sat on the uncomfortable "company" chairs, carried in earlier by Tom—who, of course, was not invited to this select assembly.

Baldwin stood up too quickly when Shelby entered, which made her back hurt more. If Charlie hadn't called ear-lier to say that Shelby was fine, Baldwin would have contact-ed the police. But now here she was, unkempt and exhausted, wearing that ridiculous coat and barging into a secret meet-ing about which Baldwin wasn't entirely at ease.

However, she had energy enough, would always have energy enough, to instruct her granddaughter on manners.

"This meeting is confidential, Shelby Howell! You can't just walk in here! You run along now and do your things!" The weight Baldwin had lost caused her skin to sag like a balloon losing air.

Shelby ignored her grandmother, nodding pleasantly to the men she knew and the two women she didn't, but direct-ing her primary attention to Julien, whose perennially pleas-ant expression fell with the finality of the guillotine when Shelby walked into the room wearing his cashmere coat.

"Well, *Julien*. Hello there," she said, as though he were just the man she wanted to see. "I hear you had a terrible time in New York City. That Negro must have been *huge* who was swinging at you with a machete or a baseball bat or a two-by- four. I've heard various versions. And your nose looks awful. It's all taped! Does it hurt? Will it be crooked forever?" Julien winced when she di-rected a playful air-punch at him with her sapphired fist. His fingers began to crawl toward his wound, then quickly retreated.

"By the way, my friend, Max . . . I know you remember Max . . . sends her best, along with your silver flask you left at our apartment. It still has some bourbon in it." Julien's eyes darted everywhere but at the woman whose hand trembled slightly when she removed the flask from her pocket and placed it on the lid of her great-grandfather's desk. All eyes turned from Shelby and became fixed on the initialed, silver flask.

"This must be a very busy time of year for an undertaker. Lots of people crashing cars. You must be shoving bodies around. Holding bodies down. But then you're good at holding bodies down."

"Shelby Howell . . ." Baldwin stammered, her hand on her heart. "Why are you here?"

The room had become quiet, the men listening with the alert head-cock of experienced hunters. They had heard about Julien and the theft of his fine coat, which looked a lot like the too-large coat Shelby was wearing. The women sat by their husbands, excited by Miss Little Rock's entrance, but also making mental notes about how shabby the house looked inside, so they could tell their friends.

Shelby wrinkled her nose adorably and leaned a bit toward Julien. "I was so looking forward to a visit after our . . . encounter . . . in New York City. But you never seem to be at home when I knock on the door. Are you hiding from me?"

"He didn't see you in New . . ." at which point Baldwin's eyes widened and she clamped her mouth shut.

"So this is my lucky day!" Shelby exulted, then puffed her lips in a sympathetic pout. "But I was so sorry to hear that your shoes and your coat were stolen, though you do still have your. . . ." She flipped an insouciant hand toward the toupee, which seemed to compel Julien to lift his own hand in the same direction, and then immediately hide the hand behind his back as though that appendage didn't belong to him.

"And hello, E.J." Shelby's voice was filled with so much

good cheer. Julien's shoulders sagged with relief when Shelby turned from him.

"I don't think I've seen you at our house unless you were delivering groceries at the back door where the colored also go. I *did* see you drive by Tom Self's house last night. Your dogs were barking really loud. But they would never hurt Tom, would they? Everybody in this town loves Tom Self. People would be very angry if anything bad happened to Tom."

E. J. shot her a furious look.

"And hi, there, Bruce! You must be exhausted with all of these secret meetings, and Kate being so pregnant! And . . . Mr. Reynolds . . ." Shelby paused to speak respectfully to Joshua Reynolds. "I'm surprised to see you with this group."

Joshua Reynolds looked thoughtfully at Shelby, who had already turned to smile again at the ladies, who squirmed in their chairs, uncertain whether they should smile back. Then her roving eyes latched on to Buster Crosby.

"And Mr. . . . . *Crosby*, isn't it? We've never met, but I saw your picture in the paper at an Orval Faubus rally. You were smiling, but I'm sure you didn't use brass knuckles to sock that man lying on the ground, even though the *Gazette* reported you did. That *Arkansas Gazette* is such a lying newspaper. Isn't it?"

But Buster Crosby wasn't looking at beautiful, bedraggled Shelby with the dark circles beneath her eyes. He was staring at her coat.

"I don't think I've met these other ladies and gentlemen. Introduce me to your new friends, Baldwin. These are . . . different people."

Shelby smiled graciously and twirled the edges of the coat so that the red satin lining, now muddy at the edges, was briefly exposed. The thin-lipped men stared at the coat, and the ladies stared at it too. Shelby's performance had become much more interesting than the house and its furnishings.

Baldwin, her voice strained, shooed at her granddaughter with a hand that seemed too fragile for the pink diamonds that weighed it down. "You get out of here right now, Shelby Howl! We have a lot of business to do tonight!"

Julien's funeral manners vanished when he thought he had an ally in Baldwin. His deep voice boomed from his short body, and he rocked back and forth on his toes. "Yes, ma'am. Maybe we'll hear from you another time, Shelby Howell!"

"But these meetings are too much for you, Baldwin. You look tired. Don't you agree, Julien?"

All eyes turned to Baldwin, with the exception of Buster's, who was still focused on Shelby's coat.

"Doesn't she look tired, Julien?" Shelby insisted.

Baldwin's voice thundered in response, energy crackling from her bunioned toes to the top of her holiday permanent, where her curls bounced like little sleigh bells. "Tired my hind foot! I have more energy in a minute than you have in a year, Shelby *Howl!* And this is *my* house! I'll do what I want in *my* house!" Baldwin jammed her left thumb across the other fingers on her left hand, as though trying to snap them all at once. "You go visit Kate! She needs company, doesn't she, Bruce? She'll have that baby soon."

E.J. stood up, face red, neck stretched like a turkey's. "Didn't I tell you, Miz Baldwin?" His veins bulged. "Shelby's got too big for her britches, ain't she, using those big vocabulary words, and calling herself Korzeniowski after all these years, and sitting out there behind my business with that nigger boy hugging her up. . . ."

Baldwin heard nothing beyond "Korzeniowski." That name was spoken so unexpectedly, and in public, she had to grab the edge of her father's desk to steady herself. Something monstrous was pressing against her windows. Something heinous was happening in her father's beautiful study.

Shelby's Arkansas accent rolled out of her mouth. "Well, I'm not using that name any more, you hear! And I may be in New York City for a while, but New York City ain't in me! And I did *not* hug Saracen behind your store, E.J. Hanson! You're a big liar, E.J.!"

"Here, here...." Joshua Reynolds interjected, rising from his seat.

Shelby bit her lip and gave Reynolds a hasty wave. "I'm so sorry, Mr. Reynolds. I shouldn't have yelled like that. I'm a little tired tonight. Please forgive me."

Joshua Reynolds was a founding member of the Good Government Committee that had reformed the city's institutions. He was also a member of the Arkansas Industrial Development Commission that was hoping to further revive the State's dwindling economy . . . with help, of course, from the deep Republican pockets of Winthrop Rockefeller, who had moved to the state, eager to compete with his brother in New York and make his own political mark in Arkansas.

Reynolds was now standing at attention like the army major he had been. He was ill at ease in this mixed social strata. He agreed that integration shouldn't be allowed to destroy the last vestiges of civilization that were found only in the South. However, in spite of Governor Faubus's private request that he attend this meeting, and in spite of Baldwin's presence in her father's venerable study, he was now wondering if he should seek a more congenial group to further this enterprise. He couldn't tolerate messy confrontation with white inferiors any more than he could with coloreds.

For instance, this grocer, E.J. Hanson, seemed unable to keep himself in hand. Everyone knew he dynamited the river for catfish to sell, which was against the law, as well as being totally unsportsmanlike. As for Eldridge Cartright, he could barely make a living selling motorboats, mostly used, and the man in the ill-fitting suit with his belly hanging over his belt was a rabblerousing Baptist preacher.

Reynolds was also reassessing his opinion of Julien Hutchins, who couldn't keep his hands off his hair. The man must have had a negative encounter with Shelby Howell in New York City, and this lovely young woman, barely in control of her nerves, seemed intent on making him suffer for his sins. And Josh Reynolds found himself hoping she would succeed, though not in his presence.

"Joshua's right," Buster Crosby nodded, with a big wink at Reynolds. "Let's keep this orderly, E.J." Crosby spoke with his chin to his neck, which made him sound like a self-centered man in the process of being strangled.

Crosby's familiar wink further irritated Reynolds. Until this evening, Crosby had never dared call him by his first name, and the man had no right to presume. Reynolds was also bothered by the feral way Crosby was inching toward Shelby, as though positioning himself to pounce. If Reynolds had possessed a whip, he might have used it.

"Mind if I take a look at your lovely coat?" Crosby smiled, his big eyes goosing Shelby. "That cashmere looks like the best there is." He had the look of a man who knew his cashmere. "But it's the lining inside this particular coat that interests me." Buster rubbed his hands together as though the feel of the expensive red satin was ingrained in his fingertips.

"You would only find some initials." She smiled sweetly at Julien who looked like he might levitate from the propulsion of his rapidly blinking eyelids.

"I'm just wondering how the designers for ladies' clothes are copying this style. It sure looks like the one that got ripped off your back in New York City by that big nigger, don't it, Julien?" Buster's smile was oleaginous. "The one you bought from me this fall? But that was a man's coat that has your initials in it, and this one right here is some fancy, New York City lady's coat, ain't it?"

Shelby felt dizzy. She needed to scream the news of Julien's treachery, and she needed to extricate Baldwin from this awful group, and from the pitiful residue of both their lives. What was the expression? Better to light a match than curse the darkness? Shelby had cursed the darkness long enough. She was ready to light the match.

"Let's help Baldwin get Shelby out of this meeting, Buster." Julien's usual perfect pitch was sounding off-key. "Maybe Bruce could take her to visit Kate. Or, listen, she could use my Caddy. The keys are in it, and the tank is full. She could drive it anywhere she wants to." South America would be just fine from the tone of Julien's voice.

When Shelby spun back to Julien, her platinum hair swirled like a sail's jibe in a wind. Her audience followed the path of the golden curve that gripped their hearts as only the unexpected sight of natural beauty can do. The men wanted to touch the hair, put their faces in the hair. The women wanted to pull it out.

"No! Julien! You help *me* with Baldwin!" Shelby demanded. The high pitch of her voice astonished her. In fact, all sounds in the room seemed amplified to her: clocks ticking, people breathing, Julien's tongue swishing back and forth between his teeth. "I should take off this coat right now, so Mr. Crosby can examine the lining."

Julien patted his hair feverishly.

"It's still up there, Julien," Shelby grinned.

His face flushed, and he pressed both hands to his sides as though he had been caught fondling something more intimate than his wig.

"You ever notice how perfectly combed Julien's hair is?" Shelby addressed the room. She was feeling slightly feverish, slightly dizzy. "His part always looks just so, doesn't it? How do you get it so perfectly *coiffed*, Julien? I sure wish I could *coif* my hair like that."

Everyone looked at Julien's hair with new eyes.

"What's come over you . . ." Baldwin's alarmed voice stopped before she could say, "Shelby Howell," now unable to address her granddaughter by that exalted last name. She was still struggling with the news that Shelby was using the accursed Polish surname, *and* with the news that Julien had visited Shelby in New York City. The possibility of so much deceit made her feel faint.

"What is it you want?" Julien asked. He was reduced to addressing Shelby directly in front of so many eager eyes.

"I told you," Shelby shrugged her shoulders and insisted too innocently. "Leave Baldwin alone. Let her get some rest. Have the meetings at your house. Leave us *all* alone in this house."

Baldwin began to sputter again, and Shelby said very earnestly, "You look awful, Baldwin. These meetings are bad for your health, *and* your soul. Your friend, Adolphine Terry, called me. She said these meetings were bad for your health *and* your soul, that there are dreadful people in this town bent on doing terrible things, and that you should stay away from them. She's got something in mind about this racial issue with a group of her lady friends. She thinks it will interest you, and she needs help organizing. They want to save the good teachers at Central High. You're great at organizing."

"Dolphine doesn't give a fig about what's happening to this town's good white citizens. And these meetings are secret, Shelby Howell, so you must go! Now!"

"*Nothing's* secret in this town, Baldwin." Shelby turned back, pointing to Julien authoritatively. "Have the meetings at the funeral home, Julien. There's lots of room there. Lots of quiet. Baldwin needs to rest."

Everyone turned to stare at Baldwin, who did look paler and less steady on her feet than she had when Shelby entered the room.

Joshua Reynolds picked up his coat. "I have to be going." He was very polite. Good manners were so important. "Thank you for the eggnog, Miss Baldwin. I'm sorry I couldn't eat your fruitcake. I had dessert before I came. And maybe you should listen to your granddaughter. These young people can make sense."

"Oh, you mustn't go, Joshua!" Baldwin cried. "I told you I couldn't take this on without your help!" Baldwin's coy nature struggled to resurrect itself, as she straightened her skirt and pushed back her hair. "And I'm perfectly fine. I have more energy than anyone in this room!"

"I'm just thinking of your welfare," Reynolds replied with utmost courtesy. "You'll excuse me if I say that you do look a bit peaked. Neither of us is a spring chicken any more. You really must take care of yourself, Miss Baldwin. Good night, ladies and gentlemen. And Happy New Year."

Reynolds picked up his coat and hat, bowed to one and all, and walked out of the library and down the hall with progressively longer strides. Julien looked baffled, then rushed after him. But Reynolds pulled off in his Chrysler Imperial before he could be corralled.

Baldwin's eyes jumped from Eldridge Cartright on one side to E.J. Hanson on the other. The truth was, she didn't feel comfortable with these men, and she could barely speak to the women, who didn't know enough to set their drinks on top of the doilies. And it irked her to see them sitting on her mother's needlepoint cushions, probably pulling out threads with their fat bottoms. She was glad that they rose obediently when their husbands did.

Bruce Norton stopped in front of Shelby. He took one of her hands between both of his, squeezed too tight, and enunciated his cold words carefully. "Whatever those Yankees did to you, you better not let it rub off on my Kate." Then he turned on his heels, leaving Shelby breathless.

Only Buster Crosby remained. He swooped toward Shelby,

lifted a side of the coat, and grinned broadly. "Hey, Julien!" he chortled down the hall, his eyes locked on Shelby's. "Come back here, my man! Your initials and my label are inside Shelby Howell's coat! Did you buy this coat from a big nigger mugger in New York City, Shelby *Korzeniowski?*" He shot his French cuffs with their gold cuff links, and moved closer to Shelby with a flirtatious swagger. "Or can we presume a little something's been going on between you and Julien? You can tell *me* about it. I always kept your momma's secrets." Buster's grin was lascivious. "Your momma and I used to be *very* good friends."

Shelby suddenly began to shake from rage and fatigue, and from all the cold creeping through all of the cracks in the old house. It had taken too much energy to stand up to the group in her great-grandfather's study. She wanted to collapse on the rug where the pile was worn soft as satin. She wanted to rub the rug with her fingers as she had as a child. She wanted comfort and respite from the years of sadness in this house.

Julien dashed back into the room for his coat, and Buster wheeled toward him on the slick soles of his Italian shoes. "Hey, ole buddy! I knew this was your coat the minute Miss Little Rock sashayed into the room! Gave you a fright to see it on her beautiful body, didn't it, ole buddy!"

Buster was grinning, his stance wide like a Las Vegas emcee's. "I know my own merchandise, my man! Her coat is just like that replacement you're putting on right now! Stand by him, Miss Little Rock!" He reached to pluck a long, blond hair from the coat she was wearing, as though he had a right. "By God, I wish I had my camera! I'd take a color photo of the two of you and put it in my store! Wouldn't I sell coats then? And navy is your color, Shelby. Platinum hair, green eyes, navy-blue cashmere coat that any man would like to put his. . . ."

"Get out of here, Buster Crosby!" The words exploded from Shelby's mouth. "Get out! You're not welcome in this house!".

"Ah, but I used to be." Buster grinned more broadly, imbibing her insult like a buzzard. "Where's your momma tonight?"

Shelby knew exactly where her momma was, and the thought made her more furious. Her green eyes blazed. "And if you ever show yourself on this side of the property line, Julien Hutchins, I'll do far more than tear your toupee off your pitiful head!"

Julien swiped feebly at her words.

"Toupee!" Buster slapped his trouser leg. "Of course! I knew it!"

"And take your damned coat." She slammed the coat at Julien, who jumped with the high step of a man avoiding a snake. The blue cashmere with the red lining looked lovely against the Persian rug.

Julien rushed toward the front door, but Buster Crosby clamped a strong hand on his arm. "Inside your house or inside my car, Julien, my friend. Lettie can join us if you want, but yours is a tale I am going to hear on this cold winter's night. And I want the truth!" The two men walked outside together, Julien still under Buster's thumb.

Baldwin, who had been slumped at the desk, forgotten, hobbled past her granddaughter. She picked up the cat, who had crawled from beneath the couch, but the burden of the cat seemed almost too much for the old woman.

Shelby gasped when she saw Baldwin, surprised and appalled her grandmother was still there.

"Is that Julien's coat?" Baldwin's voice was barely audible. The grandfather clock's ticking seemed so loud that, had the hour struck at that moment, all the glass in the house would have shattered. Baldwin had tried to have her granddaughter aborted, and nearly caused her daughter's death. She had also tried to lobotomize their memories of the man named Korzeniowski. She was so prejudiced against Negroes she was willing to ally with scum like Julien. And while Shelby knew Baldwin loved her, she also knew she would not sugarcoat the truth again to protect her grandmother's feelings.

"Yes, it's Julien's coat. He left it behind when he tried to *rape* me in New York City. He tried to *rape* me! He's an *evil* man, Baldwin. You have got to stay away from him and those racists. *Julien beat me up, and tried to rape me, and he would have if my roommate hadn't come home in time to save me!* See my bruises!" Shelby shoved up her sleeves. "There's worse on my big breasts! And did you know he's after your house, and may get it, because you haven't paid the taxes? He's a monster! He'll devour us if we let him, *which we cannot do!*"

When Shelby said the word "rape," Baldwin clutched her hand to her heart, and looked toward Julien's house where the sound of men's angry voices carried on the cold, clear air. Then she shuffled toward the stairs, holding to the bannister with one hand, and clutching the cat to her bosom with her other, as though the cat was all she had left in the world.

48

THE EYES IN THE masks were not blinking. Saracen opened the front door very quietly, but hackles rose on the back of his neck when Tom's voice rumbled in the dark, "I been waiting for you."

"Has there been trouble?"

Tom's hoarse words spilled from his mouth. "They's always trouble when Teddy comes to mind, and you got to hear me tell it. That child stirred it up in me last night, and you're old enough to bear it now. I cain't carry this burden alone to the grave. I cain't do it!"

Saracen dropped onto the couch, his body diminished in the way of someone under a great strain. "I knew there was something else," he muttered.

Tom also appeared to have shrunk. Even his pupils had shriveled like dried seeds, and his voice was grudging, as though he were being forced to speak. "I kilt Teddy," he blurted.

Saracen sat up straight.

"God *know* I didn't do it a-purpose." Tom looked to heaven, as though he was always pleading with God to absolve him of that guilt. "Eulalia in the crazy house, and Baldwin screaming on the phone in the middle of the night for me to get on over there, 'cause Teddy come to take Shebbie asleep from her bed. So I go over."

"Speak more slowly, Daddy. *Please.* It's hard for me to understand what you're saying."

"And where that Polack fixing to take that little girl?"

Tom leaned toward Saracen, demanding an answer, but not ceasing the torrent of words that streamed from his mouth. "Over to that foreign place, leaving us behind? And how he going to feed that little girl? The man don't have no money, and he don't have no aerioplane; he done crash the thing, and he already in big trouble for stabbing ole Meyers. He hiding from the law already." Tom bent over, folded his arms, and rocked his body, his voice muffled, aimed at the floor.

"But Teddy don't listen to a word I say, just keep punching me like the devil hisself," Tom demonstrated the punches he took, hard jabs from the right and the left, "knocking over Baldwin accidental so she suffer in her back to this day. I try to hold him back gentle, but the man won't stop his punching. He too angry that fretful night.

"*Let me have my little child,* he kept crying, mixing up real words with them foreign ones. *Git outn my way,* he yell, *git outn my way, I'm taking what's mine.* And I say, you got to leave her be, or I have to hit you back.

"And I be dog if he don't flip out that belt knife on *me,* his *friend,* same knife he cripple ole Meyers with." Tom began to wring his big, calloused hands. "So I have to give him a little sock, aiming to slow him down, more like a shove, you know, not hard; but I surprise him, I reckon, he don't think I would do it, and he stumble and fall and hit his head on that little iron bedstead where Shebbie sleeping, that little three-quarter bedstead in the attic to this day, and she turn over a time or two, but thank Jesus, she keep on sleeping.

"And the minute he hit that bed, her daddy passed. I'm telling you, he passed! Gone to God, just like that!" Tom snapped his old fingers with a sound so loud, sparks seemed to scatter in the dark room. "One minute we knocking each other around, and the next minute the man *dead!*" His big head dropped to his chin as though he had been felled by the same blow. "I couldn't let him take that child," he pleaded to his son, "Could I? Don't he see that? But I got to be a miserable sinner on account of I kilt a good man who just gone crazy for a spell. And Teddy my friend!" Tom wailed.

Saracen inhaled so deeply he must have been holding his breath. "Then what did you do?"

"Baldwin behind me breathing hoarse like she got the croup, I can hear it to this day, till she bust out with, *We got to bury him*. I can hear her say them words day and night. *We got to bury him*. And I say *No, ma'am, we got to call the law*, and she say, *They treat Nigras awful bad at Tucker Farm; they got a lot of shallow graves down there. You be lucky if they hang you by the neck. We got to bury him.*

"And that woman up and leave me sweating like a hog with that poor man lying on the floor, his eyes still open and looking at me surprised, like asking how come I kilt him? And his child still sleeping like a angel, and me begging the Good Lord not to let her wake her up right then, and I'm praying to my Jesus to *please, bring him back to life, please, sweet Jesus, make a miracle in Your name. You can do it, Jesus, my only God!*"

And Saracen was thinking, Where was love in the world, where was forgiveness? Was life so hopeless that good men like his father had to suffer endlessly for one simple act of friendship?

"Then Baldwin comes in dragging two old army blankets smelling like moth balls, yammering at me to pull him on outta here, hurry up, hurry up; but, no ma'am, I cover him careful and hoist him over my shoulder, and he heavy too; but I ain't dragging him on that cold ground, and there wasn't a moon, praise the Lord, no sound but them crickets; and we go down to them back acres where folks can't see us, keeping far from that *Julien's* house, till we get to where there's that naked statue spouting water in that pretty little pond filled with frogs cherlumping as loud as daylight, *Sinner, Sinner, Sinner!*

"And the minute I lies him on the ground, I go down on

my hands and knees and prays to the Lord my God, *forgive me, Lord!* But Baldwin hissing, *You ain't got time to pray! You got to dig us a grave while it dark!*

"So I fetch the shovel outn the shed, and I dig. Warn't hard 'cause I fix them flowerbeds with lots of good cow hockey, and I dig deep and put Teddy's baseball cap back on him like he was wearing, and I cross his arms and straighten out his flying suit, and I tie up them boots just right, and I wrap him up better in them blankets, and I lay him in that hole gentle as a baby, and I cover his face with the tail end of them blankets so dirt won't get in his eyes or his mouth. But I got the dirt in my own mouth, I still taste that dirt, I choke on that dirt, and then I say the Lord's Prayer, never mind Baldwin, and I say the Twenty-third Psalm, and I would of said more, but Baldwin clawing at my shirt like a tiger to get up and drive on home. So I did what she say, and I go home and crawl in my bed and I stay there. And I don't go back to work for a good long while."

After Tom quit speaking, the room was silent. Tom's head was bowed like a penitent's, and Saracen's head was flung onto the back of the couch as though ready to be lopped off by the executioner.

Sometime during the next hour, Tom began to wail an old gospel hymn, repeating the same phrases over and over, the sound thin and reedy like an aged Indian's chant to the spirit world. Saracen clamped his hands to his ears as the song persisted, but he didn't ask his father to stop.

> *"There is no hiding place down here,*
> *No hiding place down here,*
> *Oh, I went down to the rock to hide my face,*
> *The rock yells out, "No hiding place.*
> *No hiding place. No hiding place."*

The words continued to whirl in the room, even after

Tom stopped singing.

No hiding place.

No hiding place.

And all the while Saracen grieved for Teddy, and he grieved for Eulalia, and he grieved for Shelby, and he grieved for his good-hearted father who had gone about his daily chores all those years, haunted by the thought of Teddy's body buried behind the house. And knowing that, Saracen loved his father more.

Sometime in the middle of the night, Tom cried out, "Ought I tell her? Ought I break her heart again? Ought I tell Eulalia?"

Saracen slumped when his father spoke Eulalia's name, then rose, bones creaking, stretching his long arms until they nearly touched the ceiling. He walked to his father's chair, put his arms under Tom's arms, and almost lifted him onto his feet. And Tom didn't object.

"Don't try to walk yet. You've been sitting too long, Daddy. You've got to get your balance, get your feet moving." The old man obeyed, shuffling his feet and moving his arms obediently while his son supported him in a loving embrace.

"And this is what I think," Saracen said, easing Tom back into his chair, and seating himself on the couch again. "You did what you had to do. Teddy's death was one of those unbelievably horrible accidents that are mourned forever. But I know . . . and *God* knows . . . you didn't mean to kill him. *God knows you didn't mean to kill Teddy Korzeniowski.* You've got to get that into your head, Daddy. It was a terrible, *terrible* accident that was *not* your fault. And God knows that to be the truth.

"As for telling Shelby . . ." Saracen paused much too long before he repeated, "*As for telling Shelby. . . .*" thinking to himself that his world was already so crazy he could never sort it out, much less ease his father's nightmare. It would destroy his beautiful Eulalia to hear that Tom had killed her husband, no matter how innocently, and that the man she had mourned to the point of insanity, was moldering just down the hill from her bedroom window.

And Shelby . . . Shelby would go on a rampage if she heard about Teddy's death and where he was buried. The tragedy of what happened and what she might do if it were made known to her was beyond grotesque.

Saracen had to keep his own addled, dead-tired mind clear enough to think his way out of the maelstrom and find the right words just to *begin* to soothe his father's pain, to *begin* to help this good, old man put his frantic mind somewhat to rest.

"Shelby will be going through hell absorbing what she learned last night. She might forgive *you* for . . . for what you did. But I'm not certain she could forgive Baldwin, and that would be tragic." He swallowed hard, and cleared his throat again. "I . . . I don't know what Eulalia can forgive. She's trying to leave it all behind, but I don't know what this news would do to her. I . . . I just don't know.

"And what if Eulalia and Shelby wanted to dig Teddy up and give him a proper burial?" Saracen's attempt to laugh got strangled. "Maybe we should just let him rest in peace where he is. It's still pretty down there. Overgrown, but lots of flowers."

His father grunted skeptically.

"But I do know that Shelby needs to hear that you love her. She'll be choking on the stuff she learned tonight about her parents for a long while. She'll put her anger to rest after a while, but in the meantime, she'll need to feel that someone in the world loves her, no holds barred. And that has to be you."

Then Saracen announced to the room and the world beyond, as though it were important to get this much straight: "But they were all good people in that family. Even Baldwin was good enough. They just didn't know how to figure things out without destroying one another. What in God's name makes us hurt one other so deeply when we love one another so much?"

Saracen sighed and fell back onto the couch again with such finality it seemed he might never rise. "I guess . . . I guess you and I are what's left to be their family."

"Family?" Tom turned toward Saracen. "You say *family?*" His voice was suddenly harsh. "Don't you think I know what you been doing with Eulalia every night, boy! I ain't blind yet! Colored boy like you and white woman like her, older by eleven year? You call running around with her momma on the sly being *family* to Shelby Howell?"

Eastern light had begun to flood the room with wintry rays, and sounds were heard that could be counted on at the beginning of a new day: roosters crowing, the rattle of bottles in the milk truck, the slap of newspapers landing on stoops, the 5:30 a.m. whistle of the freight as it slowed around the bend.

Saracen rose to his full height, glowering, his mouth stretched furiously, and for a moment it seemed he might do Tom bodily harm. "I *love* Eulalia, Daddy. Do you think I *wanted* to fall in love with her? Or she with me? You think I don't know how complicated this is?" He gave a mirthless laugh. "Maybe our love is Teddy's vengeance!"

But Tom wouldn't stop his screed. "Don't you hear what I just told you? I kilt Shelby's daddy, and now you gonna make Shelby feel like her momma's kilt too!"

When Tom quit his coughing fit, he could barely whisper. "We both miserable sinners, boy. You understand what I'm saying? There ain't no hiding place for us. There never gonna be no hiding place for you and me.

49

WHEN CHARLIE STEPPED outside his front door the next day, Saracen was waiting for him. There was a glint in his weary eyes, and a staccato tempo to his hoarse voice.

"I'm Saracen Self, but I think you know that. You left me a packet of photographs at my father's door, and those photographs helped save a good man's job. Actually, they saved his and his family's lives. It took me a while to figure out who the Good Samaritan was, but now I've come to thank you for that good deed.

"I admire your approach to righting wrongs, and I have another project in mind regarding Julien Hutchins. I think you and I could work together quite effectively on this undertaking." Saracen's laugh was quick and ironic. "No pun intended."

Charlie stared at him for a moment, then extended his hand in a firm shake. "It's good to meet you. And you're right. We do have a lot to talk about. Please come inside."

50

ON HER RETURN to New York City, Shelby knew she was different.

She felt angrier, braver, more curious. She didn't stop to wonder if this was a permanent change, or whether she would spend her life seeking answers or revenge. She only knew her father had become her nemesis in a way, and she needed, even more urgently, to find him. She didn't stop to wonder whether it might be a futile search. She only knew she had to find him.

The weather was cold and the areas she searched often had an overlay of suffering, and the streets seemed to reek with secrets.

Last autumn she had knocked on the doors of a few of the Korzeniowskis listed in the phone book. Ben had been her guide, though he thought she was searching for relatives of the great Joseph Conrad, which had amused him. Now, on weekends and between part-time jobs, Shelby hit the trail by herself.

She wore her shrunken coat and no makeup and a wool hat to cover her hair, in an effort to become part of the passing scene where one didn't see blondes. But she took off the hat when she knocked at apartment doors, holding up her father's picture, hoping to confirm her mission before doors could be slammed: a tall, blonde young woman with piercing green eyes and a fierce expression, holding up a photograph of a smiling man who looked just like her and who seemed to beckon to the person in the doorway.

The occupants all said, *No Teodore here,* though finally, someone mentioned a "Korzeniowski" who he thought lived on the East Side.

So Shelby sloshed through snow and rain into the East Seventies and Eighties and Nineties, where Europeans had emigrated after the war, and she ate smashed peanut butter sandwiches she had encased in waxed paper and stuffed in her pockets, and she drank steaming cups of burned coffee or sweet tea in smoky restaurants where English wasn't spoken. Occasionally, she would gorge on exotic pastries sold in shops by people who had bad teeth. But the languages she heard on those streets were a polyglot of sounds that filled her with hope, and if a word was vaguely familiar, she would close in on the source, her antennae alert, and snatch off her hat and hold up the photograph. People stared wide-eyed from the young woman's intense face to the image she held up like an icon.

When finally there came a frown and a flutter of recognition from a woman about Eulalia's age, Shelby's heart began to race, and she pushed her way into the room, begging, then *demanding* the woman tell her what she knew about the man in the picture. The woman, stronger than she looked, pushed her back into the hall, with Shelby shouting, "Wait! Wait! I'm his daughter! I have to find him! Please tell me where he is!"

The woman's accent was as thick as the foul odor in the air. "He should be in hell by now," she snarled and spat on the floor to seal the curse. But when she looked again and saw Shelby's woe, her tone softened some. "He might be in Greenpoint. He had a woman there too, but I heard he left her. He always leaves. He left you, didn't he? His own daughter? You should forget about that man like I have. He leaves his women!"

But Shelby knew she would never forget the man, Teodore Korzeniowski, and she knew this woman wouldn't either.

She followed the signs that led her toward the rumbling, dark underworld of subways, and when she emerged in the sunlight, she was in Greenpoint, which she roamed with a lighter spring to her step. It was not so foreboding as the East Side had felt. The weather was a bit warmer, the East River was closer, and it was easy to see the horizon. If you weren't near the river, it was hard to see the horizon in Manhattan. Life seemed more hopeful if the horizon was visible and the sky could spread out like a big blue eye.

There were a few small apartment buildings, some large nineteenth-century homes, still dignified in spite of their disrepair, and smaller houses on fenced-in lots piled high with snow that was almost clean. The place flirted with the feel of a village, with signs announcing *Mowimy po Polsku: Polish Spoken Here*. The stores were warm and noisy inside, with aromas of sauerkraut and pierogis and kielbasa and babkas, and the air hummed with the bewitching sounds of the language she hadn't heard since she was six years old.

She felt a surge of excitement when she whipped out her father's photograph, her smile as broad as the man's in the worn picture that she carefully slipped from its envelope.

"This is my papa," she would say. "Have you seen him?"

But people didn't smile back, even in Greenpoint. They had their own woes, and they eased away, trailing remnants of their mother tongue, and looks that said this strange girl might be crazy. They didn't identify the photograph of Theodore Korzeniowski, but without the photograph, there existed the possibility her father, whom she needed to find and destroy, might never have existed. In spite of his sins, she needed to see the philandering savage who could barely make a living flying stunts, and who had married her mother, who became a vengeful whore, but only after he had made her pregnant and deceived her repeatedly.

Eventually, she quit Greenpoint and took long bus rides

to LaGuardia airport. But again people stepped away when the earnest young woman, clad in clothes that might have belonged to a beleaguered tramp, pulled a framed photograph with no glass from a battered envelope, and asked about a pilot with a foreign accent who flew small planes.

The pretty stewardesses in their tailored suits and their perky hats turned their backs, high heels clicking, stocking seams perfectly straight. But when she spoke to pilots, all men, she removed her scarf and coat and let her hair fall around her shoulders. *My father disappeared some years back,* she would say, and the pilot's pace would slow. *He was a pilot and performed in flying circuses. His eyes are the color of mine,* holding up the photograph, her green eyes plowing into theirs, trying to jog the memories of men who were more than ready to buy her dinner.

But none of them had heard about her papa.

In the spring she wanted to visit flying circuses, which might be fertile territory. Transportation was the problem, until one day Boojie, ever faithful, appeared on Riverside Drive dressed in a chauffeur's uniform, his red hair aflame in the sun, standing beside a long black car with dove-grey doors and a spare tire set in the back fender like a pearl in a platinum ring.

The car, a V12 Packard, had a naked woman's torso floating on top of the radiator, her arms caught up in her long chrome hair that flowed eternally. The ornament, combined with the sleek lines of the car's chassis and the flashy chrome teeth on the radiator snout, summoned the drama of smashed barriers at European checkpoints, and border guards shooting at the car's wake as it roared away.

Boojie's hand stayed on the horn until Shelby shoved up a cranky window and stuck out her head. He waved a triumphant fist at her and shouted, "Once more into the breach, dear friend! Let's go look for Teodore!"

"Where did you get that limo, *and* the uniform?" she shouted back.

"I released it from my parents for a few days! They're on the Riviera and won't miss their V12 Packard for months! I borrowed the uniform from their chauffeur, who is my friend. So dress to the nines and come down, dear Shelby. Let's go see some flying circuses!"

They arrived in all their glory at country fields that thrummed like bumblebees with the engines of small planes. People were waiting for the show to begin, but when they glimpsed that V12 Packard, they dashed over to it for a closer look.

Boojie (he was the chauffeur) would open the door with a flourish, and Shelby (she was the movie star) would exit, one high-heeled long leg at a time, holding up the photograph of her father, and shouting from the diaphragm: *I'm looking for a flying circus pilot who looks like me! Have you seen him?*

But no one had.

She had tried to describe her need to find her father to Charlie on that memorable evening, but for reasons she couldn't understand, she didn't answer his sweet letters or take his phone calls. She didn't answer anyone's letters from home, which made her feel like a castaway on an island. Alone. She was all alone.

51

March 30, 1957

Dear Shelby,

Whatever did you do at Baldwin's meeting over Christmas? It must have been something terrible, because when Bruce came home that night, he told me I had to stay away from you! Can you imagine? And you my best friend in the whole world and he shouting like he was my lord and master! But you ran back to New York City without even telling me goodbye, and I haven't heard a word from you since. That hurts my feelings, Shelby Howell, and it has taken me a while to write to you, I can tell you that.

But then I've been real busy. Bruce Caldwell Norton III arrived at 10:14 p.m., January 18, and he is the cutest little thing! I wanted to tell you the good tidings right away, but I waited until I could be nice. Big Bruce is a little bit put out, because little Brucie looks so much like me. He really is adorable! I love the nursing part, and I'll tell you this and nobody else . . . so does Big Bruce! But don't you dare tell anybody that little secret! He says mother's milk gives him more energy!

And you're going to be real glad I'm still such a good friend, because the latest news bulletin from Little Rock is HUGE and I know it all. At Bobby Kingston's funeral, which was open casket, there was a toupee on Bobby's head that looked just like Julien Hutchins' HAIR! . . and Julien was Bobby's undertaker!! Isn't that the meanest thing you ever heard anyone do to a dead person? And now everyone in town knows Julien wears a wig! People say maybe he was born bald and his head just stayed that way. I think he was just born weird. I never did like the way he looked at us. Like he wanted to take a bite or something.

Bobby's family was furious, of course, and I hear Julien was so apologetic he practically crawled into the coffin with Bobby! But then the same thing happened at Lester Clark's funeral, and everyone knows he was bald as a billiard ball! Of course, I was horrified. I didn't get to Bobby's funeral, but I sure went to Lester's, even though I could barely walk after the baby and all. Having babies really hurts, Shelby. You should keep that in mind. One baby is enough for any human woman.

But, as I was saying, a few weeks later when Vivian Walters died, Julien didn't leave her coffin for a second. There was standing room only at that funeral, even though Vivian was so mean, she didn't have many friends. But when I went for the viewing . . . and I was first in line . . . there was a toupee on top of her head, and she was covered with a navy-blue cashmere coat just like Julien's! Isn't it awful? Whoever is doing this stuff must be a magician!

After that second terrible mess-up, Julien is losing business right and left. I told Bruce to put it in my will that Julien can't lay a finger on my dead body. Nobody wants an undertaker who can't keep control of his bodies!

Bruce is plain disgusted, because Julien's problems with corpses have pushed the nigger issue at Central High to the back of people's minds. But that NAACP thing filed a suit because the number of nigger kids who wanted to enter Central was cut back again, and you can thank Bruce for that cut-back victory.

I hope you'll write me quick about that cashmere coat with the red lining you were wearing over Christmas, so I can set people straight on that subject. People are wondering about it. And to tell the plain truth, your face didn't look so great while you were here. Like someone had hit you or something. I told people you were just tired from your schooling up there, it being so far away and having to mix up with actors and coloreds

365

and other weird people.

Do write soonest. You know I won't tell a soul about anything private you tell me. I miss my best friend! Best friends are hard to come by.

Love, Kate

P.S. I'm on my way to the post office with this letter right now!

52

"WHO ARE YOU? You have no idea who you are in this scene, do you? And for God's sake, what's your objective? Will you never learn that you have to have an objective? Even this playwright, Beckett, has objectives, if you have the wit to understand them."

Liebmann sighed and removed his glasses with such delicacy, he seemed to be peeling off skin.

"You've learned nothing in this class, Billy. You declaim, and then declaim more. And the same goes for you, Monique." Liebmann nodded his head, but didn't look at her. "I can't do more for you. I've done all I can for both of you."

The other students froze in their chairs.

Monique's makeup seemed to crack, and she took a step back, dumbstruck.

Billy Spencer blinked rapidly, then jabbed his finger at Liebmann. "I'm not inhibited," he protested, thrusting his swarming hands in his pocket, even though Liebmann had just instructed him to stem that mannerism.

Liebmann rolled his eyes. "You can't stop those hands from hopping around, even while they're in your pockets. Relax, goddammit. *Relax!*"

"I *am* relaxed," Billy almost squeaked. The change in his pockets jingled, and his bones seemed to clack against one another.

"Don't argue with me!" Liebmann roared. "And take your goddamn hands out of your pockets!"

When Billy jerked his hands free, money fell to the floor

from holes his fingers had made during their desperate confinements, but he ignored the clatter and raised his chin defiantly.

"I *am* an actor! I'm just not a slave to your *method* of acting!"

Liebmann slapped his hand on the desk with angry satisfaction. "And there you have it, my friend. You're threatened by what I have to offer, which, in the distant future, might have helped you become an adequate performer. But you're terrified of what you might reveal about yourself, which means you'll never grow as an actor. You'll jiggle pennies in your pockets and maintain every bad acting habit you had before you came here, because if you let them go, you fear you'll drown in the muck of your own opprobrious thoughts. So keep all of your pitiful crutches! *Declaim in hell and get out of my school!*"

The dreaded words hung in the air: Get out of my school. You're no good. You're not an actor.

You might as well be dead.

Shelby couldn't breathe. To be kicked out so cruelly and in front of everyone was unspeakable. She wanted to take Billy in her arms, and yell at Liebmann to stop saying such hurtful things. But she didn't have the guts. Instead, she sat very still and trapped her hands beneath her butt.

Billy's Adam's apple raced up and down his long throat like an agitated frog. "What do you mean?"

"I mean I can't teach you anything!" Liebmann pointed to the door with his arm fully extended. "I mean get out and don't come back!"

Billy's twitching nose and upturned chin seemed the only reason his glasses stayed hooked to his ears. "But I can't leave." He sounded desperate. "I belong here. I'm on the G.I. Bill, and my tuition's paid for. . . ."

"D'Arcy will give you a check," Liebmann interrupted.

"She's done it before." He tossed his cigarette toward the ash-tray, but missed, which he never did.

The ever-vigilant Stanley was staring openmouthed at Billy's plight, and ignoring the lit cigarette on top of the wooden table.

Billy looked as though he had witnessed a terrible accident, but he was the victim. He turned toward Monique, who stared straight ahead, one palm spread toward Liebmann as though fending off evil. He looked at Robert, who was studying the floor as though his life depended on finding a hole he could fall through.

Then Billy slowly shuffled toward his briefcase, thin shoulders twitching. The sense of doom in the room was palpable. Most heads were averted from Billy's agony.

Except for a quiver in his nostrils, Liebmann looked unmoved, but his cigarette holder still lay on the desk, the embers slowly charring the wood. The ever-vigilant Stanley continued to stare, horror-stricken, at the vanquished Billy, oblivious to the rising wisp of smoke.

Shelby couldn't avert her eyes from Billy. She should do something to help him, be kind to him, take his hand, but instead she watched, with everyone else, as he removed his rimless glasses with trembling fingers and placed them carefully in his pocket. Then, before astonished eyes, he thrust his briefcase before his weak face like a battering ram, and charged toward Liebmann, howling, "*I am somebody!*"

The loud, pitiful cry masked a mournful growl coming from Bernard.

Stanley was almost as frail as Billy, but he leaped to his feet and thrust his thin shoulders in front of his lord and master at the same time that Robert and Hank grabbed Billy, lifted him beneath his shoulders, and dragged him from the room, pocket change dribbling down his legs.

The growling from Bernard had become louder, and

the whites of his eyes were almost eclipsed with rage as he pounded across the room, got down on his hands and knees, collected every penny of the meager sum, and started to stalk after Billy, returning the money with an open palm.

"*Wait.*" Liebmann commanded.

Bernard stopped at the door, quivering like an animal at his master's command.

But it was Monique who faced Liebmann, tears muddy with makeup. Her voice, beginning deep in her throat, became increasingly strident. "You are a vicious man. You make us feel disgusting so you can dominate us and make us suffer! I don't care that you're a good teacher! You're mean and you're . . . you're cruel!"

At first Liebmann turned icy eyes toward her; and then suddenly his face broke into a jubilant smile.

"That's it, Monique! *That's* the passion you needed in the scene with Billy. We're getting somewhere. Finally!"

Monique seemed briefly disoriented by his remarks, but Bernard spoke, one big fist closed tight with pocket change, one hand squeezed on the doorknob. "She's right."

Monique looked gratefully toward Bernard and found her own voice again. "I'm not staying in this class either."

She began to stuff papers into her large purse, shouting, "You're a crazy bastard who's using our emotional pain for your own vicarious pleasure! *And I defy you!*"

But Monique's tirade seemed not to bother Liebmann. He lifted his arms, his pirate sleeves billowing like sails. "Defy me! Fine! But I do get it, and so do you, my darling girl! *Finally* you get it, as you did a few years back. You're going to act again! So listen to me. I want you, with Bernard, to begin that same scene, but this time you'll have a true actor as your partner. And class, watch carefully. Monique will keep the preparation she has just created, and Bernard will improvise the lines. You've watched this scene enough to improvise, my dear Bernard. You're good at that. So enter stage left, and the two of you . . . *begin!*"

But Monique pushed in front of Bernard, turned the doorknob with an angry twist, and rushed from the room, with Bernard following her, muttering, "She got it right about you, old man. I don't want what you got to give, either. I've had enough of what you got to give."

Boojie clattered down the platform after Bernard, imploring eyes lifted to Liebmann with a silent plea, *I've got to try and save him. Someone has to save him.*

Shelby rose just as quickly and followed Boojie, not daring to look at Leibmann.

Stanley finally, but absently, poured water from Liebmann's glass onto the smoldering cigarette, and, with small, urgent sweeps of his hands, motioned the remaining students to leave.

Liebmann sat motionless, staring at the ceiling, his teeth clamped to his empty cigarette holder.

53

My dear daughter,
*Please write to me. Or call. Anytime. I've bothered you with
too many phone messages and letters, but I'm desperate to hear
your voice. I'm glad Charlie saw you when he was in New York
City, although he says you were too busy for more than a cup
of coffee. Charlie loves you, but you must know that. He's such
a fine young man. If you care for him, let him know. And soon.
I think he's becoming restless.*

    *I've learned that Julien assaulted you in New York City,
and I am so very, very sorry, my sweet girl. He is a disgusting
little man who should rot in hell. As a consequence of his cruelty toward you, Saracen Self and Charlie Billington, who, it
appears, have become fast friends, have organized some dreadful effort to humiliate Julien. I should have dissuaded them,
but he's been such a cruel antagonist to me and mine, I let it
happen. God forgive me, I hate the man. My only hope is he'll
move far away.*

    *Also, and I've waited too many months to write about this
matter. It's so hard for me to do. . . .*

Shelby nearly cried out in relief. Her mother was going to
confess that Saracen Self was her lover! At least that betrayal
would be out in the open.

    But, no. . . .

*I've also learned that Tom told you the pitiful story about your
father and me. I've said to myself so many times, she's old enough
now, she needs to know what happened. But your image of your*

father would have been shattered, and your love for me destroyed. You are my daughter, my one and only darling daughter. I couldn't live without your love.

"Ah, but you have Saracen Self. Say it! Spit it out!" Shelby shouted to the empty room. "Admit you're no better than my father was!"

The ridiculous part about the whole sad episode was that your father and I loved one another deeply, and we always loved you. You were our treasure, and still are mine.

And I have more awful news that will be hard for you to believe. Baldwin is spending too much time in bed with her hot water bottle, and with Alfred, whose once-fine tail has become a string. I fear she'll roll over on that old cat and smother him. They look about the same age, and have the same meager energy.

She hasn't said a word about it, but I think she's suffering about what Julien did to you. She sits at her bedroom window and stares at the back acres, hour after hour. My hope is, with spring coming, she'll rise from the chair and march outside to plant and prune and order Tom around like she always has. She needs to get her hands in that earth, spread the roots of plantings and cover them with her own perfect mix of soil. I'm convinced she can hear seeds pushing to the surface from deep underground. The earth is her true mother. I think it calls to her.

The crocuses are emerging like baby birds, and the tree branches are looking muscular and nearly bursting with juices. They seem to tease us with hope for the future. I love the notion of engorged seeds pushing toward the surface from deep underground to surprise us with beauty. I wish you were here to see it happen.

Also . . . your grandmother is drinking too much hard liquor.

Baldwin? Staying in bed and drinking *whiskey*?

She must be finding some of your great-grandfather's cache.

*God only knows how she drags her old body to the hiding plac-
es. If you were here, I think she would restrain herself.*

Shelby knew she had to subdue her anger and go home.
But she also knew she had to complete The Acting School se-
mester. Liebmann had been cool toward her since she walked
out of class, and she needed him to help her find work after
classes ended.

*On a very different subject, I've been doing a bit of spying.
I'm the unobtrusive mouse at the State House, the mere secretary who obediently types Faubus's papers, but it's depressing to
learn he has so little compassion for the people he represents.
Saracen Self tells me I'm naive, but I think I'm becoming quite
good at the spy business.*

Saracen Self. Her mother wrote the name again as though
Saracen were a mere passerby who stopped by her desk for
an occasional chat.

*Do write, my daughter. Please write. Or call. I love you, my
darling. Momma*

*P.S. I'm thinking of going to Paris, France next fall. I know
it's a heady thing to consider, since I've never even been to Paris,
Arkansas. But why not go to France? Maybe live there? Why not
go to Hong Kong, for that matter? I once received a postcard from
my grandfather postmarked Hong Kong. It seemed so exotic to a
young girl. Do you remember the postcards your father used to
send? I'm sure he printed in capital letters so a little girl who waited for the mail to fall through the slot could read them before her
mother did. I loved . . . and hated . . . to see them, and yet I missed
them so much when they stopped coming.*

*It must sound strange, my nattering like this. I've never
nattered before. But I feel as though I've been shocked back
into life, the present, and also the past. But whatever happens,*

I'll keep writing, and maybe someday you'll write back to me.

> *I'll love you always, my darling.*
> *Momma*

Shelby ironed her mother's letter flat with her hand. Then she ripped it apart, put her hand out the window and watched the pieces flutter to the pavement.

54

"THERE! SEE HER? In the dark glasses and the big hat? The woman near the corner?"

"Oh, Booj . . . that's not Greta Garbo. That woman looks haggard, and Garbo could never look haggard. Her bones are too great."

"It's Garbo! I could spot that face a mile away! A reliable source told me she walks miles in this city every day, rain or shine. It's Garbo, alright. Maybe she'll give us an autograph."

"You don't have paper for her to sign!"

Boojie ignored her and started after Garbo, but Shelby and Hank continued to walk toward the Village Vanguard, hoping to find Bernard, who never missed a chance to hear Miles Davis play.

Boojie teetered for a moment between his friends and Garbo. Then, with a sigh, he gave up the great actress to drift down the sidewalk with his friends.

There was goodwill among men and women when the weather was perfect in New York City, and this was a perfect night. Music floated from street corners, bongos thrummed the air, restaurant doors were wide open, lovers walked hand in hand, taxi drivers smiled.

Suddenly Hank shouted, "Across the street! There he is!"

And there he was, indeed. Bernard, was watching them from the other side, moving when they moved. But his step was unsteady.

"Oh, God," Boojie moaned. "He's smoking too much tea."

"Tea?" Shelby asked.

"Marijuana, you goof. Pot. You never listen when I explain things. I just hope it isn't anything stronger."

Shelby made a soughing sound. "He's so skinny. Do you think he's eating anything?"

"His fingernails, probably."

Each time the three took a step, Bernard did the same.

"This is too weird." There was no way Bernard could hear him, though Hank lowered his voice. "Is he still installing lights at his place? The last time I was there, the ceiling was covered with light bulbs."

"He's working on the walls now."

"And he was doing something with his hair. Spreading goop and covering it with a net. And that other jar he had. What was that?"

"The goop is hair straightener. The other stuff's supposed to make his skin turn white."

Shelby gasped. "My God! Make him stop, Boojie! Remember how I nearly burned my skin off when I tried to dye it black? It took me weeks to recover."

"You didn't tell *me* about that," Hank said enviously.

"I didn't tell you, because I knew someday I would read about it in one of your plays. I still have a scar from that stuff. Go tell Bernard, Boojie. Hurry!"

"*You* tell him. He'll do what *you* say." Their eyes stayed pinned to Bernard as they continued their curious dance along opposite sides of Seventh Avenue.

"Hey, 'B'!" Boojie yelled over the noise of the traffic. "Come on over! Let's go see Miles Davis!"

Bernard stared at them, cars blocking, then revealing his forlorn figure.

"Come on over, 'B'!" Boojie yelled again. "This is the best side to be on!"

Bernard continued to stare.

Shelby's voice was as low as Hank's had been. "Before he

dropped out of the Playhouse, he had become obsessed with this racial business in Little Rock. He never reveals his feelings about anything . . . unless he's acting . . . but this time he sounded so sad. His smart niece is one of the seventeen who'll integrate the school, and he's afraid she'll get hurt in more ways than one. He wants her family to move near a good, safe school, and when I asked him where, he moaned, '*We got no better place.*'"

"*Call* to him, Shelby," Boojie pleaded. "He'll come if you call."

Shelby gave Boojie a fierce look, but she obeyed.

"Hey, Bernard! I'll race you to the corner and meet you at the stoplight!"

She began to jog down the sidewalk toward the light, with Boojie and Hank following. Bernard did his unsteady best to keep up, but when they reached the light, he wasn't there.

"Damn," Boojie sputtered, and followed Shelby as she ran across the street to search for Bernard.

Hank stayed put, teetering on the curb. "Should we spread out?" he called.

"Keep your eyes peeled over there! He may come over before we can find him over here!" Boojie called back, scanning faces, talking more quietly to Shelby. "I went to his place the other day, and all the lights were lit on the ceiling and the wall, and a record was playing on his portable, but he was *gone*. He must have a secret escape route when he doesn't want company."

"That *Invisible Man* book is driving him nuts. He takes it too seriously. Soon he'll be waving a sword and riding a horse down Fifth Avenue, like the guy in the book."

Boojie looked at her. "You read it."

"So?" she said defensively.

"So . . . let's not worry about Bernard. He'll be okay."

But a cloud covered the moon, lovers began to quarrel,

and the city no longer seemed peaceable.

When Boojie and Shelby crossed the street to rejoin Hank, Bernard reappeared on his side. Boojie whistled and Hank and Shelby waved their arms and shouted, until they gave up and walked to the Village Vanguard, without Bernard, to hear Miles Davis play.

55

"WE'VE CREATED A MONSTER."

It was one of those hot, windless southern evenings when the crickets were almost as loud as the mockingbirds. Saracen was sitting on a brown leather chair in Charlie's first floor study, one long leg thrown over the chair arm. He was jiggling his foot, and jabbing forefinger prints onto a chilled bottle of Griesedieck Brothers beer.

"Julien sits in his yard all day long in the hot sun with his binoculars focused on Baldwin's house. He looks banal, but evil can be banal. As long as he was king of the caskets, he could swagger about town and scare black folks in his spare time; but now spying on Baldwin's house out in the open seems to be his full-time job."

Charlie craned his neck from a window, trying to see where a mockingbird was perched. "We may have ripped off his civilized mask when we ripped off his wig. We humiliated him, which wasn't a smart thing to do. Now the aggrieved man wants revenge. Though I've heard rumors he has another business in North Little Rock."

When the bird burst into another round of intricate embellishments, the men turned to listen, enraptured by the crystalline sounds that lingered, as though the warm air was reluctant to release that perfect beauty.

"That bird sings pretty good, but I hate him," Charlie said. "Every time I mow the lawn, he swoops down at me like a kamikaze."

"You probably disturbed his nest," Saracen said

matter-of-factly.

"Have you noticed how quiet a lot of the white business-men in this town have become? They're afraid. Afraid for their families. Afraid for their businesses. Afraid for their nests. Sort of like what happened in Nazi Germany, I imagine. When I walk into a store they growl and pretend they don't see me. They didn't used to growl like that. Most of the big cotton and rice farmers make no bones about their rabid feelings. They're threatening out loud to transfer their money to banks in Memphis if the schools in Little Rock are integrated."

Charlie nodded. "I've told you before we white folks are used to being in control of society. We grew up knowing we were better than people with dark skin. It was like a lullaby we heard in our cradles. Rockabye, white baby, you are superior."

"But you don't feel that way."

"Lots of people around here don't feel that way. They just don't talk about it. They hide their feelings. Afraid to speak out. If I didn't respect Negroes when I was a kid, I got paddled. Believe it or not, my daddy is not as prejudiced as you might think. He's doing his best to calm down some of the crazies in Arkansas. I never told you he was the one who arranged to have those pictures taken of Judd Meyers and the hookers . . . but not until after the title of the delta land was in the Billington lockbox. The man can be ruthless. But I understand him."

Saracen waved his Greisedick at Charlie. "Your daddy's a practical man. I'm drinking to your daddy. And did you hear about that white guy, J.C. Johnson, who owns the big junkyard on the Hot Springs Highway? Word is, when a Klan member tried to solicit money from him, Johnson told the guy that cowards who hide behind white sheets would have sheets tied around *their* necks someday. So, of course, the junkyard is boycotted, like a lot of other places in town."

"But I can give you a list of whites who are sticking their

necks out for you and yours, Saracen. Old Adolphine Terry, the richest lady in town, is tutoring the Negro kids who are planning to enter Central, and the *Gazette* is losing money hand over fist because of its stance on Negroes."

"Oh, yeah. That editor, Harry Ashmore, writes as melodiously as our mockingbird sings, but he thinks schools should be integrated as long as there's no *social* segregation. Keep my kids away from those niggers after school hours. He'll never ask *me* to his house for a drink, even though he knows my name and pumps me for information with a 'good ole buddy' slap on the back."

Charlie's grin was ironic. "I've got news for you, ole buddy. Everyone in town knows who you are. You don't exactly hide behind a tree."

"Okay, okay. And that's not a good thing if you're black. But the man who really disgusts me is Orval Faubus. He has this animal sense for weakness in others that I thought *perhaps* he would use to black folks' advantage. He comes from a hard-scrabble background. I thought he might understand us. But the 'Negro problem' is threatening his ambition, so he's turned his back on us. He let that law pass last fall that orders the NAACP to list all its money and membership, and the *law,* mind you, that allows whites to withdraw from integrated classes. And don't forget the order of interposition. Don't forget that beauty! I even hear Ike's a racist at heart." Saracen slumped in his chair, the beer bottle pressed against his forehead, as though stemming the boil of his blood.

When the mockingbird perched on top of the chimney and held forth like a mad coloratura, Charlie grimaced, but not at the bird. "Without power, Faubus is just a redneck from Greasy Creek. He told me privately when I went to his office that he has no choice but to exploit the race issue. Otherwise that true bigot, Jim Johnson, will win the race for governor! Can you believe that sophistry? He even said he would have voted for the Brown decision, but when a reporter called later to confirm, he laughed and said, 'Just because I said it, doesn't make it so.' I don't know how to stop the bastard, except to shoot him. Same way with the mockingbird. Same way with Julien."

Saracen set his beer down very carefully, his eyes narrowed to small green slits. "Say that last thing again."

"What?"

"About shooting Julien."

Charlie gave him a cautious look. "I don't mean actually *shoot* the sonuvabitch."

"Of course not. We couldn't do that, could we," although there was a modicum of doubt in his voice. "But maybe we could set him up in business somewhere else, somewhere like . . . *South Africa*. Yeah . . . he could spit on Kaffirs day and night in South Africa."

Charlie became very still, chin puckered, eyes thoughtful, as though he were taking Saracen's idea seriously. "He won't move that far, but he *might* move to another town. Become an undertaker in Mississippi, maybe, where he has relatives. The idea would have to be presented *very* carefully, and by someone he trusts. But . . . oh, for God's sakes! The guy wants his revenge here in Little Rock, and he's plotting it now! He'll never move away!"

He took a long swallow of beer and changed the subject, as though ridding himself of temptation. "When I had that meeting with the governor the other day. I told him, very diplomatically, that his dance with the devil would surely bring bloodshed. And he told *me*, with a face as straight as mine, that he *has* to play the race card. 'It's just logic, Charlie, my boy, *political* logic. And by the way,' he says to me, 'you should watch your back. I hear certain bad actors don't like the way you're cozying up to the coloreds.'

"'Is that a threat?' I asked him, and he looked way too shocked. 'Of *course* not, my son,' he said, and grinned like he had swallowed a canary. 'Of course not. I would never threaten you.'"

Saracen stabbed a finger harder on the beer bottle.

When the mockingbird recommenced his song, Charlie rose and yelled up the chimney, "Shut up, bird!" And the bird obeyed. The silence that followed was broken only by the soft swish of Saracen crossing and uncrossing his legs, until he blurted, "I'm going to tell you something that's very confidential. *Extremely* confidential."

Charlie pulled back in his chair as Saracen leaned closer and almost whispered, "Eulalia Howell and I are in love. We want to get married. Shelby doesn't know."

There was a pause before Charlie answered, his voice curiously restrained. "I'm very happy for you. As for Shelby . . ." he paused longer, "Shelby knows about you and her mother."

Saracen sat up very straight and stared, not at Charlie, but at a void. "But we've been so careful."

Charlie shrugged uncomfortably. "The night she had dinner with Tom and you over Christmas, she saw Eulalia walking toward your car, guessed what was going on, and came to me, almost hysterical. It was quite a night."

Saracen slammed his bottle onto a side table. The smell of spilled beer sharpened the turgid air. "*Damn!*" He slapped angrily at the mess with his handkerchief. "That's *another* reason she hasn't communicated with me or her mother!" He slammed the sopping handkerchief into a wastebasket as though it were the cause of all his grief.

Then Charlie said, "Call her. *Apologize.* Tell her you wished you had confided in her sooner. I think it's hard for her to trust anyone these days." He cleared his throat uncomfortably. "Including me."

Saracen responded with a sarcastic lilt to his voice, "I have to tell *you*, Charlie, Shelby's a pistol compared to Charlene at the TV station. No offense toward Charlene, she's a great looker, but there aren't many Shelbys in this world," adding ruefully, "thank God. And yeah, I know . . . Charlene's none of my business."

The men's anxious thoughts collided with the effortless beauty of the birdsong, until thoughts and song were obliterated by a brick exploding through Charlie's front window and landing at his feet. The brick was painted with big red letters. *Nigger Lover!!!* The crash was followed by the sound of a heavy engine taking off at high speed.

Charlie squinted at the brick, lifted it with delicate fingers, and slammed it back out the broken window as hard as he could.

But Saracen sprang to his feet like the reporter he was, threw open the front door, and began to lope silently down the street, tracking the sound of the car.

It took a moment for Charlie's anger to surge, at which point he began to yell at the top of his lungs and follow Saracen's long, quiet strides to the street. Sure, Charlie had ruffled a few white feathers in town, but he was the cream of Little Rock society, the most eligible bachelor in town, the hope for the state's future. *He was Charlie Billington!* He could sit in his elegantly furnished, nineteenth-century home with anyone he chose!

Saracen slowed down, then stopped abruptly, but Charlie rocketed past him, still yelling. Lights popped on up and down the street, and neighbors shouted, and police sirens wailed in the distance. The mockingbird appeared from nowhere and began to dive at Charlie, swooping back and forth, and diving again. Charlie waved his fists, cursing the bird as fiercely as he cursed the thug who had robbed him of his peace of mind. When the bird finally quit the onslaught, Charlie began a ragged walk back to his house where Saracen was in his MG, switching on the ignition.

"Did you see that?" Charlie sounded incredulous. "Some goddam crazy tried to kill me with a brick, and that goddam mockingbird attacked me in the *dark!* That damn bird is crazy! This whole town has gone crazy!"

"Like I said, you disturbed the bird's nest."

"The bird is harassing *me!* And the sonuvabitch who broke my window invaded *my* nest, big time!"

Saracen revved the motor.

"Wait a minute! Hold on! Where are you going? " Charlie shouted.

Saracen put the car in neutral. He was so tense he could barely speak. "For one brief moment, I forgot it was dangerous for a black man to chase a white man, especially in the dark, even if another white man was leaving the scene of a crime in a speeding car after he threatened a white man in that white man's swell house. But when the white man barreled out of his house, yelling and cursing at the top of his lungs, it looked like he was chasing the black man who was running down the street, who happened to be *me*, because, of course, the neighbors thought the black man had committed a crime. And that explains why I have to get out of here."

"Don't go! The police can't do anything to you! I won't let them!"

Saracen's laugh was bitter.

"I will *not* let those bastards get to you, Saracen! I won't!"

"My friend, Julien threw that brick. I know the sound of his hearse, and he'll be so hopped up with that little victory he may be on his way to Baldwin's to do something even more stupid. I have to get over there before the police come to *your* house, jump to their own conclusions, and lock me up."

Charlie ran to open the door on the passenger side as Saracen slammed the gears into place and wheeled the car onto the street in a racer's slide.

"I won't let them! *Wait, goddammit! Wait!"*

But Saracen didn't wait.

56

"DON'T HANG UP, SHELBY! *Please* don't hang up!"

And although she wanted to, she couldn't slam the receiver on that voice, even though it hurt her eardrums.

Hurt her heart.

Saracen spoke more rapidly than usual, pausing for Shelby to respond, which she didn't, wouldn't, couldn't.

"Your mother and I should have told you about our relationship. For a while we couldn't believe this feeling we had for one another could be true." Another pause, as though he were shaking his head at what had happened. "That it really was . . . *love*." Sounding still in thrall at the possibility. "You must admit it was a tough subject to broach to you."

He made an impatient sound at his awkwardness.

"I'm truly sorry I waited so long to tell you."

Shelby heard a clock strike in the background, and her anger spiked at the thought of him sitting in Baldwin's house and running up her long distance phone bill while he tried to flimflam her granddaughter.

"This would be a lot easier if we could talk in person. But I can't leave Little Rock now because of my work, so I hope you'll come down here. No. *Please* come down here." His laugh was rueful. "'Please' is a word you seldom hear from me."

Shelby's lip curled in agreement, and she sat back in her chair.

"Not for my sake," he added quickly, "for Baldwin's, and your mother's. They need you to set them at ease. You're torturing them with your silence, Sheb, and it's not like you to be mean."

They deserve to be tortured, she retorted silently, though somewhat less assuredly.

He spoke more hurriedly. "And, yes, I hope you'll forgive me, sooner than later. I doubt we'd be in the fix we're in now if I had been straightforward with you at Christmas. I'm fully aware that in this city, your mother's and my . . . situation . . . is potentially dangerous, especially now. But we're very careful. No one knows about us but you. And Charlie."

Don't say "your mother"! Say "Eulalia," or some lovey dovey name I know you have for her! And, of course, the relationship is dangerous, you imbecile! You've put us all in danger!

He spoke more hurriedly. "And I regret to tell you this . . . I sound like I'm delivering one of those telegrams from the War Department, don't I?" He barked an uncomfortable laugh. "But on bad days . . . and they're increasing . . . Baldwin withdraws within herself. She just . . . disappears."

Shelby's lips tightened. Now Saracen's chicanery was just as bad as Julien's, and worse on some level, because Saracen Self was . . . whatever he was, or had been, to her family. Her grandmother couldn't be so very confused and withdrawn. Her mother had gone down that path, but Baldwin never would. A confused Baldwin was more inconceivable than the notion of Eulalia going to live in Paris, France. Baldwin Josephine Shelby Howell had a tight rein on her mind. It wouldn't dare wander. She would tug up her girdle and move on with her life.

"It sounds impossible, doesn't it? When she comes up for air, she's her old self, ordering Daddy to put up a high fence on the property line between her house and Julien's, which Daddy is doing with as much vigor as he can muster. He's as old as she is, but he loathes Julien; and by God, Daddy's going to build his own Great Wall to keep out the barbarian who tried to hurt his Shelby. Daddy and Baldwin have a tight relationship.

"And Julien . . . Julien recently crossed a dangerous line with Charlie. Julien may move to another state in the near future. Charlie and I are doing our best to make that possible."

Shelby felt a flicker of dread. Julien could slither past anyone.

"Poor Lettie hasn't a clue why Julien acts so strange, or why Daddy is building the wall. She just blithers and drops packages of food at Baldwin's front door the way Alfred used to leave dead mice for you."

Shelby's dogged silence helped her maintain her balance in the power struggle with the man with the muscles on the other end of the line. But in spite of a Herculean effort to suppress it, she gave a loud sneeze. She closed her eyes furiously as Saracen's voice continued to flow, now with a bit of humor.

"If I were closer, I would offer my white linen handkerchief."

He was winning, she thought dumbly. He would always win.

"Daddy," Saracen's voice slowed, humor banished.

Shelby knew by the sound of that one word that he was worried about Tom. *Nothing must happen to Tom. Nothing must happen to Baldwin.* Shelby could survive as long as they were alive and well. She held her breath at what Saracen might say next.

"Daddy isn't able to work much in the garden. I'm not sure he even notices the weeds, he's so focused on that fence." Saracen's resumed cadence informed her he wouldn't exhibit weakness a second time. "Consequently, the garden has become a jumble of thirsty flowers and big weeds with puffballs primed to release seeds at any moment."

Shelby's heart ached at her vision of the mournful garden. Minute pests could lay waste to every plant on Baldwin's two acres. For a horrifying instant, it occurred to her that a humiliated, broken-hearted old woman could take to her bed and shrivel up like her desiccated flowers.

"Ernestine is driving us nuts, demanding to see her darling big sister whom she now says she adores. She even comes to Daddy's house, tapping that tennis racquet on the front porch floor like a machine gun and ordering me to have her darling sister sign a few papers that Ernestine just happens to have with her. She thinks that since I'm just a Negro, I should jump to do her bidding. But the only thing I'm in awe of is the force these two sisters possess between them. Plug in that combined will, and it could light up the world, though it's true Baldwin's generator isn't working too well these days." His voice became sad, even wistful. "I'm more aware of her recent diminishment, because she's become sweet to me like she was when I was a kid."

The phone connection hummed for a while, providing time for more guilt to seep through the wires and into Shelby's veins. Saracen was playing her just right. He knew his customer. But she was determined to remain silent.

"So, dear Shelby . . . am I trying to make you feel bad? You bet I am. The people who love you most, need you, and *soon*. Baldwin should be weeding that garden, not rocking in her momma's chair, cradling a dying cat, and staring out the back window."

Still silence.

"You're the only one who could get her moving, Sheb."

She knew he was waiting for her to absolve him, absolve all of them, *which she* would *not do*. *Why am I the one who has to take responsibility for Baldwin?* she wanted to yell in his ear. *Why am I the one who has to be the adult?* I'm the youngest. The innocent. *And how dare you sleep with my mother! How dare you!*

She was so deep into her own outrage, misery tinged with

jealousy, that she gave a start when he spoke again.

"The line hasn't gone dead, so I take it you're still there."

Shelby fumed silently.

"I hope you are," Saracen said quietly. "I want you to be there."

She hated his humbug at the same time she was hammered by the memory of how sometimes he would purse his lips before he spoke.

"So here's another reason to come home." Saracen's voice was filled with renewed energy, determined to tether her. "The politics down here are sizzling like grease on a hot iron skillet. You'll say this has nothing to do with you, and I'll quickly answer, ah, but it does. This is *your* place, as you've often reminded me, which is a part of *our* country. And everyone in *your* place is taking polar sides on integration.

Virgil Blossom, who used to be so high and mighty about his integration plan, is begging for police protection, and lots of people, whites and blacks, sleep with loaded guns by their bedsides. People are afraid for their living, afraid for their families. It's heartbreaking, really, because even I realize that Little Rock is a decent place that just needs wise leadership to keep prejudice at bay. Not wipe it out, I doubt that will ever happen, but at least keep it in the cellar with the rest of the rot."

Shelby closed her eyes when she heard Saracen's deep sigh.

"As a last-ditch measure, Faubus is hoping to get a state court injunction to put the Blossom plan on hold. That way he can blame the Feds for the delay in integration." His forced laugh at Faubus's scheme was a pale version of his usual infectious boom. "Your momma sees so much of his conniving firsthand at the State House, it's about got her doubled up. That, and the way Baldwin is fading.

But most of all she needs your love. She's hurting bad

because you won't talk to her."

Saracen's deep voice was pleading. "If it will help, I can get a doctor to send a letter to The Acting School saying you have a crisis in the family. Which is most certainly true. And I will send you a train ticket."

This time there was an even longer pause on the line. Finally, Saracen hung up the receiver very quietly.

57

My beloved Shelby,
Saracen told me you didn't speak when he called. It breaks my
heart that I have hurt you so grievously. Again.

I should have told you about Saracen and me at Christmas.
If I only had the words to describe how lonely and afraid I've
been for so many years, and how wondrous it seems that I've
found a man as kind and as good as Saracen. Yes, he's a few
years younger than I am, but he's far wiser than I am and smart-
er . . . and yet he loves me. He does, Shelby. He loves me.

And, yes, he's a Negro, but his color just doesn't matter.
He's a man, and a good man. My heart will break if you can't
understand.

Shelby's face flushed. You can't trust this man! He flirted
with me, too! Did he tell you how close we came . . . how we
very nearly. . . .

He told me he has always thought of you as a friend, and
regretted kissing you when he was in New York City. That he
apologized as best he could. That you've always been and al-
ways will be his friend. His best friend, actually.

Ah, yes. Best friends.

You may not want to hear anything so personal about your
mother, but perhaps you'll understand my situation a bit better
if I tell you something about my state of mind. For so many
years, even after I got out of the hospital, I was terrified I might
have to go back. I did my pitiful best to be a mother to you for

as long as I could. I wanted to be like the other mothers . . . Ah, but that's not exactly true. I didn't like most of them, and they were wary of me. I was the crazy lady with the foreign husband who dumped her and disappeared. My real world consisted of Baldwin, Jessie, Tom, Saracen, and always you, which was enough for me. Or I thought it was.

Baldwin couldn't watch me day and night, and she knew my deranged presence would harm you. She had to put me in that hellhole hospital, but she or Jessie came to bathe and feed me every day. I'm certain I would have died otherwise. As soon as I began to make some sense, she and Jessie brought me home.

It wasn't until this last year that I shed the residue of those crazed feelings. But it is Saracen who has willed me back to health. My heart will break if you can't understand my need to be with him.

And, my sweet daughter, if you want to make a final connection with Baldwin, you must come home very soon. I'm so very sorry to tell you this news. Her mind is becoming more and more fragmented. I think she's willing her death like one of those old Indians who disappear to die in the woods, never to return. But the woods are in her head.

If she saw you, if she heard your voice, I think she would make a greater effort to stay with us in this world, at least for a while longer. When her head is clear, she talks about you constantly.

Shelby raised her eyes from the letter and stared out the window at the river below where, amazingly, a man in a small, red rowboat was serpentining his way in and out of big, relentless scows.

Would he make it? How did anyone in the world make it?

Saracen said he told you about the high fence Tom is constructing on the property line between Julien's house and ours. Tom pounds those nails as though he were building Julien's coffin, while Julien sits in a lawn chair all day and watches through his binoculars. Slowly but surely, Julien is being blotted out by the wall. He keeps lifting those binoculars higher, trying to see over the fence.

I don't look at the garden. I don't have time to tend it, and Tom is so obsessed with the fence that the garden has become a jumble of weeds in this late summer heat.

I'm enclosing a Greyhound bus ticket, just in case. The agent said you can go all the way from New York City to Memphis on the same bus. You would just have to change one time at Memphis. The ticket is good for any day of the week. I know it's a long, hard ride, but the man said there are lots of rest stops.

If you let me know when you'll arrive, I'll be so happy to pick you up at the station. And please come soon, my dear child. For Baldwin's sake, if for no other.

I pray you'll forgive me for so many things.

I love you. Very, very much. Mom

58

"HE'S DEAD," Hank whispered.

Bernard's body lay sprawled on the floor. With the exception of the body and the overflowing sink, the small room was tidy. Two shirts, a pair of jeans, a worn sweater and two pairs of socks, all folded precisely, lay on top of an orange crate. The worn sheets on the thin mattress on the floor were smartly tucked, and an open, wet copy of *Invisible Man* was lined square to the pillow. Even Bernard's toenails were carefully trimmed, and though one leg lay askew in an unnatural position, the pant on the extended leg held its crease.

Shelby and Hank stood jammed together at the doorway. Tall Boojie peered over their shoulders. When Shelby moved toward Bernard, Hank grabbed her arm. "Don't!" his voice cracking. "The electrical wire beneath his hand may still be live!"

Their eyes stayed fixed on the dead body, but they moved further back, very quietly, so as not to wake the dead. Shelby whispered as though Bernard might hear, "He *can't* be dead." Then louder, "*Do* something, Hank," and almost hysterically, "You know what to do! You're almost a doctor! Do it!"

"But he's dead. *Can't you see he's dead? I can't do anything!*" Hank wailed.

The charging energy and brute strength that had always pulsed through Bernard's being had been obliterated. He looked totally vulnerable, no longer able to swat at the invisible blows that battered him while he breathed. It was embarrassing to see such a private man so exposed.

But the three couldn't look away from his face, or his legs that had fallen in a primitive pose Ana George would have been proud to choreograph. He was more beautifully composed in death than he had been in life.

Shelby's voice was small with hope. "But what if he's still. . . ."

"*I've seen plenty of corpses! The electricity blew those holes in his heels!*" Hank's mouth twitched. "I'll call an ambulance, but you must *not* touch him. You could die too if you touch him." He pointed a stern finger at Shelby, his mouth twitching harder, before he turned and raced down five flights to find a phone and cry in private.

Shelby couldn't take her eyes from the body. Bernard should get up now and tell them he was just rehearsing a scene. He should smile, though he seldom indulged, and say he had convinced them he was dead, hadn't he?

When the single hall bulb flickered, Shelby yelped and hooked her eyes to Boojie. "It was an accident, wasn't it. It *had* to be an accident. And what if he's not really dead? We can't just stand here staring at him!"

Boojie knotted his arms around her waist and rested his quivering chin on top of her head. "I shouldn't have let him out of my sight."

"How could he live in this hole?" Her whisper was sibilant in the silent space. "This is a *hole. I should have let him live with us!*"

The light flickered again.

"He's trying to talk to us." Shelby's voice trembled.

"Maybe we should wait downstairs," Boojie said tearfully.

"But we can't leave him alone!"

Boojie gulped air. "He liked sirens. Hank will tell the ambulance driver to turn up the siren."

"He killed himself, Boojie! *Electrocuted himself!* I should have let him live with us like you wanted!" She wrenched herself from Boojie's arms and turned unsteadily toward the stairs.

Boojie snagged her arms. "This is *not* your fault. Bernard was in horrible pain. He was trying to figure out too many mysteries, especially about skin color. He could *not* understand why people cared so much about his damn color. Sometimes I'd catch him staring at his hand, and then at my hand, as though trying to understand the distinction, when there was none but the color! He thought if he came North, it would be different, but it wasn't; and when the Little Rock thing began, he kept moaning that it would never be different for those Negro kids either, that their hearts would break like his had." Boojie clutched Shelby like a lifeline. "If only he could have performed on a Broadway stage! People would have seen *him* and not his color. He was a brilliant actor!"

"He could have been as good as Brando, couldn't he?"

Boojie looked briefly tormented by that possibility. "I don't know. He was born to act, like Brando was. Liebmann recognized that. But I think the great teacher resented that his prize find didn't need him to learn the skills. He became obsessed with Bernard's talent and his sexuality, which began to gnaw at Bernard. He was young. He wasn't even certain which sex he was.

"So he glommed onto that Ralph Ellison book to escape his woes. 'Our task is that of making ourselves individuals,' he would quote with such certitude. And on that classroom stage, he was a unique individual, and he knew it. If he could have stayed on stage forever, being somebody else, he might have been happy."

"We could have done so much more for him," Shelby muttered.

"Oh, Sheb. He was never going to leave this place and move in with us. It's too dark to see, but he installed light bulbs all over the ceiling and the walls, and he was working on the floor like the guy did in *Invisible Man*. When he'd walk in here, he'd flick some switches and the whole area would light up like Forty-Second Street. Then he'd lie on that mattress with the lights blazing and listen to his Louis Armstrong records, the same way the Invisible Man did in his lit-up basement. When Bernard began to run out of space to install more lights, maybe he decided it was time to quit everything.

"I just wish . . ." and Boojie sighed, "I really wish we could chop out a piece of that wall with the light bulbs blazing and place Bernard on top and carry him out of the building with Louis playing his trumpet on that old Victrola over there."

Shelby's eyes were still glued to the body. Was Bernard's face becoming a more neutral color? Maybe that happened at death. Maybe all of God's children became the same color after death.

But it didn't make her feel any better. She wanted to kick the body, make it come to life, make Bernard speak in his awesome voice. She wanted him to promise he would live with them, that he would give up electricity and become the great actor that was his destiny.

"*Get up!*" she suddenly screamed. "*Get up!*"

Boojie clutched her tighter, and they both began to sob, mourning the kind man who had harmed no one, who only wanted to be seen as a human being, who had only wanted to act on stage as a man, but whose final role was of a dead body lying on the floor of a tenement building, a part he was performing to perfection.

They heard the sirens drawing closer and voices yelling. The electricity to the building was turned off, and footsteps pounded up the stairs. Boojie and Shelby drew back against the wall and waited silently in the dark until a stretcher was carried into the room by two big men with torches attached to their headgear that swept through the space like prison searchlights. Their voices were loud and joking. Hank, a part-time ambulance driver himself, knew them. His voice broke when he admonished them to be quieter, saying, "He was my friend, guys."

"He's just a nigger," one of them shrugged, but then they whispered instructions, respectfully covered the corpse with a sheet, hoisted the heavy stretcher onto their strong shoulders, and proceeded with their burden down the narrow staircase in pharaoh-appropriate fashion, with Hank leading the way with a torch that created eerie shadows on the walls.

Then, "Wait!" Boojie shouted. "Wait!" And he ran into the room, wound up the Victrola, and put the needle on the Louis Armstrong record. Louis's trumpet began the slow, funky beat of a New Orleans funeral march, and the procession continued down the narrow staircase. By the time it reached the bottom step, the trumpet was silent. When the ambulance was loaded, Hank got in the front seat with the two men.

"Did Hank just take out his notebook?" Shelby asked incredulously.

"He's making notes."

"With Bernard lying dead in the back?"

"Writing is his best friend. He needs his friend now."

Hank put down his notebook, said something to the men, and when the sirens began to blare with operatic intensity, Boojie and Shelby stood at attention, tears streaming down their faces until Shelby whispered out loud, "*I've got to go home.*"

She began to hurry down the sidewalk with a startled Boojie trotting after her.

"*I've got to go see my grandmother.*"

59

Dear Shelby Howell,

This is absolutely your last chance, and believe me, It's really hard to keep from getting my nose totally out of joint with you. After all, I'm the person who goes behind her husband's back to keep you posted on the latest news. And believe me, there's plenty of news!!

First of all, I'm sorry to be the one who tells you this, but Charlie has been seen all over town with that television weather girl. Her name's Charlene, and she is plenty cute. You better think about how cute and rich Charlie is and get yourself back down here in a hurry!!

Also. There's more hurly-burly in Little Rock than I bet there's been since the Civil War! I love it when the air is boiling before an Arkansas-Texas football game, but the battle to keep niggers out of our schools has become even more exciting!

Remember that nursery rhyme about the ten little Indians? Well, there are just nine nigger kids left to enter Central when school begins, so there are lots of signs around town that say, AND NOW THERE ARE NINE! Some niggers dropped out because they're scared, and others . . . and this is really private . . . because Virgil Blossom is practically begging them to drop out! The nine little Indians was mostly Bruce's idea. I don't mean to brag, and you know I never brag, but my hubby is really smart. He's practically quit real estate, he's so busy with this nigger undertaking, and he's got people coming up here from all over the South on the day those niggers try to get into Central. People are just petrified white children will have to use the same bathrooms as the niggers. Being in the know up there, you've probably already heard that the Nat King Cole TV show was shut down because he kept touching white lady singers. Can you imagine the nerve of that man?

And I'm especially excited, because I have an important project to work on with this group called The Mothers' League of Little Rock Central. Bruce says these women are beneath me, but I'm tired of him having all the fun. After all, I am a mother!!!!

So. We Mothers are going to the courthouse to tell the judge he has to enforce our own state laws that stop what the Bible absolutely forbids. Orval Faubus himself will testify that people are buying guns and knives all over the state . . . mostly niggers, of course . . . and that swarms of armed white men are coming from other states to bring this undemocratic stuff to a halt!! Faubus is turning out to be someone we all just love, which we didn't used to do. Though I wish he wouldn't say that blood will run in the streets because of the niggers. Bruce bought us a good supply of guns right away, and I'm going to this practice range with a bunch of the other Mothers!! It's a lot of fun, but a little scary. I close my eyes when I pull the trigger, but don't tell Brucie!

I'm thinking real hard about what to wear to court, because there'll be TV cameras! I definitely think something red, white and blue. But should it be a red skirt and white blouse with a blue belt, or a blue dress with a scarf that looks like a Confederate flag? You may even see my picture in the papers up there in Yankee land!

Oodles of love from your busy Kate.

P.S. I'm taking all that love back if I don't hear back from you immediately!

P.P.S. Mary Nelle saw Julien the other day out near Maumelle. She didn't recognize him at first, because he wasn't wearing his wig! Remember what a clothes horse he used to be? She said he looked just awful. I've always heard that when a man starts to slide, he can go downhill in a hurry. And listen to this . . . rumor has it that for years Julien has had a ring of prostitutes in North Little Rock! Can you believe that? And WHO are these ladies of the night? Anyone WE know??? They say the you-know-what takes place in an ordinary looking house. Mary Nelle and I have been driving around town to try and find which house it is. Bruce says he knows, but won't tell me, the beast. But I'll get it out of him at night, if you know what I mean!

Kate's letter made Shelby feel queasy. She hadn't always sounded so silly and so prejudiced. Or maybe she had, and Shelby's judgment of friends, and of so many other things, had always been wrong.

She called the bus station for the departure time to Memphis. She would have to pack in a hurry, but if she kept very busy, she might, however briefly, put aside the image of Bernard lying dead on that cold wet floor, and of her grandmother lying drunk on that big, Victorian bed.

Or of her mother lying in Saracen Self's arms.

60

THE MONEY PROBABLY was coming from Charlie's rich daddy, Herbert.

Julien wasn't a dummy.

Didn't those fops in Little Rock realize by now that he could outthink them? He had lost his business, even lost his *hair*, goddammit, but did they think that mattered to him? He could look any way he wanted, wear anything he wanted, while those SOBs were stuck with their hoity-toity lives in their hoity-toity houses, with their hoity-toity uptight wives, having to do everything like their next-door neighbors.

But hubbies still sneaked off to screw his girls every chance they got, and he had pictures to prove it, and would make them public, if necessary. So just *who* was the smartest? Julien would like to know.

Jennings Reed explained the plan to Julien, but Julien knew that on the deep sly Jennings was one of Herbert Billington's gofers. And it didn't take long to notice the bodyguard Herbert hired to protect his son after Julien crashed the brick through the society boy's window. It had taken a lot of guts *and* strength to throw that brick across the yard into the window, and make his getaway clean as a whistle.

So Julien would outsmart the bodyguard and Herbert too, like he had outsmarted Charlie boy with the brick.

Charlie didn't seem to realize the goon was his bodyguard, which gave Julien a good laugh. The goon was a professional, for sure, most likely from Hot Springs, maybe Chicago, some Mafia tough, and he was good, very smooth, looked ordinary, kept a very low profile. But Julien spotted him. Julien knew his type.

At least he thought that was who the guy was. Julien was acquainted with several pros who looked like that. Big guys, sunglasses, tailored suits, looking around. They would visit with his girls in Maumelle, even though there were plenty like that in Hot Springs. But the boys liked a change and paid well, and they knew Julien's girls were clean, and would do damn near anything the boys wanted. The girls knew they better do.

But that guy guarding Charlie didn't have eyes on every side of his head. If the guy was who Julien thought he was. Anyhow, Julien might lay off Charlie for a while, take time to figure how to scam that Billington money and still stay in Little Rock. He was beginning to enjoy Little Rock again, now that he had a new, well-paying vocation.

First thing, though, he would settle the score with Baldwin. He had been so nice to that old bitch, and she still wouldn't sell her house to him. He was sure that goddam Charlie Billington told her not to, which made Julien even more excited about what he was going to do to Baldwin, and then to Charlie. The old biddy wanted to get back at him just because he tried to fool around a little with her skinny little granddaughter. And after that one little happenstance, the ugly granddaughter told Charlie and that big nigger, and they made a public fool of him! *Made him lose his hair and his business to boot! God, how he hated that old woman!* But she would get hers, and he knew exactly which day it would happen. Saracen Self might be next . . . after Charlie . . . but, of course, Saracen was just a nigger and could wait his turn.

It really tickled Julien that "interested parties" wanted to set him up in business almost anywhere but Little Rock. He got a good laugh thinking about it. Not an open-air laugh, but an inside, private giggle, though the giggle would pop out at unexpected moments, which gave some folks a start. Like there was another Julien hiding inside his belly.

Jennings Reed had quoted a healthy sum of money that the "interested parties" would provide to get him started. A very healthy sum. "Interested parties" knew his business had gone sour in Little Rock. They also seemed certain he couldn't relocate anywhere else in the state. Julien figured out right away that "interested parties" had arranged that particular blackball.

But "interested parties" *could* arrange for him to buy a nice funeral home anywhere in Wyoming or Montana, say. Jennings even showed him a list of towns that had funeral homes on the market. And think of this . . . places overseas offered an even bigger bonus. *Like South Africa!*

The mention of South Africa did cause Julien a moment's pause. They knew how to treat niggers over there. That might not be such a bad place to live.

"So", Julien asked Jennings, 'interested parties' are offering this good deed out of the goodness of their hearts? Good Samaritans with no names who just want to help me get back on my feet? Was that the sum of it?"

"Pretty much," Jennings said. "Provided you don't come back to Arkansas. That's the one little tickle. But new places are always exciting, don't you think? Me, I'm always wishing I could take off for a new place, but I don't have this kind of money. The kind of money 'interested parties' are offering don't grow on trees. The figure they're offering almost knocked my eyes out," Jennings said.

"And what are you getting out of this little deal, Mr. Jennings Reed?"

"Not a dime," he replied, solemn as a frog. "I'm relaying this good news to you, because you're a friend."

So . . . in time . . . Julien would "take care" of Jennings too. The list of folks to "take care" of was growing, but first he would get his hands on that money "interested parties" were so eager to provide.

In the meantime, he would take care of Baldwin. That old woman deserved the hell she was about to endure.

61

SEPTEMBER 2, 1957

ORVAL FAUBUS SENDS IN NATIONAL GUARD TO PREVENT NEGROES FROM ENTERING LITTLE ROCK CENTRAL HIGH SCHOOL

SHELBY CAME TO an abrupt halt when she saw the bold headlines plastered across the tops of the New York City newspapers. She snatched up a paper without paying and stood by the stand, reading that the evening before, on Labor Day, September 2, 1957, at 10:15 p.m., the day before Central High was to open for the school year, Orval Faubus had announced on television that Central High would close its doors to the nine Negro students the next day.

It had become apparent, Faubus proclaimed, that the Little Rock citizenry had not been adequately informed of the plan for integration. He had also learned that the sale of weapons in the area had greatly increased; that a vigorous phone campaign was in progress to assemble a large, anti-integration crowd at the school the next morning; and that caravans of angry, armed men were headed for Little Rock that very night to oppose integration. As a result, he announced, "It is my opinion . . . yes, even a conviction . . . that it will not be possible to restore, or even to maintain order and protect the lives and property of the citizens if forcible integration is carried out tomorrow in the schools of the community."

Therefore, he had ordered the National Guard to prohibit the entry of Negro students to Central High. He also decreed that the State Police would serve as an armed militia with the Guard. The Guardsmen were already in place, carrying unloaded weapons, but with live ammunition strapped to their belts.

He didn't mention that one of the laws the State Legislature had passed would excuse white students from integrated classes, but he did let it be known that a federal judge had recently declared unconstitutional all of the laws the State Legislature had passed opposing integration, and opposing Faubus's desire to test them in a state court . . . which, he privately hoped, would place the blame for the immediate closing of the school on the federal government.

According to the editor of the *Arkansas Gazette*, Faubus had created "the most serious constitutional question to face the national government since the Civil War."

Shelby stood stock-still, dumbfounded by what she was reading.

Many Arkansans interviewed for another article rejoiced over the course of action taken by their governor, declaring that Faubus should become President of the United States for his brave stand, that they needed a tough leader like him in troubled times: a devout Christian who would keep his word, a man who would interpose himself, if necessary, between the great state of Arkansas and the dictatorial government of the United States of America!

Interpose. *Interposition.* That was the word that drunk Julien had tried to say last December in the taxi. Shelby now thought she understood what it meant: that Faubus thought it was okay for a state to thumb its nose at the Constitution.

"Buy the paper, lady!" the vendor demanded. "This ain't a library!"

"Sorry," she mumbled, and in a fit of frantic extravagance, she bought a copy of all the different newspapers, and stumbled to the side of a building where she slid down to the sidewalk to devour their texts. As she read, the image of the school and its great trees and the street in front and the prim houses across the street, and the image of the lone, frightened Negro girl walking down the sidewalk in front of the school haunted her mind.

An outdoor Billy Graham crusade near Times Square had just ended, and thousands of people were marching down Broadway, singing fervently about God's love. But Shelby's eyes were fixed on the photograph of the lone Negro girl, who was surrounded by faces so wrenched with hate they looked like some of Tom Self's more foreboding African masks. It was hard to look away from that photograph, but when Shelby did, she read that Elizabeth Eckford, dressed in the brand-new, first-day-of-school clothes she had made herself, had stepped off a city bus to be confronted by a howling mob. The stunned girl's face showed no emotion. Her eyes were concealed behind big sunglasses, as she made her way down the long, and what must have seemed to her, endless city block.

She had said that her ambition was to become a lawyer like Thurgood Marshall.

The nine young Negroes chosen to break the color barrier had been told in a meeting with the Superintendent of Schools himself that they should enter by the front door. So in spite of the cruel clamor all around her, Elizabeth walked obediently past the lovely fish pond in front of the school to one of the concrete paths that led to the winding stairs on either side of the impressive front doors of the building.

But at each of the paths to the school that loomed like Oz beyond the lovely sward, helmeted soldiers, not much older than Elizabeth, snapped to attention and barred her way with rifles equipped with bayonets.

Shelby paused her reading to stare sightlessly at Billy

Graham's marchers, thinking that in the newspaper photographs, Elizabeth's skirt was similar to the full skirts of the white girls, and her shirtwaist blouse was like theirs, and her shoes were like theirs. She even held her school books the way they did. The only real difference was the color of Elizabeth's skin and the composed expression she struggled to maintain, as though determined not to cry in front of the wide-open mouths of the white faces spewing hate at her.

Shelby jumped to her feet in horror, yelling, "My God!"

And Billy Graham's marchers heard her, and beckoned to her with enraptured smiles. They understood the sudden need to extoll the glory of God! But Shelby, deaf to their entreaties, slid back to the sidewalk and continued to read that Elizabeth had managed to walk across the street to Ponder's drugstore, hoping to find safe haven. But Ponder's door had been slammed and locked in her face so fast the glass rattled.

Elizabeth's remaining recourse was to sit on the nearest bench to wait for a bus, which she did, and where, finally, tears began to flow from beneath her sunglasses. A reporter, a man of slight build from *The New York Times*, slid beside her, offered his handkerchief, and whispered, "Don't let them see you cry."

And that brave kindness helped Elizabeth staunch her tears.

Shelby, who was nearly crying herself, thought, *Cry, Elizabeth! Bellow! Screech your lungs out! Tell them all to go to hell!*

Rumor had traveled like the hounds of hell in Little Rock, and the fired-up crowd turned on the brave reporter, screaming that he was a "Yankee Jew nigger lover from a Jew newspaper and should be castrated and hung from a tree!" When the frenzy reached its dangerous apex, the crowd was suddenly diverted by a white woman who elbowed her way to the bench and raised her powerful voice above the noise,

"Hang your heads in shame!" she cried. "Leave this child alone!"

Then the woman grabbed Elizabeth's arm, and pushed the two of them onto the city bus that had just pulled up like a chariot from God. Angry people banged on the door that never had been slammed shut so fast, and the people screeched at God's chariot, *"Git the nigger! Git the nigger-lover! Lynch the burrhead!"*

But the big bus lumbered onward, nosing aside the angry mob.

Shelby jumped up from the sidewalk, grabbed her newspapers, broke through the startled crowd, and raced to catch the No. 1 train at Grand Central to go to the West End Bar. Shelby needed to see Elizabeth's walk before Central High School, had to see it to believe it, and she knew the West End had a television set.

That kind of ugliness might occur in Mississippi or in Alabama, but never in Arkansas. People obeyed the law in Arkansas. It was against the law to *jaywalk* in Arkansas. What was that hillbilly, Orval Faubus, doing to her place? *How could he stir up that kind of hatred in her place?*

She pushed her way through the crowded room of the West End Bar to be with Boojie, who was already there, and who grabbed her in a silent hug and pointed to the television screen where a recorded version of last night's speech showed Faubus announcing that, by his authority as Governor, and to protect the citizens of the state, he had been compelled to call out the National Guard, his good-ole-boy manner relaying to his white friends that he was one of them, that he was a God-fearing Christian like they were, and that he, as their governor, would keep their peace white.

Jimmy, a fellow actor tending bar part-time at the West End, asked if Shelby needed a Coke with a lot of ice, but she only murmured *"Look. . . ."*

And there on the TV screen was the grand neo-Gothic, five-story, buff brick building that unfolded like a regal fan the length of two city blocks. It was the most beautiful high school in America, deemed so by the National Institute of Architects.

"Look at my school, Boojie!" And Shelby turned to the crowd of TV watchers and commanded that they all "look! That's my school! It's the most beautiful high school in America! See the pond in front reflecting the school's columns! See the great stairs winding on either side of the main entrance where rather strange Greek goddesses . . . or were they gods? . . . preside above the doors!"

AMBITION PERSONALITY
OPPORTUNITY PREPARATION

But Boojie and Jimmy and everyone else in the bar only saw Elizabeth Eckford being goaded by the mob.

And it was terrible to see a lone, terrified Negro girl cringing in front of the most beautiful high school in America. It was odious to see that stately school surrounded by rifle-bearing soldiers who weren't much older than Elizabeth.

Shelby and Boojie clutched hands and whispered, "*My God. . . .*"

The windows of the school were open on that hot day, and if the sounds the crowd made had been less strident, it would have been possible to hear the students reciting the pledge of allegiance:

One nation under God, with liberty and justice for all. . . .

And if the cameras had focused on those open windows, Miss Finney's troubled face might have been revealed, the vein on her forehead pounding at the forbidden seas that were crashing against her world.

How could she save the white children who would soon begin reading the adventures of *David Copperfield*? How could she save the black children so they could read the wonders of *Moby-Dick*? How could a high-school English teacher, who secretly called herself Oceana, escape a fearful future, because she wanted to teach the intricacies and beauties of the English language to all children, black and white?

Shelby's eyes blurred with tears. The life she knew was being threatened by beasts crawling from fetid swamps. And yet if anyone, friend or stranger, denigrated Little Rock, she would have pounded them with her purse, stabbed them with her piercing green eyes. She was overwhelmed with the need to go home, go to her place. It was all tragedy, all pain, intertwined with the memory of her tormented parents, and Bernard's anguish, and the thought of an old woman lying drunk on her dead parents' grand four-poster bed.

John Chancellor was a brave young television reporter, standing in front of Little Rock Central High School, and continuing to report, even though he was surrounded by an angry mob. "I have learned that Faubus's pronouncement last evening necessitated a change of plans to ensure the safety for the nine Negro children who would enter Central High. However, it was impossible to inform Elizabeth Eckford of plans altered at 2 a.m. this morning. Her family doesn't have a phone, and an exhausted Daisy Bates, the organizer of the black children, tragically forgot to drive to her house later this morning with the news."

When Chancellor's cameraman was shoved to the side, the camera focused briefly on a man's feet, shod in black and white two-toned shoes with slightly pointed toes. Buster Crosby wore shoes like that until the weather got cool, and when the camera steadied, it caught Buster's full figure and his shiny black hair and his shiny black eyes and his shiny black shantung suit, all of which made him look like a dandified devil.

The next day Faubus announced with grim satisfaction that the white woman who had pushed Elizabeth Eckford onto a bus was a known Communist.

62

Rocking the torpid cat made her hot and sticky, but the old woman didn't notice. She smelled a little musty, like rotting leaves in a dark wood, but she didn't notice that either.

Julien was in her garden again. She couldn't see him, but she knew he was there. She had a preternatural sense of his presence. She had done what she could to stay the day of his villainy, but she knew the time was nigh. And she was ready.

She loved her mother's rocker. It was old-fashioned, with slats on the seat and back, padded with tufted, faded green pillows tied with bows to the rungs, just the way her mother had left it. Baldwin could sit on that rocker for hours, keeping her vigil. She made a curious half-whispered whistle between her teeth as she rocked the cat in her arms. She couldn't walk so well any more, but most of the time her hearing was okay and her eyesight was still acute. So most of the time life was good enough.

She didn't protest when Eulalia bathed her with a warm cloth and pulled a clean nightgown over her scrawny body. She didn't even mind when that tall Nigra with green eyes told her stories. She couldn't quite place him, but sometimes he reminded her of that little, green-eyed darkie who used to run errands and make her laugh with his made-up poems. She thought he was the one who had tried to rescue the elephant from the zoo. Wonderful boy. Brave too. He had kidnapped that elephant by himself, led him down the highway in the dark.

This big darkie's hands were gentle when they picked her

up and placed her on her bed. Sometimes he sang songs to her in his deep voice. The songs from the Great War were her favorites, though they made her sad; and she couldn't remember why.

And that lovely girl with the long, quicksilver hair who used to be around the house a lot? What was that girl's name, and where was she now? She would like to see that girl. She would like to brush that girl's hair and make pigtails for her. The girl liked green ribbons tied on her pigtails. Green ribbons matched her eyes. But what was her name?

The answers to those curiosities were stuck somewhere in Baldwin's mind like phlegm. She would sneeze hard and try to dislodge the answers, but it never worked. Anyhow, she didn't like to soil the fine linen handkerchiefs, embroidered with someone's initials, that were always placed on a table by her chair along with a glass and a pitcher filled with sun tea. Sometimes she would drink the tea with a strong shot of whiskey, if she could pull herself out of the chair and creep down the stairs to seek out a bottle of J.W. Dant.

But the thing she really missed was gardening. Missed the feel of the loamy soil, missed the soil's fresh pungent smell, missed pushing the earth around the seeds, ever so gently. Patting them like she would a baby. She loved the earth. She yearned to organize her earth. The return of spring was the one promise that was always kept.

And she missed the sweet fatigue after gardening, and the good long soak in the tub. Though crawling into the tub had become too difficult, and crawling out impossible.

Still the tub waited like a big fat Buddha, challenging her to lift her legs over the side that was slick and cold as ice. Her daddy once sent her a little Buddha made of ivory, but it didn't have clawed feet like her tub did. She wished she could find that little Buddha with its tiny toes. She would hold it in her hands and rub its tiny tummy for good luck.

The Nigra said he would set her in the Buddha tub, if she wanted. But she couldn't have that. To be seen naked by that man? Held in his arms, naked? That was not right, not right at all. The nice girl swabbed her good enough. That nice girl with the short black hair and the strange white streak at the forehead made her feel plenty refreshed.

Someone had caught her rings that would drop from her skinny fingers and try to escape like little mice. The nice girl was quick and she caught those rings, and now the old woman could stroke them on the gold chain that hung around her neck. She would watch them sparkle for hours. Or maybe minutes.

Time had no meaning any more.

But it didn't fly, like people said. It meandered.

And a day didn't pass but a bowl of fresh flowers was placed on her bureau in her favorite crystal vase. She couldn't remember the name of the flowers, but she could see they were her favorite. Big blowsy whites and pinks and blues. She would start down the alphabet thinking she could creep up on the name, but the letters would turn into snakes, though they didn't bite, thank the Lord.

So life was not all that bad. Most days.

The really good thing was she didn't need to eat much anymore. Eating took so much time, and she didn't like her thoughts to be interrupted by the effort of lifting a heavy fork to her mouth. Sometimes slices of plump tomatoes appeared that Tom had grown from seed every summer since the start of time. She always knew who Tom was, which was a comfort, and she loved those tomatoes, would nibble them like candy. They were sweet as sugar and should never be salted. Sometimes there were Snickers bars, and praise the Lord for those small favors. Though she only licked them. And the cat licked them.

What she wanted most was a taste of her daddy's whiskey. She loved sneaking through the house, playing the secret game her daddy had called "hide the bottle," when, as a child, she had caught him doing just that. Though truth be told, the walking and the bending required for the game had become too difficult.

Maybe she would tell the tall Nigra about the whiskey. He had the look of someone who enjoyed games.

Occasionally, she got lost and forgot what the goal of the game was and why she was dressed in her mother's nightgown in the daytime. But eventually someone came to lead her back to her chair.

She would even forget why she was so determined to stay at her post at the window. Then it would pop back into her mind like a gremlin. It was annoying that her mind treated her like that, especially when she could see Teddy grinning up at her from the bottom of the slope where the bindweed and the blackberry vines had smothered the earth.

It used to be so beautiful down where he was. Flagstone steps all the way, lined with a flowering vine. If she could just get down there, she would pull out that bind week and have Tom dig up those nasty blackberry bushes. She would feel so much better if she could get that mess cleaned up, and have a proper tea with Teddy.

She was so sorry he got himself killed. And she had watched it happen, heard the thud when he hit his head. She suffered dreadfully when he had to be buried so hastily, but Tom would have gone to jail, and her family would have endured more trauma, more gossip, and she couldn't let that happen. She had to think of . . . *what were the names of those girls she had to think of . . . the one with silver hair and the other with that silver streak at her forehead. Were they twins, those beautiful girls?*

But never mind.

It was true that guilt could pull you down with the dead,

which was what Teddy had tried to do every day of her life since they laid him in that hole. Rattling his bones at her, year after year.

It was not nice to rattle his bones, and he knew it, but he had always been a tease. She could admit that now. Sometimes she could even hear him laughing at one of his own jokes. It seemed only fair, however, that he should be the one to curb that Langley dog, since it was his own bones that were endangered. Teddy should also do his part to watch out for that Julien. It was a day-and-night job, and it was wearing her out. If Julien found those bones, the whole town would hear about them in a nonce, and Baldwin was certain Teddy wouldn't want to give that awful man that pleasure after what he had tried to do to their sweet Shelby.

That was her name! Shelby. *Shelby Howl!* She rocked back and forth, her eyes sparkling, whispering, *Shelby Howl, Shelby Howl.* She had to hold on to that name. It began with a big "S." Remember the big "S."

But Julien knew *something* was hidden down there. Baldwin saw him sneak over to look every chance he got. Trespassing on her property.

She did, however, have to admit that Teddy, bless his heart, was more on guard lately, telling her it was almost time to wreak her vengeance, reminding her where to find the gun, refreshing her memory about how to fire it, beckoning and grinning, in his devil-may-care way, even dancing a jig, ready for her to pay him a visit so they could laugh about it together.

And why not? Maybe she would do just that. She needed a change. It would be nice to have tea in the gazebo with him. Baldwin had to admit he had always been a charmer, with nice teeth, though she wondered if they were still white, those teeth, being underground so long. She hoped that mangy Langley dog hadn't carried them off. She didn't like to imagine that handsome man without his teeth.

The really big plus was that Teddy didn't like Julien any better than she did, and between the two of them, they would take care of that little pimple.

She leaned back in the rocker, but couldn't get comfortable. When she leaned back too far, the lump bulged beneath the pillow. There were no two ways about it, an old Smith & Wesson police special was a lumpy thing to sit on. But Baldwin had never been a person to complain. Her daddy had taught her not to complain, just as he had taught her how to fire that pistol. She hadn't pulled the trigger for many years, but when the time came, she could do it. Teddy would help her. And she could do anything she really had to do. If she could only remember to do it.

It agitated her, though, when she forgot to open her mouth to drink her tea, and a long, brown stain dribbled on her gown. It was so important to look clean.

Some days her head would clear, as though she had surfaced, refreshed, from a very deep lake, and she would remember everyone and everything, especially her beautiful granddaughter, Shelby Howell, who was far away in New York City with those actors. She missed that child so much. There were so many things she needed to teach her: How to prune roses. When to dig up the dahlia bulbs. Where some of the silver was hidden. How to fire a pistol. She yearned to see that beautiful face, and . . . yes . . . tell her that she loved her. But love was such a hard word to say out loud.

Suddenly the glaring light of reality grew too intense, pounding at the old woman's head until she wished she couldn't recall anything, wished she could prolong the feeling she had sometimes of drifting down an old river in a primitive land where there was nothing to think about, no troubles, just the soft lap of water and the wonderment of unearthly beauty and the bliss of eternal fulfillment.

But she mustn't let herself go all the way down that river yet. She still had things to do, and the one thing she absolutely had to keep in mind was that the awful Langley dog was digging down the slope behind the house, like he was doing right now. She had to tell Tom the dog was a danger, that he might make people wonder where he was getting those bones.

What sign could the old woman leave herself to recall the dog and the bones so she could tell Tom?

And at that very moment her memory began to jumble, as she imagined Teddy's bones were jumbled, with rot and roots and night crawlers in the grown-over garden. She looked around frantically, imploring the air with trembling hands. *Who will help me remember when it's time?*

Maybe the girl with the long silvery hair would help her. She had always been fond of that girl. Wherever she was. Whatever her name was.

Then the old woman quit rocking, fingering her diamonds. Staring at nothing for an hour or so. Drifting down the river.

63

Tell your momma,
Tell your pa,
I'm goin' back home to Arkansas

WHEN THE GREYHOUND bus driver turned the key, and the big engine began to rumble, Shelby closed her eyes and whispered, *Contact,* remembering another takeoff long ago.

She endured the lengthy gloom of the Lincoln Tunnel by muttering the Lord's Prayer until she was suddenly birthed in the morning sun of the other world where the horizon brought comfort, and the countryside became rural, and the sky was big and blue with huge white clouds that looked like elephants holding up the earth. For a giddy moment Shelby thought she was leaving her troubles behind, even as she hurtled toward them.

The bus turned from the main highways, rumbling through rundown sections of towns, and Shelby's good feeling diminished. Her seatmates came and went, their belongings in wrinkled brown paper bags. But the biggest difference was the Negroes who walked quietly to the back rows of the bus, and went to the "Colored" side of stations when the driver stopped for bathroom breaks. When there wasn't a colored bathroom, they wandered off. Somewhere. Shelby tried not to think about it.

She needed to sleep, but couldn't, and she perspired so profusely her blouse stuck to the back of the plush seat. When the bus reached the Virginia countryside, the heat became worse, but her tension eased at the sight of hills that dipped and swelled with the comfort of breasts and cradle-songs. The landscape looked like a primitive painting, with old streams serpentining lazily around green fields, and the steeples of prim churches splitting the clouds, and cows standing in muddy ponds, turning their ponderous heads to follow the bus with big, moony eyes. Blackberries were ripe on the bushes, and wild flowers bloomed everywhere: bright red poppies and Queen Anne's lace and black-eyed Susans and orange butterfly weed, but only chicory, its blossoms an outrageous blue, was tough enough to survive by the edge of the busy road.

Shelby might have slept, but that aching, throaty, melancholy yelp of country songs seeped through the air from a passing car radio. It was the music of hard times and lost loves and lonesome roads, reminding her of where she was born and where she was returning. She hung an arm from the window and kept time with her palm against the side of the bus.

That night, the driver shifted gears on narrow roads that wound around mountains, where a dark ocean of invisible trees seemed to beckon hypnotically. Once entered, it could have drowned them all, with only Shelby awake, alert to the danger. But when sheets of rain dropped from the sky, snoring mouths clamped shut, and people snapped awake, swallowing hard with dry mouths, their eyes big with fear.

Her weary spirits lifted the next day when they passed Sunday-morning, cinder-block churches topped with clangorous bells and filled with booming voices that spilled from open windows onto the big red cannas outside.

"*Help somebody today,*" the voices sang.

A deep bass echoed, "*today . . .*" and the congregation took a fulsome breath and resumed the stanza.

"Oh, help somebody today. . . ."

Shelby took the words to heart. She would honor Bernard by observing the opening day of Central High, and she would lure her grandmother into the garden again. She would find the wretched whiskey and throw it away. *She would help somebody.* As for her mother . . . Shelby closed her eyes and tried to go back to sleep.

The bus passed small trees festooned with empty, colored bottles that clacked in the faint breeze. The haggard woman seated next to Shelby had putrid breath and a black eye the size of a large fist. When the woman asked in a timorous voice, "Do you know what those bottles mean?"

Shelby replied, "People say they capture bad spirits and ward off evil."

"Evil?" the woman repeated fearfully.

"Or sometimes people just collect bottles because they're pretty," Shelby added hastily, sensing the woman's fear. "Sometimes . . . sometimes . . . things have no meaning."

When the windstream from the bus caused a bottle from one of the trees to fall and shatter against a rock, the woman gasped and scuttled to another seat.

She saw billboards along the road advertising cigarettes. Billboard-sized girls, semi-clothed in bathing suits, with long legs kicking backward and lovely arms extended, seducing wayfarers with smokes and exclamation points.

CHESTERFIELDS: JUST AS PURE
AS THE WATER YOU DRINK!

OLD GOLD'S SPECIALTY IS TO GIVE YOU A TREAT INSTEAD OF A TREATMENT!

MORE DOCTORS SMOKE CAMELS THAN ANY OTHER CIGARETTE!

Shelby gave her foot a backward mental kick. Maybe she could get a job posing for cigarettes. She had been paid a small sum to pass out packets of cigarettes at Columbia football games, but posing for ads probably paid more.

Then she grew very still, thinking of her costume at Honey's Hot House, and of Julien's glittering eyes. She would never wear a costume like that again in her life.

The deeper the bus traveled into the South, the greater the number of small gospel churches along the highway, topped with Sears Roebuck mail-order steeples: The New Life Baptist Church, and The Full Gospel Church, and The Mount Airy Church of Christ, and The Miracle World Ministries, and The Assembly of God. *The Wages of Sin is Death* and *God Only Loves the Born Again* were proclaimed frequently, in case travelers forgot that the same admonitions had been posted up and down the highway during the last mile.

The closer she got to Little Rock, the harder she prayed, and the more she feared she had lost Charlie, because for a crazy time, Ben's unpredictability and slick charm and the smoldering black of his eyes had seemed far more exciting. And he was a Broadway star!

Her thoughts swerved to the safety of Charlie's confident grin and his cocky, broken nose.

Dear God, please keep this bus safe until I reach home!

It was Charlie who was kind.

It was Charlie who liked Louis Armstrong.

It was Charlie who had long, lovely fingers.
It was Charlie who would never fly away.
Maybe the red-headed weather girl would move to Texas.

"They're cramming integration down our throats!" Faubus was shouting in a tinny voice from a tinny radio inside the station at Knoxville, Tennessee, "but the Federals are making us handle the enforcement of their orders, while the President of these United States is on a fancy vacation in Newport, Rhode Island! He issues a command from a *golf course* to have me arrested for doing my *duty!* My friends and neighbors, the crucifixion of Orval Faubus begins today!"

Catalpa trees with white-washed trunks in barren front yards were as numerous as the tombstones in the many burial grounds along the highway. Occasionally, grand Victorian homes were pitched up on deep lawns like stranded steamboats, and more and more frequently, sullen-faced men stood by trucks with gun racks in the cabs and signs plastered on tailgates:

THEY WANT OUR WOMEN!!!!

When the bus stopped near Parkers Crossroads, Shelby stretched her cramped legs toward another ten-cent hamburger joint where, in a live radio interview, Louis Armstrong was declaring in his rough voice that Ike had no guts, and that, "If the United States can't take care of those little children in Little Rock, then to hell with the United States!"

The hamburger stand owner grabbed his shotgun from beneath the counter, and yelled "Turn off the goddamn radio before I blast that nigger to pieces!" while outside, the Negro passengers hurried away from the window that had "Colored food" scrawled above it and returned to the bus with empty stomachs.

But they had heard Louis.

64

AT MEMPHIS, very early in the morning, Shelby changed buses and crossed the mighty Mississippi, her spine jolting each time the former school bus bounced over a highway joint. But she was distracted by the sight of the alluvial soil of the Arkansas delta, flat as the palm of God, where Charlie's father had traded his soul for a few acres of that rich dirt.

Cotton fields were rampant with bolls, and pickers trailed elephantine bags that hung like long, white goiters from their necks. A few miles later, the landscape changed to reveal irrigation ditches that snaked alongside rice stalks almost ripe for harvest, where red-tailed hawks, perched on fence posts, poised to dive for mice that scrambled for the grain.

The peaceful landscape overflowed with the earth's bounty. It was hard to imagine that violence lurked just over the same bridge that Teddy Korzeniowski had flown beneath as a young man, and where a billboard above the bridge declaimed:

WHO WILL BUILD ARKANSAS IF
HER OWN PEOPLE DO NOT?

A homemade sign flew like a buzzard beneath the billboard:

Two, Four, Six, Eight,
We will never integrate!

65

SHELBY STEPPED OFF the city bus and walked slowly down the block toward Baldwin's house, where Tom Self was balanced on a ladder with his back to her. He was pounding nails with a sledge hammer into tall uprights hewn to ugly points.

Tom climbed that ladder to pound at his abomination every day except Sunday, when he went to church. In this neighborhood, rose vines covered the walls that had been built low between the lovely old homes, with their broad front porches, and their immaculately kept flower-bordered lawns, walls low enough for children and dogs to hop over. But Tom's tall fence looked ugly and foreboding, as offensive to dignity and property values as Baldwin's neglected garden and the presence of black Tom himself.

Shelby shuttered her eyes to him, and the fence, and the thirsty garden, and the wisteria that was trying to strangle the pillars of the wide front porch. She crept up the steps to the house, and opened the door cautiously. But the bell, always vigilant, emitted its jangle.

"Is that you, Saracen?" her mother called, her light steps rushing down the stairs. When she saw Shelby in the hall, she gave a joyous cry and ran toward her daughter with open arms.

But Shelby backed away, and Eulalia stopped, uncertain, nervous fingers skirting her mouth. "I would have picked you up," she said, attempting a quivering smile.

"I managed," Shelby replied, unsmiling. "I've learned to

manage." She let her suitcase drop to the floor.

Eulalia sighed and sank onto a chair. "My letters made things worse," she said to the ceiling, "I don't know what else I can do." She shrugged her shoulders in resignation and looked up at Shelby. "What happened between your father and me was ugly beyond belief. But it's been so long ago, my daughter, and life has to move forward. The past can smother your entire life, if you let it. I learned that the hardest possible way. I don't want that to happen for you."

Shelby's voice cut through the air. "Where did he go? Tom said New York City, and I looked for him up there. It was horrible, looking for him."

The pounding outside grew louder with a sound like a tom-tom. The two turned in that direction as though Tom might be relaying the answer.

"I was afraid you would look for him. When you were little, you searched everywhere . . . under the stairs, beneath the beds, inside closets, in the basement. Even inside drawers, as though he might cram himself inside to tease you. And why not? We both thought he could do anything. I was terrified, even then, you might run away to find him. And, finally, I suppose you did."

Then her voice rose in a way Shelby had never heard. It was an angry voice from a woman who never expressed anger. "If I had any idea where he had gone, *I* would have found him! *Don't you realize that? Something awful happened to him! He might have screamed goodbye, but he would have said goodbye to me!*" She paused, grew calmer. "He wouldn't have left me forever wondering where he was. He wouldn't have done that to me.

"I know I heard him screaming my name one night when I was in that gruesome place. I know I did." Her voice sounded like she was inside a cavern. "It wasn't one of the terrifying, evil voices I heard so often inside my head. It was *his* voice.

I became hysterical and an attendant tied me to the bed and said it was the devil jeering because of my terrible sins. She said I would hear the voices until the end of my days.

"And when finally, *finally* I accepted that Teddy was gone forever, I felt great relief. The demons that constantly clawed my mind disappeared . . . reluctantly, but they crawled back to hell, I hope."

Eulalia released her clenched fists, and looked at Shelby.

"The one thing I know for sure, my dear daughter, is that you mustn't go through the rest of your life obsessed with your father's vanishing."

She locked her eyes to Shelby's. "He wanted you to possess the joy that buoyed him high in the sky. *Look at our beautiful earth! Look at our sky!* he would say when we were up there together. It was always *our* earth, *our* sky, as though we owned the world. You, me, him . . ."

Shelby looked away from her mother. "But you're having an affair with Saracen Self. And he's a Negro, Momma. *A Negro.*"

Eulalia's face reddened. "Saracen's a *man,* Shelby. *A human being!* If we're to remain mother and daughter, you will never forget that I love this man!"

Shelby snatched up her bag, furious at . . . at what? At being caught out, even to herself? At spitting out feelings so angry she could almost taste their bitter ooze? Still Saracen's accusing eyes, and Bernard's tormented face, and the image of that young girl pursued by the mob in front of Central High School encircled her mind like sisal, and it was agonizing to have the sisal dig deep into her putrid thoughts.

In the midst of her fury, Shelby turned to see a ghostly figure in a worn white nightgown descending the stairs, one wobbly step at a time. At the bend in the stairs, the colors in the stained glass window transformed the strange figure into a vision of unearthly beauty; but after the bend, the figure's face became almost featureless, like a dahlia bulb that had endured the ravages of a hard winter above ground. The voice that emerged was weak and gravelly, as though unaccustomed to speaking out loud.

"Shelby Howl?" The old woman's head wobbled on its stem. "Can that be Shelby Howl come home to me, Lalie?"

Eulalia came to with a start and a breathless, "Yes, Momma. It's Shelby. She's come home to you." She turned to plead silently for mercy from her daughter, but Shelby's shocked eyes were on Baldwin.

"It's me all right, Baldwin." Shelby tried to clear her choked throat. "I've come home." She let her bag sink to the floor, and when the bag fell, it seemed she might fall too. But she stood upright, alone, forlorn.

Baldwin's face flooded with an eerie radiance. "From up there in that city?" Then she demanded, almost like her old self. "Don't you go back up there, Shelby Howl! That place is filled with scallywags! *This* is your place! We have lots to do in this place!" She stared at her trembling fingers for a moment, as though trying to remember the things they had to do, then she changed the subject. "Where's my star sapphire?"

Shelby stretched out a grubby, trembling hand to show the blue of the ring. "Right here, on my finger. It took care of me when I was away from you."

Baldwin grabbed at the finger with sudden energy. "I've got my momma's pink diamond rings around my neck. See how they sparkle? Lalie put them on a chain, and Saracen hooked it around my neck. He was the one kidnapped that elephant, Ruth, the elephant's name was. He kidnapped Ruth when he was a boy. Do you remember?"

Eulalia and Shelby both stared at Baldwin, mouths agape.

"You see my momma's engagement ring here in front on the chain? It's the biggest diamond. I love it the best."

Shelby didn't dare look at her mother. She placed a careful arm around her grandmother's fragile body. "I love *you*,

Baldwin. That's why I came back. I love you. I will always love you."

But even as the words were uttered, the old woman's eyes grew blank, and she shrugged off the arm and tottered toward the sound of the hammer, nodding her head to its beat. Nod, nod, nod, as though hypnotized by the sound.

Shelby turned to her mother like a fretful child. "Can't you make Tom stop that noise?"

"He can't stop, not for long. That's what he does now. He's trying to save us from harm."

When Saracen entered the room, Baldwin made a wobbly sound, and Eulalia reached out to grasp her waist.

"Looks like you ladies could use some help," he said, and, with great gentleness, he lifted an unprotesting Baldwin and carried her up the stairs.

He wasn't out of earshot when Shelby almost shouted, "Does he *live* here now?"

Eulalia's eyes didn't waver from her daughter's. "I love him, Shelby."

"You're completely vulnerable to him!"

"I was much more vulnerable before he came into my life. If it weren't for the heartache about Baldwin . . . and you . . . I would be happier than I've been for many years."

"You know that if Baldwin were in her right mind, she would scream if Saracen picked her up like that! She would call the police!"

"Oh, honey." Eulalia grimaced as though Shelby's retort hurt her physically. "Saracen doesn't live here. When he comes by, he slips through that old entry in the cellar so no one can see him enter. And even when Baldwin is herself, she's pleased to see him."

When Shelby realized that Saracen had reappeared as quietly as he had entered previously, the room suddenly seemed too hot, too crowded with ghosts yammering and moaning about Negroes besmirching the honor of the Howell name, no matter that grandfather Howell had deserted his family and took a yellow-skinned foreigner as a wife when he already had a wife in America. But those things happened. After all, he was white and male and blood kin. *But a male Negro who might marry one of their own white-skinned beauties?*

"Your mother and I have made plenty of mistakes and we regret them. But we love one another. It's that simple. We love one another. We can't change the way we feel."

What Shelby needed was to lean on something. Anything. The cupboard was closest, but she was afraid it might collapse with its weight of family treasure and history, and, even in her current state, she didn't dare break a piece of Baldwin's Canton china. She sank onto the couch in an exhausted, petulant sprawl, and she sounded petulant, as though she were being forced to capitulate. How could she give up her anger? Anger had helped her survive during the past months.

"Okay. I should have written," she muttered petulantly, determined not to take more than her share of blame. "But you behaved badly."

"You're right," he nodded. "I did behave badly."

He seemed so relieved Shelby was speaking to him he might have agreed to anything.

Eulalia rushed to add her own confessional. "And I should have told you about my relationship with Saracen when you were here over Christmas . . . I should have told you what happened between your father and me years ago. You must have been stunned by Tom's outpouring of your parents' sordid history. I'm so sorry, honey. So very sorry. So much of your hurt is my fault."

"Ahhhh," Shelby moaned. "Let's don't talk about guilt! I'm up to my ears in guilt. Baldwin's illness is . . . it's unnerving

435

for all of us. She's always been such a force in our lives. So difficult, so bossy, so impossible, so . . . amazing. And so loved. And I always loved you, Momma, even when I ran away in December. I was angry and hurt and confused, but I loved you, and I will always love you, no matter what happens."

66

CHARLIE HADN'T CALLED Shelby since she had returned to Little Rock. And he should have, she thought. That would have been the right thing to do. After all, he was the man. He should make the first move. She wouldn't let the thought surface that she had hurt him profoundly, that she was the one at fault and should apologize until his silence became so loud in her ears she finally mustered the courage to drive to his house.

She couldn't call first. What if he hung up?

She drove by his house, saw his car, assumed he was there, parked a block away, and sat for a while, calming herself, working up courage. Finally, she got out, walked slowly, then faster, determined to knock on his door, which she did, timidly, then louder, then rang the bell, looking up to the second-floor window, where she saw the red-headed girl, smiling triumphantly down at her.

Charlie opened the door, saw Shelby, and they were both silent, stunned, perhaps, by awkward proximity. Shelby broke eye contact first, looking upward, hoping for release from all the hurt in her life, only to be faced with the red-headed television weather commentator still up there, her perfect teeth still revealing that triumphant smile. Shelby gasped, wheeled around and fled stupidly toward the safe haven of her mother's red Volkswagen. She gunned it to life, stripping gears and squealing tires, frantic to leave embarrassment and lost love far behind, knowing she deserved her fate.

67

CENTRAL HIGH HAD BEEN scheduled to integrate on September 3, 1957. Faubus was well aware of the potential for violence, but he flew to Sea Island, Georgia, to attend a governor's conference, where he knew he would be hailed as a hero. He dumped the volatile crisis in Little Rock in the hands of a lame-duck mayor.

The racially prejudiced chief of police placed his deputy in charge of the department on the day integration was to commence, and the chief himself stayed at home. The fire chief declared he would resign if he were ordered to use high-pressure hoses on the mob he knew would assemble in front of the high school, even though hoses could control a mob. The combined dereliction of duty by its political and public defense leaders left the city vulnerable to violence.

When the morning of September 23 finally arrived, phones rang off the hooks at the State House in Little Rock. Eulalia tried to allay people's fears, even though she, too, was increasingly concerned about a mob, and about Baldwin, as well. Shelby had mentioned her need to be at the school, but now Eulalia had a feeling that Baldwin might not be safe by herself, even briefly.

Eulalia knew Saracen was already on his way, reporter's notebook in hand, so she couldn't ask him to check on Baldwin. Tom, who was looking very tired these days, had told her in a determined voice that he, also, had to be at the school.

And, of course, Julien would be at the school to create

havoc.

But what if he saw everyone leave and knew Baldwin would be alone?

Eulalia took a deep breath and did what she had to do. She called Charlie. The call was a bit awkward. She didn't think Charlie had been by the house since Shelby had returned. But when Eulalia explained the situation, asked him to drop by the school, find Shelby, and take her back home, he agreed immediately.

68

A LOCAL RADIO REPORTER was having a hard time being heard above the screaming crowd in front of Central High School:

"Most policemen have stayed at home, and another just threw his badge on the ground and joined the protestors! Listen to the crowd roaring approval!"

The announcer was almost chortling. *"Those nine Neegrows think they'll get into Central High today, but I have a feeling it'll be a LEETLE bit harder than they bargained for!"*

In the background a woman wailed, "Ain't we got trouble?"

Very little traffic appeared on this usually busy Monday morning. The possibility of violence had alerted people to danger the way the approach of wildfire does to animals in a forest.

Bernard's image needled Shelby's mind, and she picked up her speed. *Three more blocks, Bernard, and I'll be there.* She had been hacking at weeds in the hard earth and almost forgot her promise to Bernard to be his witness on Central's day of integration. But as she drew close, she came to an appalled, heart-rending halt at the sight of the frenzied, sign-waving throng.

Hang 'em High!
Keep the Monkeys in the Trees!
Two, four, six, eight! We ain't gonna integrate!
What God Has Put Asunder Let Not Man Put Together!

Race mixing is Communism!

The prospect of violence seemed almost palpable. Shelby was ready to turn back, when Bernard whispered in her ear, *You promised to do this for me!*

The imposing buff-colored brick school rose haughtily above the furious clatter. AMBITION, PERSONALITY, OPPORTUNITY and PREPARATION, pilasters that adhered to the walls, gazed straight ahead, aloof to the chaos.

Shelby's arms prickled when she saw Buster Crosby. Buster was clad in his shiny-black, shantung suit and his famous slick-soled black-and-white shoes which he always wore until the weather got cool. Buster was gliding around like a man about to shove a shiv in his neighbor's back, stopping to listen to his walkie-talkie, and relaying instructions to the big-bellied men by his side, who then disappeared into the crowd, blackjacks in hand.

She backed away from Buster's line of vision. Buster was chief executioner today, his eyes gleaming with self-importance as he ordered thugs to knock down reporters and stomp on cameras. A few reporters were able to race to the pay phone at the Magnolia Mobil Station on the corner, because Gene Smith, the brave deputy who took the place of the chief of police, patrolled his men with an eagle eye, doing his best to protect the nine black children, and order his reluctant warriors to perform their jobs.

Across the street, a woman pounded at a reporter with her broom. "Get your Yankee bee-hind out of my yard!"

"But, Madam," the man objected indignantly, "*Ah'm from Alabama!*"

When someone yelled, "The Niggers are over here!" the crowd swirled and converged with Buster and his bullies until they encountered a small group of Negro reporters, whom they shoved and kicked, almost dilatorily, before moving on, because the black reporters weren't their real goal. Those nine children who would defile their white progeny were the goal, and the flushed-faced zealots raced toward the entrance their prey would likely enter.

Buster assigned three ruffians to stay behind and do the dirty work, a chore they carried out enthusiastically, kicking a Negro reporter to the ground, even as he called out, "I'm an American too! I fought for my country too," all the while holding on to his fine hat.

The toughs were so absorbed in their single-minded task, they didn't see Saracen Self, dressed in a proper suit and tie, with reporter's notebook in hand, racing down the sidewalk on the opposite side toward another melee. But when he heard a man cry out in pain, Saracen turned to see the Negro reporter being pummeled. He hesitated, calculating the precious minutes he had, or perhaps the odds, because he didn't want this fight, didn't have time for a fight with three big, enraged white men who were good at what they were doing. Then he sighed, stuffed his notebook in his pocket, and walked across the grass toward the hapless reporter.

Like a fool! Shelby muttered when she saw him. *A fool!* But she didn't call to him, nor did she call to the three men to stop beating the Negro. She was white, she was still Miss Little Rock, they might have listened to her. Instead she stood, slack-jawed and gutless, while Bernard implored her to *Help the man, Shelby! The man needs help!*

The thugs were so absorbed with their savagery they didn't look up until Saracen's shadow fell over them.

"Stop," he said. He didn't shout, but there was something in that deep resonance that made them obey . . . until they looked up and saw a dressed-up black man who had tricked them by sounding like a white man. And even in their rabid state of mind, they knew who he was. They had seen him driving around town in that fancy yellow convertible like a white man, and they had heard stories about the arrogant Negro who traveled to strange places and practiced witchcraft, and now had the *gall* to divert them from the satisfaction of smashing the head of the fallen Negro. They were so distracted by Saracen's sudden presence, the dizzy reporter had time to stagger away, trailing blood, but with his precious hat still in his hand.

The men looked at one another in silent agreement and advanced toward Saracen, emboldened by numbers. They wouldn't be deterred by a lone Negro with strange green eyes, who defied the white man's rules, not while there were three of them to fight him.

"*We can take this nigger easy, boys,*" the biggest of them bragged, and they began to taunt and feint, rushing forward and stepping back like prize fighters.

But they still kept some distance, as they would with a wild beast they had never encountered, and they might have retreated from the queer energy that radiated from Saracen's being, had not E.J. Hanson caught sight of him and the men he was holding at bay.

E.J. recognized Saracen, and, inspired by the odds, he tore through the crowd and across the grass, swinging a claw hammer at the back of the head of the big black man, who heard the footsteps and turned just enough to avert a more terrible blow. But that one blow was enough to make him stumble and cause blood to flow from one ear.

Then the three bullies and E.J. snarled like wolves and banded together to lay siege to the wounded Negro. They burned with the need to reclaim their superiority over an inferior species, who had briefly subverted their right to wreak havoc in an unfair world. It wasn't an honest fight, but neither was it an easy one, because even a groggy Saracen could hold his own for a while against these odds, and he fought, until, finally, he fell with a sickening thud, his fine suit torn and splattered with a mixture of blood from one black man and three white men.

Shelby bent toward the awful sight, her hand to her mouth, Bernard yelling in her ear, *Help the man, Shelby! The man needs help!* Finally, she took a deep breath, tore her hair loose from its rubber band, tangled the silvery mass with her grubby fingers, drew in a deep breath, and ran full tilt toward Saracen, screaming, "MOLLY PANTS! MOLLY PANTS!" at the top of her lungs, just as someone, Charlie maybe, *Yes, it was Charlie!* Charlie caught her arm and shouted, "NO!"

But Shelby tore away from Charlie, crooked her fingers like Ana George's *Medea*, and hurled herself in front of Saracen's bleeding body, still shouting, "MOLLY PANTS! MOLLY PANTS!" astonishing Charlie, astonishing the attackers, astonishing herself.

The mob was now stalking the high school entry, screaming, "*Git the Niggers! Kill the Niggers!*"

E.J. guessed right away who the bellowing specter was; he had heard she was back in town, and his fury grew greater than the consequences of what might happen if he grabbed her from behind, swung her around like a discus and dropped her with a resounding thud. Which he did.

They lay at angles, Shelby gasping for air, Saracen absolutely still.

E.J.'s fellow assailants had been stupefied by Shelby's gyrations, and then by E.J.'s aggression toward her, but none of them noticed Charlie until he hit E.J. so hard in the face, shards of yellow teeth flew from his mouth and globs of blood splattered on the green grass.

The other three ran for their lives toward the greater growl of the crowd. They recognized Charlie, knew he was a nigger lover, but they also knew who his father was. It wouldn't do to mess with Herbert Billington's son.

E.J. was bleating, "You bwoke m'nose! You bwoke m' teef!

Y'bwoke 'em t'piffef!"

A furious Charlie, trying to shake the pain from his bleeding fist, yelled back, "And I'll break more than that, you lily-livered shit! *RUN, you pusillanimous coward! RUN SO FAR I'LL NEVER SEE YOU AGAIN!*"

E.J. could only hobble, but he hobbled fast, writhing with pain and self-pity.

Then, out of nowhere, Tom Self roared across the street, the old bear come to save his cub, and he shoveled up Saracen with the miraculous strength granted to parents in moments of greatest need, flung his wounded boy over a shoulder, and shambled away.

A woman screamed, "Oh, my God! The niggers are in the school! *Git my baby out of there!*"

E.J. ran toward her in a tortured half gallop, inspired by the need to save white supremacy, but most of all to escape the man who threatened to knock out more than the rest of his teeth.

Charlie sucked up his pain, called Tom to follow him, and half-carried Shelby to his car. He eased her onto the front seat while Tom did his best to drape his son over the back seat, jimmying Saracen's knees against the door, then lifting his son's head, blood oozing all over the fine leather upholstery, and squeezing his own self inside. He placed Saracen's head gently onto his lap, then leaned back with a groan that had the timbre of a death rattle.

It was not a good day for a bleeding Negro to seek treatment in a Little Rock hospital, even in the black wing, so Charlie raced to Ponder's Drug Store where Elizabeth Eckford had been turned away three weeks earlier. But Charlie was welcomed. He was, after all, Billington's son. However, if the owner had realized Charlie was calling John

Samuel, the only white physician in Little Rock who would treat Negroes, the odds were great he would have locked Charlie out of his store the same way he had locked out Elizabeth Eckford.

69

ALFRED WAS DIGGING his claws into Baldwin's thighs, which was as unusual as it was annoying. She shoved the reluctant cat from her lap, shifted her weight, and dragged the gun from beneath the thick pillow. It took a while to catch her breath, but she was proud she could drag out that heavy gun by herself, and it was much more comfortable to sit in the rocker without the gun beneath her backside.

The gun was still a beauty. She smiled at the hand ejector model with its walnut grip handle, and she wished her daddy was there to admire it with her. He had loved that gun. He was also the person who had taught her how to shoot it.

The pounding of Tom's hammer had been a comfort to Baldwin. It was like a clock ticking countdown to the time for revenge. But today, boards were dropping like bombs outside the window. Tom would never bother her with that kind of disturbance, but Julien would. Baldwin was sure he was up to some terrible mischief. Today would be the day to use the revolver.

Then, with no warning, the cat arched its bony back, propelled himself to the sill of the open window and sailed into thin air, landing on the ground on all four feet and taking off down the hill with an unearthly shriek.

The old woman wasn't startled. She smiled, proud of the cat, proud she could hold the gun in a now-steady hand, and proud Teddy had come to be with her at such an important moment. They had a good chuckle at the thought of the cat screeching through the yards. The neighbors would be having fits.

And they chuckled at Julien who had stopped in his tracks at the cat's awful sound, and scurried around faster, like a wild-eyed monk with his tonsured head. And . . . *look at that!* . . . he had turned his head to present a perfect bull's eye!

Teddy helped her rise from the chair and walk to the window where she raised the revolver and put her finger on the trigger. But her good friend, Teddy, whispered, *Hold it, Baldwin . . . hold it. . . . Aim for the heart. That's how the evil bastard should die. Shoot him in his cold, hard heart! I know* you *can make that shot. You always could.*

A frisson passed through her old body. Teddy shouldn't have cursed, but then he was a foreigner. And he made her feel young, and while she couldn't do much, she knew she could still see enough to aim at the target and pull a trigger.

Julien was bobbing and weaving and splashing more kerosene on the scraps of lumber he had scattered next to the house. When he paused to rest from his labors, he looked up at Baldwin's window, saw that she was watching, lit a match, and raised his arms triumphantly.

He didn't see the gun, didn't suppose for a second she might have a gun.

Which was when she pulled the trigger.

70

EULALIA SPED HOME in the old convertible, anxious about Baldwin. Anxious about Shelby. Anxious about Saracen. She sensed they were all in danger.

When she saw smoke rising from the front of the house, she forgot about Shelby and Saracen, and she kicked open the stubborn Volkswagen door, even before she turned off the ignition. The car banged into the walnut tree stump, engine still stuttering, as she raced up the back-porch stairs, two at a time, yelling Baldwin's name, and shoving open the upstairs door with an urgent fist.

The carefully crafted timbers of the house had begun to consume themselves, even as they raged against their own demise. Their purpose, after all, had been sanctuary, not immolation.

When Eulalia shoved open her mother's bedroom door, she saw Baldwin superimposed against the fire that flickered outside the window. As the old woman's white hair lit up, her bones seemed to glow through her skin. She made a feeble gesture, waving her daughter from harm's way with what looked like an old-fashioned pistol, though, of course, it couldn't have been, and she coughed out words that sounded like, "Teddy helped me."

Yes! The first word was "Teddy," Eulalia was sure her mother had said "Teddy."

Baldwin then fell to the floor with a horrific scream.

71

SHELBY WAS STILL groggy from E.J.'s pounding, but her eyes opened wide when she saw the fire. She ignored her throbbing head, and before the car had come to a full stop, she yanked open the door and ran toward the house.

But the heat was too intense. She had to move back, crushing lilies sparkling with embers, burning her hand on the shovel she had thrown aside earlier, knocking over hydrangea bushes whose drought-dry globes burst into flames.

She whispered, "Baldwin," and when she saw the Volkswagen sputtering against the tree, she moaned, "Momma," screamed, "Baldwin!" again, and raised her arms defiantly at the inferno she tried to enter.

But Charlie had also jumped out of the car, and he grabbed and held on to her. At the same time, Saracen crawled from the back door of the Oldsmobile and reeled toward the burning house, calling, "Eulalia! Eulalia!" like a desperate man searching for a loved one lost at sea.

Tom, his face a strange grey, didn't move.

When Eulalia burst through the screen on the second-floor side door and fell down the stairs, Saracen staggered toward her, gathered her in his broken arms, and carried her out of harm's way before he collapsed with his precious burden.

The leather-bound books Eulalia clutched to her bosom fell to the ground.

72

WHEN JULIEN IGNITED the fuel by the ballroom, the fire was meticulous on its journey, leaping through the side window onto the spectacular ballroom floor, constructed of honey-colored cedar, edged in an elaborate parquet of dark mahogany, and never again duplicated in the United States of America. The fire had lingered there, lapping up decades of *Arkansas Gazettes* and *Saturday Evening Posts* and *Ladies' Home Journals* and United Methodist church bulletins, flinging off ashes like the chimneys of Auschwitz before it lunged into great-grandfather's study, set fire to his cherished Confederate officer's desk, caused the French Comtoise grandfather clock to explode, slurped the varnish from the China trade paintings, entered the dining room, burst rows of Steuben crystal with a series of rather musical pops, and caused the treasured Canton china to glide serenely down the burning shelves of the cupboard, one plate after the other, crashing like Kamikaze pilots. Then, in a frenzy of flames, the fire wasted the Collard & Collard piano, roared up the stairs, buckled, then melted the stained glass window imported from England, swallowed Grandfather Shelby's portrait in a fiery gulp, and arrived triumphantly at Baldwin's bedroom door.

During the entire conflagration, the silver front doorbell clanged belligerently, until, finally, it melted.

When a pumper arrived on Baldwin's street, it was too late to save the house, or save Baldwin Josephine Shelby Howell, whose body was burned beyond recognition.

Alfred, the cat, was never seen again.

73

LETTIE WAS WEARING an old robe and slippers when the policeman arrived to find out why she was screaming.

Lettie had always tried to do the right thing. When her third grade class went on a field trip to watch a man shear a sheep, she had won the prize for best manners. She attended church at least twice a week, and she tithed with the small sum Julien gave her for household expenses. She fixed his pot roast with lots of gravy and potatoes, the way he liked it, and made him buttermilk biscuits, even though she preferred baking powder biscuits. She ironed his undershorts that always tore at that particular place, and she mended those tears, never asking why they tore in such a private place. She hated his toupee, and hated to see it hanging on the bedpost at night. But, of course, she didn't mention that she hated it. It reminded her of a possum, and she hated possums.

It had been hard to see what looked like that same toupee on the heads of corpses in Julien's funeral home, but she had lifted her chin, sat with a straight back and stared straight ahead, as people snickered. It had become increasingly hard to make do with less and less money, and harder still to watch Tom build that fence next door, which broke her heart. Lettie had no idea what she had done to make her best friends angry. Her only friends, really.

And it had been beyond horrific to huddle all alone and watch the fire consume Baldwin's house, which had collapsed with less sound than seemed appropriate for such a stately structure. It never occurred to Lettie she might be in danger, and if it had, she might have welcomed the flames.

When Julien didn't appear after the fire, Lettie locked the doors, pulled down the shades, ate from jars of food she had preserved, and nibbled at bread she had baked. Or she didn't eat anything. Food had never been important to her.

Julien had always written the checks and bought her clothes. He bragged that it was his job to drive the hearse and Lettie's to wash the dishes. She didn't much like that way of doing things, but she had learned the hard way to keep her mouth shut. And after the terrible events at the funeral home with the corpses and all, Julien had stopped speaking to her, and, more astonishingly, stopped wearing his toupee, which neither of them mentioned. He looked quite strange without the toupee. In fact, Lettie thought his naked head looked obscene, which she tried to put out of her mind, and, of course, she never mentioned that to Julien.

Then the sedan disappeared, leaving only the hearse in the drive.

And, finally, Julien quit going to work at the funeral home, because, really, there was no work to go to, which was when he donned an old pair of overalls and hardly ever took them off. The town forgot, and so quickly, that he and his daddy before him, had been the finest undertakers in the state, *and* in the country, Julien said.

A Nigra even had the nerve to walk right up to the house, knock on the front door, and make an offer for the funeral home, which had so outraged Julien, his almost-hairless head turned purple, and he had run to get his shotgun. But the Nigra must have planned ahead, because a car was waiting for him with a driver at the wheel and the motor running. By the time Julien got outside with the gun, the car was gone.

After that, Julien didn't speak to Lettie or sleep at home, though he did appear every day to sit in a chair in the yard and stare at Baldwin's house through his binoculars, which scared Lettie nearly to death. Why would he do such a thing? She didn't know where he stayed at night, and, of course, she didn't ask.

Her only remaining family was in Oklahoma, but after her parents died and left her all the money, the Oklahoma family quit visiting. They thought they deserved a share, since they were blood. Julien used the money for his business, which was his right, he was her husband; but there was no one for Lettie to turn to after he left.

When big planes thundered overhead on the night of the fire, Lettie got into bed, pulled the covers over her head and hummed one keening note as loud as she could to drown out the noise, knowing God would take care of her, would always take care of her if she prayed hard enough. But she felt sick to her stomach and trembled mightily, even with God by her side.

When she finally ventured outside to go to E.J.'s store for essentials, she blinkered her eyes to the ruin next door, and scurried past Julien's hearse that was still in the drive. The hearse was filthy with ash from the fire, which would make him very unhappy when he came back. He always kept it so clean.

But a smell from the hearse became stronger than the scorch from the fire, and it frightened her so she hurried back inside the house for two more days and ate saltine crackers. She had stayed far from Julien's business, because, frankly, between her and no one else, dead bodies and hearses made her feel a little sick to her stomach. She had attended the services Julien directed, because it was the right thing for a funeral director's wife to do, but funerals and hearses and possums, and a lot of other things, made her feel sick.

She finally forced herself to take a timid look in the front windows of the hearse, but there was nothing unusual to be seen, and no one to open the back doors that concealed the main source of the smell. Opening those doors was something she simply could not do.

Baldwin and Eulalia weren't at home, since it no longer existed, so they couldn't help. Lettie didn't know where they had moved, somewhere fine where they had lots of friends, she was certain. Tom Self, who had always performed small chores for her without charge, wasn't around, and of course, she couldn't seek him out in niggertown.

But when the smell grew progressively worse, Lettie donned an old raincoat, buttoned it to her neck, and slipped on some worn gloves. She was shaking so hard, she could barely push down the big handles in back of the hearse, and when she opened the first door, she nearly fainted from the rush of putrid smell into her nostrils and her mouth, even through the raincoat and all the pores of her skin.

When she saw the body, she began to scream and couldn't stop screaming, because Julien was sprawled against the gurney he used for corpses, his head dangling in a funny way. His hands were badly burned, though that was not the cause of death, according to the policeman who responded when neighbors reported Lettie's hysterical cries. The bullet lodged near his heart was the cause of death, but who had pulled the trigger was a mystery.

The police, however, were looking into the matter.

74

LITTLE ROCK'S MAYOR SENT A message to President Eisenhower, pleading for troops to restore law and order. The President responded the same day.

The ominous roar of the military transports that carried one thousand 101st Airborne paratroopers to the city was the cause of the noise that made Lettie cower in her bed. The "Screaming Eagles" landed at dusk at the Little Rock Air Force Base outside North Little Rock, and proceeded to Little Rock Central High School in a long convoy of trucks.

When they arrived, the soldiers raced to set up pup tents and field stations on the football field, with whistles shrieking and loudspeakers blaring at the angry gathering of Little Rock citizens:

"PLEASE RETURN TO YOUR HOMES OR YOU WILL BE DISPERSED!"

Soldiers marched and hammered and shouted, even at suppertime, when families should feel safe in their homes. The school's coaches milled about the edges of the field, raging at the disruption of practice for the football team's usual winning streak, and they raged louder when the riot-trained soldiers ignored them and surrounded the school with double-time boots that echoed all through the night. The soldiers ignored the catcalls from groups of locals, and they ignored the woman who re-emerged from her house to wave her broom and yell at the soldiers to take their Yankee bee-hinds back north where they belonged.

But the members of the newly federalized Arkansas National Guard were glum when ordered to snap to attention and stamp rifle butts to the ground, even when people yelled, "Hiya, Hitler!" at them. And this time the Guard had been ordered to *protect* the nine Negro students who were inside the school.

"We are now an occupied territory!" Orval Faubus raged from the television screen. "In the name of the God we all revere: in the name of liberty we hold so dear: in the name of decency which we all cherish . . . *What is happening to America?*"

75

THE MILITARY TRANSPORT planes that terrified Lettie and shook the windows, even of the Little Rock Baptist Hospital, didn't disturb Eulalia, who floated on a sea of white bandages and the numbing bliss of morphine. The undamaged side of her face looked so serene one might imagine the terrible injury on the opposite side had absorbed all her worries.

The doctor told Shelby he feared her mother would be scarred permanently, unless there was a miracle.

But Shelby had to believe in miracles. After all, her mother was *alive*, which was a miracle, the doctor said, and Shelby was convinced, *had to be convinced*, that Saracen, who was also badly injured, could restore himself and her mother to perfect health. He had those miraculous gifts, didn't he?

Charlie moved to the window to try and glimpse the planes, but Shelby remained transfixed by the side of the antiseptic-smelling, strangely peaceful creature who was her mother. She leaned closer to make certain the creature was still breathing, and realized with a sharp inhale that she, Shelby Howell Korzeniowski, had been holding her own breath.

In fact, the daughter looked almost as vulnerable as the woman on the bed, except there was no repose in Shelby's aching body, and wouldn't be for a long while. The ten-by-fourteen space in the room was her space now, her cosmos, and the cot on the other side of her mother's bed would be Shelby's bed for weeks to come.

A compassionate nurse had provided a surgical outfit in lieu of Shelby's own filthy clothes, but the baggy blue top and trousers were at least two sizes too big and had to be tied around the waist with a double-knotted cord to keep them in place. The clothes, and the black circles beneath her eyes, and her disheveled hair, and the way she was mumbling made her seem oddly old, like the beautiful young woman in the movie about Shangri-La, the young woman Boojie obsessed about, who had aged hundreds of years when she stepped into the cold, real world.

"*I love you, Momma,*" Shelby whispered again, praying that if she spoke the words often enough her mother might hear them in the deep recesses of her brain. "*I love you so much.*" She swallowed a sob. "*And I love Baldwin too. She is . . . she is. . . .*"

Shelby couldn't say Baldwin "*was.*" And her mother shouldn't hear the truth about Baldwin, when, in fact, the only thing that remained of Baldwin were her ashes and her trunk that was still safe in New York City, along with a few of Teddy's books up there, and the books her mother had clutched to her bosom when she fell down the stairs; those leather-bound books, now scorched, with feathery writing in the margins in the beautifully discordant language that would always haunt Shelby's dreams.

Hospitals should be quiet, especially at night, though they seldom are, but on this particular night; at the Baptist State Hospital in Little Rock, Arkansas, there was the constant swish of white uniforms, and the patter of running footsteps, and bells ringing from rooms, and patients calling out, having been made more agitated in their illness by the dreadful sounds of war. When Eulalia added a moan to the sad chorus, Charlie hurried to find a nurse, and Shelby leaned a bit further toward the bed, whispering her litany: "I love you, Momma. I'll always love you. Please come back to me. I love you, Momma. I'll always love you. Please get better."

459

76

ON THE DAY of the memorial service for Baldwin Josephine Shelby Howell, a Russian satellite circled the earth like a long-legged spider with a silver belly that emitted A-flat beeps audible on shortwave radios. It was rumored the beeps were timed to trigger atomic bombs in the United States, causing people to flee to their recently built bomb shelters. For a short while, the fear of atomic attacks created an even greater dread in Little Rock than the thought of Negroes going to school with white children. Attendees at Baldwin's service would be safe, they felt certain, because they would be in God's house, with the added benefit of being close to the fallout shelter, recently constructed in the church basement.

Sputnik was only visible in early morning or early evening, but people still strained for a sighting as they walked toward the church entry for Baldwin's midday service. It was a shame such a major distraction should occur on the day commemorating her departure to the most foreign of countries. But Shelby, wretched as she was feeling, almost smiled at the thought of her wayward father sitting astride Sputnik and waving an ironic farewell to his mother-in-law. He would have loved the view from up there.

The agony Shelby was enduring was also relieved by a crazy but growing conviction that her grandmother had been, at least partly, the deus ex machina for Julien's demise. The bizarre notion offered a bit of distraction from her unrelenting guilt at leaving Baldwin alone at the house. Had Shelby been there, Julien couldn't have created the fiendish bonfire that desiccated the great Victorian manse like the funeral pyre it became.

The police had concluded that Julien had been killed by a single bullet, not self-inflicted. When Charlie relayed this interesting news, Shelby was jolted by a childhood memory of Baldwin aiming a pistol across the garden at a copperhead poised to strike Alfred when he was a kitten. Her copperhead kill had been the talk of the neighborhood for months.

Sure, the old woman was often addle-headed, but some days her mind emerged like a great fish geysering from the sea. When it happened, Shelby wanted to shout, "Welcome back! Please stay!" She clung to the image of a clearheaded Baldwin standing up straight for the last time, taking aim, and shooting Julien so close to his heart he could only crawl into his hearse and die in agony like the monster he was.

Of course, there could have been another marksman. Lots of people hated Julien. But few had the old woman's resolve, her keen eyes, and her fierce need for revenge. Over time, the possibility that Baldwin had exacted just retribution with her father's ancient revolver crystallized into a certainty in Shelby's mind; and that truth . . . Shelby's truth . . . helped her endure heart-rending days and sleepless nights.

When Kate gathered Shelby in a chattering hug outside the church, Shelby could barely refrain from kicking her in the shins. But when Miss Finney shuffled forward, the vein on her forehead swelling like a frog's big throat, Shelby embraced her teacher and called her Oceana, which made them smile before they both burst into tears.

Ernestine was much more restrained after the fire. Not even she could have wished such a thing, though it was apparent her grief for the loss of the house was greater than her grief for her sister. She insisted on buying "an appropriate dress and shoes" for Shelby to wear for the memorial service, and Shelby relented, first because she had nothing decent to wear, and, more importantly, because she knew Baldwin would want her to show people how fine her granddaughter could look. However, Shelby ignored Ernestine's outrage over the decision to scatter Baldwin's ashes on the site where the house had once presided, and where the Quapaws had "merely squatted." Her aunt sputtered repeatedly, "*This will not do! We Shelbys have always been buried at Mount Holly!*"

But granddaughter Shelby was legally in charge, and refused to look at the top-of-the-line copper coffin found in Baldwin's name at Julien's abandoned funeral home. Instead, Baldwin's ashes rested comfortably in her mother's enameled jewelry box, the one her husband had shipped from China, and where the diamond rings had been stored before Eulalia strung them on a long gold chain and clasped them around her mother's withered neck. The enameled box was, miraculously, found intact inside the old, fireproof safe, along with another faded, fingered photograph of the mysterious young soldier in his World War I uniform. Ernestine said she had no idea who the man was, but Shelby knew she was lying.

Aunt Ernestine also vehemently objected to Saracen and Tom's presence at the memorial service. "*If they have to be seated anywhere in MY church, it will be in the balcony, and NOT in the front row of the sanctuary with the family! I SIMPLY WILL NOT HAVE IT!*"

But Charlie Billington, who was richer and more socially prominent than Ernestine, smiled at her and placed the Negroes on either side of Shelby, with Saracen on the aisle so he could prop his cane and stretch his damaged leg. Charlie was on the other side of Tom. A visibly disgruntled Ernestine fretted and huffed, and pursed her lips, and stuck up her chin, and fingered her purse straps on the other side of Charlie.

Tom Self looked awful, but no one suspected he would die from a heart attack in two weeks' time. Everyone knew, however, why Saracen had one arm in a cast, and why he limped badly, and why his once handsome face was covered with slow-healing wounds that would leave disfiguring scars. Many in the congregation seethed at being forced to confront the consequences of their bigotry while attending a funeral in *their* church.

The feeling of unbrotherly love clouded the sacred air, even as the minister praised Baldwin's fine work with the Methodist Missionary Society, and praised her valiant efforts to enhance the gardens at historical sites in Arkansas. When he finally paused, people adjusted their backs and their butts, and looked around, more or less discreetly, to see who else was there.

Their ease was interrupted by loud rustling in the balcony that encircled the sides of the formal space like open arms. To the surprise of the minister and everyone else, person after person, most of whom weren't even church members and weren't fashionably dressed, rose to commend Baldwin for her good works on their behalf: the soup and the flowers she brought to the sick, and the food and clothes she provided the needy, and the bills she paid in hard times. She was always accompanied by Tom Self, and that's our Tom, one pointed, right down there in the front row with the family. Their Tom would perform whatever chore was needed without charging a penny and depart as quietly as Baldwin.

Silent tears flowed down Saracen's cheeks, and Tom, whose face was already shining with grief, bowed his noble head. He and his son were the only ones in the church, or in the world, for that matter, who knew the deeds were acts of atonement for the death of a man whose body was still lying, at that very moment, behind the ruins of Baldwin's house.

Shelby tried not to bellow out loud, though it was difficult to suppress her surprise. She could imagine such kindness from Tom, but who would have thought her grandmother could be so generous and not crow about it? Shelby needed desperately to tell Baldwin how much she loved her. But she would have her turn to do that a bit later.

When her turn to speak came, Tom put his big hand on her elbow and gave her an upward boost. As she made her way to the podium, she clutched the handkerchief Saracen had handed her as she high-stepped over his wounded leg, but she walked with her back straight, head high, new dress swirling above her new high heels.

So on this day, Baldwin's day, Shelby gathered her courage to recite lines, first giving her nose a good blow on Saracen's handkerchief, clearing her throat and standing tall.

"I want to talk about family and love, and how both can prevail, even in the most difficult circumstances. Even when it seems family and love would be torn asunder. And don't worry. This won't be a sermon. It's mostly about life with Baldwin.

"She could be very difficult, Baldwin Josephine Shelby Howell could. Many of you know that. You may have experienced it. She was feisty, oddly vain, and snobbish. But she was also hard working and loyal and, in her own way, fair, and today I, along with all of you, learned how quietly generous she could be. Who of us knew, except my dear friend, Tom Self, who is seated by me in the front row? Tom knew about that generosity, and I'm not at all surprised he was part of it." Shelby smiled at Tom who was looking at Shelby with a face filled with sorrow and love.

"I'm going to recite a bit of her favorite hymn. I was always surprised to hear her humming this hymn. She was very proper, Baldwin was, but when she was happy, or when she was sad, she would sing this old-fashioned hymn's words, a hymn usually bellowed loud in an old-fashioned Baptist church. I know the words, because I heard them often. I have a terrible singing voice, so today I'll just say the words."

Shelby tried to smile at Miss Finney, who nodded encouragingly. Shelby cleared her throat once more and began.

"Far below the storm of doubt upon the world is beating,
Sons of men in battle long the enemy withstand;
Safe am I within the castle of God's word retreating,
Nothing there can reach me . . . 'tis Beulah Land."

At this point, faint singing of the refrain was
heard in the balcony:

"I'm living on the mountain, underneath a cloudless sky,
(Praise God)"

And the singing voices grew louder:

"I'm drinking at the fountain that never shall run dry,
O, yes, I'm feasting on the manna from a bountiful supply,
For I am dwelling in Beulah Land."

And Shelby continued:

"Let the stormy breezes blow, their cry cannot alarm me,
I am safely shelter'd here,
protected by God's hand;
Here the sun is always shining,
here there's naught can harm me,
I am safe forever in Beulah Land.
I'm living on the mountain, underneath a cloudless sky,
(Praise God)
I'm drinking at the fountain that never shall run dry."

As Shelby said the words, others in the church, especially
in the balcony, now sang the chorus of the hymn as loud as
their voices could carry and clapped their hands to the beat,

"Oh yes, I'm feasting on the manna from a bountiful supply
For I am dwelling in Beulah Land."

When the singing stopped and it was Shelby's turn again, her voice began to quiver. She stared at Tom and Saracen and Charlie, trying to absorb the collective fortitude they were sending her. Her nose clouded with the hurt of stopped up tears, her voice choked with phlegm, she lowered her head a moment. When she raised it again, she stood straight and cleared her throat, and she spoke from the diaphragm in a voice that was loud and clear: "We're on this earth such a short time, and while we're here, we *must* try to do the right thing, the *moral* thing, I guess you could call it. In her own way, that's what Baldwin Josephine Shelby Howell was still trying to learn to do right up to the end of her life. She was an old-age learner up to the day of her death. "

Shelby felt a great calm, as though God and Baldwin had placed their hands on her shoulders. She also felt a surprising rush of affection for those before her, even the bigots who seethed in their seats, but were still there, and stayed, if not to honor Baldwin, at least to bear witness to her passing. Something greater than mere politesse had brought these disparate people together in the overflowing church, something even greater than the solemnity of the occasion. Perhaps it was concern, if not shame, about the horrible events that had taken place in Little Rock; perhaps it was about the horrible wounds Eulalia was suffering; perhaps it was thoughts of their own dead, or *their own* death that would surely come; *perhaps* . . . or perhaps not . . . it was guilt about their past behavior toward Baldwin and her family, and people of color in the community.

Or they might have come simply to honor the horror of her ending, along, more likely, with a silent plea to God to spare them and theirs from such evil carnage. For some, it was a silent recognition, as Shelby had said, of how quickly life flows by in everyday moments that seem insignificant until there are no more moments to squander or savor: Time, that most precious and fleeting ephemera that we take for granted until there is no more time left, no more time for words that can be said. Words like: "I love you."

Or perhaps some people just felt safer to be in God's house while Sputnik threatened the skies above, and Negroes threatened their "white" way of life just outside the sanctuary doors.

Whatever the reasons and whatever their thoughts, Shelby, at least, was feeling better, and was clarion-voiced when she continued.

"I loved my grandmother. She was the bravest person I'll ever know. I wish I could have talked to her more, heard more stories about her past, her history, because it's my history too. But since that can't be, I hope something positive will be gained from the unspeakable way she died, *and* by my mother's terrible wounds, *and* by the trial, by another kind of fire, the nine Negro students, children really, endure every single day in our high school as they are kicked and shoved and knocked down and spat upon and called horrible names by students, and even by some teachers. I hope on this very day something positive will at least begin to happen for them, and for all of us here in this church and in this city."

There was a grudging hush in the room until Miss Finney stood and began to clap, which one never did in a white church, and the people in the balcony followed her lead, and then Charlie stood and clapped, and Tom clapped his big, calloused hands, and Saracen lifted burn-damaged hands in silent tribute.

The clappers didn't include Aunt Ernestine, who was twisting the straps of her purse into a shape that looked like a noose, even as the organist and the choir commenced a joyous chorus of "Dwelling in Beulah Land," and people began to sing and clap their hands to the beat as though they were Baptists.

But it didn't take long after the service for word to spread in some circles that the shadows beneath the former Miss Little Rock's eyes weren't only from fatigue. That dark color seemed to be seeping into the rest of her skin, and everyone knew what that meant.

Come to think of it, her Polack father, who had disappeared all those years ago . . . wasn't his skin darker than usual? Now that people thought about it, he must have been part Negro.

77

SHELBY HAD AVOIDED the block since the fire, but she felt reasonably calm when she stepped onto the ravaged earth where the great Victorian house had dominated the neighborhood.

Then, in the afternoon silence, Shelby was certain she heard Baldwin pleading from every flame-filled window:

Save me, Shelby Howl! Save me!

Charlie was with Shelby, and surely he, too, could hear the old woman wailing:

Save me, Shelby Howl! Save me!

Shelby tried to grab the walnut banister, worn smooth as skin beneath a knee, and race up the stairs to save her grandmother. But the banister wasn't there, and the stairs weren't there, and the clocks were rubble, and the silver bell had melted.

Was she losing her mind? Would she wind up in the State Hospital like her mother once had, and where Lettie Hutchins now wandered the halls?

Then the voice that was Baldwin's reversed course, as it so often had when she was alive. *Do what you came here to do, Shelby Howell! Take the box from Charlie! It's time.*

Shelby grabbed the jewelry box from a startled Charlie, knelt down and opened the lid. But when she spotted lumps in the ashes, her chin wobbled, and she forgot Baldwin's injunction. As she knelt closer, a bit of ash escaped, eager, it seemed, to converge with the familiar earth. She jerked herself to her feet and thrust the box back at Charlie. "Baldwin's *bones* are still in the ashes!"

Charlie's usual composure deserted him. "I . . . I don't know about cremated ashes, but I'll call the crematorium first thing tomorrow. Don't worry. We can come back here another time."

But Shelby continued to tunnel the ashes. "There couldn't have been much left of her body. They could *at least* have cremated what was left of her body!"

Charlie peered over her shoulder.

Then Shelby's face blanched, and she dropped back to the ground, hunched over the ashes like a woman protecting a child. "My God," she whispered. *"Oh, my God. . . ."*

Charlie tried to lift her, but she wouldn't budge.

"It's a *diamond*, Charlie. This bone is a *diamond*, and I think there are others!" She began to laugh incredulously, hysterically. "They couldn't burn up her bones, but they couldn't burn up her diamonds either! Look, Charlie!" She waved some pieces of smut. "Look at Baldwin's diamonds!"

Charlie's picked up the dirty blobs with fastidious fingers, dropped them in his palm, wiped them with his clean white handkerchief, and squinted. He polished them more thoroughly. "My God," he murmured, running fingers around each piece. "You may be right. I can feel facets. Isn't that what the cut edges are called?"

He turned to Shelby, his excitement growing. "And this big one has a fancy shape. Can you see it?" He was now nose to nose with Baldwin's remains. *"You're right! These are diamonds!* Can you believe this?"

He wiped the biggest stone on the side of his trousers, as though human ashes were no more than dust, and he grabbed another and squinted at it, talking more to himself than to Shelby. "The guys from the crematorium just stuck everything in the oven they had shoveled up. . . ."

Shelby squatted beside Charlie, and rubbed her fingers over the big, pink diamonds, holding them up to the sun like a child playing with pretty glass.

"You could sell these things for a lot of money, Shelby."

Shelby gave him a look. "Oh, Charlie . . ." She spoke with affectionate disdain. "Charlie, *Charlie* . . . I could never sell Baldwin's diamonds! They belonged to her mother, and before that probably to God! If I had the guts, I would toss them all with her ashes. She should have any comfort she can get, and these beauties gave her great comfort. So, listen . . ." Shelby was very excited. "Here's what we'll do . . . we'll throw them with her ashes! You and me!"

But Charlie clasped her laden hands between both of his. "No! Don't you get it? The diamonds are her blessing to you! And what a blessing! They are her final gift! Put them in your pocket! Do that for Baldwin! No holes in those jean pockets, right? And I'll drive you straight to Worthen Bank to rent a safety deposit box!"

Shelby spoke to the diamonds with a half smile. "But they might yield a crop. Baldwin's soil is very rich." Then she abruptly changed the subject, as though she knew something even more astonishing than finding a trove of diamonds in a dead woman's ashes.

"She shot Julien, Charlie. Baldwin shot him through the heart."

Charlie sighed and looked away, as though nothing more could astonish him.

"*She did! She shot him.* Finding the diamonds is extraordinary, but Julien's . . . demise . . . *that* was her greatest gift to me." Shelby's eyes grew blank as once again she heard the old woman's voice pleading, *Save me Shelby Howl! Save me!* She shook her head until the bleak landscape came back into focus.

"Not long before she . . . died. . . ." Shelby spoke more quickly to rid herself of that desolate word, "she muttered something about shooting Julien. And, yes, I know she rambled a lot, and I half-listened most of the time, but this time she also talked about her father's gun. She had his gun, she said. And I think she found that gun and managed to shoot that freak while we were all at Central during the troubles. That was when the fire began and the house burned down, and she burned with it."

Charlie's voice was very gentle. "Shelby. The chief of police told me Julien killed himself. The *chief* told me; and no, I don't like him either, but he didn't lie to me. Anyhow, you know Baldwin couldn't lift a gun, much less walk to a window and shoot that bastard dead."

"Well, *I* think she did. She found her father's bourbon the same way she found his gun. Maybe God thought she deserved some vengeance." Shelby's eyes brimmed with tears. "I know, *I really do know that she shot Julien!*"

Charlie took both of her ash-covered hands in his and said very softly, "Okay. Okay. . . "

"Saracen will back me up when he gets those stitches out of his mouth. *He* will believe me." She was trying hard not to blubber.

"But think about it, *please.*" Charlie reasoned, "Could she shoot a pistol with the skill of a sniper at her age and in her state of mind?"

Shelby snatched her hands back. Her voice was guttural. "She could still see like a hawk. Her vision amazed the doctor. She didn't always know my name or the doctor's name, but she could see my fingernails were dirty from across the room and insist I clean them. Immediately. If you had a far-out theory about something this important, I wouldn't shrug it off. I would think about it. Investigate it. *Again.*"

"Okay," Charlie said gently. "Okay. I will."

Shelby wiped her tears with the back of her hand, stood up, drew her fist back, and threw a diamond as hard and as far as she could. Then she picked up the enameled box with the ashes, lifted it toward the late fall sun, and swirled the box in dizzying circles, platinum hair flying in the ashy scrim. The astonished young man with the slightly crooked nose stood up in a hurry, prepared to catch her if she fell.

"You're a dear man, Charlie Billington," she yelled, still whirling. "I treated you badly this past year."

She came to a breathless stop. "I treated a lot of people badly. And, yes, I'm feeling crazy these days, but when I tell you I'm sorry for my behavior, it's the truth." She raised her arms, amid the lingering elixir of her grandmother's ashes. "But whatever happens, fuck it! *Fuck it! I'll survive!*"

Charlie stared at the beautiful, bereft young woman, reached to close the lid to the enameled box she clutched to her bosom, took her arm, and maneuvered her over the scorched earth toward the back acres that many years ago had been Baldwin's favorite place in the garden. In the summertime, she and Shelby had sat in the cool of the gazebo to drink tall glasses of sun tea that they stirred with the tinkling sound made by Baldwin's father's antique silver swizzle sticks. And all the while the neutered Italian cupid had spouted water into the pond where exotic goldfish swam.

The spot was blackened now. Desolate. Nevertheless, it was Shelby's chosen place to scatter what remained of Baldwin's ashes. When they reached it, however, Charlie stopped so suddenly it caused Shelby to stumble, drop the box, and look down at the ground where he was staring. The vegetation had been burned away, but the confounding sight had to be confirmed by bending further and peering closer, until there could be no doubt that what they both saw were the remnants of a flight jacket and a dirt-encrusted buckle with a tiny rusted object sticking out from the side. Some creature had dug at the lower part of the skeleton, but the top half of the skull was covered with rags of what might have been a hat, and the eyeholes, filled with moss, stared up with a greenish glow at Teddy Korzeniowski's daughter and the man who caught her when she started to fall to the earth.

MARGARET DAVIS MOOSE

Margaret Moose is a writer whose previous novel, *Happy Days,* was published to critical acclaim by Simon & Schuster in 1974. She was born and raised in Little Rock, Arkansas, graduated from Little Rock Senior High School, Barnard College and the Neighborhood Playhouse School of the Theatre, and lives in Alexandria, Virginia.